P9-EDW-447

CENTER DOOR FANCY

Center Door Fancy

BY
Joan Blondell

DELACORTE PRESS / NEW YORK

FOR
SANDY, SCOTTY, GUNNIE
AND
JOANIE

PART
ONE

THE PIANIST in the pit turned toward the red glow of a cigar in the dark, empty theater. "Should I commence, sir?" he called.

"Let 'er fly," John Marten answered from back of the glow.

The pianist banged out a downbeat and kept repeating it until he heard the stage manager's strident voice from on-stage. "Awright, girlies, calm yourselves. My name's Joey. Pleased to meet cha. Now, leave us have a little close atten-shun. Line up for the parade, and cut the crowding, you'll all get a crack at it." He took a deep breath that made him cough, and then continued. "In other words, line up and shut up, like I said."

Sitting alone in the theater, John Marten, producer-writer-director of *Through the Middle of the Earth*, kept twirling a cigar around in his mouth, and with one eye squinted, leaned back to watch the march of the girls across the stage.

He needed twenty for dancing, and ten who could walk—better still, slink,—to keep the Tired Businessman awake.

The piano pounded out one of the songs he had written for his show, and the parade started. Across the footlights the girls walked one at a time.

Johnny sank farther down in his fourteenth-row seat. His hat was pulled half over his eyes, and he chewed the end of his cigar.

Across the stage they came, all sizes, shapes, colors. Flashily, gaudily, demurely, brazenly they came. All types of femininity, some well dressed, some shabbily. And still more girls in the wings, grouped like a bouquet, waiting for their turn to parade.

Sometimes there were surprises under ill-fitting clothes, so after the girls walked, their legs and other anatomical wonders were inspected. Talent came last.

Sammy, the dance director, slid into the seat next to him with his pad and pencil.

"Number five," Johnny said in a low voice.

"Five it is."

"Seven's not bad—eight—eleven—that blond, both brunettes, the redhead—number twenty . . ." It took about an hour.

Johnny relighted his cigar and went out to the box office, while Joey gave the bad and the good news to the aspiring chorus girls. "Sorry, sister." "You, stay." "Sorry, sister." Johnny wanted no part of that.

Next session was legs. The happy chosen lifted their skirts and walked in a circle. Then more of the "Sorrys" and the "Stays." By five o'clock Joey's voice said: "Attenchun! Girls that hear their names called be here pronto at nine A.M. in the morning. Ya hear that time? I said nine A.M. in the morning, and in rehearsal clothes. Shut up, will ya? I said rehearsal clothes, and don't make it on the town tonight because nine A.M. in the morning is hard to be ready. Yer gonna get a workout from Sammy, and it's up to him if you stay. So brush up on yer high kicks and yer time-steps, and we'll see ya at nine A.M. in the morning here, rehearsal clothes. Dismissed."

Joey jumped down off the stage to join Johnny and Sam. "We're ahead of the game, don'cha think, sir?"

Johnny nodded and lit a fresh cigar. "Go ahead, fellas, leave the work light on. I'm going to sit here awhile and do some thinking."

"Nothing more we can do?" Sammy asked. Johnny shook his head, and they filed out.

The theater was quiet. Johnny stretched out in his seat, his eyes closed, and thought about the jugglers. They were great, but he didn't need the whole act; he only needed them for their big finish—about four minutes. Still, four minutes of them was bettter than a whole act from most other jugglers, including the ones with whom he had shared a dressing room in his Barnum days.

He thought about his circus life whenever he got depressed; he could even remember his first day at Barnum's. He had come straight from a carnival, where he had been the barker for the snake act.

"Yes, sir, Mr. Barnum, I've had years of experience," the fifteen-year-old boy bragged. "I've handled venomous reptiles, strippers, magicians, wizards, and sorcerers. I've sold parlor games, souvenirs, feather rubbers, and cure-all syrup. I can walk stilts, shoe horses, and paint merry-go-rounds. I've been a straight man, and barker. I can hoof and sing, but I'd like to be a clown best of all." Johnny had gulped for saliva.

Barnum had looked at the eager boy with amusement. "Know what a water boy is, young man?" he asked.

Johnny nodded.

Barnum called to another youngster who was braiding a pony's tail. "Scott, come over here and meet our new water boy. What's your name?"

"Johnny Marten, sir."

"Johnny Marten, this is Scott Kent. Get him started, Scott. The wages are nominal, Johnny, but the prestige is tremendous. You'll be feeding wild animals. Treat 'em with respect, or you won't be around long."

Johnny watched Barnum light a fat cigar and head toward the bareback riders.

"I've been with the circus ten months," the boy standing next to him said.

"I've been with it ten minutes." They both grinned.

"I'll help you, Johnny. I know the ropes."

"Thanks, Scott." Johnny looked up at the dome of the Big Top. "Those men are busy as switch engines!"

"Yea. They're putting up braces and guy wires for the acrobats. They're riders, tumblers, clowns, or balloon vendors. Nobody has just one job in this circus."

The wagons in the distance were unhitched and settled-looking. Flags of all nations were flapping in the summer breeze. The newly put-up billboards modestly announced "THE GREATEST SHOW ON EARTH" in brilliant ten-foot-tall letters.

It all looked as though the whole shebang had been on the property forever. No one would guess that this world of performers, animals, carpenters, musicians, wardrobe women, and cooks had ridden over dusty roads from town to town just to get a show on and then move on.

A gong was humming. "Groceries! Let's run, Johnny. First come, first served," Scott cried.

Out they tore into the fading sunlight, Scott leading. Side-swiping horses, ladders, performers, scenery, and dogs, they were almost first in line for the big pot of steaming hot beans, rice, diced pork fat, and peppers. Johnny helped himself to a two-inch slab of baked ham; next cold chopped tomatoes and onions, vinegar and oil to pour over it. Then thick rough bread, butter, jam, and barrels of cold milk and hot coffee. Indian pudding for dessert.

Blonds, brunettes, grayheads, redheads, short, tall, skinny, plump, fat, young, old, eager, disillusioned—the troupe lined up to get their dinner before starting a run-through of the show, a run-through that would last all night until curtain time the next day.

And Johnny, with his stomach full of warm food, decided he wanted to stay with the circus forever and ever.

It was two years later that Johnny and Scott, now closest friends, rehearsed for the matinee opening of "The Kent Brothers." It was Scott who had dreamed of becoming an acrobat, with Johnny as his partner.

"Anybody can be a clown," Scott had contended. That had confused and hurt Johnny, because he loved every minute of the act he had perfected in Barnum's employ. He'd been donning a red wig, chalk-white makeup, red rubber nose, mammoth black eyebrows, a huge varicolored satin suit with ruffled collar for two years now. And as he walked around the ring making faces, turning cartwheels, stealing candy from the children, kissing the ladies, hitting the fake pig with a bladder, squirting big tears from a hose under his costume, balancing fifty white plates, tripping over nothing, acting frightened, bashful, giggly, brave—the laughter that rang in his ears surged right through to his heart. But if Scott, his pal, his hero, wanted him to be an acrobat, an acrobat he'd be.

The boys had been rehearsing the gymnastics for a year under the careful tutelage of the Wadleys, a team soon to leave the circus to retire to their native land, Germany. They used the tent each morning before the matinee and many times after the night show. The Wadleys hovered over the future acrobats, corrected them, warned them.

All through that year they still worked their current spots; Johnny the clown, Scott the Wild West rider. Barnum gave them no particular encouragement to change their acts, for he considered each boy box office in what he was doing. But neither did he discourage them, for he was losing the thrilling Wadleys, and Johnny and Scott would cost less than sending to Europe for a replacement.

The boys had two great years of a companionship neither had known existed. They shared their secrets, their dreams— Johnny's to be a great clown, to get married and have plenty of kids; Scott's to be the world's foremost aerialist and a bachelor.

"You can't mix show biz and a family, Johnny."

"I bet *I* could. I'll make money enough to troupe 'em with me. We'll live in nice boardinghouses, and they'll see the show from the front, where it's clean and fun. And they'll wait for me in the park, and look in windows along the street and skate and go fishing. . . .—They'll live normal."

"Big-time thinking."

"It'll be a long time yet, so don't worry, Scott. I'm going to get very rich first and give them the best of everything, like royalty!"

TAAAAA RAAAAA!—a mammoth drum roll; then: "ATTENCHUN, LADIES, GENTLEMEN, AND CHILDREN OF DULUTH! This matinee, for the first time in any ring, we are honored to present two young men who will show you that we Americans, as well as Europeans, have daring and brawn. Give them your attenchun, please—Barnum proudly presents the inauguration of that fantastic new acrobatic team—the one and only—KENT BROTHERS!"

I gotta pee, Johnny thought, panic-stricken.

"Okay, buddy, let's go," Scott called. And out they ran, head-on into the ear-splitting sound of another mammoth drum roll. Dressed in white tights and bugle-beaded jock straps, they ran to the center ring, bowed low, making a complete circle. Scott marched to the right, Johnny to the left, and each grabbed his own swinging ladder.

The music had segued from the drum roll into "The Skaters' Waltz." They were at the top, each on his own platform. A deep breath, then air whirring through their ears as they grabbed each other's young, sure, strong hands.

They twirled, they twisted, they pulled, they dove and—Hallelujah!—there it was, applause! As they clambered down. Deafening applause. They collided in the center of the ring, and instead of bowing, they hugged, slapped, pummeled, and whacked each other, laughing, crying at the same time.

They were parading up Battle Creek, Michigan's Broadway, a prologue to the opening day there.

For eight months Johnny and Scott had filled the star spot in the show, and therefore had the flashiest wagon. It was rigged with a trapeze, a riot of colorful plumes and spangles decorating the four sturdy white horses that pulled it through the streets. In the back of the wagon two amply chested blonds were holding the banner that heralded "The Incomparable Kent Brothers." The boys were standing erect, waving to the natives lining the street, their great physiques getting gasps of admiration from the ladies. "Padded," sniffed the men.

When the parade reached a busy intersection, Johnny and Scott whirled around on their poles, drawing rounds of applause from the onlookers.

"Gesundheit!" Johnny said when Scott sneezed in the middle of a somersault.

"You're welcome." Scott smiled. "Alley-oop!" He was standing on Johnny's shoulders. "Case the tomato with the big floppy tits." He threw her a sharp salute. "They look like overgrown jellyfish under that blouse. Me, I like 'em hard."

"Me, I like 'em hard, soft, medium, or rare," Johnny bragged. The two boys turned head over heels and landed on their feet, arms outstretched toward the crowd.

Scott sneezed again.

"Gesundheit," Johnny repeated. "You get caught in a draft?"

"Guess so."

When the parade returned to the circus grounds the two boys changed to bathing trunks, grabbed a towel apiece, and bicycled to a shady area a mile from the tent, where a small waterfall greeted them.

They rolled over and over and kicked and lolled in the water.

"Do you know that there are fishes that climb up places like that?" Johnny said, pointing toward the high rushing falls. "And they scale walls and bounce over dry land to get to their mates when they want to have babies?"

"Salmon." Scott was staring at the waterfall. "And I know how a salmon feels, Johnny," the confirmed bachelor sighed.

"About what?"

"About climbing up water and bouncing and scaling to get to their mate to have babies."

"Ethel?" Johnny asked.

"Yeah."

"I knew it, Scott."

The falls whooshed, the water lapped, the air rustled the trees as the boys lay on the shimmering grass grinning at each other.

"Johnny, you remember how burned I was when Ethel wouldn't let me get lucky with her—and I stayed away, wouldn't even look in her direction?"

"And you patted every female butt in the show to make her jealous." Johnny's voice was disapproving.

"But," Scott said slowly, "she didn't *get* jealous. Something very dignified and classy about her, and that's what I want."

"Jeez, Scott—that's great. Get married right away."

"She's only seventeen."

"Hell yes, but you're twenty. Propose to her tonight after the show—go ahead, Scott . . . we'll have a big wedding with the whole troupe . . . her ma and pa will give her to you, and I'll be best man. . . ." Johnny said it all in one breath.

"Funny, me getting married first, when you're the one that wants to so bad." Scott looked at his pal.

"Hell, I didn't find an Ethel yet."

"Well, hurry up, so all our kids can be born together!"

Johnny put his hands down in the shallow icy water and lifted his legs and arched his back. His wet body had patterns on it from the sun through the trees. "You lucky stiff. You damned lucky stiff!" he said, head down.

Scott was doing push-ups, his body over the water like an expansion bridge. "She's going to quit work right away, too. The Famous Thoston Bareback Riders will be only two now. You think her ma and pa will mind?"

"No, Scott, I've caught 'em looking at you as much as

Ethel does. They want their girl to be married to a nice guy like you. I know it. I would. To hell with an act!"

Scott got to his feet on the nineteenth push-up. "I feel scared. I don't know why. It's a big move."

Johnny, looking at him from an upside-down position, said, "I'd be scared, too, in a way."

"Boy, am I in love!" Scott spread out on the grass, hands behind his head. He sneezed three times.

"Three sneezes. That makes it true."

"Cripes, my stomach's jumping, and I feel hot and cold at the same time, now that I've made up my mind."

Johnny looked at Scott. "The bridegroom willies! I've got them myself, and *nothing's* happening to me."

Scott shivered and wrapped the damp towel around his shoulders. "I'm going to ask her to be my wife tonight."

The boys shared a dressing room with the Leo Brothers, aging jugglers, whose one weakness was gambling. Their professional days should have been over, but their betting losses were so heavy that they had to plod on long after their dream of retirement. David was sixty-two, James sixty-nine. And it took all the strength they had to do each show. The brothers knew their days with the circus were numbered. But they never voiced it.

They were extremely fond of Johnny and Scott, and told jokes while they were all making up in the dressing room the four of them shared. "Know the difference between a snake and a flea?—A snake crawls on its *own* stomach—a flea ain't so particular!" Or "The word pants am an uncommon noun because pants am singular at the top an' plural at de bottom."

Johnny and Scott would laugh, no matter how stale the joke, because they genuinely liked the old fellows.

All four of them were seated, looking into the mirrors, putting on greasepaint. The dressing-room lights blinked three times.

"Half-hour," Scott sang out.

David looked at him. "What makes you so high?"

"Let's tell 'em, Johnny."

"Go to it, Scott, everybody will know by midnight tonight anyway."

Scott stood up and cleared his throat. "Gentlemen, I am about to enter into the holy bonds of matrimony."

The tumblers jumped to their feet with spirit, hugged and swung Scott around the room, crying their congratulations.

"'Tis better to have loved and lost; Than wed and be forever bossed," David cautioned in a basso-profundo voice.

"Many a man in love with a dimple makes a mistake of marrying the whole girl," was James's gleeful contribution.

Then the lights blinked twice—fifteen minutes until showtime—and the boys dived into their costumes, laughter still high in the room.

Johnny and Scott limbered up backstage of the arena, then walked to the aisle that led to the center ring and bounced up and down to keep themselves hot until the drum roll.

"Ladies and gentlemen," the megaphoned voice boomed.

Scott turned and caught the clear eyes of Ethel. She was in her tutu leaning against the wall. Tonight after the show he would ask her to be his wife.

Scott vaguely heard: "THE INCOMPARABLE KENT BROTHERS!"

"Lift your dogs—that's it!" Johnny tugged on his arm. He heard Ethel call, "God bless you," as Scott sneezed on the way to the spotlight.

Up the rope ladders the two climbed, higher and higher, until they reached their opposite platforms at the top.

They dived, then twisted around on the bars of their swings. Now hanging by their bent knees, heads downward, bodies arched, now joining hands, swinging higher and higher, Scott holding Johnny, his one bent knee holding the weight of the two of them.

Applause and—whoosh!—mid-air flipover, and they were back on their platforms drying their hands with a cloth attached to a pole. The music stopped for their big finale. Without looking, the boys knew the breathless audience held their faces upward. Even children were still.

Johnny took his position, hands strong on the bar of his trapeze. Off he went, swinging back and forth slowly until he gained enough momentum to whip his body around and stand on the bar. Then he swung faster and faster—ARUMP! His knees were over the bar, holding him, his head down, arms outstretched.

On the upswing, Scott grabbed his hands and the two friends swung wider, until the *pièce de rèsistance:* a double flip-over by Scott, and then the wonderfully strong, accomplished feeling they had when their hands gripped and the cheers from below began.

It was the same as always. Scott double-flipped, but in the flash of lightning that crashed through Johnny's brain, he knew his friend had missed his hands . . . "No! God, please, no!" he screamed.

Johnny never knew how he got to the ground—or whose arms held him upright in the ring.

"He's okay," someone said to him. "Scott's okay, Johnny." He felt many hands touching him. Someone was slapping his face to make him stand erect.

Someone was talking in a loud voice. "Only minor injuries —back tomorrow—partner started as a clown—will entertain you along with the rest—until the stage is set for the wild animals. Keep your seats, please. Scott Kent is all right."

Johnny was propelled to the center of the ring. "I can't." He didn't know whether he said it aloud or not. "I can't."

"Sit him in a chair and make him stay out there and do something. He's got to—for his own sake." It was the voice of Lazy Lou, the white-faced clown.

Johnny sat because he couldn't stand, while Lou took the lipstick from his own mouth with his fingers and smeared it on Johnny's nose, then put his peaked hat on him. The spotlight was blazing down. "Just make your faces," the clown whispered. "Make 'em laugh. Scott's okay."

Johnny started to get up, but he slipped and fell. Sitting on the ground, he waved weakly to the blurred bleachers. "Scott's all right. They said so." He got up slowly and started around the ring, a strange figure in his spangled tights, red nose, and clown hat. He took a bag of popcorn from a little girl. "Scott's all right," he mumbled. He gave the popcorn to a boy in the next aisle. "Scott's all right." The section laughed at the popcorn switch. He encircled the arena. "Scott's all right," he said to himself as he chased a stray dog, kissed an old lady, "Scott's all right." He took a man's program away, borrowed a match from the girl next to him, and set the program on fire. "Scott's all right." He did somersaults with a stolen balloon in his hand. "Scott's all right, Scott's all right, Scott's all right. . . ."

Applause—giggles—yoo-hoos from children as each step took him farther around.

At the exit, Ethel's mother took him by the hand and led him outside the tent. "Sit in this chair, dear."

Johnny struggled to make her face focus in his eyes. "He's dead," he said in a whisper.

"Ethel said he looked feverish, like he had a cold, when he went on. She said he sneezed and his eyes were too bright. Yes, Johnny, Scott's dead."

Johnny rejected the arms that tried to comfort him, and walked into the darkness. Long after, lying on the ground, the splash of their afternoon waterfall was soft to his ears. He felt someone covering him gently; he felt his head being lifted and something soft put under it.

Through his burning half-opened eyes he saw the black trees outlining a moon-drenched sky. Then he saw old David and James, coatless, sitting on the ground.

They sat with him until dawn.

2

JOHNNY MARTEN opened his eyes. A girl was standing alongside the work light in the center of the empty stage. They looked at each other for a long moment. Johnny rose. The girl held his gaze but didn't move. Johnny pushed his hat to the back of his head, relighted his cigar slowly, then walked jauntily down the aisle to the pit. He looked up at her. Jesus Christ, what a beauty! he told himself. Aloud he said, "Do something for ya, miss?"

"I'm frightened," she said.

"So am I." He grinned and whipped himself up on the stage.

He stood close to her, looking hard into her eyes. She held the look.

"What's going on?" he asked. And he managed another grin.

She dropped her eyes and looked at her pocketbook. "I told you. I'm frightened."

He didn't answer, so she looked up again. His stomach flipped. "Let's get out of here," he said. He grabbed her hand and pulled her across the stage through a low doorway and up the aisle of the darkened theater to his office.

"Sit down," he ordered. He went behind the desk and sat in a swivel chair. Looking at the tip of his cigar, he said, "You want to be in the show?"

"Yes. I want to be an actress."

"Can you act?"

"Yes."

"Experience?"

"No."

Silence. He puffed on his cigar. Finally: "You didn't audition."

"No. I was afraid."

He opened drawers, took out papers, put them back. Then he walked over to her, and with his hands on his hips and his feet spread apart he said, "I'm starved. Let's get something to eat."

"All right, Mr. Marten."

"Your name?"

"Cecilia Quinn."

He took her to a place called Leonardo's. There was an exchange of words between Johnny and the maître d' and they were ushered to a balcony and into a private dining room. Round table for two, candles, flowers, couch in front of a fireplace.

Johnny took Cecilia's pocketbook from her hand and removed her gloves. He looked at her breasts as he unbuttoned her green velvet coat. The waiter lighted the candles and the fireplace and turned the champagne around in the ice bucket. Johnny ordered the food, and the waiter left. "No hurry," Johnny called after him. Then Johnny poured the champagne. "Sit there." He motioned her to the deep sofa.

I've got to say *something,* Cecilia told herself, but my throat hurts and my voice will sound funny. If any one of her seven brothers knew she was there . . . But she had made up her mind. She wasn't going to be babied by them any longer. She was almost sixteen, and she was going to become a great actress—and marry Johnny Marten in the bargain. She'd seen his picture on the cover of some sheet music, and had fallen in love with it.

He touched his glass to hers. And she swallowed her first taste of wine. It tasted like vinegar to her. They sipped in silence, the fire warm and crackling. Every time he took a sip, she took a sip. He hummed bits of a tune she didn't know. He refilled their glasses. They drank in silence. They hadn't really looked at each other since they left the office. She started to feel silly and warm, and her legs felt weak.

He took her glass from her hand and put it on the floor next to his, then brushed his lips on her shoulder.

He was gently touching her thigh, his head on her breast, and she could feel the heat from his breath through her blouse. She was floating, relaxed, floating. Someone tapped on the door, and she grabbed his hand to hold it there.

"Stop now," he whispered, "but we're going to keep this going all night, all day, all night." He ran his fingers through his hair and went to the door.

"I can serve your supper, sir."

"Come in."

The waiter worked swiftly. Johnny gave him a lavish tip. "That's all—no hurry."

He seated her at the table. Then he pulled her back against the chair and put his hand inside her blouse until he found her nipple. She was looking up at him, he down at her. Her mouth was open and yearning toward him for their first kiss, but he took his hand away, touched the back of her neck with his lips. "Eat now, and have some Burgundy." He sat opposite her.

She looked down at her plate and toyed with the food.

"You're not eating," he murmured.

"Neither are you," she said primly, and cleared her throat again.

He got up and stood over her. "Let's get out of here." He pulled the tasseled gold cord alongside the draperies and helped her into her coat.

"Where to, sir?" the cabby asked.

"Up to Central Park."

They rode in silence. The night was clear and crisp, and the clip-clop of the horse's hooves hid the pounding of her heart—she hoped. She leaned back and closed her eyes—and tried not to think what her brothers or anybody else would say.

They rode in silence for a long while. Her breathing became more regular. She loved the smell of his cigar. She wanted to feel the contact of his body again, so she let her head fall to his shoulder, pretending to be asleep. He put his arm around her and cupped her full breast.

"Go to the Murray Hill Hotel, cabby," he said suddenly.

"No, I shouldn't," she said.

"Shush—be quiet, I'm in charge here."

They entered the ornate lobby.

"Wait by that palm, then go up with the bellboy. I'll be there right after." He touched her hand and went to the desk.

The room was large. The boy lighted the pink-and-gold-fringed lamp by the four-poster bed.

"Good evening, madame," he said with a bow, and left.

She removed her gloves and stood there, wondering what to do next. Then Johnny was in the room. He took off her coat, then his own. He pushed her down on the bed and lifted her skirts. His body was hard on hers as he fumbled with their clothing.

As he entered her body, his mouth, hot and wet, met hers in their first kiss.

His back was toward her. "Why didn't you tell me you were a virgin? Good God, why?"

She looked at the tight olive skin of his naked back.

"Answer me," he said.

"I don't know. Is it awful to be a virgin?"

"How the hell old are you?"

"Almost sixteen."

"Oh no!" He whirled around and sat upright, staring down at her. "Where're your mother and father?"

"Dead."

"Thank God—I mean, that's too bad."

"No, it isn't, really. I didn't know them. They died when I was an infant. My brothers brought me up."

"That's funny. I'm an orphan too. Some people took care of me for a while, but I ran away when I was a kid. I joined a carnival. Hey, you look older than sixteen."

"I know. I'm overdeveloped."

"You can say that again!" He was leaning on his elbow now, looking at her body. "What made you so eas—I mean, how come I didn't have to put up much of a battle, if you'll pardon my French?"

"I knew we'd be married all along."

"Married!" He sat upright again. "Look, honey . . ." He slowed down. "Now, what do ya know! Your name escapes me."

"Cecilia Quinn!" She smiled up at him.

"Holy smoke, you're beautiful, Cecilia Quinn." He smiled back and had a wild desire for her again.

He dried their soaking bodies with the sheet; they lay there, just looking at each other.

He was thinking a lot of puzzling things. Aloud he said, "I haven't had a cigar in four hours—you must be pretty good. I mean *that's* pretty good!" He got up and wrapped a bath towel around his middle and lit a fresh cigar. He walked back to the bed and looked down at her. "I've never seen skin like yours. It's so white it's almost translucent. You just drink milk and eat peaches?"

She giggled, and he leaned down and kissed the side of her nose.

"You smell good," she said.

"We smell good together," he answered. He walked to the window and pulled the heavy rose-colored drapery, and streaks of the same color from a newborn day came into their room. He opened the window and took deep breaths of the crisp air. "I'm starved."

"So am I."

"It's still very early, but I'll get us a feast."

He was talking on the phone. "We want coffee, hot muffins, eggs basted, ham, potatoes, jelly. WHAT? Now, nothing's impossible. George lives in the annex, doesn't he? Well, get him up. Tell him it's for me, John Marten, and I'll see him before I leave. Thanks, friend." He hung up, not waiting for the answer.

She wrapped herself in the wrinkled damp sheet and hobbled past him to the bathroom. He touched her arm as she went by.

The warm water felt wonderful. She put two bars of soap in the tub and kicked her legs to make suds. He will do that to me all the time, she thought dreamily, except, of course, when I'm on the stage or posing for pictures, or giving stories to the newspapers. She lay in the sudsy tub, looking at her full breasts, rubbing soapy hands between her legs. "More . . . more . . . more!" she whispered breathlessly, and patted her hands on the water like a child.

They had made love again, and now the warm sunlight poured into their room as John Marten tried to figure out his feelings: I'm thirty-seven, but she makes me feel like a kid, he thought.

"Now, Mademoiselle Quinn," he said, as he blew out the rich smoke he had inhaled, "what happens?"

"What happens?"

"I've got an audition at nine A.M. You wait here for me? . . . S.I.B.?"

"What's S.I.B.?" she asked.

"Stay in Bed."

She giggled.

"Or," he continued, "buy pretty clothes? Or what?" A pause. "Want to be in the show, or what?"

"I want what you want."

"Shit, I'm stuck," he muttered.

"What?"

"Pardon me, beautiful one, pardon me. And just don't look at me like that—I'm . . . I don't know . . ." He grabbed her roughly, and his body wrapped around hers. "Listen, you—you wouldn't know—I didn't find—I've never found . . ." He swallowed. "All right, now, I'm afraid of a lot of things, mostly afraid of believing . . . and I don't know why."

The roof of his mouth was uncomfortably dry. "I'm homesick," he continued.

"Right now?"

He gathered her closer so that their naked bodies were tight together, and once more he wanted her.

"No, baby, not homesick now—unfortunately." He rocked her in his arms, then in a whisper said, "You—Cecilia, you say you wanna marry me?"

"Yep," she answered loud and firm.

There was a knock on the door.

"Breakfast is served, sir."

Cecilia sat upright. "Oh, goody," she squealed.

"Should I commence, sir?" the pianist called toward the red glow of a cigar in the darkened theater.

"Let 'er fly," from the voice in back of the glow.

The pianist banged out a downbeat and kept repeating it until he heard Joey's strident voice. "Awright, awright, girls—listen with attenshun! . . ."

Johnny twirled his cigar around in his mouth. I want her this minute. He leaned his head on the seat in front of him. I haven't belonged to anyone since Scott. Now suddenly I belong to her. She's my Ethel. See, Scott, I've found my love.

Every spot in the parlor seemed to be occupied by the enraged brothers. David standing by the window; Ernest and Patrick on the sofa; Norton standing tensely against the fireplace; Henry and John on straight-back chairs; Joseph pacing slowly, deliberately, one foot down firmly, then the other. The clock struck three. They all looked at their fob watches. Though the shutters were closed, the bright, warm sun fought its way through, to make pretty dancing patterns on the rug. The hand-delivered message announcing the arrival of the newlyweds was lying crumpled on top of the piano.

They heard the sound of horses, and all seven of them rose to attention. But the horses kept going, so they resumed their positions.

"Here I am, my brothers, Mrs. John Marten."

The brothers stared. Her arms were outflung, and she glowed. They were stunned at her full-blooded joy.

"Where are you, Johnny?" she called.

"I'm putting the packages on the dining-room table. We're going to celebrate."

She ran to him and pulled him into the parlor. The boys were standing close together now in a semicircle, expressionless.

Holy Jesus H. Jumpin' Christ, Johnny thought, they're all nine feet tall! Bravely he strode up, and reading from left to right, pumped their hands. "Pleased to meet ya, pleased to meet ya." He said it seven times.

Silence followed that performance.

"We can't use *this* for a finish," Johnny muttered. Then he proclaimed, "Soup's on! Champagne, caviar, *Pâté de foie gras,* brioche, sturgeon, smoked oysters, Brie, Camembert, nuts, and fruit. We must drink to my glorious bride, don't you think, fellas? Come on, let's dive in." His voice was too loud, but he couldn't seem to lower it.

The brothers were drawn, dumbly, to the dining room. This was not what they'd planned.

"Pass the glasses, sweetheart," Johnny said to Cecilia. He tore open the packages, popped open the Champagne. "Happy New Year," he joked, then poured the wine into the glasses that Cecilia had stuck in their hands.

"To my beautiful bride," he toasted. "Now have a hunk of caviar—and taste this—great sturgeon—I know a guy—whoops, nearly dropped it!"

"Look here, Mr.—"

"Marten's the name—and I'll lay you two to one you're Joseph."

"I am."

"Ceeley said she didn't know which brother was the handsomest, but she thinks you've got a little the edge on 'em. And you paint houses—you're the one, aren't you?"

"I am," Joseph said stiffly.

Johnny turned to the youngest brother and continued: "And I'll put up a deuce you're Patrick—Patrick, and a hero no less. Ceeley told me how you saved that child. Caught her before she hit the asphalt. Nearly broke your own arms doing it. Have some more wine. There's plenty where this came from. Let's sit down. I'm so hungry my belly button's where my backbone used to be."

He laughed alone, but the brothers all sat as ordered.

Cecilia had brought plates and silverware, and Johnny passed the food as fast as he could. Then he picked up his glass. "A toast to the greatest bunch of brothers-in-law ever wished on a bridegroom—God bless 'em all!"

Down went his drink. The brothers sipped and remained speechless.

"Ernest?" Johnny questioned. "Oh, there you are. You pour the next round. You're the printer, and I bet you're going to run your own newspaper before you can say Weber and Fields."

Ernest poured.

"A great feat of engineering, Niagara Falls," Johnny continued. "That's where we go for our honeymoon. David, since you're studying engineering, I know a guy—he's looking for bright, young men like yourself—soon as we get back we'll make a contact. . . . Drink up, Norton. You're too quiet. Read too much, but that's how you got your brains, and I'm for it."

Cecilia threw her arms around Johnny's neck, and they kissed.

Seven throats cleared. Henry rose and tapped his glass.

"Speech, speech," Johnny called.

"Mr. Marten," Henry started.

"Call me Johnny, for Pete's sake."

". . . er, John, we, my brothers and I, were shocked beyond words that our beloved and only, and very young"—he belched slightly—"sister did not conform to our—a—desire to have her remain—un—a—unhampered—until such a time that we could—my brothers and I—choose—a—er—a choice both suit—"

"You're the orator. Henry! You're Henry!"

"Well, I, I've always . . ."

"You should be an actor. You have the resonance of John Drew."

"Not really," Henry denied lamely.

"What d'ya mean, not really? Really!" Johnny opened another bottle and was making the rounds.

"Pass the caviar," Norton said.

Plates, bottles, and glasses went from one end of the table to the other as the feast was consumed. Johnny eyed the boys and grinned to himself. Then he said, "Pack a bag, Ceeley mine, and let's go. We've got a train to catch. Don't take much, though. There're great shops in Niagara. It's the honeymoon spot of the world!"

Cecilia ran out. "I'll hurry!"

After an awkward moment of silence, Johnny looked at

each of the brothers gravely. "Will we have more privacy in the parlor?" Reluctantly they filed in.

"All right if I slide these doors closed?" Johnny closed them without waiting for an answer. The brothers took the same positions they'd had before.

Johnny faced them and cleared his throat. "I'm saying to myself, 'I wanna put into words what's sitting in my heart—I wanna be able to express how I feel toward your sister.'" He took a deep breath. "Y'see, gentlemen, I just looked at her, and there was my love. And I know that all the love and protection I can give her will have to be multiplied by seven. Yeah—I know that. . . ." He cleared his throat again. "I solemnly promise—look at me, please—I solemnly promise I will care for her as you have done, I will—"

"Johnny!" Her voice interrupted him. "I'm ready—let's go!" She ran to her brothers one by one and kissed them, then gaily pulled Johnny out the door and down the stoop. "Run, we'll be late."

Johnny helped her into the carriage, then momentarily stood still, his back toward the house.

"Hey!" a voice called. Johnny swung around. Joseph stepped down from the stoop, his hand outstretched. Suddenly all the brothers were shaking his hand.

And as the lovers pulled away, fourteen arms were waving, and "Godspeed!" and "Happiness to you!" filled the sun-warmed air.

3

FOR JOHNNY, the first year of their marriage was bewildering. He worshiped Cecilia, but it was a colossal shock for him to realize that his breathtakingly beautiful wife was a selfish brat who demanded twenty-four-hour adoration. She was used to it. Her brothers had catered to her, coddled her, brought her presents, attended her needs, treated her as a beautiful ornament.

Now her never-ending desires, complaints, and her hot temper had him in a spin.

She became enraged about that musical he was in the throes of producing. "You stay in that dark theater all the time rehearsing all those dumb girls. Well, just you wait, Johnny," she threatened, "when I get rid of this awful stomach, I'll leave you and be a star, and then you'll be sorry."

"God, Ceeley, you talk like a silly infant," he answered impatiently. But he worried that her continued dissatisfaction might affect their expected baby, so he canceled his show.

He took her to every glamorous event in New York, but her constant desire to be entertained and her excessive spending frightened him.

"Ceeley, I've just lost a lot of money cancelling the show and paying off the cast; I'm near broke."

"You have a big glob of money in that Philadelphia bank. You told me so."

"That's for our future, our family. We're not going to touch that."

"You don't think I'm pretty," she cried, tears welling up in her eyes.

He folded her in his arms and laughed. "You're more of a baby than the baby you're carrying. Come, let's pack, we'll go to Saratoga for a vacation."

When they had returned from several such vacations, Cecelia, having taken to bed, sent Johnny to Baltimore for an antique cameo she had heard about. He returned to their New York brownstone just in time to hear a voice blast through the beaded portières that separated the bedroom from the parlor.

"Congratulations, John, it's a boy!" Dr. McCarthy called as he tugged on the broad, olive-skinned shoulders of the child. He gave one more gentle pull, then, taken aback, corrected himself. "Oops, I mean a girl."

"My stomach's flat again, Johnny, feel. I can be an actress now, can't I?" She giggled with delight as she pulled him onto the bed with her.

"I have *two* babies," he said contentedly, "Ceeley and Nora."

"Tell me I can be a star now, please, Johnny," she whispered in his ear.

"There's no star anywhere—on a stage or in the heavens—as beautiful and as glowing as you."

Cecilia took full advantage of her convalescence, insisting on a full-time nurse for Nora; daily visits from Dr. McCarthy; weekly deliveries of imported gowns, furs, cosmetics; and hourly attention from Johnny.

After two months the doctor cornered Johnny. "Listen, John," he said, "your wife and daughter are strong and extremely healthy—have been for quite a time. Dismiss me, for Pete's sake, and go about your life."

"Thank you, Doc, I will. I'll go to work now."

"Sure, Hell, a man's got to be the boss, eh, John?"

So Johnny booked his act, and played for two seasons in every key city in the United States and Canada, but this time with a family.

He had been in vaudeville ever since Scott died. At first he wrote songs and comedy situations for other actors. Then he went back to his clown-pantomime act and worked it into a single in vaudeville. In time, the clown became a country rube in red wig, baggy knickers, suspenders, and oversized shoes—and the pantomime was interspersed with stories about farm days.

He made such a success on the Orpheum, Keith, and Pantages circuits—and abroad—that he saved enough money to try his wings writing and producing his own show.

But that was over now, and it was back to vaudeville—his wife and daughter, Nora, with him.

PART
TWO

1

WAS the happiest Marten. My first awareness was the sound of laughter and applause, the scent of powder, perfume, greasepaint; and as the months passed, my world became a kaleidoscope of music, colors, and lights, the rhythm of train wheels pressing the tracks, the wail of a whistle, the exquisite harmony of the orchestra playing, the exquisite discord of the orchestra tuning up, the cadence of that familiar call, "Peanuts, popcorn, Cracker Jack!"

The performers would tap-dance for me alone; they would sing silly songs to make me laugh; magicians' cards would disappear before my eyes. Stagehands showed me how they pulled the ropes to raise and lower the curtain.

I fed the trick dogs and ponies and elephants. I pulled off my dad's red wig when he finished his act; I played with the spangles and feathers the other acts gave me.

We opened in a different city each week, which meant a

new backstage, a different hotel, an unexplored park to play in between shows, and strange children to watch.

The act had been expanded into a comedy sketch. Johnny had hired a buxom woman as a straight lady. She played an elegant society woman—and he continued as the innocent country rube she was trying to seduce. To no avail. He was too innocent to know what she was after. When she said to him, "Nobody loves me, and my hands are so cold," he answered, "God loves you, and you can sit on your hands."

He called the act "John Marten and Company in 'The Boy Is Gone.'" The "and Company" was because he didn't want to have to change his advance press releases every time the lady in the act got drunk, married, or bored with travel and left.

Mom was not contented.

"I want to act. I want people to applaud me the way they do you," she complained to Dad.

"Someday, sweetheart," Johnny promised, but that was not his prime worry. He had seen the way other men looked at her. He became increasingly uneasy after he'd seen her whispering to Joe Ralston, a young singer who was on the bill.

One night he made his decision. "Ceeley, when we finish this tour I can book a couple of years through Europe and then Australia. I'll rewrite the act, and you can play the society woman."

"Will that make me a star?" she asked.

"Well, er—a . . ."

"Goody!" She whirled, bowed, and threw kisses over Johnny's head to an imaginary audience.

From an act in "one" it became full stage with a "center door fancy"—that ornate painted archway—for their entrance.

He wore the same makeup, red wig, and baggy pants he had worn in his single act. Cecilia wore a lavishly beaded white evening dress which showed off her figure. He played the eighteen-year-old country rube, she the rich society girl.

Johnny booked four extra weeks in small, out-of-the-way places to break in the new material, and he was delighted that Mom was warmly received by the audience. She was thrilled with her success, and with the stage-door Johnnies who stared at her when the family left the theater.

The U.S. tour ended, and we set sail for England. Johnny spent everything he had to make Cecilia happy. We lived in the finest hotels in England. He bought her elegant clothes and jewelry in Paris. But the more alluring she looked, the more she flirted.

For me, France meant riding in carriages drawn by shining black horses, running through lobbies with crystal chandeliers, riding down a long marble corridor astride a white Russian wolfhound, sitting high on my father's shoulders looking down at upturned faces as we toured the crowded streets.

I had my third birthday in Vienna—and my first taste of fear.

I was in a huge tub playing with a sailboat when my mother burst into the room. "Don't ever touch yourself anywhere, or you will die," she said, "and don't let anyone else touch you, and don't look at yourself—it's vain—keep covered. You understand?"

"Yes, Mama," I said, not understanding at all.

After I was in bed I heard my parents quarreling.

"If that bastard ever touches you, I'll break his goddamn neck! Has he? Has he ever . . . ?"

"No, no, NO, I told you!"

"I'm warning you, Ceeley, you quit giving the come-on to guys. I've seen you, and so help me God, I'll—I'll . . ." He stormed out and slammed the door.

I chewed on my nails and wondered about the mysterious "touching."

The voyage to Australia was tranquil, and the ten acts that played the Williamson Theater in Sydney were excellent:

four jugglers; a quick-change artist; a soft-shoe team; a magi-
cian; a tramp monologue; a soprano and her canary; James
Flaherty, songs (his showstopper was "On the Road to Mandalay"); and next to closing, John Marten in "The Boy Is
Gone," assisted by Cecilia Quinn; a unicycle act finale; then
the afterpiece—all the acts reprising.

John Marten and Company played the same theater for six
months, and somewhere in the middle of the run Mom started
coaxing Johnny to let me appear in the afterpiece.

"Nope," he said. "No show business for her. She's going to
marry someone not in show business, have a home, live a
normal life in one spot, and that's it."

"Please," Mom cajoled, "Nora can imitate any one of the
ten acts—you've seen her. Please?"

"No, Ceeley, she's barely five years old."

That was it until the day Mom went to the doctor's. Johnny
and I were at the hotel, and Johnny was showing me how to
make a rabbit out of a dinner napkin, when the door flew
open and in stormed Mom. She threw her hat at Johnny, and
followed it quickly with her shoes, her bag, and her fur piece.
"I knew it, I knew it, I knew it! You louse, you! Another
baby—a rotten, fat baby!"

Dad grabbed her. "Oh, thank God," he cried.

"Thank God, my ass, thank *you*—you louse!"

He had her on his lap and was rocking her.

"There, there," he said.

I had hidden behind a door. When I peeked out, my mother
looked at me with red, swollen eyes.

"Mommy, will you don't cry if I go on the stage tonight
for you?"

"Good idea, Nora," she answered with a wicked grin. "You
go on the stage tonight." Mom stuck her tongue out at Johnny,
and he smiled.

All three of us were wrapped together in the armchair.

Johnny took me to the theater and rehearsed me until
showtime. When the lights blinked the five-minute warning

he steered me into the darkness back of the curtain, knelt down, and looked up into my eyes.

"Listen, Nora, there's an arch in the middle of our set, it's called 'center door fancy.' You will enter through it, so take command of yourself, then step right out on that stage with confidence. Keep your head high and your feet firm on the boards." He paused. "Now, then, feel the audience—understand, Nora? *Feel* 'em and know they want to love you. They *want* you to make 'em happy. They *want* to applaud you. It's your chance to make a lot of people feel better." He took my chin in his hand. "Sometimes, Nora, we fail. I don't know why. I can never figure it out. But if we fail, there's only one thing that will keep us going—one thing—and that's if we know we did the best we could do—the best."

My eyes were solemn.

Johnny laughed. "What am I saying to a baby?" He stood me in front of the entrance. "There's your music. Center door fancy, Nora, up and at 'em, and the best you can do. . . ." He spoke so softly I could barely hear him.

"Yes, Daddy, center door fancy."

I marched through the arch toward the footlights. Looking down, I saw the conductor and the shadows of men in the orchestra. The pull of the spotlight was drawing my face up—the pull of the light and the warmth of the people in the darkness.

" 'On the road to Mandalay—hay!' " I sang, my left hand on my chest, my right hand in back of me.

My afterpiece impersonations were doubled by popular demand: Cecilia's. Johnny's consolation was to whisk his wife and daughter out of the theater and into the parks. We saw more of trees, gardens, birds, and squirrels than of actors and dressing rooms.

For me, the trip back to America was a very exciting time. Christmas came in the middle of the ocean on a bright and sunny day, and it seemed everybody on board gave me a present. A miniature deck chair, candy with a Santa Claus on the box, beads, perfume, books, hankies with lace. From Johnny, a big teddy bear on wheels.

Cecilia gave me a pearl-handled manicure set, and I manicured everybody who failed to resist my offer; there was an epidemic of sore and bloody cuticles.

I loved the creak of the ship as it rolled in the night, the splash of the waves as I lay in the upper berth of our cabin, the muted music from the ballroom, the salt smell from the ocean, the fruit smell from the piled-high bowl—and the beautiful purser with gold braid on his cap and gold buttons on his uniform. I hid behind columns to get a peek at him. He'd always catch me peeking, and smile. One day he hugged me and said, "Hello, platter eyes."

He touched me, I thought in terror. Sitting stiffly in a big, leather chair in the writing room, I waited to die.

Later that night, Mom was crying. I heard it from my upper berth, and it caused again that miserable feeling of fear.

"Never again will I be this ugly."

"You're beautiful carrying the baby."

"I'm not. And I hate it. I'm young—you forget that. And I intend to have some fun."

"Aren't you?"

"No."

"What kind of fun?"

"Acting, dancing, going places. I don't want to be stuck with kids, not yet."

"You've been places. Almost all over the world."

"And I've been pregnant most of the time."

"Now, Ceeley, the baby'll be born in a few weeks. Then you can have all the fun you want. You can get into your pretty Paris clothes again, and we'll see all the shows in New York. We won't take more bookings until you've had a lot of fun."

"I'll get even one of these days. I'll make men take notice of me and see how you like it."

"Don't talk like that. Nobody's ever going to look at you that way—nobody's ever going to touch you but me!"

I flipped over on my stomach and put the pillow over my head. "Nobody's going to touch you but me," Dad had said. Uneasily I wondered if Mom ever told *him* about touching and dying.

I flipped over again and concentrated on earlier that night when Johnny and I had taken a walk around the deck. The ocean was choppy, and the boat had rocked from side to side. A man was leaning over the rail, throwing up. As we neared him, the man straightened and braced himself. He held his handkerchief over his mouth and said to us, "I was wondering if the moon was up yet."

Johnny put his hand on the man's shoulder. "It is if you swallowed it!" They both roared laughing—me, too.

Fun to think about that as I lay in my berth. My dad always makes people laugh. And that was my favorite sound.

Johnny rented an attractive oceanfront house at Rockaway Beach, New York, so that Cecilia could wait out in comfort the weeks prior to the birth of their second child.

Across the street lived a little girl my age. Gertrude Lean was my first friend. We ran along the beach, swam, collected stones, popped kelp together.

A forever friend, I thought. No leaving. Each day you wake up, you have the same friend. Rockaway Beach is my favorite town forever and ever.

Mom's time was close, so Dr. McCarthy and a nurse came in from Manhattan to be with her. Johnny arranged for me to stay overnight at Gertrude's house.

"When you come home tomorrow, Nora, you will find a wonderful present. God is going to drop it down the chimney into your mother's arms."

"What's going to drop in Mama's arms?"

"A baby."

"I hope Mama doesn't get burned sitting in the fireplace," I said, and ran off with Gertrude.

The next morning, before anyone was out of bed, Johnny's excited voice woke me up. "It's here! It's healthy! And it's ours!"

"What?" Gertrude and I were asking. Gertrude's parents, still in their nightshirts, were yawning and scratching. "What is it? Boy? Girl?"

"Boy—boy! It's a boy. Scott Marten," Dad yelled, waving his cigar like a madman.

He grabbed my hand, and together we ran across the street and into the bedroom.

Three weeks later, one twilight, Johnny, his heart heavy, held my hand as we walked along the ocean's edge.

"Everybody's movable, Nora; we open in Cleveland."

I stiffened. "Could Gertrude be in the act, Daddy? I'll show her how," I said in a small voice.

"No, baby." He sighed. "Nora, look, we'll quit one of these days, and you'll have a home and friends."

"Gertrude?"

"Yeah, Gertrude, maybe. Oh, God, Nora, are you crying?"

"No, Daddy, I just need to blow my nose!"

Scott occupied the crib on top of the theater trunk. He was strong, wiry, and bellowed lustily. I changed him, dressed him, undressed him, sang for him, played with him until it was time for my entrance. "My doll has much better manners," I grumbled. "Boys are a mess."

But taking care of my wildcat brother was better than the frightening lectures my mother would spew at me unexpectedly. "Don't ever touch yourself. . . . Don't ever let anyone else touch you. . . . Don't ever look at yourself with your clothes off, Nora—or with your clothes on," she'd add bewilderingly.

"No, Mom," I promised, "I'll never do those things."

There were more years of continuous travel: Boston, Trenton, Philadelphia, Concord, Indianapolis, Tampa, Topeka, Dover, Springfield, Des Moines, Detroit.

"The Gerry Society won't let her work in this town, Cecilia, and that's that. They're gonna make her go to school."

"School?" Cecilia was shocked.

"It's against the law for children to work, and the Gerry Society forces them to go to school if they catch up with you," Johnny said. "Schools had better be good to her," he warned the ceiling. "We'll give teachers free seats to the show to ensure it. Anyway," he said proudly, "here's a letter from Governor Julian of New York. Got him to write it out that night he, Jolson, Jessel, Cantor, and I played poker." He read the eight-line document aloud:

To Whom It May Concern:

Nora Marten, daughter of John and Cecilia Marten,
shall hereby be permitted to attend
any public school in the United States
of America for one week, if it is necessitated
by the profession of her parents.
I do hereby set my hand and seal.

Governor Julian

Johnny folded it with care. "The Gerry Society's representative swooped down on me this morning. I couldn't make the crank laugh once. So it looks like the fair state of Michigan gets our baby first."

"It's only for a week," Cecilia said; "maybe that society won't catch up with us again."

For my entrance into the field of education, Mom bought me a plaid taffeta dress of blues, greens, and yellows with a wide, white, Irish lace collar. But my palms were wet as Mom dressed me.

The school was a small, rural building, two stories high. Set back of a green lawn, framed in huge trees. Detroit Public School No. 9.

Cecilia made me blow my nose before we entered the principal's office. After a short, nervous wait, we were seated before a severely dressed lady whose glasses balanced precariously on the tip of her nose. The glasses trembled with each question.

"Child's name?"

"Nora Marten."

"Age?"

"Seven and a half."

"Father's name?"

"John Marten."

"Profession?"

"Actor."

The principal's pen remained mid-air for a moment, then dipped disapprovingly into the inkwell.

"You're the child's mother?" she continued.

"Yes."

"Name?"

"Cecilia Quinn."

"Quinn?"

"That's my maiden name and stage name. I am Mrs. John Marten really."

The pen stopped in its tracks again.

"You are an actress?" The glasses shuddered. The pen scratched: Actress. "Permanent address?"

"None."

"What does that mean?"

"We travel. We just stay a week in each town."

"The child, too?"

"Yes."

"Madame"—she put the pen in its inkwell—"we do not take children for one week."

Cecilia reached in her bag with a crooked smile, then waved a sheet of paper in front of the glasses.

I had to go to the bathroom. I wiggled on my chair.

"Here's a certificate from the governor of New York. Read it," Mom said grandly.

The glasses sat stiffly on the principal's nose as she read. After a silence she rose and banged on a bell. She caught her eyeglasses before they hit the desk.

"Mary, take these people, Mrs. Marten and Nora, to one-B."

"Yes, ma'am."

I had to go to the bathroom bad.

"Mrs. McKinney, this is Mrs. Marten and Nora, who just enrolled in your class," and Mary bowed out.

"What a dear, dear little girl, and what a lovely smile! We have fun here, Mrs. Marten. She will love us. Come, Nora," the teacher said in a singsong voice.

I flung myself at Cecilia in the terror of parting.

"Now, Nora, you're a big girl. I'll pick you up at three. Today's Friday, and there are no shows Saturday—I mean— no classes." She wiped the tears from my eyes and walked sadly down the hall.

"Children?" the teacher called. All the moving and talking and punching and bumping subsided. The teacher continued: "We have with us a dear, dear little stranger. Take her unto your heart, as I have. Just look at that pretty dress and those big, big eyes. And I see by this card that her name is Nora Marten. And—what is *this?* Actors! Actors? Where?"

"Pantages."

"Oh—oh, my! Vaudeville—well, how exciting. I've something to confess, Nora. My aunt—a dear soul—played the organ in a cinema theater in Montreal for a week once. Gwendolyn LaFayette. Will you ask your parents if they know her?"

"Yep."

"Now, children, all together, say, 'Welcome, Nora.'"

The "Welcome, Noras" were lost amid catcalls, boos, and raspberries.

"Very good, children," Mrs. McKinney said absently. "Dear Nora, sit there."

I sat.

"Now, children—we will continyouway. We study a smattering of French, you know," the teacher told me.

As the morning crept on, I leaned on my desk, my fists tight. I'll split if I don't wee-wee soon, I thought, but how do you ask a teacher? And where do you go? I watched several children raise their hands, but they were answering the teacher's questions. Don't they ever go to the bathroom? If I raised my hand and asked, maybe they'd make fun of me.

Another hour passed. "Nora, dear," the teacher interrupted my misery, "step to the blackboard and write bird, cat, and dog."

I stood up and started toward the blackboard with a hobble. In despair I realized that I couldn't hold it any longer, so I ran out of the classroom door, my pants dribbling wet. I galloped down the stairs, and there it was, a door marked "Girls." I ran in and hid in one of the six cubicles. Leaning against the door, my body shook with sobs of shame. The wet had gone down my legs, even into my shoes.

"Nora, come out, please. We wish to speak to you. Don't be afraid—we just want to ask some questions," a voice coaxed.

I pushed the door open.

"Do you do that often?" the principal asked as her eyeglasses quivered. The room teacher was looking at my drenched socks.

"No, ma'am."

"You do it at night in your bed, don't you?" Mrs. McKinney smiled tenderly.

"No, ma'am."

"Do your mother and father scold you a lot?"

"No, ma'am."

"You're not alone most of the time?"

"No, ma'am, never."

"You see strange things at the theater, don't you?—back of the stage?" the principal asked.

"Huh?"

They leaned toward me, the principal repeating, "What do you see back of the stage?"

"Well—costumes, dancers, or acrobats working out, the mail box, spangles to pick up, nails, ropes . . ."

"Go on."

". . . the call board, the stage hands shooting crap—"

"Ah-ha! Go on," Mrs. McKinney said.

"Sometimes dogs or ponies . . ." I tried to think of everything. "Way down in the basement, the musicians tune up."

"And?"

". . . and they play cards between shows."

"Do they ever paw you?" the teacher asked.

"Paw?"

"Touch." The principal smiled.

"Oh yes, they sit me on their laps—" I stopped. There it was again—"touching." The women moved closer. "But I never die!" I felt proud saying it. "They show me pictures of their little girls or boys, and sometimes they let me plunk on their banjo or show me how to play 'Marcheta' on the flute."

"What do you mean, 'never die'?" the wobbly glasses asked.

"Well," I fumbled for an explanation, "here I am, see? I'm not dead."

"Your parents have you in a dreadful atmosphere—no wonder you did what you did, you poor little thing!"

"I'm not poor. I—"

I had had enough, I drew myself up and used my best British accent to say: "I have nevah thrown up in public befoah." Then I marched out, down the hall, through the front door, and ran for blocks until I saw the glorious sign that said "Pantages Theater."

Johnny was stalking back and forth in the dressing room. "All right, dammit, you had an accident. You wet yourself, and no wonder—having to go to school! And those owls that asked you those lousy questions—they haven't got enough juice in them to pee in their pants."

My schooling ended temporarily with Detroit. It was many weeks before the Gerry Society caught up with me again. But those weeks—going from Kansas City to Omaha to South Bend to San Francisco to Salt Lake then to Chicago—were unhappy ones. The nervous pacing of my dad, the shrill snapping of my mother's voice, gave me an ugly lump in my stomach.

Even the fun in the dressing room dimmed. My parents put makeup on in silence, and there were three shows a day instead of two. There was seldom time to go to parks, and little Scott was restless. Between the supper show and the evening one, when Scott was asleep, I would lie on a rolled-up ground cloth that was against the wall of the big, empty backstage. I'd watch the "backwards" movements of the actors on the movie screen, and listen to the organ music playing for the picture while the orchestra was out having dinner.

My comfort was my satchel—that fine tiny case that Johnny had given me. He'd had it handmade, a miniature edition of a grown-up's. It was never away from my reach except when I was on the stage. It was my private world. In it was the first curl ever cut off my brother's head—I'd picked it up from the barbershop floor and tied a blue ribbon around it. And in there too was a huge splinter that I'd gotten in my toe at Loew's 83rd Street Theater—it rested in a tiny drawstring to-bacco pouch. Pouches held all the gay-colored spangles: the pearls, diamonds, and rubies that fell off costumes. My collection grew whenever we played on a bill with girl acts, for many a spangle was lost during the dances, and I was right there to pick them up. I figured I had more jewelry and sparkles than a queen.

I'd kept one sea stone from every beach all over the country; and a snapshot of my friend, Gertrude, of Rockaway. I was thinking of Gertrude now as I lay backstage on the rolled-up rug, the flickers of light from the movie screen dancing across my face. The organ was pounding out "I Love You Truly," and the sound made me feel lonely.

I was sad, too, thinking of what had happened between shows with the little boy who lived over the drugstore next to the theater. He had a bean bag, and he'd tossed it back and forth to me in the alley of the theater.

"Come to my house," he had said; "I'll find another bean bag and give it to you for keeps."

I ran to the dressing room to ask permission, but the door was closed, and I had heard the fighting.

"Just quit it, hear me? Quit hanging around that crummy xylophonist."

"I think it's fun to watch him, and he isn't crummy. Tossanetti is billed as 'The World's Greatest Xylophonist.'"

"What he is and what his billing is are two different things. You know what I'm talking about, Ceeley. I don't want to keep punching acts in the nose because you give them the eye, goddamnit."

Mom started to cry, so I tiptoed back to the alley.

"You can come up?" the boy asked.

"Yes."

He took the steps two at a time, with me following. His home smelled of garlic, and there were pictures on the walls, and fringed lamps all around, and a long-legged doll with a gold lace dress sitting on a cushion that said "Asbury Park" in purple paint.

"I played there," I said.

"Well, well, well—company," said his mother, coming from the kitchen. "What's your name, little girl?"

"Nora Marten. What's his?" I asked, pointing at the boy.

"Jimmy Mulhoon. Want some strawberry pie?"

"I'm gonna give her a bean bag," Jimmy said, as he ran from the room.

"Sit down, and I'll bring the pie."

I sat and looked at the pictures standing on tables: babies, girls dressed like brides, old men and old ladies—even a dog.

Mrs. Mulhoon returned with a whole pie covered with whipped cream, a bottle of milk, plates, and glasses on a tray.

"Here it is," Jimmy yelled, and tossed me the bean bag.

"I surely do thank you," I said shyly.

"Eat, kids," Jimmy's mother said. "Where do you live, Nora?" she asked.

"The Winston Hotel. We have two rooms. One for my mother and dad, and one for my brother and me and the trunks and cooking."

"Been in Chicago long?"

"Nearly a week. We go to Milwaukee Sunday night. I don't know where, maybe a boardinghouse if Dad can find one," I managed between bites of the pie.

"Your dad a traveling salesman?"

"No, ma'am. He's John Marten and Company in 'The Boy Is Gone,' assisted by Cecilia Quinn. Cecilia Quinn is my mother, and I am the 'and Company.' "

"What?" Mrs. Mulhoon asked.

"On the stage, next door," her son said, his mouth full of pie.

"Oh—vaudeville! How wonderful, I love it," she said. "What an exciting life! You travel a lot, don't you?"

"My sixteenth trip across the continent," I announced as snootily as Cecilia would.

"Oh, my, no!" Mrs. Mulhoon gasped, "and *I* haven't even been to Evanston yet!"

We finished the pie, and Jimmy and I played "bean bag." A little later I ran up the alley with a bean bag of my very own.

Cecilia, at the stage door, gave me a cuff and marched me to the dressing room.

"Now, where were you?"

I tried to explain.

"Were you alone with that boy?"

"Well, we played bean bag. His mom gave us some pie."

"Did he touch you? Answer me—did he?"

"No, Mom, no—I promise you. He just gave me a bean bag!"

"Wash your face and stop crying. Here comes your dad. And don't go near that boy again."

The organ droned on, but the music didn't wipe out the sound of the voices of my parents in the dressing room.

"Those pictures, those goddamn pictures, moving like that —people are getting to want them more than acts," Johnny said.

"We can't work more than we do," Cecilia reasoned.

"But the handwriting's on the wall, and it's bad. Damned moving things!" He coughed hard. "We've got to put more money away. We can't keep on going to expensive hotels."

"You've got eighty thousand dollars in that Philadelphia bank."

"That's for Nora and Scott and the new one on the way."

"Don't mention that or I'll scream."

"Ceeley, don't—I'm sorry."

"We'll have so many kids we can book the ten acts ourselves," Cecilia cried. "Especially if the new baby is a trained seal!"

"That's why I'm gonna put a new line in the act: 'The stork's walked around our house so much he's worn his legs down till he looks like a duck.'"

2

ON TO MADISON, Charleston, Cheyenne, Seattle, Richmond, Austin, Columbia, Providence, Portland, Raleigh, St. Paul, Annapolis, Frankfort, Tallahassee, Hot Springs.

Vaudeville was taking a nose dive. The expensive living quarters, first-class transportation, meals in all the best restaurants, big salaries, "Ten Acts—Ten," the lush days started slowing down, and a chilling mist of worry settled over all vaudevillians.

The Philadelphia bank went broke—closed—and with it Johnny's savings of a lifetime of trouping were gone.

The day of the bank closing Johnny was doing four shows. The baby was due soon, and so Johnny was working his single. He kept the news of the bank's failure from us and managed to appear happy and excited as he said to Scott and me, "We're going to buy a brand-new baby, so save your pennies, kids."

"No," Scott said, a big bubble-gum bubble muffling his voice. "No, I wanna dog. I don't wanna baby."

"I want a baby," I said.

Johnny donated the pennies, dimes, and nickels that went into our portable bank shaped like the Flatiron Building.

Toward the end of that week a hired nurse took Scott and me to the park, a toy store, a zoo, a restaurant, a movie, and a "legit" show starring Nat Goodwin. The management of the drama asked us to leave, for Scott had climbed over every empty seat in the theater, and the patrons had risen in a body and demanded his removal.

Scott had stuck his foot out and tripped a harassed waiter carrying a tray of hot soup in the restaurant; he had gone to the bathroom eleven times during the movie; he had cranked a locomotive in the toy store and steered it into an old lady's shins; he had been lost for twenty minutes in the park. The hired nurse looked older as we headed back to the hotel at nightfall.

Johnny met us in the lobby. "I thought you'd never get here —hurry—it's a girl—Judy's her name!"

He had run from the theater to the hotel in his makeup, red wig and all. Everyone in the lobby was staring at him.

We looked at the wrinkled, red face of the baby. Scott broke the silence. "I told you we shoulda bought a dog!"

A month later, we were in Memphis, and I was entertaining Scott between shows. He was sitting on the floor, and I was doing a time step for him on top of a large theater trunk.

I was humming "Beside a Babbling Brook" and getting ready for the big finish when my foot slipped, and off the edge I went, hitting myself a terrible blow between my legs.

My screams could be heard throughout the backstage, and all the performers ran to our dressing room. Johnny and Mom, who were getting a breath of fresh air outside the stage door, pushed their way through the crowd. "She's bleeding down her leg," the Bird Lady told them. The crowd left, taking Scott with them.

The doctor was rushed to the dressing room, and my screams became more piercing than ever as he examined me. Even though all he did was take a flashlight and look.

"She got a damn good blow, but I wouldn't worry, Mr. and Mrs. Marten; she'll just be sore for a while."

"But she bled, doctor; does that have anything to do with her virginity, please God no?" Johnny asked.

"I can't get close enough to examine her, she fights and kicks so."

I let go with another scream.

"All right now, Nora, he's not going near you again. But, Doc—I want a letter from you telling what happened, how and when it happened, in case it *did* happen."

"Well, Mr. Marten . . ."

"I'll be at your office right after the show, doctor. *I'll* write the letter, you just sign it. Goddamn it, I must have something with authority to give her husband someday."

Johnny ordered ice-cream cones for everybody backstage as a token of appreciation for their concern, and I walked like a bandy-legged cowboy for about a week. But Johnny got his letter.

During the next few years, shuttling from coast to coast, I was forced by the Gerry Society to enroll in sixteen different schools—one week at each. But the terrifying experience of Detroit never repeated itself. I had become more practiced. As soon as I was seated I'd spot a girl who looked friendly, then at recess I would tell her that I, Nora Marten of "The Boy Is Gone," could recite and do impersonations and dances. When the moment arrived for the teacher to ask questions in arithmetic or grammar or history—questions that would draw a complete blank in my mind—I'd give my accomplice the nod. And up would fly my new friend's hand. "Nora's an actress. She can *recite*."

"Oh?" from the teacher. "What do you recite?"

"Little Orphan Annie," I'd answer in a confident voice. "Annie" was a great favorite of mine—and it was well broken in; I knew where the laughs were. Sometimes, with only a halfhearted invitation from the teacher, I would march quickly to the front of the class, bow deeply, and in a voice shaking with emotion, open my act.

The verse had four stanzas, lots of action, and it was Johnny's coaching that made the laughs so sure-fire.

"Oh, no, Dad, I can't do *that*," I'd said to some of his mad pantomime.

"Do it," he'd said. "It's a 'belly.' Even *kids* know a belly laugh when it comes along."

He'd written plenty for an encore—jokes, songs, and a tear-jerking scene "exclusively for schools, thanks to the goddamn Gerry Society." He had me carry a small American flag to wave for a finish. I'd exit to my seat amid cheers. And many times an assembly was called for a repeat performance.

Johnny still didn't want me to work in the act, but as he said, it was better than seeing me enter an edifice of torture named P.S. something-or-other. When I *had* to go to school, Johnny saw to it that I was fortified. "Then get off *fast*," he cautioned. "Let 'em mull it over till the three-o'clock gong!"

I got excellent grades.

So it went—a week of school in Trenton, Dallas, Sioux City, Denver, Seattle, Pittsburgh, Washington . . .

"I don't think she's really learning anything, Johnny," Cecilia said.

"F'rinstance, *what* is there to learn? Is arithmetic anything to *laugh* at? What's so funny about grammar? History she'll make. She can read every marquee and billboard we've ever passed. Geography she knows. What other kid of her age has been all over the world, and across the U.S.A. sixty-seven times?"

On days when there was no school Johnny would see that

I was free to walk lovely, tree-lined streets, to peer into shop windows. I loved to see people sitting on the porch of a house. Every day—all the time, winter and summer—those people lived in the same house on the same block. What an exciting life they had!

My own security came from the theater dressing room, its smells, colors, and sounds: greasepaint; L. T. Piver lotion; Cashmere Bouquet soap; Smith Bros. cough drops; putty; Yardley's sachet; the towels heavy with the scent of makeup; Mumm tobacco; Yankee Clover toilet water; Fels Naphtha.

With fascination I watched Mom "bead" her eyelashes with a toothpick dipped into the black wax, Cosmetique, heated in a pan held over a candle. Lump after lump, and presto-chango her lashes looked a foot long. Then she dipped her pinky into a jar of red greasepaint and painted her full lips and rubbed them together until they were smooth and perfect. And that skin! Wherever Cecilia went, people would speak of it.

Looking at my mother, I yearned to be beautiful, too. My eyes shifted to my father's mirror. My skin is dark—so is his. And our eyes are alike—not soft golden brown like Mother's, but sort of gray-green and too big, I decided. People mentioned the "bigness" of my eyes so often that I wished I could take a needle and sew them up on the sides. It was miserable when grown people stared at me and said, "She's got such white teeth." "Her eyes are enormous." "What thick hair." Miserable because Cecilia always said, "Don't be vain, Nora. Don't look at yourself."

Johnny smiled broadly into the mirror to see how he'd appear to the audience. The light globes around the mirrors blinked: it was a half-hour before they were due onstage. They'd blink again for fifteen minutes, then for five, the signal to wait in the wings for their music cue.

One day at the hotel while Cecilia and Johnny were out shopping, Scott broke my beloved doll. He used a pewter water pitcher to smash it. After picking up the pieces of my doll's face, I locked myself in the bathroom and cried. I decided to take a bath and let the tears fall into the water. There I sat, trying to sob hard enough for the rising water to cover my head and drown me. But the process was too slow. So I got dressed and set about finding a quicker way to make my brother suffer. I would melt a Hershey bar on the radiator and lick off all the nice soft goo from the silver paper and not let him have even a taste.

I knew it was wrong to leave Judy and Scott alone while our parents were out, but I had to run down to the lobby to get the candy. I had purchased a Hershey bar and was just about to go back up when I heard a woman screaming. "There's a little boy on the window ledge! His legs are dangling over, and he's looking down! About the fifth floor. He'll fall out, he'll fall out!"

"Oh, God!"

"Got a passkey?"

"Call the Fire Department!"

"A net, a net—that's what we need!"

Crowds gathered in the street. I didn't wait for the elevator. I galloped up the five flights of stairs. "Please, God, don't let him fall; please, God . . ."

My heart was thumping out of me; there was a knife of pain in my side when I opened the door. There he was, bending out toward the street, his legs dangling over the ledge, one hand barely holding the sill.

"Lovely candy, Scott," I whispered, "and we will cook it soft. You can have it all to yourself." I was tiptoeing toward him, and as he looked around I held the Hershey toward him and tried to smile. "All for you, Scott, because you're such a good—" I grabbed the back of his shirt and pulled him to the floor. I threw myself over him as the manager, bellboys, and guests came running in. Someone shut and locked the window.

"He threw the screen to the street."

"Save the rod, spoil the child."

"He should be spanked within an inch of his life."

I held Scott in my arms and looked up at them all. "Kindly leave, please. *I* have charge here."

I stared them down. They filed out, muttering, and the manager muttered with them: "They're actors' kids, what can you expect?"

Judy was gurgling happily and banging her rattle against the crib.

I looked at Scott. "Now we'll cook the Hershey bar, and like I said, you can have it all!" I kissed my brother and went into the bathroom.

"Thank you, God," I blubbered.

3

J OHN MARTEN and Company was playing split weeks, and that meant getting up from a warm berth in the middle of the night, dressing ourselves stooped over, whispering so as not to awaken the passengers who stayed aboard the train. We'd wait huddled together in a depot in the dampness of the night, while Johnny went to look for a place for us to live.

Stations are pretty much alike, I thought, lights that hurt your eyes after sleeping; a lady sitting holding a crying baby; raggy-looking men asleep with their mouths open; a redcap leaning against a wall, staring into space; long benches with used newspapers or candy wrappers on them; a man writing behind a caged booth, bands on his shirtsleeves to hold them up, a green eyeshade to dim the hard light; the slow choo of a train starting, as if all of its strength was needed to move out of the station; men swinging lighted lanterns in the darkness to signal the train on its way; the call of "Booooooord," then the silent movement of people picking up luggage and packages.

"Memphuss—Nashbill—Reanning—Deloot and all-points-sout," would slur through a megaphone. I never knew where the voice came from, nor could I understand the towns it called. I was amazed that anyone ever caught the right train.

And a dog—a skinny, mangy dog—was in every station, snooping in empty bags, looking, sniffing listlessly and almost hopelessly for food and water. My heart ached for each of them. Someday I'm going to be rich and gather up all the depot dogs in the world and make them full and happy, I told myself.

Sometimes the stations would be mystifyingly still. Nothing moving or happening. Everything just waiting. No sound but the faraway toot of a train whistle. But inevitably there was a Harvey House, and we'd all pile in for some hot cereal, tossed at us by a waitress who seemed annoyed that people ate.

Johnny would come back from his search for a place to house us, looking as though something great was in store. His jaunty walk and smiling face never failed to make us confident that we would soon have warm clean beds, hot sudsy water, and our trunks in the room. "Allez-oop," he'd boom, and off we'd start in the cold dawn. On the way he'd recount his experiences, as though they were fun.

"So this skinny witch came to the door with curl papers matted in her hair. Her breath smelled like mildewed socks and nearly knocked me down the stoop.

" 'Two rooms,' I said, and followed her bony behind up three flights of stairs. The rooms were fair—you know, not the king's palace, but fair and pretty clean.

" 'How long?' she asked. 'Three days,' sez I. 'Write your name,' sez she. 'John Marten and Company,' I put in her book. 'What's that, "and Company"?'

" 'Well, my wife and I and three more of us.'

" 'Children?'

" 'In a way.'

" 'No children allowed,' she said through her nose, and her lips drew up to the size of a wrinkled pinhead.

" 'I mean, they're the size of children, but they're full-grown midgets.' She was backing me down the stairs to the front door.

" 'I don't know about midgets, but if they're the size of children, they're children. And no children are ever coming into my establishment.'

"I saw it was no use, so I jumped to the finish, smiling with all my crockery. I said, 'Tell you what I'll do—I'll take them to a lake and drown them, then my wife and I will come right back and enjoy your hospitality.' Her mouth flew open and let out the mildewed socks again as I threw her a kiss."

He grinned at his family. The three of us kids laughed, but Mom didn't.

"Where are we going now?" she asked.

"I got us a hotel."

"Expensive?"

"We'll save the difference next jump," he said. He clamped his teeth on the end of his unlighted cigar, and the veins stood out on his forehead.

4

TAKE this letter, Nora, and do exactly as I say, "Cecilia whispered. "Put it in your bloomer leg, and don't let your father see it. Go straight to the mailbox on the corner and look around you. If you see Dad or anyone else from the bill, keep walking—keep walking until no one is around, then drop it in the box and come right back. No one must see that letter or see you mail it. And never, never mention it to your father. Now, go. Hurry."

I felt weak in the knees as I walked toward the corner. I didn't like having a secret from Dad. But I did as I was told. People were passing, but no one I knew from the theater, and not Johnny. As the letter fell into the mailbox, I saw my mother's handwriting—"Mr. José Mazzo."

It happened again and again, and the letters were always addressed the same. In Detroit, New Brunswick, Portland, Oakland, San Diego.

We'd played at the Orpheum Theater that week in San Diego, and I worked. One night after the show Johnny said, "Kids, your mom and I have talked it out, and you're going to stay in San Diego for a while. Maybe two months. It's time you met some friends and had a home. I'll pick up someone here to take Mom's place in the act and finish out the time. Then I'll come back and get you, and maybe we'll stay a week more."

"Will we stay in a real house? I mean with nobody else in it, and a porch?" I asked.

"Yes, sweetheart, and maybe a backyard."

"And you're going to school and have friends," Cecilia said.

"Friends?"

"Yes, your own age."

"Like Gertrude?"

"Who?"

Scott interrupted. "I want a dog."

"And you'll have one, son. There is a place called a 'pound' where your mom will let you pick one out."

Scott did an Indian war whoop, and Judy and I joined him. "A house, a dog, woo-oo."

Johnny looked at us, his eyes moist. "Oh, God, if only that money wasn't gone, we'd live in one spot always." He seemed to be talking to himself.

The rest of the week we kids were on our best behavior, anticipating the glorious future. Even Scott did so little damage that Dad took his temperature several times to see if he were sick. I kept Scott and Judy in the park between shows while Johnny and Mom went house-hunting.

On Friday they found it: a cottage in the suburbs of San Diego, overhanging a canyon at the end of a dead-end street. It had a big porch and three bedrooms. A huge gnarled pepper tree in a large backyard, and two swings. The section was called Ramona Hills, and Mom said it was "residential." The grammar school was only ten blocks away.

Oh, that first day of getting settled! I had my own room with a white bed, a white dresser, and a white rocking chair. The wallpaper had rosebuds dancing all over it. And there was a low window looking out toward the pepper tree.

I unpacked my precious satchel. Carefully I laid my "jewels" in a design on my dresser—rubies, diamonds, pearls, spangles. And I took out the picture of homes and of beautiful babies I had cut out of magazines.

After that I helped Mom unpack and get Judy and Scott in play clothes. By sunset I was free and standing on the edge of the canyon, my head filled with plans that bumped into each other. We'll have picnics; we'll collect stones; we'll build a hideaway. Then I turned and looked at the long street—our street. The sidewalks were paved; the middle was wide and made of sand and gravel.

A boy ran out of one of the houses, picked up a stone, and threw it high in the air, then galloped across the street, yelling: "Melvin—hey, Melvin, c'mon!" Out the door flew another boy about the same age as the first. Then, as though a whistle blew, boys spilled off all the porches and clunked together in a mass. I hid behind a bush and peeked at them. The boys were swinging a bat. They were going to play baseball.

Scott ran out to see what was going on, and then settled on the curb to watch. I sat cross-legged behind the bush and separated the branches to get a better view. I knew about baseball from watching actors play in the alleys of theaters on nice spring days. They'd let me bat the ball sometimes, and they'd taught me a fancy wind-up for pitching.

The game was in progress.

"Ball one." Pause.

"Ball two." Pause.

"Boy, do you stink!"

I froze. Everyone looked at Scott. Good nightshirt! I thought, we'll never get to play this neighborhood again!

Would anything wipe that smug twist off my brother's mouth?

"Who are you, punk?"

"What's it to ya?"

"I'll tell you what. We're the best team in San Diego, that's what. We're the Cincinnati Reds, and he's the best pitcher anywheres, so button up your lip. You don't belong on this block anyways."

"Go pee up a rope," Scott retorted.

They'll get into a fight, I thought, and they're all twice the size of Scott. I ran from my hiding place and went up to the indignant pitcher. Taking a deep breath, I said, "We live here," and pointed. "I am Nora Marten of John Marten and Company in 'The Boy Is Gone.' This is my brother, Scott, and he's just sticking up for me because"—both teams were gathered around me—"because, well, you see, *I'm* a pitcher."

"A pitcher?"

"Hey, nonnie-nonnie!"

"Tra-la-la, a girl pitcher!"

"Don't make us laugh, pop-eyes."

They all spoke at once.

I was not dismayed. I had been throwing my voice to the balcony for some time, so I did it now and brought about silence.

"And my brother would make a great shortstop—he's faster than greased lightning." I held their attention, my arm around Scott's shoulder.

The team expressed themselves:

"Holy smoke, nutty neighbors!"

"Bats in her belfry!"

A man pushed his way through the noisy crowd.

"Now, kids . . ." He had a pleasant voice and was good-looking. "That's not the way to greet our new neighbors."

"But, Dad, she said she was a *pitcher!*"

Dad looked surprised. "Well—er—a—fine. Let her pitch!" Then he addressed me. "I'm James Tenant. Those two are my sons, James Junior and Arthur."

"How do you do. I'm Nora Marten of John Marten and Company in 'The Boy Is Gone,' assisted by Cecilia Quinn. And this is my brother, Scott, and I have a little sister named Judy, and that is my home."

Suddenly Mom was there, asking pleasantly what was going on.

"You're Mrs. Marten?" Mr. Tenant smiled.

"Yes—is there something wrong?"

"No, just a misunderstanding. Your daughter said she can pitch a ball, and—"

"Yes," Mom said, "she's very good at it."

I was so proud. My mother looked beautiful standing in the pink of a sunset sky.

"Well, come on, kids, let Nora have a chance at it."

Mom and Mr. Tenant were smiling at each other.

"Awright, fellas," Arthur said. "Let 'er pitch just once, then we'll get on with the game; it's gettin' dark."

We all took our places on the diamond. The disgusted pitcher handed me his glove and ball. I whispered in his ear, "I'm not good at it, really. It's not my profession, you know."

I was standing erect, with all eyes upon me. I spat daintily in my left hand, then the right, and rubbed them on the side of my dress. Slowly I put on the mitt. Then I looked at the catcher. He was bent double punching his glove. The batter was cutting the air choppily with his bat. I wound up. Around and around my right arm swung, stiff, and from the shoulder. My left leg kicked high in the air and— Brummmmmmp!

"Strike one!" the umpire bellowed.

Silence—except for the crickets. Once more I wound up, the leg lifting automatically.

"Strike two!"

A dog barked, and a soprano called, "Theodore, time to come home!"

"Strike three. You're out!"

It was suddenly almost dark, the lights twinkled on in all the houses, and everyone drifted away. The day was over. I sniffed the evening air happily.

Grabbing my hand, Scott said, "Let's sit in my pepper tree!" As we set off toward our first backyard, I barely noticed Mom and Mr. Tenant standing on the front porch.

Cecilia took us all to the pound, where we bought Queenie for a dollar. "Genuwine collie," the man said, "about three years old, I guess—was pretty thrashed up when we brought her in."

Cecilia said she doubted the dog being "genuwine," but no matter—our first dog was loved desperately from that moment on.

The days following were filled with other "firsts."

"My name's Andrea. Want to climb my loquat tree?"

"Oh, yes, thank you," I answered.

New experiences happened so fast they tumbled over each other: walking to school with girl friends while they rattled all kinds of exciting plans: "You sharpen the pencils Mondays; I'll sharpen them Tuesdays." And their gossip: "Helen's got a crush on Alfred, but he likes Augustine." We exchanged sandwiches at lunchtime: "I'll give you a half a peanut butter for a half a jelly." And at recess: "You can sit on the grass with our group, Nora. Eleanor's group are dumb bunnies." And the school play: "Mom, Mom! They gave me a part in *Little Women!* I play Amy. Marion picked her pimples during rehearsals, so the teacher made her an usher. It isn't a 'single,' Mom. It's a whole lot of us together. We open next Wednesday in assembly, and parents are invited. Will you come?"

More firsts: pulling wild oats on the walk home from school and bouncing them up and down in my open palm until they disappeared; chewing on sour grass; putting buttercups under a chin "to see if you like butter"; waving at girls and boys passing on bicycles; hopscotching on all the squares of pavement.

And the inside of our home. I wanted to pat every inch of it. For the first few days, I took my little suitcase to school, but I was asked so many questions that I decided to leave it in my top drawer at home. After school I'd take it out and sit in my white rocking chair looking over my possessions: my own dresser, my own bed, my own window, the poppies I had picked in the canyon. I could stare at my room forever, I thought. And, heavens to Betsy—the "Cincinnati Reds" let me pitch now and again!

And Mom stopped sending those letters to that man, and was almost always happy. She sang a lot and cooked fine meals. Mr. Tenant sat at the kitchen table sometimes and watched her cook. I wondered why Mrs. Tenant didn't come, too, but Arthur said his mother was visiting her parents in Iowa.

The days flew by. Judy was getting a wonderful color from being out in the backyard all day. Scott did comparatively little damage to San Diego, although one day he nailed my shoes to the floor so I was late for school. He urinated in the bathroom sink until I explained that this was not a theater, so he was to use the toilet. And he put live caterpillars in Judy's bed. Still, Cecilia could write Johnny that Scott was taming down.

Then there was the principal of the school, Mr. Van Buren. I thought he was the nicest principal of any school anywhere, and he liked me. When I did Amy in *Little Women* and said "Cologaney" instead of "Cologne," he laughed louder than anyone. "I did it on purpose," I explained to him, "because there were no laughs, and it was getting near the finish."

He took a great interest in me from then on, and many times after school he'd ask me into his office and question me about my life. He was crippled, which made me like him even more. He had an awful limp, poor man.

He chose me to deliver corrected papers to the various classrooms during the last period. And when I reported back to his office, he asked me to stay awhile. "Don't you get tired of different hotel rooms all the time?"

"I like my home here better than anyplace, but it's fun to fix up our adjoining rooms at a hotel."

"What do you mean?"

"Well, we have five trunks, you see. One for the theater things; one for cooking utensils and dishes; one for Mom and Dad's clothes; one for our clothes; and one filled with toys and all my decorations."

"Decorations?"

"Dad bought me pink spreads for the beds. I put the pearl-handled manicure set and brushes out, and cover the hotel trunk with flowered cretonne. I have cushions and dolls and vases for flowers. And Dad invented a rubber thing so I can hang up our pictures without putting nails in the wall. It's like a plunger. It only takes me ten minutes to make the rooms look pretty. I hang a line in the bathroom for our wash. Handkerchiefs go on the mirror to press them. And the bottom drawer of the dresser is where we keep our groceries. Most times we eat in the room. Mom cooks over a Sterno, and we stuff cotton in the keyholes so the management doesn't smell the food."

"You can't have many friends, spending only a week in each city."

"Scott and Judy are my friends—and my case and my doll."

It was fun being listened to. I ran, skipped, and hop-scotched home.

One day I had a very sore throat, and the school nurse sent me home. The front door was locked, so I went around to the kitchen door, and Queenie jumped up to greet me. I went right to my room to drop my books, and was surprised to find Judy taking her afternoon nap there. I tiptoed out to look for Cecilia, but Mom wasn't in sight, so I went to her room. The door was locked. That's funny, I thought. "Mom,

Mom," I called softly, so as not to wake Judy. I heard moving in the room, but no answer. "Mom," I called again. The door opened. It was two o'clock in the afternoon, but Mom still had her nightgown on, and her hair was mussed.

"Why are you home so early? Come in the kitchen."

"I have a sore throat."

"Well, goddamn it, why don't you keep your sweater buttoned?"

"I'm sorry, Mom."

"Pick up those papers in the yard, and I'll get your bed ready. Stay out there till I call you."

"Yes, Mom."

I picked up the papers, and Queenie gave me a kiss every time I bent down. I felt dizzy and could hardly swallow. I threw Queenie's ball toward the side of the house, and it landed in the bushes.

"I'll get it for you, Queenie girl."

I was on my knees looking for the ball when I saw Mr. Tenant climb out of the side window and crouch down. Then I heard my mother's voice call from the kitchen door.

"Nora, come in here this minute."

One morning before school Mom called me. "Sit here," she said, putting a chair in front of the mirror. "And don't look at yourself—it's vain. I'm going to fix your hair another way."

I kept my eyes down, and Mom yanked my long curls and braided them so tight that my eyes filled with tears. With horror I felt the ends being snipped off with scissors, saw my curls on the floor.

When I got to class, I was bombarded with: "Your hair looks awful!" "Where are the pretty curls?" "You look like you're Dutch now." My head ached, and when the teacher asked, "Where are your lovely curls?" I excused myself and went to the girls' room. I looked fully in the mirror.

"I don't like you, Mom, I don't, and I hate Mr. Tenant, and I hated mailing those letters. You're mean, you're a mean mother!" I washed my face. "I'll tell Mr. Van Buren that I'm going to run away and take Queenie and Judy and my case and my doll." I was undecided about Scott. Maybe I'd send for him when he grew up.

On my way back to class I saw Mr. Van Buren coming out of the library hall.

"Why, hello, Nora," he said. "What did you do to your beautiful hair?"

"Mr. Van Buren, may I come to your office after school? I'm going to run away."

"Of course, I'll wait for you." He smiled and patted my head. "And don't look so sad. It couldn't be as bad as all that."

When I got to Mr. Van Buren's office with my aching head and my slicked-back, cut-off hair, I didn't tell him about Mr. Tenant and Mr. Mazzo, but I did say I felt very terrible and wanted to go far away and have my own room.

"You're just growing up," he said, and took me in his arms. Next to Dad, he's the nicest man in the whole world, I decided. Then it happened. He had his hand between my legs and was hurting me. "Hold still," he said, breathing hard. I screamed, and he clapped his hand over my mouth. I fought and hit at him, and finally got out the door. I ran fast, toward home, then past it, and hid at the top of the canyon. I stayed there until it was almost dark, not crying, not thinking, just throwing up and whimpering, and not knowing what to do about the pain.

When I finally got home, Mr. Tenant was there.

"You're out too late, Nora. Wash up—dinner is ready," Cecilia said.

Two weeks later, Johnny was home, and we were off to Salt Lake City, and I never had to see Mr. Van Buren or Mr. Tenant again.

5

THERE was Waco, Milwaukee, Concord, Sheridan, Wheeling, Cleveland, Boston, Peoria, Tulsa, Augusta, Baltimore, Hartford, Buffalo.

Buffalo. I was glad to get out of Buffalo because of what happened to Judy. Cecilia had taken Scott to the dentist: he had got a penny stuck between his two front teeth. I was playing house with Judy at the hotel. When it was feeding time, I heated the cereal over the Sterno and started to feed Judy. But when I tested it, it tasted so dull that I decided to give the baby a change: potato chips, my favorite food. Judy started stuffing them in her mouth. She gurgled, swallowed, and began to choke. I banged her on the back and shook her, but nothing happened. My sister's face started to turn blue. I ran into the hall with Judy in my arms just as Mom was coming out of the elevator with Scott.

"She's choking," I screamed. "Mom, Mom—help her!"

Cecilia dropped her packages and quickly stuck her finger down Judy's throat and pulled away the potato chip lodged against her windpipe. Judy cried, but she was all right.

I sank to the floor. Mom picked me up gently and laid me on the bed and put a cold cloth over my eyes. "Now, Nora, stop shaking like that. Your sister's all right."

"But I hurt Judy!"

"There's no harm done, except to you. Your face is pure white."

I threw my arms around her. My mom's so good, I thought. It's the best feeling in the world when we all love each other.

Johnny came in looking tired. Scott brought him up to date on the near-tragedy, and wound up by saying: "Anyways, those were *my* potato chips. Nora stole them."

Johnny lay down on the bed next to me. "Judy's all right. You mustn't blame yourself, it was an accident, and they happen. After dinner we'll take a nice long walk and look in the store windows. We don't open until tomorrow."

The transoms were closed; there was cotton in the keyholes, and Mom was preparing weiners and carrots. I set the "kitchen" trunk—put the celluloid dishes, the ketchup, salt and pepper, and the tin utensils on top of it. We owned a batik tablecloth, a gift from Mrs. Benson of Bensons' Trained Dogs. We used hotel towels for napkins, and the stools and chairs from both rooms. I put my vase of artificial daisies in the middle of the trunk and a lighted candle in a pink pottery holder.

Later the few leftovers went down the toilet, and I washed the dishes in the bathroom basin and put them away. I used the toy broom and dustpan Johnny had bought me to sweep up. And when the cretonne cover was back on the trunk again, the hotel management would not be the wiser.

After dinner Scott and I went into the other room to play. We turned the chairs upside down and spread a sheet over the top of the legs to make an odd-angled tent. I never tired of picturing the inside of the tent as a thing of beauty—just like our San Diego home. I set miniature dishes on top of a cigar box for "tea."

Johnny called me. "Your mom wants to write some letters, Nora, so put Judy and Scott to bed, and you and I'll walk to the theater and check the props. Bring your skates. We'll look for a park on the way back."

More letters, I thought. For two months now I'd had to mail letters to Mr. J. Tenant, P.O. Box 1120, San Diego, and I hated it.

A soft light stalled in the sky as Johnny and I strolled hand-in-hand toward the theater, Johnny talking. "One of these days we're going into a solid business, Nora, in one spot. No traveling at all. You'll go to the same school and live in the same house, like San Diego." I looked up at him; his eyes had filled with tears. "And—well—you'll have friends who will last a lifetime, and you'll marry someone solid, you know, in business—a man who'll be kind to you, a man who can stay in one spot," he added.

"I just want my own room—and Queenie." I swallowed. We both walked along silently for a while, thinking of that heartbreaking last day in San Diego when we drove Queenie, in a borrowed car, all the way to Imperial Valley. An elderly fortune-teller who had retired from circus life and was living on a small farm had said she would take our dog. The parting was awful. We couldn't forget the look in Queenie's eyes as we drove away.

At daylight the next morning the owner of the borrowed car was in front of our home, waiting to drive us to the depot. I backed out of my room so that I could see it as long as possible, backed out through the dining room and living room, and then I heard Scott's voice yelling hysterically, "Queenie, here's Queenie—Queenie's come home!" We all knelt on the grass and kissed and hugged and laughed and cried over the worn-out, mud-spattered dog. Queenie had done the impossible—found us, somehow, from five hours away.

But we knew we could not take her with us. She just *had*

to be left behind. The sound of our sobbing was more than the owner of the borrowed car could stand, so he gently took Queenie. "My wife and I will take care of her for you. I give you my word. Come on, now, you'll miss your train."

Johnny broke our painful thoughts. "Look at those skates," he said, pointing in a store window. "They have rubber tires. I'll get them for you when the store opens tomorrow." He wiped the tears from my eyes, and I smiled up at him.

At the theater he told me to go backstage, while he talked to the manager out front.

"Good evening," I said as I passed some of the performers standing in the alley, getting a breath of fresh air before going on the stage. "We open tomorrow—acoustics any good?"

"Not bad—picture stinks, though, so the houses haven't been good," from a strawberry-haired woman with purple spangles on her costume.

"What act are you, Moon-eyes?" a man in a tuxedo asked.

I noticed his collar and cuffs were frayed. But it'll never show from the front, I decided. "John Marten and Company in 'The Boy Is Gone,' assisted by Cecilia Quinn."

"Great act," the dwarf said with a grin.

"None better. John's got the best laugh act around. You'll do business next week," the nice frayed man said.

"Having *Flesh and the Devil* with Norma Talmadge ain't gonna hurt none," Purple Spangles snapped.

I went through the stage door and right to the mailbox in the basement. I always felt adult and important going through the mail. Seldom, though, was there a letter addressed to John Marten and Company.

"Come on, honey," Johnny said. "Let's go to the park. I've left the prop list, and we'll rehearse the music in the morning."

It was getting dark, but we found the park, and Johnny helped me on with my skates, under a lamppost. "That's a nice hunk of pavement, go to it." He sat on the bench and watched me. I skated, but stayed within his sight. He was awfully blue. I wished I could think of something funny. I skated in front of him and went into an off-balance arabesque, my eyes wide with pretended fear. Then I twirled around and around, and, as though I were dizzy, I grabbed at the air and stumbled crazily. He laughed. I skated happily along the path.

After about fifteen minutes I sank on the bench beside him. He put his arm around me, and I relaxed on his shoulder. An indescribable feeling of safety and confidence filled me. He's the strongest man in the world. There is nothing he can't do, I thought.

His voice was comforting. "Y'see, Nora, things are not like they were. They're not paying salaries anymore on account of moving pictures, so it's tough to save. But don't you worry, we've been careful, and it won't be much longer before I'll have two thousand dollars in my money belt. And we'll open something—a store, maybe."

"A store?"

"Yep. A ladies' ready-to-wear or something. You know, something everybody's got to have—like toilet paper. We'll find a nice small town that looks like a boom, and we'll settle there and have an income. Then, by God, no more packing and moving!"

I looked at his face in the lamplight and knew that whatever he said was right and would come true.

Suddenly a gust of cold wind made us scurry for the hotel. "Gee whiz"—and Johnny grinned—"the weather's so changeable, you don't know *what* to hock!"

There was San Francisco, Portland, St. Louis, Bar Harbor, Wilmington, Worcester. The Orpheum and Pantages circuits had cut many cities on account of moving pictures, Johnny growled. "And it's not bad enough as it is—the frigs are starting to talk!"

There were more split weeks, and one-night stands. The

"solid season" stopped. But the packing and moving, cold trains, colder stations, didn't stop.

I learned from my sporadic schooling that I could tell the principal I was in 6-A when in reality I'd never been near 4-B. All I had to say was: "My credits from Cincinnati will be here soon," and into 6-A I'd go. By the time the credits arrived, the Martens would be playing Butte, Montana—or some other city.

"The Board of Education was fouled by vaudevillians," Johnny smugly proclaimed.

Nevertheless, he kept updating the act I performed at each new school. It eased me to hear the strange children laugh, to have their applause. But recesses and lunchtimes were rough on me. Usually I hid in the girls' room until they were over.

For the children, in separate bunches, would become silent when I approached. The girls would stare, the boys would whistle and point. I understood. They all knew each other, and I was a newcomer who had to prove myself before I could belong to them. But how could I? They had started school together from the beginning. They had learned to belong to each other—all at the same time. I had only one week to make it in. So it was easier for me to hide in the girls' room until those periods were over. Then, in the next town I'd skip a grade or two, if I felt like it. There I had it on them; it was my secret.

Salisbury, St. Cloud, Biloxi, Gary, Pocatello, Hot Springs, Corpus Christi, Clinton, Dubuque, Cedar Rapids. We were in Seattle now, and Johnny was tapping on a water pitcher in the Sullivan Hotel. "Meeting'll pleez come to order," he said, rocking back and forth on his heels, stroking an imaginary beard. We kids sat cross-legged on the floor in front of him. Cecilia rubbed night cream on her face as she sat in the armchair. We gave Johnny our rapt attention. He took an impressive pause. Scott belched. "Jesus," Johnny said, forgetting his subject matter, "maybe he needs an operation. I never even heard such wind come out of a fat man, let alone out of a wiry little frame like his. What d'ya think, Mom?"

"Stop worrying. He does it deliberately—practices all day. On with the meeting!"

Johnny looked at Scott for a long moment, worried.

"Meeting, meeting, meeting," Judy squealed.

Johnny cleared his throat. "Ladies and chentlemen—var vas I?"

We cheered and applauded him.

He raised his hand to silence us. "Pleez—mein friends—jokes aside, kids, here's what I've got to tell you. You're going to have a home. A home. We're going to live in one spot. We've got two thousand dollars you've helped me save—two thousand dollars right here." He whacked his belly and sides and made us laugh again. "We just have to play four more dates, but I booked 'em in *that* direction. We have a big jump from here, but we're going to get there—to Waterville, Texas. That'll be our home. It's a boom town. Joe Walker of Walker's Midgets told me York and Queen told him they were stranded there once and heard from the natives that there was plenty of oil under the dirt. They couldn't stay, because they'd already booked Canada, but they told Walker about it." He paused impressively. "So, kids, we're going to open a ready-to-wear store. Y'see, that's what everyone has to have —ready-to-wear. And you're going to meet friends and go to the same school, and live in the same spot. And you'll have a dog, and cement to skate on. And, Mom, you won't have to wash and cook and be a million things and an actress, too. You'll just be ours, and I'll make it up to you."

Scott was pulling in air through his mouth, trying to belch again. Judy poked him to stop it. Cecilia was still rubbing the cream into her face, but she was smiling lovingly at Dad.

I hugged myself and rocked happily.

"So, kids, there it is—'the sun shines bright in our Waterville-hill home,'" Johnny sang.

We all jumped up, and everybody kissed everybody.

"Let's have chop suey—no cooking in the room tonight."

We weren't to open for two days, but we jumped ahead to Cedar Rapids because, as Johnny said, "They have a hell of a park."

So two whole days were ours, and the park had a zoo. We skated, ate hot dogs and popcorn, and fed peanuts to the animals.

Early the second day Mom packed jelly sandwiches and milk, and while Johnny went to the theater to check his props, Mom and the three of us went to the fountain in the center of the park to sail the boats we'd made out of hotel stationery. Suddenly there was a deluge of rain, and we scurried to gather our belongings. We had to go four blocks to our streetcar line, and we thought we'd drown before we got there.

"Never saw anything like this rain since we were in Honolulu," Mom said to me. We stopped to wipe the water out of our eyes and looked longingly at the porch of the house in front of us.

A woman came out the door. "Come on up, you people," she beckoned to us.

We didn't need a second invitation. We turned into the walk and ran up to her.

"You poor dears, you're soaking. I'm Mrs. Lyndon. If you come in, I'll get you some towels."

"My name's Cecilia Marten. These are my children, Scott, Judy, and Nora. We'd love to dry off, but can we go to your kitchen so we won't wreck the place?"

Never in our lives had we seen such a kitchen. It even had a fireplace.

A maid appeared with towels, and then went back for an armful of bathrobes.

"Take off your wet things, and Alberta will press them dry. We're about to have tea, so come in the drawing room when you are ready."

We dried ourselves in silence. When we were wrapped in

the robes, we walked down the wide, lavish hall and found Mrs. Lyndon with her husband.

"Sit down and relax," he invited us. "You're absolutely right," he said to his wife. "I never saw such a resemblance."

We bumped into each other getting to the sofa. Mrs. Lyndon poured tea, while Scott eyed a trayful of dainty sandwiches.

"Boy, I'm so hungry my stomach thinks my throat is cut," he said. And he was kicked in both shins by Mom and me.

We all took a sandwich, and then Mrs. Lyndon turned to me. "Our daughter, Audrey, will be down in a minute. You'll know what my husband was talking about when you see her." Just then, a young girl came into the room.

"Audrey, this is Nora." We smiled at each other, then stared. We both saw our amazing resemblance to each other.

Two hours passed. The rain stopped, and we were back in our dry clothing.

"Don't forget, tomorrow, Nora, in time for lunch. I'll be waiting for you," Audrey called as we waved good-bye.

The two of us spent the whole week together—in the park, at picture shows. "Do you recognize the profession?" I would ask the ticket taker solemnly. Then I'd proudly take my friend's hand and march us in free of charge. The Lyndons were guests of the Martens at our own theater, and Johnny took them for chop suey later.

Audrey and I marveled over our resemblance—even to the identical twin moles on our cheeks. "Maybe we're long lost twins," I said hopefully.

It was Easter vacation, so there was no school, and Johnny cut me out of the act to free me for my new-found friend.

I prayed that closing day would never come. But it came, and Audrey and I had to say good-bye. The train was to leave at midnight.

I went to the theater to help pack. The talkie *Noah's Ark* was on, and it was two hours before the final performance. I fussed around the dressing room, then took my case and doll and walked out on the empty stage and over to the ground cloth by the wall. I lay down on my stomach and let the tears fall. Before long I felt a hand on my back, rubbing it gently. It was Johnny.

"Don't, honey, for God's sake, don't," he said, and took me in his arms.

"Oh, Dad, I can't leave her. I can't. She's my friend . . . I love her."

"I know, I know . . ."

My body trembled as he rocked me. Suddenly Johnny said: "Go to your mother. Tell her I'll be back in time for the show."

When Johnny came back, he sat at the dressing table. I noticed his hands were shaking so much it was difficult for him to put his makeup on. When he was ready, he turned to me. "I tried to get her for you to keep. I tried—they understood." He put his hand over his eyes. "I said they could have the whole two thousand dollars I've saved in my money belt— I guess I'd have shot somebody that said that to me, but they were kind . . ."

The lights blinked.

"Onstage, Dad," I said, and kissed the back of his head.

During the show a bouquet of roses came addressed to Miss Nora Marten. The enclosed card read:

> Dearest Nora,
>   Your father is a wonderful man.
> We'll miss you.
>   Audrey, Susan, and Jim Lyndon.

6

MOM HAD a miscarriage on the train. The conductor wired ahead for an ambulance to be waiting at the next stop, Des Moines. Johnny, desperate with fear, tried to get a room for Mom instead of the lower berth, but it meant carrying her through four cars. The women passengers who were clustered around us advised against it.

I took Judy and Scott to the ladies' room to be out of the way. It was past midnight; we had three hours to wait. I put towels on the floor for us to sit on. "Now, let's say our prayers for Mom."

"Geez," Scott groaned. "It ain't bad enough you got me in the ladies' room, I gotta say my prayers."

"Please, Scott, Mom is very sick. Let's be quiet awhile and just know that God will keep her safe."

We were quiet—just the train noises. And I thought how hard all of this traveling was on Mom. All those diapers she had washed in small basins on trains, in hotels and theaters—all those bottles she had heated and sterilized under impossible conditions. And she was constantly mending our clothes and finding ways to appease our appetites. Yet she always looked so beautiful—she should have been a princess. No wonder she was so mean at times.

My eyes were closed. "Please, God, don't pay any attention to those letters she writes or, you know, those things."

It was bitter cold dawn when Cecilia was carried on a stretcher to the ambulance. Johnny turned to us and in a strangled voice said, "Here's ten dollars, Nora. Get our baggage and a taxi to take you to the Chatham Hotel. I'll call—I'll . . ."

"John, don't worry about the kids. I'm takin' 'em under my wing. You stay with Ceeley." The woman's voice was warm, husky, reassuring.

"God bless you, Sophie," Johnny managed to say. Then he jumped into the ambulance, and they pulled away.

I turned to the woman. "Thank you, Miss Tucker."

"Come on, now, get in the car and warm up. There'll be hot chocolate and sandwiches for you at the hotel. You'll sleep like cherubs—because your mother has a great doctor. He's a long-time pal of mine, and he knows his stuff."

In the car she kept talking: "Dawgonedest way I heard about it. After the show I couldn't sleep, so I went down to the lobby to see if there was an all-night café. The gent at the switchboard said he'd send a boy for some vittles for me. Well, I stayed there gabbin' with him till the food came. Guess those guys got nothin' much to do during the night, so they listen in to calls to break the monotony. He told me there was an emergency call from a train—lady sick—people from the theater. I had him call the hospital and found out it was your mother. Well, I called my pal, Dr. Marshall, and told him to take care of the situation, and he promised." She chuckled pleasantly. "Worked the bill many times with your dad before you kids were even born—great guy. He worships your beautiful ma. . . . That, Dr. Marshall, and God's help will get her well."

The famous singer of songs, belter of lyrics, talked on. "I caught the stuttering-maid bit you broke in in Chicago, Nora. You do the toughest thing on the boards—you feed a comic delux—and brother, straight men are tough to come by!" She smiled at me.

We were at the hotel.

Mom was in the hospital for two weeks, so I went on the stage in her place. Mrs. O'Dell of Remick and O'Dell altered Mom's white, beaded dress to fit eleven-year-old me—leaving the material inside so it could be let out again when Mom was well. I bought high-heeled white pumps and smeared an overabundance of greasepaint on my face. Then bright blue over the lids, a dot of red lipstick in the corner of each eye, red inside my nostrils—why, I didn't know. My blond curls were piled high on my head, and I stared at myself in the mirror and grinned like Johnny always did.

I'm sort of pretty, I thought, then looked away quickly, not to be vain. But I glanced once in the full-length mirror and felt my face flush, for I noticed the way I stuck out in the chest.

Johnny was delighted with the way I looked, and he smiled for the first time since Mom took sick.

The lights blinked one last time: onstage. Johnny and I walked to the wings. "Don't be nervous, honey. Just come through center door fancy, aching to please. They'll feel it and respond. Push out all the humor and warmth you've got, till it reaches the last man in the third balcony."

Then he added, "Sometimes, no matter how hard you try, it doesn't seem to work." He paused. "But don't let it take the starch out of you. You've tried—and that's the best any-one can do." He looked at me. "I told you sort of that when you were a baby," he said.

I smiled up at him. "I remember."

Johnny made the first entrance. The music—"The Sheik of

Araby"—was up forte until he took his hand out of his pocket, then pianissimo until he sat on the sofa, then out. He was on the stage for four solid minutes alone, not saying a word, and the audience rocked with laughter all that time.

I stood listening, caught in the wonderment of his panto-mime. Finally my cue came, and I smiled and entered.

As best I could, I imitated my mother's society woman, copying her timing and her gestures. Most important, Johnny got his laughs, and he was delighted with me.

The week went fast.

Between shows the four of us would go to the hospital to visit Mom. We children picked flowers for her from the front lawns we passed, so her room looked very cheery. Johnny brought her a paper box of chop suey, but the doctor was afraid it might be gassy, so Johnny ate it for her. The acts playing on the bill took turns visiting and brought her presents: a bar of tar soap; talcum powder; two magazines; a sack of gumdrops; a nail file; licorice shoestrings; and a small, live turtle. Mom named the turtle "Miss Carriage," and she and Johnny thought that was a great joke. Eventually Judy fell heir to the turtle, and Miss Carriage slept with her from then on.

Mom progressed, but the doctor told Johnny that she must have rest for at least a month. A family meeting was called. "Now, kids, for just a little while longer we'll have to forget the ready-to-wear store. When Mother's well enough to travel, the doctor says we'd better take her to Brooklyn to rest. The Flying Cains are retired now, and they have two extra rooms, so Mother and Scott and Judy can stay there for a while. Nora and I will jump out and play some time around the East. We got a fat dent in our bankroll, but thank God we had it to dent." He took a deep breath. He saw how serious we were and decided to cheer us up. "You've got a beautiful mother, you know that; but once, before I met her, I almost got hooked by another gal."

"Ooooh—tell us," Judy begged.

"Who?" I asked.

"Nobody's hookin' me, ever," Scott bragged.

Johnny continued. "This fuzz-nutty booberine was any-where between fifty and ninety. She had swivel teeth, and when she opened her mouth, they spread out like a fan! Some-one told me, if I married her, I'd get everything her father had. Luckily I found out that all he had was the seven-year itch and a dollar watch. When he wasn't scratching, he was winding." We'd heard the routine before, but we cheered and applauded. "Now, let's go get some doughnuts and coffee. I'll bet you're starved."

Filing out to the elevator, we harmonized: "M is for the million things she gave me. . . ."

On the train east Cecilia asked me to sit on the side of her berth. She wanted to tell me something important.

I was fearful. My conscience was clear, but that tone in Cecilia's voice always meant something unpleasant.

"Nora, you're growing up, and you will bleed soon."

"Bleed?"

"Yes, bleed, and you'll continue to bleed every month of your life until you're old."

My palms were wet.

"Stop looking so horrified. Everyone does it. You're no different than the rest."

"All my life?"

"Yes."

"Where will I bleed?"

There was a long pause.

"Through your nose," Cecilia answered irritably, and turned her back on me.

It was Johnny and I now: split weeks; Elk's Clubs; paid benefits; one-night stands. Trying to stay near the East, we grabbed every booking we could.

Four months passed as we played a couple of weeks, then

crowded into the Flying Cains's house to visit the family, then went off again.

Judy was in seventh heaven, because she'd added a mangy cat to keep Miss Carriage company. She called it Amos, after "Amos and Andy," but she was not one bit astounded when Amos gave birth to six kittens.

Scott loved Brooklyn, particularly his school; he never attended it. He learned lovely non-show-business expressions from the guys on the corner: "Shinny on your own side"; "Yer cousin sleeps with polacks"; "She's a free hump for the monkies." He got his education on the Brooklyn streets.

"Honeys"—Johnny cleared his throat, and we knew it was a meeting—"we just have to get the act together. The bookings around here have been wrung dry, and the faster we get the two grand in the ole money belt, the faster we can open a store and retire!"

So—Hagerstown, Paducah, Rockford, Twin Falls, Fort Wayne, Springfield, Dearborn, Portsmouth, Shreveport, Evanston, Ann Arbor, Toledo, Kansas City . . .

Long hauls, near-impossible jumps, one-night stands. Everybody was in the act now: Mom was back, and Scott and Judy had been added to the Company. Dad made me the society woman's maid, and Scott and Judy were neighborhood kids. He gave me some laugh lines, gave them a song and soft-shoe dance. In the eighteen-minute act, we did everything but our laundry.

Johnny rehearsed us between shows, during meals, in the middle of the night, traveling, walking to the theater, while we were sitting on the toilet. We thought it would never end. When we were on the stage, if Johnny didn't get a laugh on a certain gag—the same one he'd used for twenty-odd years—he'd swear it was because we'd moved on it. "Don't budge an eyeball when I'm talking," he'd caution. If a tried-and-true piece of business flopped, he'd blame us all for having the wrong expression on our faces. He even reprimanded Mom for having loose beads on her dress. "If they fall, it's distracting, goddamnit!" He rewrote the story line of the sketch, added songs and tap dancing to accommodate the larger cast, but it was still John Marten and Company in "The Boy Is Gone."

"We've got to boil ourselves down to one room, kids, if we want to save." So sleeping, cooking, washing, ironing, playing, rehearsing, laughing, and crying were done in one room, with three extra cots and a box for Miss Carriage and her pal Amos.

Johnny bought an electric plate, so we had coffee and doughnuts for breakfast, meat and vegetables for supper, and doughnuts and coffee after the show. Once a week, chop suey in a restaurant. Rehearse, work, travel. Rehearse, work, travel.

7

WE WERE in Flint. A meeting was called. "Kiss show business good-bye, kids." Johnny patted his money belt. "With God's help and what's around my belly, we close here, and that's the finale! It's been rough, but I've got a stand-up family, and you've made it come true. We're going home," he finished, all choked up. We screamed and yelled and hugged and kissed. Judy stood on the bed, her arms raised.

"All together now," she warned. "There's no place like ho-home. . . ."

"There-hairs—no-ho place like ho-o-ome. . . ." we harmonized.

The train gasped into the station, shuddered, and stopped. We'd spent endless days on it. Every couple of hours we had stopped at a not-on-the-map town. You Bet, Texas, was our favorite. We'd been looking out the window at a man who was putting a sign around his neck that read, "I am blind." He had looked up and down the cars and decided to get on ours. He'd jumped aboard, but as he came down the aisle had suddenly become halt and lame, tapping a cane on the floor to feel his way. He came to a standstill at our section. "Please help me, I am blind and crippled, and I have eleven children to feed!" Johnny put a quarter in his tin cup.

"Eleven childen!" Cecilia repeated.

Johnny winked at her and said, "Don't blame the poor man. He can't see what he's doing!"

The beggar looked over his fogged-up glasses at Johnny, snorted, and moved on to try his luck with less discerning passengers.

"They even got clip merchants in You Bet," Scott said.

The trip had been grueling, the heat and stale air stifling, but we were here at last. "Utopia," Johnny said with hope in his heart.

"Waterville, Texas," a weathered sign announced.

Five weary, dirty, hungry Martens alighted, luggage stacked all around us. A bug jogged us up to a dismal-looking hotel, and there we had our first nonsandwich meal in days: watery soup; cold hot biscuits; lukewarm, tough chicken; stringy string beans; and a blob of wet hominy grits. We got it down, absconded with a glass of milk for the pets, and went upstairs to bathe and rest. Johnny set right out to find a location for our store.

It wasn't as easy as he thought, and three days passed before he announced: "I've found it! It's great! A white cottage, and we can live in the back. The landlord said if we paint the rooms ourselves, we can have it for thirty-five dollars a month. And listen to this—it's across the street from a big girl's college, and girls buy dresses, see? The store part will be in the living room and dining room, and we'll live in the rest!"

We hopped and danced around until Cecilia yelled, "Don't, the floor will cave in!"

It took us two weeks to get our new establishment ready. We had paintbrushes in our hands from morning until night. Johnny did the ceiling, Mom and I the sides; Scott mixed and stirred the paint; Judy did the doors. "For a group that never painted anything but their mugs, it ain't bad," Johnny said as we all looked at the completed job.

Bright yellow it was—and not too streaked. Johnny and Mom had picked up three secondhand clothes racks and a showcase for purses, stockings, jewelry. We rented a sewing machine, and Mom stitched up pretty yellow and white curtains. We painted a couple of second-hand chairs the color of the wall, and Mom made cushions to match the curtains.

Judy said she could paint leaves, so Johnny bought her a paint set—and it was true! From behind the showcase she painted lovely ivy running up the wall. How could a little girl who'd been on trains and in theaters all her life know how to paint? "You'll study art when you go to school here," Mom decided.

School! It was important, Johnny said, because it would be a way to drum up customers for the store. But first things first, and I was the caretaker for a day while Johnny and Cecilia went to Fort Worth to the wholesale houses. They spent a thousand dollars on merchandise.

One more week passed, and we were ready for the Grand Opening. The sign outside was in gold lettering: THE LA MODE DRESS SHOPPE. Johnny thought that sounded just French enough.

John Marten and Company were tense waiting for the first customer. Finally in she came—a young girl from the college. "Good afternoon." She smiled at the five of us.

"Good afternoon," we answered in unison.

"All right if I look around?"

We nodded.

"I want something in a flowered-print dress. I'm going home for a visit this weekend."

"Oh, dear," Cecilia said.

"My God!" Johnny said.

"We haven't got one," I said.

"Phooey," Judy said.

Scott was the first to make a move. He walked to the rack, got a dress, and held it up. "This ain't mashed potatoes."

"It's dots," Cecilia said.

"But it's quite pretty," the college girl said. "May I try it on?"

We all went into action. We also all went into the fitting room with the startled girl.

"If you don't mind, I'll just slip into this myself," she said politely.

"Of course. Get out, kids."

"Come on, Judy."

"Scott! Did you hear me?"

"Oh," the girl called. "It's very pretty, but the tag says ten-sixty-five. . . . I can't pay more than eight dollars for a dress."

"Eight's all right," Johnny answered.

"Let's see you in it," Cecilia called.

The girl stepped out. The dress fit perfectly.

"I love it," she said, and smiled into the mirror. "Thank you for the reduction."

"Not at all," Johnny said. "Nora, let's have some coffee and cake."

I ran to the kitchen and put a big pot of coffee on, then set the table for six. The bell rang over the front door. Three more girls! They looked at the dresses, but their purchase was a dollar-ninety-eight for a red bracelet.

All us Martens waited on the girls, and four of us took turns trying to wrap the purchase. Scott held out his hand for the dollar-ninety-eight.

"It goes in that drawer, Scott," Mom reminded him, "every last penny of it."

"We've got a packed house," Johnny said. "Might as well

have a celebration, so let's exit to the antechamber and have coffee and cake, girls."

We gathered every stool, box, and chair, and nine noisy chatterers sat around the kitchen table. I got our ukuleles, and the crowded kitchen rang with voices: "Every little breeze is singing and birds are winging at sundown. . . ."

Three more girls came into the store, and we Martens stopped the gaiety long enough to sell them a pair of hose— then to brew another pot of coffee. By the time that was empty and Cecilia's cake and two dozen cookies gone, there were twelve voices harmonizing happily.

"Blue and broken-hearted, blue because we parted. . . ."

By midnight the lights were out and the Martens were all lying—still awake—in the only bedroom on a double bed and three cots. The only tiny room was used for our trunks and clothes.

"Thank God for this day," Johnny said reverently.

"The place looked pretty, didn't it, Johnny?" Cecilia asked him.

"Yes, honey, and so did you." They kissed.

I smiled to myself. I didn't know just which I wanted most —my own room, or all of us happy and safely together like now—this lavish, love-filled moment. I reached out for Judy's hand.

"Hey, Nora," Scott called, "you'd better get your musical saw outta the trunk tomorrow, and Judy's kazoo."

"I thought of that," I answered.

"If the girls that come in wanna use my ukulele, I'll play a comb," he offered, martyrlike.

"Good idea, Scott."

"Let's say our prayers and get to sleep. I've got to press your school things in the morning," Mom broke in.

"Oh, no!" Scott moaned. "Not school!"

"Don't sound so dad-blasted abused," Johnny cried. "Good nightshirt, you sound like you'd been going to the damn thing all your life."

"Our Father Who art in heaven . . ." Mom started.

"I have to wee," Judy said.

"Well, hurry up!"

I led her to the bathroom and back, then covered and kissed her.

"Our Father, Who art in heaven . . ." Mom started again. Scott belched.

Johnny's voice rose above their laughing. "Dawgone it, I'm going to have that operated on. I never heard a—a—a cripple make that much noise. It's dangerous!"

"Hallowed be Thy . . . Now, stop giggling and say your prayers." Mom tried to be serious. Our voices were together now: "be Thy name; Thy kingdom come, Thy will be done, on earth as it is in heaven. . . ."

Judy broke wind. We all screamed laughing. Johnny turned on the light by the bed. "Damned if this isn't the gassiest troupe in Waterville." The five of us sat up. Scott ran to the kitchen to get an apple.

"Bring me one," I called.

"Bring me one," Judy echoed.

"Want some hot milk, Johnny?" Mom asked.

"Yep, I'm starved. How about an onion sandwich with it?"

"Let's all get up, then, and make a night of it," Mom said, as we piled into the kitchen. We pulled out everything we could find in the icebox and had a noisy, gay feast—Amos and Miss Carriage included.

"Let the dishes go, I'll do them early in the morning," I promised.

We got back into bed with full stomachs, sleepier now, and once again the lights were out.

"Thank you, God, for this day," Johnny whispered.

"Don't you think I ought to be a freshman in college this week?" I asked my mother and dad.

"You're only twelve, and don't say 'this week.' We're going to be here forevermore." Johnny knocked on wood.

"I'm going to go in five-A," Scott announced.

"Me, too," Judy said.

"Stop it, you kids," Cecilia said. "Where'll you get your credits?"

"They're-on-the-way-teacher-dear!" we sang in unison, and finished with a time step.

The grammar school was four blocks away. Mom got Judy in the second grade, and Scott sat in 5-A, not understanding a word.

I put on lipstick, high heels, and a sweater and skirt and enrolled as a freshman in the College of Fine Arts across the street. I told them I was sixteen and that my diploma from Savannah High School was being forwarded.

The La Mode's clientele grew that week, and we did an enormous business in the kitchen. The kettle was always steaming, and Mom furnished goodies to eat and drink. I taught the customers the Charleston, Off to Buffalo, Black Bottom, and soft-shoe steps. They made so much noise that the college finally sent a committee of three to see what was going on. The committee didn't approve of what it saw. The girls were told they could buy from the Shoppe if they must, but they could not dawdle there.

I told Johnny the committee was the same one that told the girls that if a man offered them a seat in a streetcar, they should fan it until it cooled off.

Johnny said, "Wow-wee, you gotta have a brain twisted like a pretzel to think that up! Good thing my kids didn't get stuck with school much."

Nevertheless, the hilarity had to subside. The singing was softer, the laughter muffled. Still our guest list expanded.

Judy brought her drawings home from school.

"You couldn't have done that—did you?" How was it possible for a little thing like Judy to draw a house and flowers and cattle—even a portrait of Amos and Miss Carriage—with no lessons? We were bewildered.

Scott was in heaven—not in class, but on the football field:

fast as a streak of Texas lightning and "so small for his age!" Possibly this was because he'd decided to be three years older for good old 5-A.

My situation at college was very satisfactory, too. I avoided mathematics, and my homework for the other subjects was done for me in our kitchen by full-stomached, happy classmates.

Three months had passed—the best we'd ever known.

One Friday, Mom and Johnny were about to leave for the wholesale houses to buy more merchandise when the blow came. Two of our customers, Alice and Connie, cut classes to deliver the news.

"Mr. Marten—it passed—they passed it—the rule goes into effect in two weeks!"

"What rule, kids?"

"From then on we all have to wear blue-chambray uniforms—no more dresses except during vacation!" Both the girls were breathless from running.

There was a long silence.

"There's no business to speak of from the natives of this burg; that means we'll . . ." Johnny couldn't finish his thought. He sank to the nearest chair. Mom just stood still and erect. The girls tiptoed out.

Mom walked to the window and looked at the sleepy street, peopleless until the end of the schoolday. This was a crisis, and she was great in a crisis.

"Johnny," she said, "get yourself on the phone and try to book the act. We'll make it—some other time we'll make it."

"The children . . ." He couldn't talk.

"The children are young."

She went into the bathroom for a wet cloth and put it over his face. "Stop it now, Johnny, and get on that phone and book the act."

Four days passed, and Johnny called a meeting.

"Ladies and chentlemen," he started.

"Hurray!" we yelled.

"Pleeze! Var vas I, Mr. Gallagher?"

"Vell, I'll tell you, Mr. Sheean," Judy sang.

Johnny tapped on his head, banging his other hand under the table to make an emphatic sound.

"Meeting vill pleeze come to order."

We quieted down.

"Now, so far, I've booked Houston, split week; Galveston, the following weekend. You can swim there—helluva beach—then six weeks of one-night stands. A new circuit's cropped up—the Gus Sun Time around California. It won't be easy, one-nighters, but the money's pretty good. And here's a surprise—we're going to drive it. I bought us a Model T."

We screamed with delight.

"I have dibs on driving it first," Scott yelled.

"Shut your faces a minute. Let your dad finish," Mom quieted us.

"It's a beaut. The latest model—almost. Only cost sixty dollars, because it's secondhand. Runs like a top. Now, here are our plans. This is Monday. We should be packed and out of here by Thursday. They only allowed us seventy dollars on the leftover stock—the bums—but the landlord is going to give us back two weeks' rent if we leave the curtains, racks, and showcase."

"How much for the paint job?" Scott asked.

"Shut your mush," Judy said.

"So," Johnny continued, "we're off! I'm going to take another driving lesson from the guy at the gas station. I can do everything but back up."

"Got a vulcanizer?" Scott asked.

"What the hell's that?" Johnny wanted to know.

"To seal up flat tires. You can do it yourself, and it's cheaper."

"They learned the damndest things on the Pan Time," Johnny told the ceiling. "You can buy a vulcanizer," he said to Scott.

Johnny closed his speech with, "Now, hop to it!" Then we all went into the action so familiar to us—packing.

Thursday morning arrived, and the natives of Waterville, Texas, joined the student body and faculty members of the College of Fine Arts to witness a sight that even Boob Mc-Nutt couldn't dream up. Five trunks were wired to the top, back, and sides of the Model T. Both front doors were rendered useless by the luggage strapped to them. Only the right-back door was usable. Mom, Judy, and I were squashed into the back seat, blankets over our laps, our feet resting on the groceries, celluloid dishes, tinware, three pots, a frying pan, the Sterno, and a box full of Amos and Miss Carriage. Scott looked comfortable in the front seat with only the ukuleles, three quarts of milk, and four rolls of toilet paper to share it with him.

Johnny stood poised, ready to crank Myrtle, as we'd named the car. Arrrraaa arraaa araaraaraaaa. He straightened up and smiled to his audience. "She's a little chilly," he said, patting the hood. Once again—arraaaa arraaaararaaaa arra. He was sweating. He took a cigar out of his pocket, lighted it, slowly exhaled the smoke, then carefully laid it on Myrtle's fender. He wiped his hand on his handkerchief, turned it to one side, then the other, tossed it into the air, and made it disappear. He bowed. The applause was fair. Again—araaa araraaa arraaarrrraaaa. Scott climbed out his window. "Let me try it, Dad."

"Get outta here."

"Lemme try."

"Try, then, smart aleck."

Arrrrraaaaaa araa brump brump brump—chug chug chug . . . "Get in quick, Dad!" The engine was bumping us up and down as Johnny climbed through his window and Scott through his.

"Let 'er fly," said Johnny as he stepped on the gas. The flivver started to move. Cheers filled the air. "California, here

I come . . ." the Martens sang for about fifty feet, then achug!—the engine stopped.

Two hours later, Sam from the gas station had done something about the choke, and we were off.

"Thank goodness they can't see us anymore," I muttered when the first flat tire took place, just five blocks from the college.

"Hot dog!" Scott said, as we tipped to the left. "Hand me my vulcanizer." He climbed out his window.

We drew a crowd of strangers, who seemed fascinated not by the flat tire over which Johnny and Scott were red-faced, but by the crazy wiring and lumps and bumps all over the car. "A newfangled radio station," one of the natives said, picking his teeth. "T. J., you're right," his friend said, and the crowd murmured its approval.

Meanwhile, Scott looked as if he were cooking something. "What in hell you building?" Johnny asked.

After burning and brewing and pounding, Scott said to Johnny, "Tell them to get out. I wanna get the rim on, and they're too heavy." But we ladies did not wish to crawl over the pots and pans with the crowd looking on, so Mom moved over to the far right, I sat on her lap, and Judy sat on my lap, her neck bent slightly so as not to push on the top.

The tire was fixed; we were all settled. As Johnny started to crank the car, he stared at the onlookers and wished they would sink through the ground. But when the engine started, Johnny leaped through his window like Douglas Fairbanks, threw them a kiss, and the Marten family was on its way.

"What happened to my cigar?" he asked as we shook our way down the street.

Nightfall—three flat tires and seven miles later—we pulled off the side of the road. It hurt us to get out of Myrtle, we were so cold and stiff.

"I'm glad I allowed us eleven days. It's two hundred and

twenty-six miles to Houston. We've got—let's see"—he took out a pencil and a piece of paper—"we've got two hundred and seventeen miles to go."

"I'm hungry," Judy cried. "So are Amos and Miss Carriage."

"We're all starved. Johnny, do you think you could build a bonfire to keep us warm, and for some light while I get our food?"

"Yep, Ceeley. Hop to it, Scott. First thing is to gather some wood."

"First thing is, have you gotta match?" Scott answered, urinating on a tree trunk.

"Don't do that in front of your sisters!" Johnny whacked his butt.

"I got my back turned, Dad. And they don't hafta look."

"Okay, shake it off, and help us gather some wood."

Mom heated a can of beans over the Sterno while I buttered the bread to go with the roast beef we had brought from home. Home, I thought, we mustn't say that—we have no home.

"We'll have to cancel *this* act," Johnny said, trying again and again to fan some life into the fire.

"We need some paper," Scott said.

"We've got four rolls of toilet paper," Judy said.

"Only three and a half rolls now," Cecilia answered. "And we've got two hundred and seventeen miles to go."

"At that rate we'd better hang on to it," Johnny said. "You know this troupe!"

Nevertheless, we parted with one roll, and Scott got a flame going. We were very dirty and tired, but the bonfire made it feel like a vacation.

"We've blown an hour," Johnny said, "and we've got to keep going till we find a place to shack up. So far we haven't passed anything that looks like Times Square, but we'll get our bearings, and there's bound to be a native who'll take us in for the night."

Five hours later the engine coughed to a shuddering stop.

Johnny climbed out the window—quite unlike Douglas Fairbanks this time. He was nearly frozen.

We were all nearly frozen, and feeling strangely dizzy and sick. "Pile out, everybody, and jump around, even if it shivers your timbers. The circulation is good for what ails you." Johnny tried to sound cheerful.

"We're all dying from monoxide gas," Scott said.

"What's that?" Johnny eyed him with suspicion.

"The gas fumes are coming up at us—there's a leak. And like I said, we'll all be dead soon," he informed us serenely.

"Smart aleck," Johnny snorted, though he looked worried.

"Shut your face, you don't know everything," Cecilia reprimanded her son.

We took turns behind a bush. Judy, squatting there, called: "It's so cold my wee-wee will turn into an icicle before it hits the ground, and I'll have to put a hole in the middle of my pants to get them up." Our laughter warmed us a bit.

"While we're jumping around, let's have a meeting." Johnny didn't wait for an answer. "The next light I see in one of these burgs is where we're going to stay, and that's it. I'll pay 'em extra, and I won't take 'no' anymore, even if we sleep on the floor."

"Everybody thinks we're dippy with this top-heavy contraption," Mom said. "They're afraid of us."

"I'll jiggle the throttle, Scott, and you get a good hold on the crank. Allez-oop!" Johnny cried, as we ladies scrambled back into Myrtle.

We jogged over the narrow dirt road. The headlights were weak, and Johnny's eyes ached from squinting into the starless night. Because of the deep ruts and crevices in the badly kept, almost deserted road, our highest speed was ten miles an hour.

No singing now. No jokes. The jerking, the bumping, the revolting sweet smell of leaking gas, the hateful chills that shook our bodies, kept us silent in our struggle to ward off nausea. Hours later we pulled over to a shack—combination groceries—notions—hardware—outhouse. The place was dark except for a dim light in the back.

"Ouvray la fenetra!" Johnny cried, depleting his knowledge of French. "And damned if we didn't make it! Get some air in your lungs, and we'll hole up in there if we have to do the act." His husky voice sounded reassuring to us.

We didn't know how much it cost. We just knew we were going to get yearned-for sleep now. Mom was stretched out on a couch, and Johnny and the three of us shared the small floor space, our clothes, our dirt, our empty stomach, wrapped in the thin blankets the owners provided.

Softly we mumbled the Lord's Prayer into the darkness. Our bone-tired bodies were still.

Eleven back-breaking, brutally exhausting days later we pulled into the alley of the Ford's Theater in Houston, just before showtime.

"Hurry, kids, they already called 'fifteen minutes,'" Johnny pleaded. "Give them the prop sheet and music, Nora. They'll have to do the best they can."

Frantically we unloaded the car and somehow made it, greasepaint over grime, just as the small orchestra picked up "The Sheik of Araby."

Johnny made his entrance in the kid outfit; Cecilia next in her beaded dress; then Judy and I in striped turtleneck sweaters and skirts. Scott, in sweater and knickers, made his entrance last. But he didn't come in on cue, and the family looked toward center door fancy in panic.

Evidently he'd had shoe trouble, because out stuck one very swollen, dirty bare foot, followed slowly by the other. His wild eyes seemed to enter without his face. His expression was the last straw. We broke up onstage. Our hysterical laughter transferred itself to the audience, and there was bedlam!

Johnny tried desperately to continue the act, but he couldn't. The rest of us struggled for composure, but it was useless. We were doubled up and hurting—and we couldn't stop.

The curtain was lowered with a bang.

"We'll be all right in a minute," Johnny yelled to the fly man. Facing us, still shaking with hysteria, he cried, "We've got to—we've got to stop it."

"Let's think of something sad," Mom said, her voice unnaturally high. "Let's think of the trip here."

We held our breaths for a moment, trying to picture the misery of the past ten days. Somehow that turned out to be even funnier than Scott's sore bare feet.

"Put—put on the single—we can't—we can't—make it," Johnny gasped to the stage manager. A signal was given for Owen McKnight and His Card Tricks.

We were in our dressing room now, still laughing. There was a knock on the door.

The manager marched in and shoved the five stage photographs that had been on display in the lobby under Johnny's arm. And Johnny stood there looking like a newsboy carrying papers.

"The girl act goes on next. You're fired!" the manager blazed, and slammed the door in our faces.

Judy started the crying that quickly became as uncontrollable as the laughter had been. And we clung to each other in such despair that it was some time before Mom could bend Judy's head over the sink and splash water on her face, then on mine and Scott's. She wet a cloth and gave it to Johnny, then doused her own face. She looked at us, sobbing, trying to hide from one another in the small dressing room. Then, struggling with her own tears, she forced her voice to ring out strong and clear.

"Come on, crybabies, let's pack up and get a bath and a hot meal. Then we'll leave for the next jump so we'll be there in plenty of time for a rest."

It was eleven back-breaking months of one-night stands, split weeks, and clubs, mingled with layoffs, before Johnny called the next meeting. This took place in Hotel McKinley, La Junta, Colorado.

"I don't know how to word it good, but God gave me a special glance—having you for a family. And with His help, never, never will you have anything tougher than this past nightmare. We've got the two thousand again, and it's only because you've done without even candy, even anything that kids should have. You've been tired, cold, hot, hungry, sick . . ." He couldn't go on. He gripped his nose to hold the tears back. We were embarrassed; we didn't know what to say.

Finally Mom managed, "Judy, get Dad a drink of water."

Judy solemnly tiptoed to the pitcher and returned self-consciously with a full glass. As she reached him, she tripped, and Johnny got the entire icy contents in his face.

"Bull's-eye!" he spluttered, choking and coughing, and roars of laughter came from all. As usual, we took turns going to the bathroom before the merriment subsided.

"Let's see what La Junta chop suey tastes like; we're going to celebrate!" Johnny was helping Mom on with her shoes. "We play Albuquerque next, then Flagstaff, Phoenix, Vegas, Sacramento, Fresno, Los Angeles. Then we jump to Ventura, where we settle down! And we'll open a tearoom this time. It said in *Billboard* they're the most popular places to eat in. So mark that town clearly in your heads, because it's America's next hot spot. V-E-N-T-O-O-R-A," he spelled it, "Ventura, California."

"What act tipped you off, Dad?" Scott asked.

"I don't like your attitude." Johnny glared at him. "Sammy Burns, Street Singer. What's it to ya?"

"Just askin'." Scott inhaled air deeply.

"You belch, and I'll whale your tail," Johnny warned, as he buttoned Judy's coat.

After a two-day engagement before meager, unresponsive audiences, the safari began again. We'd discovered it was best to tie all the paraphernalia on Myrtle at dawn, when we would be uninterrupted by the questions of startled and unbelieving natives. It was less embarrassing for us and for good old Myrtle, who had so nobly transported us from one theater alley to another—invariably just in the nick of time.

"My jokes are good enough for N.Y.C.," Johnny griped as he loaded the car. "The only goddamn thing they think is funny in Albuquerque are those goddamn Indian blankets they sell. Who needs this burg? Let's take it on the Arthur Duffy."

"What's that, Dad?" Judy asked through a mouthful of bubble gum.

"Pull out, get going, skedaddle."

"Oh!" She made a big bubble and popped it. "Where're we Arthur Duffing next?"

"Flagstaff," he answered, as the engine leveled into its full but dreary chug. "And we've no time to kill." Johnny's voice sounded strong, but he was tired and discouraged. It made him sick when the act didn't go.

A heaviness lay on all us Martens. We sat in silence as we passed the homes, shops, street lamps, and went into the semi-darkness of another long haul.

In the front seat Scott hunched forward, straining to see the bumpy dirt road beyond the throw of Myrtle's inefficient lights. I knew what he was thinking. He had said it often enough: "Lousy, lousy, lousy—it stinks, having no dough, no home! You can have it, buddy, I want to be nice and rich, and fix autos, and play ball, and sing."

"Memories . . . memories . . . dreams of love so true; o'er the sea . . ." Our stomachs full of Sterno-heated soup and crackers cooked en route, we were singing again.

"That's about fifty songs they sang today. Ceeley, how do you suppose they remember all the words?"

"From acts. Anyway, children just remember things."

"Once we get to Ventura and they're settled down in some school, they'll probably get one of those Cum Harry Lauders."

"What's that, Dad?" Judy asked.

"That's not really what they call it. It's a Spanish name that sounds like that," Johnny answered. "Anyway, it means when you've got smart brains in school they give you a button or a cup or something to prove it."

"Mom ought to get a prize like that for cooking such good soup in her lap in Myrtle," I said.

"While it's moving, too!" added Judy.

The men grunted their approval.

Into the night we jogged, sometimes singing—always thinking.

Judy kicked off her shoes. She was rubbing her cat's head with her toes. Amos was in an open canvas bag on the car floor. Judy couldn't wait for us to get to Ventura—so she could bury her turtle. Nobody knew Miss Carriage was dead except Judy. But Scott almost did. He said, "Something smells even worse than the monoxide gas," and that made Judy nervous. Judy hadn't wanted to bury Miss Carriage in the town where she died. It was such a blah place—the park was brown grass and papers.

Judy started to sway from side to side, her dead pet hidden in a small box in her cupped hands. "Rock-a-bye baby, in the tree top . . ." she hummed softly.

We other Martens joined her.

The miles ticked off slowly.

Scott switched his weight. "Jeeze, my butt is sore," he said.

"So's mine!" It was a cry from all of us. Judy and I gripped pinkies. "I wish your wish and my wish comes true touch blue," we said together.

"What did ya wish, kids?" Johnny asked between coughing fits.

"*I* wish you wouldn't smoke so much," Mom answered for us. "That cough of yours is getting worse by the minute." Then she turned to me. "Why are you wriggling so? You're all right now, aren't you? The pain's gone, isn't it?"

"Yes, Mom. I'm just uncomfortable."

"Lean over this way. You'll feel better."

I leaned against my mother, thinking: It wasn't a nose-bleed at all. Why didn't Mom tell me that's what would happen, or write me a note or something? And why did she say, "You're different now," and warn me again about touching?

Mom sighed. She looked as though her head was splitting. I knew why she didn't tell me. Because she didn't want to give me any premature ideas. That's what she always said. Last night Mom said to Johnny, "It doesn't seem possible Nora's grown up so fast. Men are starting to look at her. She's too darned developed for her age." Now Mom was looking at the back of Johnny's head, the blue-black hair, strong shoulders. "He's the best," she said, as though to herself, then leaned her weight toward me.

I was biting my lips, so that Johnny wouldn't know how much I hurt. He was so upset last night. "She'll never be in that awful pain again with no place to lie down. I'll keep track, and she'll have a nice, white bed to lie on when she gets those lousy periods," he promised Mom. Now he opened his window and spat out the chewed tobacco. He gripped the steering wheel harder. "God, help me hurry and make a home for us. We're all tired, tired—damn tired."

Judy's nose was pushed against the window, her eyes moving from side to side, counting the passing trees.

"Don't squash your nose against that window, Judy," I said. Then I thought, what a sister I've got. She can do more strange things you don't know where they came from—like when we stopped in that big field to wee. She just jumped on a bare horse, and off she raced till we couldn't see her—all of us running like crazy people to save her. Then back she came, the horse shiny wet and Judy's face beautiful—like she got a letter or something. Where'd she learn that? Nowhere, that's where. It's like the painting and the clay molding. She learned it nowhere, just nowhere. I reached over and took my sister's hand.

The car jerked up to a gas pump. "Pile out, everybody, and

stretch," Johnny cried, climbing out his window. We all scrambled out, and tried to get the circulation back into our stiff bodies. We drank water from a hose and splashed it on our faces. "We'll line up a place to sleep and wash up," Johnny assured us. "Must be something ahead; and we'll get a hot meal; to hell with sandwiches tonight."

On our way once more, Mom suddenly nudged me. "Move —you hear? I'm uncomfortable." I quickly leaned toward Judy.

"Yes, Mom," I said, and then, depressed, wondered what I'd done to make her cross. She's been funny to me a lot lately, dragging my hair back in tight braids again. For a while she let it be soft and curly; then suddenly there was that day she told me, "Men are starting to gape at you. Well, don't feel flattered. You're homely, you hear? So don't get any ideas!"

Scott half-turned in the front seat. He'd heard Mom telling me to move. He twisted his body restlessly. "The inside of this bus is crawling with blue notes tonight!"

Johnny agreed. "We're so cramped—sick to death of travel, sick to death of no hot bath, no hot food, wondering what town is this? I thought the dresser was over there. . . . Oh, that was the last town—that was yesterday. Let's see . . . oh yeah, there's the street below, not much different than all the others, and there's the bathroom and the transom and the rules printed on the door."

Scott picked up the cue: "Leave the keys at the desk; no cooking in room; no loud noises; no visitors of the opposite sex. 'Well, okay, Management, we won't eat, talk, or screw, and you can have your keys.'"

Johnny stopped him. "Scott, watch your verbs in front of your sisters."

Dad misses a home even more than the rest of us, I decided. That's why he always finds us a park where we can get to feeling like home. Trees are the same every place— birds, dogs, kids. You just look up at the trees, and they rustle "hello again." Dogs give you big wet kisses like you're an old friend. Children are still playin'—same as last town. Yes, Dad sees that the lost feeling gets lost in the parks.

Blammmmmmmmm!! Flat tire. We were all pleased—it meant another stretch. But the stretching and the vulcanizing were done in silence and in darkness.

Scott had become so proficient in his tire mending that he did it alone. With a weak flashlight resting on a rock, its ray of light toward the damaged tire, Scott went to work.

Johnny's arms were outstretched toward the dark sky. Judy came over and stood next to him as if for shelter. Poor kid, she cried so hard at the last stop when we buried Miss Carriage. We just chose some old spot by the side of the road. But Judy knew Mom was right. We couldn't wait for Ventura. We were all getting pretty dizzy from the smell. Anyway, Judy felt better after I made the turtle a cross and wrote it a poem. It managed to make them all laugh:

> Here lies dearest Miss Carriage
> Who didn't have time for a marriage
> Lying deep in the sod
> She went early to God
> And didn't miss a damn thing.

Johnny had laughed the hardest. "Where, oh where, did you ever get such a notion?" He shook his head. "Whew—what kids I got!"

I was kicking my legs to give them life. Suddenly I made fast *tour jetés* along the dark bumpy road behind the car. I twirled for about a hundred feet trying to forget what had happened last week on my thirteenth birthday. But I remembered it all.

Mom had made me a lovely blue taffeta dress, and Johnny had brought me a parasol. My hair was soft and curly, and I had gone for a walk in a fancy neighborhood with porches. I'd felt pretty, and as if I'd like to have someone to talk to, so he'd see my new dress.

Suddenly two boys had come toward me, had crossed from the other side of the street.

"Hi," the tall boy had said.

"Howdoyoudo," I had answered.

"You look too beautiful to be all by yourself."

"It's my birthday; I'm just taking a nice walk, and this is my new dress."

"Well," the redhaired boy said, "we came over to give you a present. Fancy that; we didn't even know it was your birthday."

The tall boy had held a piece of new, white painted wood toward me—about two feet long and two inches wide.

"Gee, that's lovely—I certainly—" I had taken the piece of wood, but the boy had ripped it away from me. Then they had run off laughing and hollering, and I had stared at my hand. "They left number two on me!" I had called to no one.

"Come, Nora, we'd better get going," Dad called now.

Once more on our way, Mom took out a vial of perfume and put some behind her ears. Johnny smiled when the lovely scent reached him. We all loved it when she did those things. It made us feel civilized and rich.

There was a clap of thunder, and I put my arm around Judy. "It's nothing, Judy, just clouds bumping because they didn't stay on the route God gave 'em—like bad kids." We smiled at each other.

Mom was fanning herself with a piece of paper. The rain, falling hard now, made it close in the car. Suddenly Mom put the paper fan over her face and started to cry.

"Mom? . . . Mom?" I was horrified. "Mom—what is it?"

"Shush," she whispered, and put her arm around me. "It's nothing. Don't let 'em hear—I just feel tired. Nora, do you think I look old?"

"Oh, no, Mom, you're so beautiful. Everybody says so."

Cecilia wiped her tears on the bottom of her skirt and gently rocked me back and forth, still whispering in my ear, "Nora, you can always wear your hair soft, and I'm going to make you a pretty red chiffon dress—like the one we saw in South Bend."

"Oh, Mom—Mom!" I was joyous.

Scott had his hand out the window catching the rain. "Dad's right," he said; "we gotta get in real business. But I'm not sure about an asshole tearoom." He let the rain from his cupped hand drip over the top of his head.

Mom looked over at Judy. My sister appeared to be asleep, her head bumping on the windowsill with every jolt of the car. "Put this scarf under her head, Nora," she said. I carefully lifted Judy's head.

"I guess she's tired of leaning my way, Mom."

"I guess so."

"Do you think we can get another Amos when we live in one spot?" I whispered.

"I guess so." We had given Amos away to a little girl, a little girl who couldn't stop petting her, and who had a nice home for her.

Judy wasn't sleeping. "At least Amos can have a nice natural life now," she said. She put her arm under her head to get more comfortable. "Kitty cats shouldn't live like actors." A tear ran down her nose. "Nobody should."

Scott started singing, "There's a long, long trail a-winding until our dreams all come true—till the day . . ." His voice sounded so soft and wonderful that the rest of us Martens just listened, asking him to sing it again and again. It kept us from thinking about the bed our frozen, aching bodies longed for.

8

J OHNNY waved his arms wildly at the truck, beckoning it down the street.

"Here it is, kids, here it is! Our 'twenny-four sheet.'" And there it was, indeed, Johnny overseeing the job of two men lifting the huge sign off the truck. They erected it in front of the gray-white, one-story, ornate cottage we had rented for our home and place of business.

It was so huge that it practically cut off the view of the cottage from motorists and pedestrians. Nevertheless, there in the bright sunshine, on the corner of a wide, willow-tree-lined street in Ventura, was the sign:

MARTEN'S TEAROOM
—*Fine De Lux Food*—
(*And Beaucoup Of It*)

Johnny, Cecilia, Scott, Judy, and I stood gazing at it

speechlessly. It was impressive—it was our dream—it was sacred.

"Ready, set, go—taaa raaa!" Johnny sang out, and there was a mad scramble to light the orange candles, one on each of the twelve tables.

Mom and I had fringed the orange tablecloths. Judy and Scott had painted the living–dining-room floor, tables, and chairs a shiny black. There had been a unanimous family vote taken for a "Halloween Motif." Slick and gay-looking, the tearoom seemed as expectant and pleased as the Marten faces. Everything was ready for the dinner opening: corned beef, cabbage, carrots, boiled potatoes, and turnips were simmering in a huge pot. Individual salads of lettuce, bananas, mayonnaise, and nuts were all prepared; hot biscuits were in the oven; coffee was brewed; there was cold caramel custard—and steaks and chops for special orders. The Martens in their best togs were all in readiness for this moment. Like trained soldiers we stood in the entrance hall, alerted for the crowds that would momentarily flock in.

Three hours passed. Flames were lowered, oven turned off, lemon juice poured over the bananas to keep them from turning brown. Candles were burned halfway down. Johnny had changed the sign on the door from "Open for Dinner" to "Open This Minute." But no one came in. I burned nearly all the sticks of Chinese punk to offset the cabbage. Our feet felt flat from standing at attention, and we were terribly hungry.

"Hell, they don't know what they're missing—let's eat," Johnny said into the silence. When we were halfway to the kitchen door, the bell tinkled over the front entrance, and we about-faced and ran headlong into the two customers. The man and woman were pulled, shoved, and pushed into chairs, and before they could exchange a word, their table was piled high with steaming food. The two people, seated at a table for four, had food enough for eight. Like a stream of industrious ants, we shuttled back and forth from the kitchen, laden

with trays of goodies. Scott brought in a jar of peanut butter
as an added attraction. Then we stood in the doorway watching the confounded couple attempt to eat.

Suddenly I let out a squeal.

"What? What?"

"Quick. Come in the kitchen—quick."

I shoved the bunch of them in the kitchen, slammed the
door, and leaned on it.

"Guess," I cried.

"Hurry, tell us, for God's sake," Cecilia said.

"What you give 'em—rat paste?" Scott asked.

"No, no, listen, all of you—know who that is?"

"Who? . . . Hurry!"

"Listen, listen to me—it's—John Gilbert!"

"John Gilbert!"

"The movie star?"

"Not a movie star here!"

"Not John Gilbert!"

"Yes, I'm telling you—John Gilbert, and the blond lady is
probably a movie star, too, but I don't know who."

"Holy mackerel," Judy sighed. "John Gilbert."

We were stunned into inaction.

The females came to first, and we fought for a look in the
bathroom mirror before returning to gaze at America's Lover
Boy.

Mr. Gilbert never before had a more attentive audience—
never while eating, anyway.

"He seems to like the groceries," Johnny whispered.

"He's so nice," I said happily. "He's smiled at us five times
already, and one just plain look."

"Been open long?" Mr. Gilbert asked politely, and gave us
another wide, quick smile.

"His teeth look like the keys on the Filman Brothers' ac-
cordion," Scott said.

"You're the opening act," Johnny said to the star. "Have a
cigar?"

"Thank you, kindly—no. I don't smoke."

"Gotta save your wind for those goddamn talkies?"

"Dad!"

"Shush."

"Oh, dear."

But Mr. Gilbert didn't seem to mind. He flashed us another smile.

That night in our dormitorylike bedroom, our stomachs full, our kitchen spotless, our legs aching, we talked over the day—the highlight being the dollar tip Mr. Gilbert had pressed into my hand. We planned to have it framed.

Johnny held a family meeting in the dark. "We've got to produce our show better than tonight. Maybe if you three start school tomorrow and bring the kids by for a snack before they go home, they'll tell the folks. Advertising—that's what we need."

"Let's put a 'Marten's Tearoom' sign on Myrtle, and I'll drive her around town," Scott said.

"Brainstorm!" Johnny applauded. "And sit on the horn so they'll be sure and look."

"Our Father, Who art in heaven . . ." the exhausted Cecilia started.

"Do you think maybe Charlie Chaplin will come in?" Judy asked.

"If so, we'll save money and give him a shoe to eat," Johnny answered her.

We had the giggles through the rest of the prayer. And the heavy breathing of deep sleep followed almost before the sound of "Amen" was lost.

The Marten Tearoom caught on. After school the kitchen bulged with children of all ages—"Classmates and Co.," Scott called them.

"Make yourselves at home," Johnny urged the kids, and that they did. "It's the gayest, happiest, whoppin'est kitchen on the west coast hemisphere," Johnny gloated, his heart high, "And it's gonna keep up forever."

The three-o'clock free "snacks" became famous. Great bowls of my soup disappeared. "What d'ya put in it, Nora?"

"Oh, sheet music, old scenery, and all my toe shoes!"

They gobbled Cecilia's pies—with ice cream, with cheese, with whipped cream. "Orpheum pies!" Johnny'd say ecstatically. Bread, jelly, fruit and nuts, meatloaf, lamb shanks, crackers, peanut butter, stew, milk—all disappeared during the "supper show," as I christened the packed kitchen.

The dining room was kept orderly for the paying customers.

Johnny knew it was extravagant. But it was the first time his family was part of a community. "At last the Martens have what all normal people have," he said, "friends, a donkey, regular hours." We bought the donkey for six dollars. We subscribed to a local newspaper and read it. We got phone calls. We talked with the neighbors. We fed the same birds day after day. A stray cat gave birth on our back porch, and mama and the twelve kittens stayed there. We had bicycles. People called us by name, and we waved to them. The smell of the ocean was near. The radio programs were familiar. The garbage man ate free in our kitchen; the postman, the milkman. Teachers had free meals. The teachers laughed there, talked there, and they cared about us because we were "homey."

I was pedaling my bicycle to Ellen Palmer's house. I was singing at the top of my lungs: "I'm in love with you, honey . . ." Because I was sure—absolutely sure—that the handsome student-body president, Kenny Snell, considered himself my boyfriend. Hadn't he proved it in so many ways?

Every noontime he would find me under the tree at school, and he would eat my lunch—every bite of it, I thought dreamily.

And he had whacked me on the back when I won the dancing contest. It had made me cough until my eyes leaked, but I got the message.

Now I was on my way to my best girl friend's house to find out about sex. Ellen Palmer's father was a doctor, and Ellen had promised to show me his medical book. "The part where it says about how to have things like babies?"

"Yep, heck yes, Dad would say 'help yourself.'"

Ellen found the page for me:

". . . the urethral orifice is important to sexual intercourse. Snugness of the tissues or hasty entrance at coitus may result in traumatism of the meatus—may be termed honeymoon dyspareunia—the penis enters the vagina and as parasympathetic vasodilator fibers arise . . ."

I pedaled my way back home. Remind me never to do *that*, I thought.

"Dad! Dad! Cue me." I tossed my script on the kitchen table. "I've got the lead in the senior play. I'm Lady Katherine in *If I Were King.*"

Johnny looked up with a mouthful of the doughnut he'd been dunking. "What act they lift it from?"

"No act, Dad. It's a play." I clasped my hands over my breast, gave him my profile, and in the deepest voice I could muster widened my nostrils and breathed: "If I were to die tomorrow, I would tell you this much tonight—I love you. These are easy words to say, but my heart fails as I say them, for their meaning is as full and powerful as the bell of doom. . . ."

"Where're the laughs?" he asked, starting on his fourth doughnut.

"Oh, Dad." I ran to Mom.

Johnny hammered up the sign on the front door:

MARTEN'S TEAROOM IS CLOSED BECAUSE
DAUGHTER NORA MARTEN IS STARRING IN PLAY
AT VENTURA HIGH SCHOOL—*If I Were King.*

ADMISSION, FREE—EIGHT O'CLOCK—ONLY ONE SHOW.
SEATS AVAILABLE—HURRY-HURRY-HURRY!
                                        The Management
                                        OPEN TOMORROW.

The play was a huge success, and I took bow after bow. Afterwards, the Martens gathered in the kitchen and talked excitedly until long past two A.M. Mom was as elated as the others. "You looked beautiful in that black velvet gown —and that picture hat with the blue feathers!"

"That's because you made it, Mom." I hugged my mother.

"I'll be doggoned if you didn't make me want to cry with those stupid speeches," Johnny said. "They ought to take the goddamn thing on the road!"

"Was that in the act when your train got caught on that cardboard tree?" Scott asked.

"Shut your face," Mom snapped.

"Nobody saw that," Judy defended me.

But Scott refused to be deterred. "And how did you get the black off your face from his moustache after he smooched ya?"

"Go to bed, son, or I'll whale your ass off." Johnny led him to the bedroom.

"You looked like you had to wee when it first started, and when you banged your shins . . ." But Johnny got him closed off in the bedroom.

MARTEN TEAROOM CLOSED FOR TODAY.
SON SCOTT MARTEN IS PLAYING FOOTBALL
AT VENTURA GRADE SCHOOL.
HURRY-HURRY-HURRY!

was the next sign we put out.

The four of us were sitting in the bleachers watching Scott play. It was Ventura against Oxnard Grammar School.

"What's he doing now, Dad?" Judy had to yell it to be heard above the cheers.

"Running."

"Where?"

"Off the field, I guess. He's got a ball." Johnny was standing on his seat waving his arms like a madman.

"They knocked him down, Dad. Why are they cheering?"

"He made a damn good try to get out of here, I guess."

"But lookit, they're still yelling—and lookit, they're throwing hats in the air."

"Yeah—now just keep still a minute, will ya?"

The cheerleaders were leading the crowd: "Marten! Rah! Rah! Rah!—Marten!!"

"You hear that, Mom?" I grabbed her arm. "He must have done something good."

"Yes, I guess so—he must have!"

Judy was talking to the man on her left. He was explaining things to her. After the conference she turned to Johnny. "Dad, he said Scott made a touchdown that will win the game, unless something fantastic happens in the next two minutes to help Oxnard—then it'll be a tie."

"Yeah?" Johnny said, reaching in his pocket. "Have a cigar, sir. That's my son."

"Thanks, don't smoke."

"Take it and save it—maybe someday you'll have a son."

"Got two of 'em in the game. Twins." The man grinned. "I'll take it in case I get a girl."

There was another play on the field; then suddenly everything was quiet in the bleachers. One of the players was lying on the ground, and both teams huddled together. The Ventura coach was bending over the player. Someone was running on the field with a water bucket. The referee started pulling the unconscious boy's belt up and down over his stomach. Another man ran from the sidelines with a black bag.

My eyes darted, squinted at the boys huddling together. "It's not Scott; they just got through cheering for him. Please, God, it's not . . ."

"What number?" Johnny asked the man next to Judy.

"What number? Please, mister, what number?" Judy pleaded over Johnny's voice.

"He'll be okay—happens all the time; it's your boy, sixty-seven, he's . . . don't be concerned . . ." He put his arm over Judy to Johnny's shoulder.

"I beg your pardon?" Mom bent forward and asked the man.

Johnny put his arm around her. "He says it's all right, Ceeley. It's sixty-seven—Scott—he says it happens all the . . ."

But Mom was gone. We saw her walk down to the ropes, duck under, then walk steadily, surely—a small, straight figure in that huge field—toward her son. We were all by the rope now, our eyes on the still body of Scott, but conscious of Cecilia on the way to him.

Judy's head was leaning on my back, and I could hear her whisper: "Yea, though I walk through the valley of the shadow . . ."

There was a mass rumble from the crowd. Scott had moved, just before Mom reached him. She did an immediate about-face, and with her head high, retraced the long walk back to her family.

Scott was taken off the field, but he walked. And he was cheered wildly every step of the way.

"Let's be home when he gets there; he must rest." I took my mother's hand and kissed it.

Scott came in an hour later. The kitchen table sagged with food. We watched him devour it silently; he didn't mention the game. After he finished, he belched.

"I'm going out."

"OUT!" we yelped.

He let the echo of it die down. "Yeah, out. I wanna meet the guys at the drugstore."

"Don't you want to rest?" "How about a little dessert?" "Listen to the radio?" "A hot bath?"

A long pause ensued. "I'm-going-to-the-drugstore. This-is-an-important-day."

We were silent before his ultimatum.

"S'long," Scott said. He started out, then stopped. He turned around and looked piercingly at Cecilia. "Don't ever—when I'm playing a game—interfere, hear me? Jeez, how stupid can a guy feel? Just 'cause yer knocked out a little, some woman comes stalking over. Jeez, was I ribbed."

Suddenly he ran to Mom. "It's just about against the law, Mom. It's so embarrassing. Don't ever do it again. Jeez—" He grinned, then ran like a streak to the drugstore.

Eight months later the phone rang. It was Johnny.

"Nora?"

"Yes, Dad?"

"I—ah—well, I'm downtown."

"Yes?"

"And—I came here to pay the meat bill."

"Yes, Dad."

"Not pay it, I mean. Just talk the guy into a down payment again—" He paused. "It was awful big—the bill—and with no business—"

"Yes, Dad, I know."

"Well, honey"—he hesitated—"the guy said, 'Want to go to jail, or will you pay?' So I said, 'If I can use your phone, I'll book the act, and then you get it in a few weeks.'"

I started to tremble, but I asked, "When do we leave, Dad?"

There was a long silence.

"Dad?"

"Yes, honey—oh, Nora, I couldn't face you. I know what it means, no graduation, again no . . ."

"Stop it, Dad. We'll have all that kind of stuff some other time."

I heard him blowing his nose. The lump in my throat was hurting badly.

"Dad?" No answer. "Dad, don't feel like that. We'll just pack quickly and go. When do we open?"

"Week and a half."

"Where?" I asked.

"Seattle."

"Hilly, isn't it?"

"Yeah."

When I hung up, I walked into the bedroom we all shared. I opened the bureau drawer and took out the box that held my precious swimming medal, then the scrapbook I'd assembled these past eight months. Turning the pages, I saw pictures taken in front of Ventura High School: the glee club standing on the steps, me grinning in the second row, the picture taken that momentous day I was elected president of the Band Box Players, the high-school dramatic club. One by one I slowly turned the pages. I saw Judy sitting under Maudie, the donkey. Judy sat under her beloved nonbudging animal when it rained. There was a picture of Scott as captain of the Ventura Grammar School football team—the smallest member of the group. There were various views of the crowded tearoom, taken during those five busy months before the city cut down the huge willow trees along Wilma Boulevard to widen the street. Now it had been two months of almost no business—no easy way of getting to the tearoom, no walking space, no parking space. The heavy trees lay there closing off the avenue.

"Nora! Wassa matter, you crying?" It was Scott.

I turned away and wiped my tears on my sleeve. "Nope—lookit these crazy things!"

"I don't think that picture's crazy." He looked suspiciously at me. "That's when you won the Declamation Contest."

Scott turned the page. The next picture was of me standing dripping wet with three blurred judges beside me, one of them holding the bronze first-prize medal just before presenting it to me. "Jeez, that was some race you won—the whole auditorium screaming for you—but us Martens had the best projection." Scott opened the velvet-lined box which held the medal. "We about blew the walls apart."

We looked at the well-memorized inscription: "First Prize,

440 Australian Crawl, Nora Marten, Ventura High School."

"Scott?"

"Yep?"

"When's the next game?"

"Three weeks."

"Who you play?"

"Santa Barbara. Tough, but we'll beat the sh—daylights outta them."

"Scott?"

"Yeah?"

I paused. "You gotta be with me when I tell them."

"Who?"

"Mom and Judy. Dad just phoned—"

We stared at each other, then I pulled Scott to me. "Don't look like that, Scott. It's not the end of the world." I gently rocked my brother.

"Nora?"

"Hmmm?"

"Where do we open?"

"Seattle."

"Hilly son-of-a-bitch."

"Yeah."

9

MYRTLE LASTED another four months. Her end came at twilight deep in the heart of a deserted road during our second swing through Texas. We were singing "Chinatown, My Chinatown" and bouncing our bodies in tempo when it happened.

"Maybe she just needs a rest," Judy said.

"Let's not bull ourselves. She ran her sixty-dollar ass into the ground," Johnny said.

We literally tiptoed out of the car and stood looking at her. The wheels were bent, the middle sagged, and there were weak puffs of smoke coming from her insides.

Finally Johnny said: "Let's unhitch our baggage, troupe, and please God a car will stop and give us a lift to Paris."

Paris, Texas, was a three-day stand, and we needed that money to get to Fort Worth—a full-week date.

We busied ourselves with our belongings. Myrtle was as

close to us as Queenie, Miss Carriage, Amos, Maudie. Doggedly we untied, unloosened, unhitched our possessions from every side, nook, and corner of our collapsed car.

"She looks decrapitated," Judy said despondently.

We pushed Myrtle under the only tree that was standing in the barren field. Johnny broke the silence. "Well, God bless you, Myrtle." He bowed his head. "And thanks a helluva lot."

I pulled up sagebrush and with Judy's help placed it artistically on Myrtle's hood.

"Write something to her," Scott asked me.

The others stood around while I sat on the ground biting the end of a pencil and thinking. Scott made a cross with the wood and wire from our baggage. Johnny looked up and down the darkening road for a lift. Cecilia nervously combed her hair.

"Hallelujah!" Johnny yelled. "A truck! I'll be a son-of-a-bitch if God isn't standing right here." He went in the middle of the road and waved his arms frantically.

The truck stopped. We didn't hear the long conversation Johnny had with the driver, but we saw him reach in his pocket, then call jubilantly: "Come on, kids—*ouvray la fenetra*—Paris next!"

The driver helped us load his empty truck with our trunks, suitcases, and boxes. "They're off!" Johnny bellowed as the engine started.

"That's what the monkey said when he backed into the—" Scott continued.

"We know—lawnmower," Johnny interrupted, and swatted his son. "Don't talk dirty in front of your sisters."

We attempted to sing, "Honey Moon, Honey Moon, wonder why you set so soon . . ." but the five of us were thinking of Myrtle in that field forevermore—with the branches of sage and my epitaph on her hood:

> The shell is here
> But the nut is gone—
>> Thank you, and love always,
>> Ceeley, Johnny, Scott, Judy, and Nora.

Paris, Texas. The picture on the bill was *Sonny Boy* with Al Jolson, so business should have been good, even though there were only two acts: a local singer who bellowed "Indian Love Call" off key, and John Marten and Company in "The Boy Is Gone." But business was bad, because everyone in town was on the square looking up at a bulletin board over the barber shop. They were waiting for news of a young man's flight to Paris, France. "Lindbergh spotted by Gander" was the last information.

I ran to the park in the middle of the square. I saw an elderly man, a black skull cap on his head, sitting alone. Maybe he hadn't seen the sign.

"He's going to get there," I said to the old man, and smiled joyfully.

"Yes, of course." He reflected my smile.

I sat on the grass and looked up at him. "This is the best day on earth! They even canceled the supper show because there was no audience—everybody's waiting for Lindy to land —everybody."

"Supper show?"

"We're at the theater."

"I see."

I was too excited to stop talking. "It's such a good feeling to have somebody like Mr. Lindbergh to love and root for— and to have ourselves, even strangers, all feeling the same feeling all at once—you know what I mean?"

He nodded and smiled.

"When Lindy gets on earth again, we will all yell 'Bravo!' and laugh and love and applaud together. You see, nobody's alone or frightened today."

I paused, but not for long. "You see, acts are lonely," I said.

"Acts?"

"Yes, acts that we play on the bill with. I know they are, because sometimes they're rigging their props before the show, and they're on the empty stage, and they say things like, 'Gotta oil up the gear—get ready to kill the people,' but they look lonely and not like their words. I think sometimes that they want to be on a porch in one spot. I think they'd like that more than killing the people."

"Go on, young lady," he said.

"Now, you take my father—he's John Marten and Company, the best pantomimist in the world, and you know something, people laugh for four minutes, ever counted that? Two hundred and forty seconds, and they laugh real hard—and he hasn't said one word." She paused to make her point. "There he is—my dad—he puts Stein's stick on his face, a red nose, a red wig, but sometimes he's awful worried, and he's tired—but whatever stage he walks on, he just sails through like that's all the day has been to him, like there was money in his money belt, like he had a good meal, a good bath—that's how he faces the audience, and they laugh. Now, you take Mr. Lindbergh, who's flying in the sky—everybody wants him safe. Y'see, this wonderful day, nobody, not even actors, are lonely!" I stopped and looked sheepishly at the old man. "Everybody says I never talk much."

The man smiled. "What's your name?"

"Nora Marten of John Marten and Company in 'The Boy Is Gone.'"

"Mine is Springold—Abe Springold."

"How do you do, Mr. Springold."

"How long will you be at the theater?"

"We close tomorrow night and jump to Fort Worth—the train leaves at two A.M." I paused. "We'll have time to grab a bite at the station. We have Harvey House stomachs," I added sedately. "That means, if we can swallow that swill in stations, we'll never get a bellyache anywhere. That's what my father says."

"I see." He laughed.

I glanced at the bulletin board. People were quiet. Maybe that meant more news soon. I separated the grass, hoping to find a four-leaf clover; it might help Lindy.

"Tell me more about people in show business being lonely."

"Well," I answered, "they get a lot of laughs and a lot of applause and hear a lot of music, but it all goes away. I mean, the audience always files out and takes those things with them. Then the theater's dark."

"But today no one's lonely."

"No, sir, the whole world's holding hands today—nothing's gone or dark. And look," I cried, "I found a four-leaf clover!"

Worry, hunger, little money, insufficient clothing, exhaustion, separation—we had them all the following year. Workless days piled up, split weeks, one-nighters, with long barren stretches between, waiting in cheap rooming houses, waiting for a letter or a wire that would get us out of whatever godforsaken spot we were stuck in. We huddled together, frightened, embarrassed, depressed, while Johnny fought it out, cajoled, promised landlords money soon: "Just don't put us out, we'll hit it before long; I have kids, I'll pay you; I'm a headliner, a responsible headliner, you'll get your money, I promise . . ."

A one-shot date would come along miraculously, and Johnny would get an advance to pay up. Then off we'd go by bus or milk train, most of the money used up, salary gone in advance—and again waiting, praying, stranded, scared.

It was Christmas Eve day in Butte, Montana. Johnny had given the landlady our only unhocked possession of value—a Brownie camera. "Let us stay—come on now—you have kids," he pleaded. "I'll send you the money—you have my word." The landlady weakened. "Two more days, that's all, after Christmas, that's all," she said.

Johnny ran upstairs, two at a time, and the old twinkle fought through the worried look in his eyes as he told us excitedly: "We can stay—and here now is a secret." From his money belt he took four crumpled, long-hidden, one-dollar bills. He straightened them neatly and gave them to Mom. "Pile out, everybody, and get us a turkey, punkin pie, mashed potatoes, cranberries—the works. Mom will cook us the best Christmas dinner since Rector's, with giblet gravy . . ." His body made a jerky triple sigh, and beads of perspiration crowded his brow, but he was grinning.

Mom took over. "Tonight's dinner will be like even the President wished he had! Lie down, Johnny, lie down till we get back; rest. The kids will go with me to carry things."

While Mom was powdering her face, Scott and Judy gleefully wrestled on the floor. I covered Johnny with a blanket and started to remove his shoes, when I saw their soles. There was almost no leather at all—holes through to his feet; and it was freezing and wet—winter. Oh, Dad . . .

Mom saw me standing there looking at the shoes. Then the children saw, too. Quietly we tiptoed out.

"There's loads of markets all piled together in this burg—I saw 'em," Scott said, leading the way through the icy streets. The raw wind whipped us.

Suddenly I stopped. "Let's stand in this doorway a minute." We huddled together, stomping our feet.

"Listen, everybody," I began. "Listen—Dad's shoes—we don't need . . ."

"Yes! Yes! Oh, yes!" Their cry was spontaneous.

"We'll get the goddamnedest pair of shoes!" Scott said, kicking his legs in the air.

"Heavy, heavy ones," Mom added.

Judy jumped up and down. "A Christmas present—a big surprise—like it's from Santa Claus!"

"Anyway, nobody's hungry," Scott said, rolling his eyes.

We laughed until we were flushed and warm, then Mom took charge. "I saw the shoes—down the street yesterday. Now, be quiet a minute. They're beauties, and heavy. . . . Wait a minute till I finish—and they're only three dollars."

"A dollar for food then!" Scott yipped.

"Yes. We'll buy carefully and have a Christmas dinner," Mom said as we started off on the shopping spree.

"Dinner is served, madams and mesewers," Judy, the perfect butler, announced.

The room looked festive and smelled of onions. I had covered our dining trunk with red crepe paper with ruffled edges. The holly berries in the center were courtesy of Scott from a neighboring back yard. Mom had made covers for the lamps from a worn red flannel nightshirt. I had decorated the edges of the celluloid plates—even the handles of the tin utensils—with red, green, and yellow sealing wax, making a batik pattern which had hardened disturbingly—never to be removed, I feared.

"That's the topper!" Scott said, pointing to the life-size face of Santa Claus peering merrily at us from the windowpane. Judy had accomplished that with her crayons.

During Mom's secret preparations of Christmas dinner, the small apartment rang with our songs: "Silent Night," "Jingle Bells," "Oh, Come All Ye Faithful."

Now we held our breath as Mom brought in the platter covered with a napkin and placed it in front of Johnny. "To keep it hot," she said, and sat down.

"All right, kids," Johnny ordered. We bowed our heads. Hesitatingly he began: "For—for—this great day, for this blessing, thank you, God—what you've given us is the best health and each other—brother, it's hard to top that—so God bless You, God—and we thank You."

There was a moment of silence, then. "Allez-oop!" Johnny cried as he ripped the napkin off the mound in front of him. There on the platter sat a pair of shiny, black-laced shoes, a spray of holly on each stub toe.

Johnny gripped his hands, and from his throat came a deep cry, like that of an animal. And he sobbed—the sound of it like the rumble of a released dam. His body heaving mightily, his head bowed, he sobbed. We'd never witnessed anything like that. Our arms were holding him—we, too, were crying—we knew not why.

Toledo, Akron, Erie, Reading, Corvallis, Grand Forks, Durham, Helena, Billings, Casper . . .

Dear Gertrude,

I'm fifteen now, and I guess you are about the same.

I just felt like writing a letter today, and although I've had three girl friends, I thought I'd write to you because you're my first girl friend. I hope you live where you were when we were about six years old—so this reaches you.

My other girl friends are Ellen—her father's a doctor and he reads dopey books. My other girl friend is Audrey. She has two moles like me and looks like me all over, and my dad tried to buy her to be my friend for always.

I hope you are well, and I bet you are very pretty. I'm not very pretty, but I have white teeth. And garbage men whistle at my chest.

We have been traveling almost every place.

I'd like to tell you some secrets, Gertrude. I'm going to be a legit actress (that means not a vaudeville one), because I've got to make some money for us. It makes me feel awful when we go to a restaurant. Dad goes in first while we wait outside. He says he wants to case the joint. That means he looks at the food people are eating to see if it's a lot and good. Then he looks at the menu to see how much it costs. Sometimes he goes in three or four restaurants before he gives us the nod. Then Dad and Mom order two dinners and ask for five plates. And the waiters look so snotty at us, like we're dirt, and slam things on the table, and I can hardly eat because Mom and Dad take the best off their plates and give it to us. Dad makes it a joke, though. He puts salt and pepper on the pattern of his plate when he finishes and pretends to be eating and eating till he about bursts and belches. And we laugh till people start looking at us, but I don't like it inside. That's why I want to be an actress on a stage in one spot, or in a movie picture. You make a lot of money, and everybody can have their own dinner.

Does your mother ever hit you, Gertrude, and say how nasty everything is? You know, things about touching? Sometimes when I'm not thinking anything, my mother whacks me and says I am. Sometimes I want to run away. How is your mother?

Remember my sister, who was born across the street from you? Well, she's so cute, and I don't want her to ever be afraid of Mom. My brother is a mess, although he's good-looking and can sing better than anyone, and can fix anything.

Vaudeville is out. Although Dad and everybody are awful worried, they act like that aren't.

We've had a lot of bad seasons in the last few years, but this last year was the worst.

I wish we had a dog. Have you?

I've got to make money, so I'm going to stop being bashful and embarrassed, and I'm going to find work to make us rich as soon as we get to New York again. I'm grown up, and it's time for me to take care of them.

I sure wish you were here. I could tell you a lot more things, because I can't write very good.

Dad has a five-dollar gold piece. A friend that was an acrobat who was killed gave it to him for good luck when they were both boys. Well, Sunday we went to church. We all agreed to concentrate on Alexander Pantages during the silent prayer so he'd think of us for booking. We also agreed to pass the collection bag quickly to Dad, who was going to put a dime in it for all of us. Well, we did, and as Dad passed it to the next customer, he let out a groan. Everybody looked around, because you know how quiet churches are. "Five dollars gone to Hell," Dad whispered. He had put his lucky piece in that bag by mistake. It was awful, but it was funny, and everybody around us got the giggles.

I love to get the giggles, don't you? I don't like to feel like crying.

Well, write soon, Gertrude.

Yours truly,
Nora

I addressed the envelope: "Gertrude, Rockaway Beach, New York," enclosed the letter, and put a stamp on it. I picked up a doll I'd made out of a bath towel, beans for eyes, nose, and mouth, and swayed back and forth in the small room singing, "Yes, sir, you're my baby . . ."

Suddenly I stopped and lay my doll on the bed carefully and kissed and covered her. Then I picked up the letter to Gertrude and tore it into tiny pieces.

Jacksonville, Newburgh, Stockton, Menlo, Salinas, Covington, Cedar Rapids, Sioux City . . .

I didn't learn about Dad's and Scott's Sioux City venture until long after, when Scott confessed. It had been all his idea.

"I tell ya, Dad, we can do the whole thing on ten dollars," Scott pleaded.

Johnny scratched the top of his hand. "I'll let you in on something, son," he said. "I've only got sixteen dollars between us and starvation. I'd die if we blew it."

Scott ushered Johnny to the park bench, then continued his pitch. "You always said, 'Have something people can't do without, like toilet paper.' Well, damnit, Dad, men can always pick up a leaf or a corn cob, but a rubber is another story."

"They're illegal, son. I don't like to have us monkey around illegal," Johnny said.

"As soon as we get to N.Y.C., we'll get legal again. It'll only take about two bucks to get to Marshall. We'll buy ten dollars' worth—they're a dollar for 144 of 'em—that's a gross —and a dollar for a room for us overnight. We can sell 'em on the way back here."

"All right, goddamnit, we'll take a flyer—till I get my bearings. But don't you ever, never, y'hear, tell your mom and sisters—"

"Don't worry," Scott said with enthusiasm. "There's a hell of a mark-up. We can get a dollar for a tin—three in a tin. Then—"

"Hold it—that's too much of a hell of a mark-up."

"But, Dad, for emergency cases, guys will be willing to pay that. You know how those things are."

"Holy jumpin' Jeez Christ Almighty—*you* don't—do ya?" Johnny asked.

"Nope, but I ain't deaf. I hear what stagehands and the Canto Brothers and the likes of them say."

"But, son—don't you ever—ever—y'hear?"

"What ya mean, ever?"

"Well, hell—not till—well, hell."

"Okay, I won't, Dad."

Thirteen hours later Johnny and Scott were sitting on straight-backed chairs beside a rickety bed in their dollar room on the outskirts of Marshall, Iowa. Their wares—nine gross of them—were piled high in the middle of the bed. The skinny bedposts were used as a base to roll the latex rubbers, then three were put into a small tin box labeled "Agnes, Mabel, and Becky."

Stopping only for a quick sandwich and some coffee, they worked through the night, and by checkout time they had two cases full of their commodity. They set out eagerly for barber shops, gas stations, pool halls, and whore houses.

Seven foot-sore hours later, they were in another small town, lying on another rickety bed, with seventy-seven dollars in Johnny's money belt. And hardly a dent in their stock.

They decided they'd better cut their price to three tins for a dollar. Since the nine rubbers cost them approximately six cents, it was still a hell of a mark-up.

Four busy days of superb salesmanship elapsed.

"I've got feet growing out of my feet," Johnny said as they returned to the dingy hotel housing the rest of us. The roll in Johnny's pocket was $374.

The lie had been thoroughly rehearsed. "Y'see, the guy owed me this dough from the show I almost produced—*Through the Middle of the Earth*—you remember, Ceeley?"

"Mmmmm," she answered vaguely.

"If I had to beat him up to get it, I was prepared to. But there was no snarl—he just shelled it out."

"Why did Scott have to go?" Mom asked.

"If there was gonna be a fight, I was gonna be the referee," Scott answered glibly.

The explanation was satisfactory to all of us, and we set out for the Sioux City chop-suey parlor.

Trying for our New York goal was like taking two steps forward and sliding back five: long layoffs; big jumps; zig-zagging north, south, east, and west; playing towns we'd never heard of for two days, one night—anything we could get. The pay in most places was so meager that Johnny, hoping to retain his status in show business, called the act "Del Hawkins and Company," so the big-time bookers would not know how little he'd worked for.

The rubber money dwindled, but Scott's suggestion to continue the "sideline" was met by Johnny's icy stare.

10

MESA, Fort Smith, Greeley, Elsmere, St. Petersburg, Lewiston, Topeka, Lake Charles, Hattiesburg, Montgomery . . .

Mobile, Alabama.

Judy and Scott each had measles and whooping cough. "Jeez, two diseases apiece—shows we're big time!" Scott moaned, then threw up. Mom held his head over the toilet bowl.

Johnny tucked Scott back in bed for the twelfth time that day. "When's that fat-head doctor coming back?" he asked Cecilia, his hand on Scott's brow.

"Which one?" Mom asked. "Don't rub your eyes, Judy."

"The one with the gray soup strainer."

"He's due back at five."

"Well, where the hell is he?"

"It's only three-thirty."

"Call the other one, then."

"Johnny, we're in trouble already, balancing two doctors in and out. People are only supposed to have one. It's ethics." Mom was giving Judy some juice.

"But they got two diseases, so we're gonna have two doctors. They're gonna have a set of prescriptions for measles and a set for whooping cough. One doctor might try to pool the two diseases and give us a rate, and I don't want no rates or slipshod stuff for my kids' sicknesses."

"Awright, Johnny, but for God's sake quit pacing back and forth. You've got me bilious." Mom sat in the armchair and scowled.

He crossed the room and kissed her. She put her hand on his cheek. "Don't get so rattled, Johnny, kids get these diseases."

"Yeah, but not two at a time."

Scott's voice came from the bed. "Next week—leprosy and clap."

"Shut up, son, you're sick—and who told you about clap?"

"The stage manager at Loew's."

"Where?"

"Chicago."

"Okay, rest now—you're sick."

I had been practically thrown into a hotel across the street, toothbrush and nightgown after me.

"I know she's already had some kind of bugs, but I don't want to book 'em again," Johnny declared as he hustled me out.

I woke up the next morning and lay there in bed, the sun pouring over me.

I was on my own, for a whole day! I stretched and pointed my toes high above me. I decided to take a bath and go to the five and ten and buy some toys for Scott and Judy, and lipstick for Mom, and then just walk and walk and look and look.

I spent seventy cents of the two dollars Johnny had given

me, and had the bellboy take the presents and four ice cream cones up to my confined family. Mom called me on the lobby phone to say the children were much better, and Johnny butted in to tell me to sign the tab and have a nice dinner in the hotel, and to be careful crossing streets.

I looked in store windows, priced silk stockings, books, paintings, perfumes, bedroom slippers. I settled myself in the back of an ice-cream parlor and had a "pineapple temptation." I bought a second-hand copy of *The Arabian Nights* for fifteen cents and went back to the hotel and sat in a big lounge chair on the mezzanine and began to read.

"Hi," someone said. I looked up. "Ma name's Mary Lou," a pretty, dark-haired girl told me.

"Hi." I smiled and closed the book.

"Are y'all goin' in the contest?"

"What contest?"

"Why—Lawd—everabody knows about the contest!" the girl answered disapprovingly. "Miss America contest. Each state enters about three cities. Raght now they're looking for 'Miss Mobile.'"

"Oh, no—I'm not going in."

"Well"—Mary Lou slumped in the chair next to me—"why not? Just buy a bathin' suit—there's nothin' to it."

"There's something to it—you got to open by being pretty."

"Y'all are pretty, and yo' shape looks O.K. How old are y'all?"

"Sixteen—almost."

"S'posed to be eighteen, but—well, tell 'em y'are. Anyway, yo' shape looks like eighteen," she added.

"Oh, Ah couldn't," I answered, then grinned to myself. I had gotten Southern awfully fast.

"What part of Alabama y'all from?" Mary Lou asked.

"New York City. We're just stranded here for a while. I mean, we're staying here till my brother and sister feel better —they've got diseases."

"Oh—well, Ah'm goin' to go in it." She crossed her legs and kicked her foot. She was really pretty.

"When will you win it?" I asked.

"Oh, you," she giggled. "Ah'm not goin' to win—but maybe Ah'll get one of the prizes. They're all pretty good."

"What kind?"

"Well, whoever is elected Miss Mobile gets clothes from every big store in this city—everything—about ten complete outfits, and a trip to Atlantic City with a chaperone—free, too —and she gets to live in the best hotel and she gets two thousand dollars in cash."

I jerked upright. "Two thousand dollars?"

"Yessireee ma'am; then, if you're Miss Amer—"

"Never mind that. When do you get the two thousand?"

"As soon as you're voted Miss Mobile, Ah guess. What's yo' name?"

"Nora. . . . Listen, Mary Lou, how long will it take—to pick Miss Mobile?"

"Here's what I found out." She moved closer. "First y'all sign up the Maynard Auditorium, then Monday through the whole week the judges look at you, and if you stay in, you try again until they pick fifteen girls on Saturday. Then on Wednesday they pick five, then they choose Miss Mobile on the next Saturday. Land o' Goshen, Nora, squint yo' eyes a little—they're gonna fall out of yo' head."

"Mary Lou, can you wait here a minute? I'll be right back."

"Where y'all goin'?"

I raced upstairs three steps at a time and grabbed the phone. "The hotel across the street, please—yes, the Madison, that's it." My palms were wet while I waited for them to get Johnny to the phone.

"Dad?"

"Yes, sweetheart?"

"How long are they going to be germy? I mean, how long will we be in this town?"

"The gray doctor said ten days, the bald one said two weeks —why?"

"Will I stay in this hotel?"

"Yes, I have enough in my money belt now to tide us over. Why? You all right?"

"Oh, gee, yes. Dad? I met a girl friend in the mezzanine— she's awful nice—"

"Where's her mother and father?" Johnny interrupted.

"They're home in her house, I guess—and, Johnny, she asked me to go shopping with her. Could I?"

"Sure, honey. I'll send some money to the desk downstairs. Just be careful crossing streets, and call up when you get home."

"How's Mom?" I asked.

"Fine, just tired of beef juice and enemas and squeezing oranges."

I was in bed by nine that night, but I relived the day until it was almost dawn. My thoughts were like a crazy quilt, thanks to all the lies I had told in filling out the entry blank:

Name: Nora Tyler.

I'd borrowed Mary Lou's aunt's name, because you were not supposed to be from vaudeville, just from a home.

Address: 14 Spring Street, Benton, Alabama.

She let me borrow her aunt's address, too.

Phone: None.

Age: Eighteen.

Eyes: Green.

Hair: Blond.

Height: 5'1".

Weight: 107 pounds.

Father's name: Sam Tyler.

Mary Lou's aunt's dead husband's name.

Mother's name: Sara Tyler.

Mary Lou's aunt's name.

Father's occupation: Milkman.

I thought that one up myself.

Ambition: Dramatic stage star.

I lay still for a moment, then switched on the light for the twentieth time and looked in the dresser mirror, involuntarily glancing around to see if Mom was watching. "Dramatic star," I said solemnly to my reflection, then sat on the bed, crossing my legs under me. Big dramatic stars, like Katharine Cornell and Lynn Fontanne, had soft beds and dogs. All right, that's it, I've put it in writing. I flopped over on my stomach and grabbed the pillow in my arms. Two thousand dollars meant we could get East. And if I won, we could pay the rest of those awful tearoom debts. And maybe instead of us opening a store, I could try to be a dramatic star now—quick. Then everybody could just rest.

I jumped up once more and ran to the mirror. "Nora Marten—I mean, Tyler—you've just been elected Miss Mobile!" I bowed and threw kisses, then turned around and around till I was dizzy, and fell back on the bed laughing.

An amplified voice rang through the crowded auditorium. "Ladies and gentlemen, after a week of owah judges' close inspection, we have chosen five girls from the ninety-three entries from our fair state—all perfect representatives. Ladies and gentlemen, from these five will emerge Miss Mobile. One lucky girl will be the recipient of the great honor of representing our fair city in the Miss America contest."

He paused to impress. "It was a difficult chore to eliminate the others—we had fifteen charmin' girls in the semifinals. The judges—Mr. Fairchild, Mr. Newton, Mr. Porter, Mr. DeKabe, Mr. Wallack, our esteemed Mayor Heffley, Mr. Condon, Mr. Boris, Mr. Taneetic, Mr. Murphy, Mr. Crooks, and Mr. Gittel—have spent long hours weighing the girls, literally and figuratively"—he acknowledged the scattered giggles—"and to the best of their ability have with honest integrity chosen the five for the finals. Those girls will be judged not by looks alone

but by personality—personality, folks—so that the winner will
be able to conduct herself with ease when face to face with
the world-famous judges who will decide if she is to be given
the highest title in the land—that of Miss America!"

Cheers!

"Dad? Mom?"

They looked up. Cecilia, scissors in hand, had been cutting
out paper dolls for Judy. Johnny, with pencil and paper, was
trying to sharpen the act.

"Honey," cried Johnny, "why didn't you give us some warning? We'd have checked with the doctors to see if you
could come in yet."

Mom eyed me. "Nora? What are you up to? You look
different."

"Listen, Mom and Dad—Judy, Scott!" I paused dramati-
cally. "Listen, I . . . am Miss . . . Mobile!"

They gaped at me as though I'd taken leave of my senses.

Then Scott said, "And I'm Miss Gawanus Canal." He put
his hand on his hip, limp wrist above his head.

"Now, listen, I'm going to be crowned at a big ceremony,
and we get the two thousand tonight, and you're my chaperone to Atlantic City, Mom, and I get the clothes today, and
they're waiting for me now to get the key to the city. I'm not
your sister, Judy and Scott, you're just friends of mine—and
Mom and Dad, you get ready for tonight!" I pointed at Johnny.
"You're Sam Tyler, milkman. You're Sara Tyler, wife." I
pointed at Cecilia. "And I'm Nora Tyler, your prize-winning
daughter!"

The stunned silence was finally broken by Scott. "Two thousand what?"

"Dollars! Dollars! Dollars! Dollars we don't have to work
for, travel for, pack for. Just two thousand lovely, lovely non-
earned dollars!"

Johnny led me to a chair and seated me. "Now, honey, calm
down. Just quietly tell us . . ."

So I told them every step, every feeling along the way. ". . . and at last there were just the five of us in this sort of ballroom with the twelve judges sitting around looking and whispering and making notes on the cards they held in their hands. I was jumpy in the stomach, Mom, because I knew I didn't look beautiful like those other girls, and I wasn't from Alabama, anyway. Those other girls were so beautiful. But you know something? It was getting near the finish—so I just took a deep breath and said to myself, 'This is like a show. It's like our act. There's got to be a punch—up forte—dazzle 'em—leave 'em laughing.'"

"Slow down, Nora. Just tell it calm," Johnny advised.

"Well, I took a good look, a real hard look at those other girls. And they were trembling from head to foot, poor things, and they had funny-looking smiles on—not natural anymore. They didn't even walk like before—they were jerky, and they kept pulling at their hair. So I said to myself: 'I'm going to pretend I'm a great actress, and I'm playing the part of the most beautiful contestant in the world. And Ah tawk Southern and Ah'm reel cute.' Well, it was time for each girl to be interviewed by the twelve men—personality, that's what was next! So when my turn came, I just thought what you said, Johnny, 'Try to make 'em happy, and they will be. *Know* they'll laugh, and they will. Do the best you can.'" I paused, ran to Johnny, and kissed him. Then, with hands on hips and a wide smile, I batted my eyes coyly. "Theyfo', Ah'm Miss Mobile, y'all!"

11

ATLANTIC CITY looks like the subway crush with sunshine," Mom said as we got off the train.

We tried to make some headway through the jammed platform toward a banner that proclaimed: "Welcome, Miss Mobile!"

There were all those "Welcome" banners trying to ripple in the hot, dead summer air. And a dozen or more small, separate bands were blaring songs appropriate to the U.S.A.'s curvy representatives. The tunes merged into ear-splitting noise.

"Put them all together they spell 'Welcome Miss Hong Kong!'" Mom yelled over the racket.

Two bulb-flashing hours later, all of us Miss Thises and Miss Thats, withered and dry-toothed from throwing kisses and smiling, were herded, armpits wet, into bannered top-down cars to kiss-throw our way to our respective hotels.

Miss Mobile was stationed at the Shelbourne. In my wake was young, good-looking Mr. Black, my assigned escort for the duration of the four-day pageant. Mr. Tanner, a prissy-faced, frail-looking man, was my bodyguard.

I shook hands with—while I smiled, smiled, smiled for the curious bystanders—the manager, the manager's assistant, the first desk clerk, the second desk clerk, the third, the night clerk, the cashier, the cashier's assistant, the bell captain, the bellboys, the elevator men, the baggage man, the doormen, and the toothy maître d', who said, "We have Miss Mobile soup on the menu tonight, basically bean. Will you autograph this for my two-month-old daughter?"

Flowers were jammed into my embrace; thorns stuck into my arms. "Smile fo' a pitcher, y'awl," one squashed-nosed photographer drawled, enjoying the laughs he got on his faked Southern accent. "Lift y'all's skirt," another requested, nudging the first with self-delight. "Just stand still for crissakes," a third man demanded as he tried to focus his camera. "Hold it, smile, wave, autograph—autograph—autograph—"

We were alone at last in our suite, the door locked.

"It's good you-all got two thousand for this, isn't it, you-all?" Mom said.

I pulled the remaining thorn from my sore arm.

We went to the bathroom quickly, because we were due at the Steel Pier, then due at the City Hall, due at the theater, due at the Fire Department, due—due—due!

At the stroke of midnight we were in our beds, too exhausted for teeth brushing. And on the dresser lay a long list of tomorrow's "due ats."

"Mom?"

"Ummm?"

"I wonder if Miss Los Angeles' mother really broke Miss Salt Lake City's mother's nose when the train stopped for Miss Chicago?"

"I dunno. The conductor said he'd get her a doctor to set it in Pittsburgh."

"I don't know how a doctor could even find her nose through all that blood."

"She didn't wipe it, just let it keep bleeding till she showed everybody on the whole seven cars."

"All because she said Miss Los Angeles' legs were bandy!"

"Yeah."

We were quiet. Then suddenly Mom laughed out loud. "I nearly jumped out of my skin when Miss New York City's mother smashed that plate over Miss Portland's mother's head!"

"That was because Miss Portland's mother said Miss New York City's curls were bleached!"

"Mmmmm," Mom said, sleepily now. "They were, too!"

I was determined to hold on to the wonderful closeness between us. "The trip was only fun because of the fights. Otherwise, it was just strange—nobody speaking to anybody, just staring like we weren't all on the same trip trying to win the same thing. It was spooky."

"Go to sleep."

"Okey-doke, but I'm not sleepy."

"Go to sleep."

"Okey-doke."

Late another night, after a couple of busy days, I was in bed rereading the messages from the family: "You're my Miss America. . . . Love, Johnny," "Land on your feet. . . . Love, Scott." "*You* have the whitest teeth, I bet. . . . Love, Judy."

"Mom?"

"Huh?"

"Tomorrow's the day! Float in the afternoon—then the American Beauty Ball!"

"Uh huh."

"Aren't you tired, Mom? You going someplace?"

"Thought I'd get some air. It's nice out. I won't be long."

"But it's after midnight."

"I won't be long."

"You look awful pretty, Mom. I love that dress on you."

"Now go to sleep." Cecilia bent over me and kissed my nose. "I won't be long."

She left a trail of lovely perfume.

I got up for a glass of ice water, pulled up the blind, and looked down at the boardwalk. I saw Mom and Mr. Black, my handsome escort, get into a wicker cart for an oceanfront ride.

I tried to sleep, but my thoughts were too vivid. Of course, I wouldn't win. And anyway, the prize was a cup—and a job with a Publix Unit, and it didn't include John Marten and Company, so I'd die of lonesomeness. I twirled around in the bed and kicked off the blankets and thought of Johnny's letter from New York: ". . . found an apartment on St. Nicklos Ave. by the week, and everything is fine and paid up, so hurry home."

Flipping on the light, I took my American Beauty dress from the closet and held it in front of me. I had been photographed in it, and the pictures had been on all the pages of the Mobile papers. "Custom-made by the famous Nighton and Sons. Cost: $400." It was the loveliest dress in the world, with yards and yards of blue taffeta and ruffles of real lace. I fondled the garlands of roses that began pink at the shoulder and became red as they followed the billowy skirt to the floor. I decided that whoever won, I had the prettiest dress. I hung it carefully in the closet and was soon asleep.

"Y'see, Dad, it was only a little while before the finale—the American Beauty Ball—when she called us on the phone. I was dressed and ready, and there was no way of checking. Everybody had left their hotels, and the streets were so jammed, I couldn't reach anybody in charge, not and get there in time." I paused to look at my pacing, outraged father. Scott and Judy were sitting on the floor, Cecilia in the armchair. The atmosphere of our small New York flat was charged with indignation.

Mom continued the story: "The little tramp—that's all she

is. It was jealousy, downright jealousy, that's all!" She leaned forward to make her point. "Y'see, Johnny, it started during the float parade. She was right in back of Nora's, and believe me, Nora was the hit of the parade. People yelled, applauded, and threw torn programs in the air when she passed. I tell you, she was the hit of the parade!"

"What else?" Johnny said, chewing on his cigar like a camel.

I took up the tale again: "But who could believe Miss Birmingham would call up and lie like that! 'Honey, y'all heah the orful news? We cain't weah owah pretty ball gowns. We hafta weah what we woah at the banquet, 'member? Yo' green and my lil' ole' beige? . . . Well, that's what the committee jes called and said—don't ast me why they din't call you. Anyway, jes don' embarrass yo'self bein' ovah-dressed. Y'see honey, Ah thought of you right off 'cause we're both from Alabama and I want us to be right—y'heah?—*right*. So Ah cawled you. Oh, Ah know yoah blue taffeta is beutiful, that's what breaks mah heart!'"

I stopped to breathe. "Oh, Dad, I felt so awful. I wore that same green dress, and there sat the prettiest dress in the world in the closet, and the dresses all the other girls wore were dreams, including that horrid Miss Birmingham. She had on a beautiful flowy red satin, not that 'beige thing.' It was beautiful, long, full, and *all* of them had on their best-of-all dresses."

Johnny stopped pacing. "Didn't help her, the crumb. You came in third. She came in nothing."

"But, Dad," I cried, "I'd just as soon of come in nothing. I don't want a cup, or a Publix Unit. I just wanted to feel right in my beautiful blue dress."

"I'll write something in the act for that dress—don't you feel bad. Crumbs are crumbs," Johnny continued. "You run into them all the time. Some crumbs are little crumbs, and that's bad enough, but when they are lying crumbs, that's the worst." He had a coughing fit, and we took turns pounding him on the back. "But don't feel bad anymore, sweetheart. It's past. We're going to have some chop suey."

He pulled me to my feet and held me close. "We have a new backdrop, the debts are paid, Mom's beaded dress has been cleaned, we're going to have new pictures for the front, and we've got two full weeks set—Detroit and Nashville. Nora, you did a man's job."

12

THE BONANZA didn't last long, and there were long
spells of inaction.

St. Joseph, Jefferson City, Greenville, Cumberland, Baton
Rouge, Manchester, Fall River, Stanford, Pawtucket, Cran-
ston, Rutland, Harrisburg . . .

And finally New York again.

"I'm going to take this filthy troupe into the washroom at
Grand Central, Johnny. We look like a band of fortune-
tellers. We can't face New York like this. Nobody'd give us
work. You and Scott exit to the men's room." Mom was in
charge.

Polished up now, we set out in search of a place to live.

Five hours later we found it: one room, ground floor on
Ninety-first Street near Lexington, five cots, three stools, gas
stove, and icebox behind dirty drapes, community toilet down
the hall.

"Meeting will pleez come to order." Johnny was futilely searching his pockets for a cigar. "Now, kids, we'll make the best of it. I'll go the rounds tomorrow, and—and—I know we'll be okay."

"I will, too," I added firmly.

"Will what?"

"Make the rounds."

"What d'ya mean?"

"Now, listen, everyone—I'm grown up," I said. "And if we can't find work together, we'll have to work separate. I'm going to where they book dramatic actresses—or movies. I'm going to find work."

Scott looked at me. "I am, too," he said. "I'll be a delivery boy or something."

"Me, too," Judy told the world at large.

The meeting lasted until bedtime. We stopped only to eat the salami and rolls Scott had run out for.

Later that night, Johnny pulled his cot next to Mom's. Scott and Judy, covered with every piece of warm clothing they could find in their suitcases, were fast asleep. The last of the five trunks was being held for nonpayment of rent in Muncie, Indiana. In the dark Mom turned toward Johnny and whispered, "Cut it out, Dad, don't keep sighing like that. The kids are all right—they want to help. I'll stay here and watch them, and you jump out. If theaters can't pay all of us, you can do a single and keep your standing as a fine act."

"Will Nora be safe?"

"She'll be safe. And who knows—maybe she's got talent."

"What d'ya call what she's had so far—chopped liver?"

Cecilia giggled. On the other side of the room, I heard the creaking of their cots with calm but immeasurable sadness. When I'm a star I'll get them a nice double bed, I decided.

13

JOHNNY was playing his single in clubs and picture houses on the outskirts of New York City, sometimes for as little as ten dollars a performance. Scott had a paper route around One Hundred and Twenty-fifth Street and St. Nicholas Avenue. He walked home at day's end through bitter-cold darkness to turn over every penny to Mom.

Mom's new interest owned the pharmacy on the corner of Ninety-second and Madison, and his name was Bernie Manning. I didn't know how long it had been underway, but I sensed the romance was in bloom the day I went into the store for a tube of Straska's toothpaste. It was to be a present for the family from the dollar I'd received for decorating the shop window. I was about to go out with my purchase when I heard Cecilia's voice, "Coffee's ready, Bernie," coming from the back of the pharmaceutical room.

"What's the matter, young lady?" Bernie asked me, as I stared in the direction of the voice.

"Is that my mother?" I asked. And Cecilia peered around the door.

"Why, Nora, what are you doing here?"

I held the toothpaste package toward her, not trusting the sound of my own voice.

"Don't tell me you're Nora!" Mr. Manning asked, pulling me toward him. "No secret where you get your beautiful eyes," he said smoothly.

"I look like my father." I jerked away from him and ran out of the store.

"Here, little boy," I said to a dirty-faced six-year-old, and put the toothpaste in his hand. "A present for you!" Then I turned and headed toward downtown Broadway. Defiantly I spent the rest of my newly earned dollar in every drugstore I passed: for a soda I couldn't touch; a movie magazine I threw away; gum I put in my shoes; and a ten-cent package of cigarettes. It was almost dark.

Then I set out for the heart of the Great White Way, turned into the Park Central Hotel, ran up the stairs to the mezzanine, and sat at a desk to write my farewell note:

> Dear Everybody:
>   I am going to commit suicide. I will never see you again. Take good care of yourself, Judy, and take care of every animal. Scott, I hope you'll make a lot of money so Johnny won't have to worry.
>   Good-bye to everybody.

I looked around the mezzanine. I was alone. I continued writing:

> . . . And I hope you stay well and happy. With all my love from Nora.

With tears streaming down my cheeks, I wrote:

> P.S. And I love you, too, Mom.

I had to address the envelope three times. My tears kept blurring the ink.

Finally, I sat in a large leather armchair and took the cigarettes and matches out of my pocket. Tears wiped dry with my sleeve, I puffed on my first cigarette. The result was extremely unsatisfactory. The mezzanine started swaying. I squashed the butt on the side of a brass spittoon and walked down the stairs toward the cashier's booth. I stood behind a man and waited my turn to buy a stamp.

Gee, he smelled nice, I thought, as I looked at his tweed coat. I got my nose as close to it as possible. Suddenly he turned and caught me as I lost my balance.

"Oh-oooh," he said. "I'm sorry." I dropped my letter. We both stooped to pick it up and cracked heads.

"Sorry again." He laughed this time and rubbed my forehead. "The least I can do after being so awkward is treat you to a stamp!"

My eyes were downward, but I'd gotten a glimpse of his face. He looked sort of like Ronald Colman, and my heart skipped beats.

"I'll mail it for you," he said, and bowed in such a gentlemanly fashion that I was speechless, until I saw my suicide note heading toward the mail slot.

"NOOOOO!" I screamed, stopping everyone in the lobby.

"Huh?" He looked startled.

"I mean—I mean—" I stuttered and grabbed the letter. "It's misspelled," I finished weakly, and ran through the revolving door.

Flustered and giddy, I scarcely felt the blocks fly by. Waiting to cross a busy intersection, I leaned against the lamppost and looked at the world's largest electric sign blinking: "Marion Davies in *When Knighthood Was in Flower*.

There I stood, unconsciously tearing my letter to shreds, as the crowds passed around me. The dreams in my eyes changed the sign to "Nora Marten in *When Knighthood Was in Flower*. And I threw kisses to the clamoring throng, and

Mr. Ronald Colman, Jr. pressed red roses in my arms as we walked hand-in-hand toward home.

But the wings on my feet fell off about Eighty-seventh Street. Nervously I told myself, "I'll get hell for being out so late."

Six weeks passed. Johnny was still away, sending us whatever he could out of his meager salary. He barely held on to enough to keep himself from starving. Scott's paper route netted about three dollars a week, and I had a part-time job at a small circulating library and greeting-card shop on Second Avenue at One Hundred and Tenth Street. I worked from eight A.M. until one P.M., then returned at four P.M. until eleven P.M. I had three hours in the afternoon to make the rounds of the theatrical offices. My pay was eight dollars a week.

Judy went to the public school on Eightieth and Lexington. Mom slept in the mornings, but she made a warm dinner for us—before she went out.

In the evenings Judy and Scott were free, and it was Judy who took the most drastic advantage of that freedom. She would race through the streets and up a littered, dark stairway until she reached the fifth-floor apartment occupied by an orphaned schoolfriend and her older brother. There Judy would change into a tight black skirt, threadbare, a rose-colored satin blouse, and push her feet into ill-fitting, run-over high heels. Looking into a cracked mirror over the grimy kitchen sink, she'd spend a half-hour applying full stage makeup: beaded eyelashes; blue lids; black eyebrow pencil; voluptuous red lips; bright red cheek rouge; all smeared on heavily over thick-coated greasepaint and powder. Then onto her ears would go cheap, dangling earrings. And for the final glamorous touch, a pair of the brother's dirty, stiff socks stuffed into a brassiere. She'd allow herself a minute to stare into the mirror, then the eleven-year-old baby face shining through the mask would smile victoriously.

Again running, Judy would cover the blocks to Loew's Eighty-sixth Street Theater in time to change into an usherette's uniform and be at work from six to eleven. Then she'd try to beat me home, and did so successfully—except once. Cecilia seldom came home before midnight, so there was no worry there.

One night Judy could not resist an ice cream on her way home. Squirming onto a high stool in front of the counter, she called out: "Banana split, please."

I was sitting three stools away. I stared in horror at the profile smothered in makeup. Stealthily I slid onto the stool next to Judy, and scarcely breathing, watched the oblivious child devour the elaborate concoction, then reach into the cigar box on her lap for the money.

I could contain myself no longer. "Judy!"

"Holy mackerel," she answered.

I grabbed my sister and dragged her through the drugstore and out to the street.

"Ouch! Take it easy, you're pinching my skin."

"I'll pinch more than that."

"Lemme be, and I'll tell ya."

I steered her into a dark doorway. "Now, what's the meaning—and hurry up."

"Well, y'see I—well—we—"

"Make it snappy." My voice was ominous. "And who is 'we'?"

Her lower lip protruded almost as far as her nose. "You spoiled the surprise—here." She held the cigar box toward me. "Here is one hundred and two dollars I got for ushering."

"Ushering what?"

"Loew's Eighty-sixth."

"When—how long? What clothes are those? Why are you made up like Theda Bara?" I asked all in one long breath.

Our mouths blew steam into the cold night air as the questions were asked and answered.

When I was partially satisfied, I grabbed Judy in tender

panic. "But you silly thing, you're a baby—it's dangerous running the streets."

We had started walking toward home when I stopped and asked suspiciously, "Judy, baby, if you've only been doing it for ten days—at a dollar a day—how'd you make this hundred and two dollars?"

"Well, I saw that other fellow in the balcony—"

"What other fellow?"

"He was an usher, too—on the other side."

"Go on."

"Well, he'd look for the rich-looking ones lined up waiting for seats—you know, fur-coat ones and jewelry."

"Go on."

"And he'd whisper to them that he had two seats or four seats put aside, and they would give him a big tip to be ushered to the seats ahead of all the others, so—"

"Hurry up."

"So I did it, too, and I made all this nice money."

"But is that honest?"

"When people just hand you money, you don't steal it," Judy said loftily, and she started to skip to keep herself warm.

"I give up! But you're never going back there again—or to that crazy apartment. I'll get your clothes and return this junk you're wearing. We'll have to say you found the money. Mom'd get mad if she knew."

We were both skipping now, and nearing home.

"You nutty kid." I smiled. "Was it fun?"

"Yep—all but three things."

"What three?"

"Well, the armpits in the uniform—they smelled awful pew-ie."

"From you?"

"Heck no—all the other ushers that wore it."

"What next?"

"Well, I had to listen to George Jessel singing 'My Mother's Eyes' way too much. I only liked it the first thirty times."

"What's the third thing?"

"All the men pinched my socks."

"Your *socks?*"

"Yep," she answered blithely as she reached into her bosom and yanked out a sock. "These!"

We were home.

It was Thanksgiving. "It's a holiday today, the wedding of the painted doll . . ." We had reason for singing. Johnny was coming home, and Judy's Loew's Eighty-sixth Street Theater loot assured us of a tremendous holiday dinner, fleecy blankets, and new clothes. The window of our flat was steamed over from all the cooking on the two-burner. Judy had finger-drawn a pumpkin on the clouded window, and her scroll lettering said: "Happy Thanksgiving, Dad."

Johnny's eyes were moist as we screamed our welcome.

I noticed that he looked worn and thin.

We all talked at once, and it was not until after the feast that we were able to settle ourselves enough to tell him all the news.

"I suppose you're wondering how we all look so prosperous, Johnny," Mom said with a smile.

"Tell it, Judy," Scott said, setting the stage for our sister's rehearsed and oft-repeated fib.

Judy stood by her stool and bowed. We applauded.

"Well, it was that early blizzard, see. . . . There I was walking, and I was freezing." She shook drastically to prove her point. "And there was a garbage can spilled, and a poor sick dog . . ." She impersonated a poor sick dog. Scott booed. "Well, the poor sick dog was hungry, and he was eating the awful garbage, see."

"Get to the verb," Scott said.

"Shut up, son," Johnny said.

"Well, you see, I didn't want him to get sicker, so I got a stick and shoveled the garbage back in the can, and while I was shoveling"—she paused—"well, see, there was a cigar box, and in the box was this money, see. . . ."

"What money?" Johnny asked.

We all spoke at once telling him what we'd bought. We showed him the new sweaters and shoes and blankets.

"Wow!" Johnny repeated time and again. "Wow!"

Then it was my turn. I told Dad all about my job at the circulating library. "Mrs. Strong, the owner, is awful nice, and she gives me full charge. I sell books and rent out books, and sell greeting cards." I described the long, narrow store in detail.

"And you, Ceeley?" Johnny asked.

"I keep busy—go to a night school to learn flower arranging," she said.

I loved watching all who came in to browse in the book store, but one young man was a special point of interest. He was so handsome he was almost beautiful. From the library card he had just taken out, I knew his name: De Witt Marathew II, age twenty-three, address 812 Fifth Avenue.

He came back four days in a row—evidently a fast reader —and every book I suggested, he took.

"I can almost see my face in his shoes, they're so shiny," I told my family, "and he has a gold wristwatch that he puts to his ear at times."

"He's deaf," Scott contributed.

"Shut up, son." Johnny said it with dignity.

"And he wears a navy blue suit—the bottoms and the tops are the exact same color, and a different tie every day."

"He's a pansy," Scott sneered.

Johnny was horrified. "Where'd you hear that word, Scott?"

"From Professor Muscles at the—"

Johnny interrupted, "Quiet, son."

"And he talks English," I continued. "You know, like 'cawn't' instead of 'can't.'"

"Woo woo," from Scott.

"Son, you hafta leave us and go to your cot," Johnny said.

"Leave you?" Scott giggled. "For where? There's my cot, Judy's got her foot on it."

"Go on, Nora," Johnny said.

"Well—there's no more," I said. "He's just fun to look at, like a pretty marble."

Two days later, after work, I flew into our one-roomer.

"Guess what?" I all but yelled it. "De Witt Marathew the Second asked me to go out with him, to the Senior Prom at Columbia, Saturday night. He'll pick me up here at seven o'clock, formal. That means a long dress—and Mrs. Strong says a prom is an honor to go to."

Mom was ecstatic, but Johnny got practical. "Where can we get you a long dress?" The Martens' finances couldn't handle more than the rent and food.

"I'll take in the sides of my white beaded dress for her. It won't be hard to let it out when we get booking again," Mom said.

"There's no coat—no coat except our raincoat, and it's worn out from sleeping in it," Johnny said.

"Let her take it off and stick it behind the front door when she gets to Columbia," Scott suggested.

"My white shoes are too big, but we'll put paper in the toes," Mom said happily.

"I'm going to buy you white gloves." Johnny's eyes were moist.

"And I know how to make a bag; we'll get a little piece of white velvet and . . ." Judy started drawing a picture of the bag she would make.

Johnny said he wanted to have a chance to talk with De Witt before we went to the dance, and to have the rest of the family meet him. So the Martens swung into action.

Judy pinned pink crepe paper over our one armchair to cover the fraying, and Scott filled milk bottles with leaves and flowers from Central Park.

Johnny pulled the trunks and suitcases out of the room and

lined them up along the hallway wall away from the door; Cecilia gave the janitor's wife her Spanish comb to ward off complaints. I dyed a towel to use as a runner on the bureau, and we put a plate of fruit in the center. Judy cut out pink roses she had crayoned and pasted them over the cracks in the mirror.

I spent the whole of Saturday afternoon getting ready. I washed my hair, and Mom brushed it dry for me.

By six-thirty Saturday night, we were all slicked, scrubbed, and sitting stiffly around the room. Judy and Scott had on their stage clothes: Judy a turtleneck sweater and skirt, and Scott knickers and a white shirt. Mom had on her Sunday best and Dad his only suit.

I was in the one good chair. I held my arms away from my body and tried not to perspire.

It got to be seven o'clock.

Then it was seven-thirty.

The Martens were as quiet as we had ever been. At eight o'clock Scott said sadly, "He was run over—even his wrist-watch was squashed."

"I bet it's the wrong night," Judy contributed.

Mom tried to smile. "You look so beautiful, Nora, you're too good for him.

We held out until nine. Then Johnny blew his nose. "Listen," he said, "nobody's gonna make us feel this bad—not Marathew the Second, Third, Fourth, or Fifth. Nobody is gonna hurt Nora. Tell you what," he brightened, "I'm gonna get us some ice cream and nuts and syrup." He was on the way out the door as he said it.

I never found out what happened to De Witt Marathew. Whether it had all been a joke, or whether he found somebody better to ask at the last minute. He never came back to the bookstore.

14

I WAS HAVING difficulty getting to sleep. My back was paining badly, and I still couldn't forget what had happened. Two weeks had passed, but I couldn't get it out of my mind. And I knew I could not share it with a soul—Johnny above all.

It had been about ten-thirty at night. I was sitting behind the desk reading a book. No one had been in the store for an hour; the storm outside had emptied the streets. Suddenly the door had opened, and a policeman had come in, shaking his coat and stamping snow off his boots.

"Good evening, young lady. Mind if I warm up a bit?"

"No, sir—come right in," I answered. "I was going to close early tonight because the weather's so awful. I was sure we wouldn't have any more customers. Now I'm glad I didn't —you can get dried off."

He removed his coat and hat. "Mind if I hang 'em back here?" he asked.

"Of course not."

He went behind the screen, which shielded a sink and the stairs to the basement. Then he lighted a cigarette and sat in the chair in front of the desk. "You haven't worked here long."

"Just about three weeks, and as soon as I get a job as an actress—my real profession," I said sedately, "I'll leave. My boss knows that, and she's very nice."

"Where is she tonight?"

"Home—playing bridge. She's very good at that. She's in a tournament, and they're playing at her house."

"I pass here every night. What's your name?"

"Nora."

"I pass every night, Nora, and I see you sitting here. There's hardly any business at this hour—seems silly to make you wait all by yourself."

"Well, sometimes somebody comes in late to pick out a book or buy some stationery."

"Aren't you afraid here all alone at night?"

"Oh, no—I'm not afraid. Mrs. Strong takes all the money out of the cash register except about fifty cents, so there's nothing to steal, except books and things—and I don't think burglars want that!" I smiled.

"True." He smiled back. "Nevertheless, I watch you every night and follow you home."

"You do?"

"Uh huh."

"Gee, that's nice—thank you—gee!"

He offered me a cigarette, which I declined.

He asked me questions about my family, and the half-hour passed swiftly.

"It's eleven now," he said. "I'll help you close up."

I tidied the desk and went behind the screen for my coat and overshoes. I heard him at the front door fussing with the lock. "I have the keys," I called.

He came back. "I'll check the basement for you."

"Oh, you don't need to—it's all right."

He flipped off the light switch.

"Hey," I giggled, "we can't see our way out."

He found the switch to the basement at the head of the stairs and turned it on. "Down here where you keep the stock?" he asked.

"Yes."

"Do you work down there?"

"Sometimes, when new things come in, Mrs. Strong lets me take inventory while she's up here waiting on customers."

"Let's take a look."

I followed him downstairs, saying, "There's not much to see—just stacked-up boxes."

"I'm interested, though," he said.

We were in the small basement now. "Over there's where we separate the greeting cards—see, birthday ones, Valentine—"

In a flash he kicked my two legs from under me with his right leg, and I hit my spine on the hard concrete. I screamed. The pain was so excruciating I nearly lost consciousness. He was on top of me, clawing at my pants. I lay still for a moment of shock, then started to scream again, beating him with my fists, kicking, rolling, pushing desperately to get him off.

"You bitch—shut up—shut up!"

I was punching violently, sick with fright. And I knew the police couldn't help me—he was a policeman.

"I'll strangle you, you bitch."

I fought and kicked, my body twisting, my arms scraping on the cement floor.

As suddenly as he'd thrown me to my back, he dragged me to my feet. My body shook so I could hardly stand.

He whipped out a gun. "All right, you lousy bitch, get out. Hear me? See this gun? If you ever tell a soul—anybody, ever —I'll get you with this. Now, get out!"

I turned to run, but the pain in my lower back was so

severe I felt as if my legs were stuck. I crawled up the stairs and, hunched over, got out of the dark store.

Now, moving carefully on my cot, I faced another sleepless night; the pain in my back seemed to get worse each day, yet I could never let anyone know—ever.

A week after Johnny's homecoming came the separation. Scott came running into Mrs. Strong's store. "Nora, you better get home right away! Mom's crying, and something's gone wrong about Dad!"

"Is he all right?" I grabbed my brother's arms.

"I guess so, I dunno. He left. I guess they had a fight."

I got permission to leave the store.

The flat was a shambles. Mom had broken and torn apart everything she could get her hands on. She was pacing the floor when we ran in.

"Your father—that bastard!" she snarled at me. "Accusing me—accusing me, you hear? That evil, rotten mind . . ." She ranted on, including us in her rage. "I hate all of you! This dump—everything! *I'm* leaving, too. I'll show him—I'll do what he thinks I do—the lousy bastard! I hate you, you hear me? And I'm going. *See* how you get along—all of you—I'm leaving this goddamn rotten place!" She grabbed her purse and coat.

I tried to stop her. "Please, Mom, don't go. We love you, Dad loves you. Please, Mom." But she was gone.

Scott sat white-faced. I sank to the floor and put my head in his lap. "Oh, Scott, I'm frightened. What will we do?"

He put his hand on my head. "I dunno. It's a mess. . . . I dunno."

Judy flew in the door and slammed it shut. "Lookee—I got a ladybug in a bottle, and she's going to sleep with me. She's mine. She's my baby." She stopped short. "Wassa matter, Nora?" she asked.

"C'm'ere." I held out my arms. Judy knelt beside us.

I pulled her close and started to cry, and Scott, digging his fists into closed eyes, joined me. Judy looked at us a moment, then without knowing anything, put her head on my breast and cried the hardest.

Mom was back early the next morning, tiptoeing about. And the smell of bacon and eggs wakened us.

"Come and get it!" she called gaily.

We got out of bed and scurried down the hall to the bathroom, laughing and shoving crazily to see who'd make it first. No mention of the past; we were just deliriously happy that she was home.

The effectiveness of my rounds of theatrical offices was weakened considerably by my shyness. Each day from one until four I looked for work and tried to behave as all budding actresses should behave—with ease and confidence—but I failed miserably time and again. The constant pain in my back added to my nervousness. And I was uneasy, too, working in the book store at night, but I needn't have been: the Law never showed up again.

I had learned that if I sat at the soda counter of Grey's Drug Store on Forty-fourth Street and Broadway, and listened carefully over a long Coke, I could always find out who was casting what. The young hopefuls and the youngsters who had already "arrived" on Broadway gathered in Grey's to share their knowledge of inside show business. It was a beehive of current theatrical information.

One day an attractive young juvenile called across to an equally attractive young ingenue: "Hey, Marie, Al Woods is looking for a replacement for *The Trial of Mary Dugan*."

"Yeah?"

"Yeah, Selwyn Theater Building, inside info."

"Gee, thanks. You're a buddy!"

I paid for my Coke and walked as rapidly as I could to the Selwyn Theater.

"Mr. Woods isn't casting today, is he?" I asked a horn-rimmed, expressionless male secretary. The secretary shook his head as negatively as I had.

"Oh, I see—I'm sorry," I said. Pigeon-toed and stiff-armed, I retraced my footsteps past the four actors lounging in chairs. Before my exit, I heard the secretary sigh mightily, then the giggles of appreciation.

I decided to take a ride in the subway and rest my back. I caught the BMT local to Coney Island, took a rear seat next to the window, and spent the ride worrying about one depressing reality after another. I had to learn to talk to people, ask questions, not be bashful. After all, everybody had a right to ask for a job. . . . I should have stayed home with Judy while she had that awful cold; maybe Mom was with her, maybe she wasn't. . . . Maybe my dress didn't look nice, or those people in the office laughed because I had a run in my stocking. . . . There was a stock company in Jersey City I could go to, but what if they asked me what I've done before? Vaudeville wouldn't count. . . . My back hurt. I should go to a doctor to have him fix it. Dad would kill that policeman. Would the judge believe me and Dad, or the policeman? . . . Mom was acting pretty blue. She missed Johnny.

The train was out of the tunnel, and I leaned my forehead against the windowpane. I wouldn't go back to work today. I'd call Mrs. Strong from Coney and make up a lie. I had enough money to go to a doctor in Coney. . . . Why didn't I tell Mom about my back? But I knew what she'd say: "See, I told you so. Touching is dirty, and sex is dirty, and men are rotten, and don't talk to them—stay away."

I stood on the platform between cars for a while to ease my back. The pain made my arms itch, and all my nails were bitten off. . . . Scott said there was a girl teaching him how to dance. He wouldn't tell me who she was. Well, Mom better not find out! . . . Just one letter—a big, thick one—came from Dad to Mom. She hid it. Did they make up? Where was he?

The conductor called: "Coney Island."

I started to get out and decided I had to go back to the book store.

I was in the same seat, still thinking disjointedly, as the train started up for the return trip.

At home two policemen were questioning Mom: "He took *all* his clothes?"

"Yes, all but soiled things—socks and things."

Judy, in bed, had a violent coughing spell. The blankets were up over her face; only frightened, watery eyes peered out. I sat by her side, gave her a swallow of cough syrup.

"Well, ya see, lady, like I said, it's a runaway case. Boys do it, y'know. Everybody does it once in his life," the tall policeman said.

"Thanks—great comfort," Mom said.

"I know it ain't a comfort, but—well, we'll keep a lookout and report the description of your son to headquarters. We'll check with you later. Don't worry, lady—he'll turn up—they all do." And the policemen were gone.

Mom put hot water in the pot for coffee, then sat by the window, her head against the pane.

We were all stunned beyond talking. The crumpled piece of paper on the table seemed the only object in the room.

"What did the note say again?" Judy asked me.

I whispered to her. "It said: 'I ran away with her, and we're going to get married—and I hope Dad comes home soon. Too bad—it's too bad. Love to all, Scott.'"

Johnny appeared one midnight when Scott had been missing for about ten days. He became gaunt and sheet-white when we told him. He and Mom seldom spoke, and then only in monosyllables, as they stayed in the flat, waiting for news of Scott.

And they were desperately worried about Judy's health. "Warmer climate . . . warmer climate . . ." the doctor insisted.

Finally Mom confessed. "All right, I did it, I'm to blame!" she yelled, beating on the walls. "I found the girl's house. I followed him—I got in—they were on the couch pawing. She was ugly, older, taller. I beat at her—I made her face bleed; and her ugly mother came from the other room, and I beat her and tore her hair and broke her glasses, and Scott was fighting me to stop. And I told them they were tramps and filthy rotten—and Scott slapped me! He slapped me and said I was evil-minded—and pushed me out—you hear? I did it, I did it!" She sank to the floor fighting for breath.

Johnny helped her to her feet. "Now, Mom, be quiet—I guess you meant well."

She grabbed Johnny. "I didn't do anything wrong with that stupid man. I swear to God, Johnny."

I covered my sister. "Turn to the wall, Judy. Leave them alone," I whispered, and grabbed my coat and ran to the street.

Whatever Mom said, Dad would believe her, I decided, as I walked to work next day. Believing that she was true to him would make Scott's going away and Judy's sickness easier. They would have one worry now, not separate ones.

And that's the way it happened. As a unit, Cecilia and Johnny made the decisions. Johnny emptied his money belt. Cecilia opened the shoe box in which she'd saved a little. And I got a two-week advance from Mrs. Strong. "Judy comes first," Johnny said. "We'll put an ad in the paper to get a ride to California. You take her there, Ceeley, and get her well. I'll take the doorman job at Casey's Theater in Barnesville, Pennsylvania—the one that Klibert offered me—and I'll send you money. When you get settled, I'll book the single and get there somehow. Nora will have to get a room and keep trying to branch out, get her bearings. Maybe Mrs. Strong will rent her a room cheap over the store. And God will take care of us—and Scott. He always has."

Thus we separated.

Mom and Judy were driven across country to Oakland, California, by a German mechanic who was joining his family there. He charged them sixty dollars for the ride, and they shared the expenses of meals and lodging. In Oakland they took a one-room apartment. It was on the ground floor, and Mom wrote that Judy spent the days in hot sunshine in the yard and was improving. Johnny sent them money from his three-month job as doorman, and then began his single again, zigzagging cross country to join them.

Scott sent two letters to me at the book store—one for me alone, and one to be read by the rest of the family.

Dear Nora,

Sudden, wasn't it? I don't know what Mom told you but it was awful rough what happened. And pretty senseless, because nothing wrong was going on. But well, hell, after Mom said damn awful things—really awful things, I'm telling you—well, you see, Nora, they are pretty nice people. Janet's not very good-looking but she was real nice teaching me ball-room dancing, and her mother gave me good things to eat and it was fun at their house.

I met them on the paper route. There was nothing wrong in it. We just kissed now and again. But, well, Nora, it's hard to explain—but after we were accused of all that stuff, we just did it. But she was a good girl, and I was the first, and she was my first—and, well—here's the blow—she got pregnant. Can you beat that—just one crack at it. She was afraid to tell her mother, so we took a bus here to Colorado. Her dad left her two hundred dollars when he died, and she took it out of the bank and we just left.

Well, it's kind of a mess—me not sixteen till July and going to have a baby. She's eighteen—but she's nice, and it's kind of fun.

I sure hope you get a job on the New York kind of stage. Is Dad back yet? Keep this letter to yourself.

I miss everybody, and hope it's a boy.

Love,
Scott

And the second letter:

Dear Mom and Dad and Judy and Nora,

I'm here in Leghorn, Colorado—my address is on the envelope. I've got a job in Woolworth's here. It's a good job. I
hope you're home, Dad, because everybody feels better when
you're around.

Don't worry about me. I m fine, and my wife's nice. It
wasn't very nice of me to run away and not help anymore,
but enclosed is ten dollars, and I will send some next month.

My wife, Janet, has got nice dark brown hair, so I guess
the baby will have nice brown hair. We're going to have one
—around my birthday sometime. I'll take a snap and send it.
I think I'll name it Johnny. How about that, Dad?

I hope you're fine, Mom and Judy, and as soon as Nora's
a star, shoot me a wire.

I miss you, but I'm grown up now. We're going to get a
dog for the baby. Write soon.

> Love,
> Scott

"How did it happen?"

"I slipped and fell on an icy pavement."

"When?"

"About six months ago."

The doctor, silent for a while, was tapping on his desk.

I felt sweaty in the dark, airless office, and I was anxious
to leave. I was due at the John Murray Anderson School of
Drama to accept a scholarship. It had been offered to me
after I'd been very successfully reviewed in *Tarnish,* a play
I'd done with a second-rate company in a tiny Greenwich
Village theater.

I wondered what it really meant—a scholarship—besides,
of course, being an honor. I hadn't had the courage to ask
yet.

The doctor's monotonous voice droned: "You have fractured your coccyx, the bone at the base of your spine. There's

nothing you can do for it now, except maybe try some hot baths. Be careful about lifting things, and I have to warn you: it is inadvisable for you ever to have children."

"Oh, I see." I blinked my eyes nervously. "Well, I better go now—and thank you. How much do I owe you, please?"

The two visits and the X rays added up to twelve dollars. I paid him, thanked him again, and left—and knew that whatever he said, I'd have plenty of babies.

As I neared the Anderson Drama School, I was afraid they'd tell me it was all a mistake and I hadn't won any prize. I turned into a drugstore for a Coke, and tried to summon up some confidence.

"May I light your cigarette?"

"Huh?" Startled, I looked into brown eyes whose whites were whiter than any I'd ever seen.

"Your cigarette?"

"Oh, thank you." I accepted the light, and said without looking at him, "I'd forgotten I had it in my hand."

"I see."

I glanced at him and caught his smile. "I don't generally smoke in public."

"Nothing wrong in doing what gives one pleasure."

"Nope—guess not." I swallowed my Coke hastily. "My check, please," I called to the counter boy. I paid it quickly, felt his eyes following me as I walked into the John Murray Anderson School across the street.

I was there two hours, and everyone was complimentary and gracious. The head of the drama department, Mr. Hornblow, said, "We offered you the scholarship because we felt you have great potential talent as a dramatic actress. Aside from *Tarnish,* we saw you in *The Miracle* and *The Trial of Mary Dugan.*"

I was amazed. "I played those in such silly out-of-the-way places, just stock companies—not Broadway."

"I know. I predict you'll have a long career," he said. "Meanwhile, we want you to take advantage of our classes:

Shakespeare, dancing, and singing. We produce our own shows here at the school, and they are covered by every big scout and producer in New York City."

He put me at ease, yet I still couldn't bring myself to ask the question uppermost in my mind: would I be paid a salary for being in the shows? Instead, I made the rounds of the school with him, visited every class, and was introduced to the students and teachers.

Out on the street again, I walked over to Central Park and bought a bag of peanuts. I meant them for the animals, but I ate them myself on a shaded bench. As I got toward the end of the bag, I put my head on the back of the bench, and with my arm held stiff in the air, dropped the remaining peanuts into my mouth.

"You haven't missed once."

I saw him against the almost twilight sky. Sitting up, I brushed the bits of shells from my skirt. He stood beside me silently until I was forced to look up at him.

"May I sit down?" Without waiting for an answer, he did. "I followed you," he said.

I looked at him. He was very handsome. "Well," I answered tartly, "you shouldn't have." And I pretended to be looking for someone.

"How can you speak for me? Have you ever been a man who suddenly saw a pair of huge green eyes, glorious shining blond hair, voluptuous breasts, and a tiny waist?"

I started to go.

"Please—wait, let me finish; and a back"—he continued as I reseated myself, still looking in another direction—"a back so straight and wide, like a Greek goddess."

I smiled momentarily, then furiously brushed at the peanut shells which were no longer on my skirt.

"Do you know how lovely you are, miss?"

I was silent.

He continued. "My name is Bill Kadiz. I teach philosophy at City College. I'm hungry, and the night will be too star-filled and balmy to let me correct papers in my room. More than that—I don't want to lose you. Please let me take you to dinner."

I looked at him as aloofly as I could.

"Please?" He smiled again.

His teeth and the crinkles around his beautiful eyes made me answer his smile. But even so, I said, "No."

"We'll go to a quiet, candlelit café I know in the Village. Let's ride on the top of a bus to the Arch—the fresh air will make us even hungrier," he said as though I had said yes.

"No, I can't—it's not right." I rose and headed for the park exit; he kept up with me.

"What's not right? Tell me."

I stopped at the corner of Fifth Avenue and Sixtieth Street. "I don't know you, and . . ." I hesitated, searching for something different to say.

"Here comes our bus," he cried, and grabbed my hand and pulled me to the top level.

The sky was streaked with orange ribbons, and we watched them fade as we rode along. He talked animatedly about his work, his pupils, and he said that he would like to take me to the open-air concert at City College the following evening. "We profs get season tickets—free—and it's great listening to music under the stars."

Oh, well, I thought, torn between guilt and pleasure, I'll sit by the exit in the restaurant.

He introduced me to many things; concert music on warm, summer nights: "You dream through the melodies—I can tell by your eyes."

"Umm hmmm."

"Tell me the dream tonight, Nora."

"Well, let's see, I was dreaming of being a movie star; then we'd—"

"I know—quote, all be together, unquote." He smiled.

"What a family gal you are!" He paused. "I wish you were dreaming of . . ."

"I know, letting you make love to me."

"Mmmm hmmm."

I put my hand over his. "Oh, Bill, don't make me tell you over and over how sorry I am."

"Tell me, I'm a masochist."

"You know I feel like it—sometimes."

"So?"

"But, and anyway, I just have to wait until it's more than just feeling like it. I have to—"

"I know—don't say it again—be in love with the guy, and married; we mustn't forget that." He seemed nervous when we talked about it.

I was silent and unhappy. He had kissed me a few times, but I had avoided having much physical contact with him. Yet the talks, the walks, the dinners in romantic, inexpensive places made me vaguely ashamed not to reward him for the friendship that meant so much to me. But I didn't love him, and besides, I wanted to give my family a home first, before I thought of marriage.

Still, I was proud to know he was in the audience when I played in neighborhood stock companies; I reveled in his delight in my performance, warmed to his encouragement.

I loved telling him about my father. "You'd think, Bill, at his age and all, it would be hard to make the audience believe he was about an eighteen-year-old, but he does it! You should see him just before he goes onstage. He takes out a pocket mirror and smiles and makes faces in it; he says it's to remind himself that he's a silly kid."

And I enjoyed Bill's compliments when I picked up inexpensive knickknacks and secondhand books to decorate my small room over the book store. I'd lived in that room ever since the Martens separated.

"You have an ability to enhance, Nora. You make this dreary little room look lovely and lived in," he said.

He helped me figure out how to manage on my meager

CENTER DOOR FANCY   •   179

earnings. I sent the bulk to Cecilia, and often—if the jobs were not too far apart—I'd send a few dollars to Scott for his son and the new one on the way.

I learned about paintings and their artists during my hours with Bill in the Metropolitan Museum.

Between theatrical jobs, and my part-time work at the store, were the hours when Bill would tell me stories by Dickens, Twain, de Maupassant, Balzac.

"You're an enigma in a lot of ways, Nora," he said. "No drive to be an actress, really. It's just a job to you that may pay off and take care of your troupe, as you call them, in style. Some kind of magic comes out of you on the stage—I can't define it. Yet it seems you're more pleased with yourself when you've placed a vase of flowers strategically in your room than—than at the sound of applause!" He looked at me tenderly. "Crazy girl, you just want a home and your family, and the only way you'll really be happy, I guess, is to have it." He threw his head back and laughed. "You're umbilical-cord-bound, damnit-to-hell, and meanwhile I'm hungry to love the delights out of my actress friend."

I smoothed his thick hair. Damnit-to-hell is right, I thought.

During our next evening walk Bill said, "Nora, there's a party Sunday night in Greenwich Village for a colleague of mine. Want to go?"

"Gee, that sounds like fun, Bill, it'll be our first party together."

We made plans. Bill would pick me up at the train from Yonkers, where I was closing that night in *This Thing Called Love*. We'd check my makeup case at the station and go to the Village from there. The party didn't start until midnight, so we had plenty of time.

As we climbed the five flights of narrow stairs, I suddenly stiffened at the jumble of voices and music coming from above.

"Now, Nora"—Bill took me by the shoulders and looked at

me sternly—"there's no need to be shy and uncomfortable with these people. They're concerned with themselves—with having fun—they'll not be criticizing you."

"How did you know I had the willies?" I asked. "It's just about my first party."

"I know. I know a lot about you after these months together. I know that you're miserably bashful, except when you're with me, or on a stage. I know that you're ridiculously immature in many ways, and as insecure a young lady as I've ever met." He gripped my shoulders tighter. "Look at me," he ordered, and I looked into his grave, clear eyes. "I know, too, that I love you." He took my hand, and we continued up the stairs.

The small apartment was literally covered with people—standing in groups, seated on the floor. Bill introduced me to a pallid-skinned girl with black hair slicked back in a bun, and to two men who were attractive in an unattractive way.

"I'm your hostess, darling. Who are you with?" a woman dressed like a man asked me.

"Georgia," Bill answered with a wide smile, "this is Nora Marten."

"Bill—my darling of all darlings," the woman bellowed, and hugged him gruffly. "You've been making yourself scarce for months. I should be peeved, but now I see the reason." She pinched my cheek too hard and continued, "So you shall have drinks, and we'll make whoopee!" Georgia whacked Bill on the back and returned in a minute with two drinks in paper cups.

I downed the entire contents of mine at once. It worked: I relaxed. I followed Bill around and listened and smiled attentively.

At one point I was cornered by a young college-type boy. "Did I see you at John Murray Anderson's?" he asked.

"Yes," I answered, "but just once. They gave me a scholarship, but I have to make money, and they don't pay you while you learn."

"Don't I know!" the boy answered. "I've been making the rounds of offices this past month because I couldn't afford to study there. If I hear 'What have you done before?' once more, I'll take up plumbing!"

"It's kind of discouraging sometimes, isn't it?"

"Discouraging! That's putting it mildly."

"I've gotten a few jobs, luckily—good parts, but in small-pay, out-of-the-way places—nowhere near Broadway."

"Well, here's hoping—"

I didn't hear the rest of his sentence, because I was looking at a girl who entered the apartment—the most startling-looking girl I'd ever seen in my life: long, thick, blond hair that hung to her waist; cream-colored skin; large violet eyes; and a deep, red, full mouth. Gold hoops dangled from her ears, and she wore a long, flowing, white chiffon dress with a gold cord around her waist, and gold, flat sandals on her feet. Looking around the crowded room, her face was taut, her eyes wide and expressionless.

I watched her go up to Bill, who was standing nearby, and whip him around to face her.

"Tina!" he cried, and turned pale.

"Which one is it?" she demanded.

"Come on." He took her arm and tried to lead her out. She started to scream and to hit at him. All conversation stopped. There was just the sound of her screaming, and the movement of Bill getting her out of the apartment.

I remained stock still, my face flushed, my heart pounding. Everyone in the room seemed to be looking in my direction.

Georgia's booming voice broke the silence. "Drink ye one and all—for tomorrow we may kick the bucket." The tension eased, and everyone went back to chattering.

Georgia put her arm through mine and led me to the bathroom. After shutting the door, she said, "I'll go down and see if everything's all right, Miss Innocent Eyes. Put some lipstick on and relax."

"What do you suppose was wrong?" I asked.

"Just a family affair, sweetie," Georgia answered, giving my cheek another hard pinch. "I'll be right back."

I stayed in the bathroom for what seemed an eternity. Finally I peeked out. I decided to make a beeline for the door and wait for her on the stairs.

On the floor below, I met Georgia coming back.

"Nasty business, kid," she said, shaking her head.

"What—what? Please tell me," I asked.

Georgia looked at me. "You don't know?"

"Know what? Please tell me!"

"Look"—Georgia reached in her suit pocket—"in case you haven't got enough with you, here are a couple of bucks. Take a cab home, and wait till Bill tells you himself." She pinched me again, this time on my hip.

Back in my own room, I paced the floor, looking out my window every few minutes for a sign of Bill.

Was that his girl? I wondered. It couldn't be. He was always wanting to be with me—never talked about anything except his mother and his beautiful sister. I shuddered. A wife? No, Bill wouldn't do that, he was too honest!

I took a hot bath, and when I crawled into bed, it was getting light outside.

I was awakened at noon the next day by the ringing of the hall telephone. It was Mrs. Strong from the store, four flights below.

"Nora, listen." She sounded breathless. "Nora?"

"Yes, Mrs. Strong, what is it?"

"That fellow Bill Kadiz—that one who takes you out . . ."

"Yes, what about him?" I was alarmed by the sound of her voice.

"Well, I can't come up, Nora—the store's alone—but the headlines say he was killed!"

"What?"

"Killed, Nora—by his sister."

"Killed? Killed!" I screamed.

"By his sister, Nora—incest, the paper says."

"Bill? No not killed—he's not dead—not Bill." I was almost incoherent.

I hung up and staggered to my bed and sat upright on the edge. I sat for a long time—numb, pretending it was something I had not heard. I would wait right there until Bill came over. I remained there until Mrs. Strong rapped on the door at five that afternoon.

"Here, honey, I brought you some soup. Got Jack to stay in the store."

I shook my head.

"Take a sip and have a nice bath. We've got to get some color in your face."

"Did you say he was killed, Mrs. Strong?" I asked in a whisper.

"Yes, honey—it's in all the papers. Headlines. His beautiful sister, Tina, did it—stabbed him through the heart with a knife, then killed herself with the same knife. She found out he was in love with somebody else, the papers said—I guess you, honey. The papers don't know who or what—and we'll keep it a secret, honey. Here, drink some soup while it's hot."

I shook my head again. "I want to go for a walk. I don't feel good."

"You ought to rest."

"I want to go for a walk."

"Well, wear your coat, honey. It's cold out now the sun's gone."

At nightfall, chilled through, I was sitting on the bench in Central Park where it all began. I tried to keep the word "incest" out of my thoughts as I looked at the changing sky. I didn't even know the exact meaning of the word, but I knew enough to remember with horror the few remarks Bill had made about his sister.

"I wish she'd find someone to love. She's beautiful—it can't go on . . ."

"Oh, Bill—gee—she's only nineteen. She's got oodles of time."

"No—no—no," he'd said desperately. Then he changed the subject.

I walked back to my room, dreading being alone. I felt dizzy and weak climbing the stairs. I untied the handkerchief hidden in the back of my dresser drawer and counted nine dollars and eighteen cents. Then I went to the hall phone and asked for the California number.

"Two dollars and twenty cents for the first three minutes, please."

The number was ringing. "Mom! Mom!" I called.

"Nora!"

"Mom? How are you? How's everybody?"

"Fine, Nora, just fine."

"You sure?"

"Yes, dear. Your voice sounds funny. Anything wrong?"

"Oh, Mom," I cried, "I'm homesick."

Later, after a warm bath and one swallow of the cold soup Mrs. Strong had left, I fell into a restless, disturbed sleep.

I worked in the book store for the next three weeks—full time.

"I want you under my nose," Mrs. Strong said, "and to see that you eat something."

The fourth week, I set out for the theatrical offices. I took the first job offered. The show was called *My Girl Saturday,* and I knew that the producer and cast had been arrested several times for lewd entertainment. They'd get short sentences, reams of publicity, then reopen to crowded, if bawdy, audiences.

The ingenue had run off with a broker and had to be replaced immediately, so I was sent over by a small-time agent, along with half a dozen coarse-looking girls. The readings were listened to impatiently by the producer, who was also the male comedy lead in the farce. He was surly and rude as the others tried out. "Get lost, babe," he'd snarl in the middle of their efforts. Watching from the wings, I wanted to hit him with something.

Then it was my turn. I took the script from the stage manager. I knew from listening to the others that I'd get the part. It just called for someone to look innocent and to feed his double-entendre jokes. I was a good straight man, if nothing else.

I began. Two "sides" later he asked, "What's your name?"

"Nora Marten."

"You got the job. Stay. We'll rehearse. You open day after tomorrow. Forty dollars. Quick study?"

"Yes."

"Well, come on, let's get goin'."

I played the part for four miserable weeks, ashamed to be in the off-color play, to be around the ugly-tempered producer and the foul-mouthed cast; ashamed, too, in front of the audience—mostly men in shirtsleeves who laughed raucously at the filthy lines.

There were terrible fights backstage between management and crew. And girls were constantly dropping out for abortions, drunkenness, or elopements.

At the beginning of the engagement the stage manager told me I had a picture in the *New York Graphic*. Excited, I bought a paper and waited till I was home, a bologna sandwich and glass of milk in front of me, to read it. There it was—my picture, all right, a big one, too—the one the Martens used in the act. Then I read the caption. "Nora Marten has replaced someone in the cast of *My Girl Saturday*. Who hasn't?"

I decided not to send my first New York clipping to my folks.

About eleven o'clock one morning on a matinee day, I was drinking a cup of coffee at the counter in Grey's.

"The joint's jumping in here, isn't it?" The remark came from a man sitting next to me.

I looked around and nodded.

"That's because Edward Murphy's casting his new play, *Dora, the Fierce,*" he said.

"The Edward Murphy who wrote *The Ego, Henry's Bride,* and *The Carriers?*"

"None other. He's casting in the Bond Building, 1560 Broadway, eighth floor. I'm going to make a stab at it myself."

I paid my check and took long strides to the Bond Building.

I got into a crowded elevator. "Eighth floor, please." It was a chorus of voices.

The starter growled, "I know," and emptied the eager job seekers on the eighth. We found ourselves in a jammed corridor of earlier job seekers: actors, actresses, milling and chattering from the outer door of producer Murphy's office right along the long hall to the elevator door.

I decided I didn't stand a chance with that mob ahead of me. My palms were wet. Still I waited, rigid and uneasy, slowly being edged ahead. About fifty feet from the magic door, which opened to an already packed office, I asked a man for the time.

"One-thirty, miss," he answered. Then he added, "It's a long wait—but even being turned down by Edward Murphy is an honor!"

"Yes," I smiled. "But I guess I can't wait to be turned down. I have a matinee."

"Try later," he suggested. "This casting will go on until nightfall. I know from experience. This is my third try at a Murphy show."

"I will." I thanked him. "And the third time's the charm," I assured him as I eased my way back through the crowd to the elevator.

After the matinee, I was back again—nearer the Murphy door this time. The dinner hour had temporarily thinned the crowd.

In the outer office at last, I stared at the man guarding the inner sanctum. After a long wait I took a newly available chair and sat like a ramrod, hands folded in my lap. And I daydreamed about being a star and giving bills of large denomination to all the unemployed actors in the world—after my family was wallowing in mansions, yachts, and tremendous turkey dinners.

"The young lady in the red beret," a voice penetrated my dream. I blinked my eyes furiously and realized, because attention focused on me, that I was the one. Still, I hastily felt the red beret, then rolled my eyes upward to check the color of my only hat. The waiting actors laughed; so did the man at the door as he said, "This way, please."

I was alone with the great Edward Murphy. I knew it was he—no one else could be so dignified, elegant, refined—like a king, I decided.

He smiled. "Sit down and be comfortable." He waited until I was in a brown leather armchair; then he seated himself behind his desk. "Relax," he said.

I let out my breath and leaned back cautiously.

He smiled at me again. "The girl in the play is named Eva," he said. "Let me tell you about her." He got on his feet, and started acting out Eva's lines, gestures, her walk, her expressions. I was transported. My shyness and self-consciousness melted away as he continued to unfold his play to me. I laughed, I wept, I shocked myself by bursting into applause. He threw back his head and laughed. "What's your name?" he asked.

"Nora Marten, sir." Here it comes, I thought nervously—"What have you done before?"—but it *didn't* come.

"Go in there, Nora," he said, pointing to an inner, inner office, "and sign the contract."

I sat motionless.

"What salary did you get for your last professional job?"

"Sixty dollars," I answered, my fingers crossed for daring to lie by twenty.

"Tell them your salary is two hundred."

I just blinked.

"Go on, Nora. You've got the part." He pressed a buzzer three times.

I stood up like a tin soldier.

"And, Nora," he said, "lower your lids a little or your eyes will tumble out of your head." He smiled and took my elbow and led me to the door and closed it behind me. I waited while the woman at the desk nodded into the phone she held. Two men were seated, silently inspecting me.

"All right, good—Nora Marten—yes, Mr. Murphy, it's done. Now, just the mother role to fill, and we're in the clear. . . . Good." She hung up.

"What's your salary, Nora?" she asked.

"Two—two hundred."

"Alrighteee," she drawled, and wrote the figure on the document on her desk. "Sign here—and congratulations—you've just landed the best part on Broadway this season."

The family was not at the New York opening—just Mrs. Strong was there. But two telegrams were pasted on my dressing-room mirror at the Cort Theater: "The best you can do, sweetheart. Our prayers and love are with you. Dad, Mother, Judy."

The other wire read: "Stick and slug, Nora, and you're the one that can do it. Love, Scott, Janet, Johnny, Joan."

During the Atlantic City and Boston tryouts the play received excellent notices, but the year was 1929, and the pall of the Wall Street crash was over everyone. Yet at opening night on Broadway, even in the face of the crash, the excitement was not dimmed. The tension, nerves . . .

"Guess who's out front? Marilyn Miller! She looks all peaches."

"Cole Porter has tails on. . . ."

"So does George Jean Nathan—and O. O. McIntyre . . ."

". . . and Katharine Cornell is in green velvet, and Jeanette MacDonald in pink tulle . . ."

". . . and John Barrymore . . ."; ". . . and Jane

Cowl . . ."; ". . . and Warner Baxter . . ."; "and Clive
Brook . . ."; "and Sylvia Sidney . . ."; "beautiful Barbara
Stanwyck . . ."; ". . . and Lillian and Dorothy Gish . . .";
". . . and Al Woods . . ."; ". . . and Florenz Ziegfeld . . .";
"and Ed Wynn . . ."; ". . . and George Arliss . . .";
". . . and . . . and . . ."

Shivering, I was pacing my dressing room, feeling sick to
my stomach. Then I sat on my dressing-room chair and
furiously massaged my big toe, yanking it back and forth.
"How the hell did that fall asleep?" I muttered. Suddenly I
became limp. "No—no—I can't—please, God, help me, please.
I've got to feel strong—please." In the half-hour before showtime, I had gone from panic to desperation to hysteria to
bloodlessness.

"Onstage," the stage manager called. Frozen, I went down
the stairs, acknowledging and returning the whispered wishes
of the cast: "Good luck"—"Merde"—"Break a leg," as I walked
to the door leading to my entrance.

My mouth was bone dry. I can't even get my lips over my
teeth, I thought in horror.

There it was. I knew the house lights were dimming because the voices out front were settling, and the sounds of
"shush" penetrated the curtain. Then silence—a few seconds
of the most deafening silence I ever heard. The whole world
seemed at a standstill. I got my cue to enter. "Our Father,
Who art in—center door fancy—" I breathed, and was onstage.

I took the subway and was in my room before I realized it,
pacing wildly, my head splitting. I couldn't stop the pacing
or the wringing of my hands as, word for word, step by step,
I retraced my performance. I'd stop suddenly, my heart
missing beats: "I didn't say that line—oh, God—yes I did, I
did *too*." Then the pacing again. "They didn't laugh—no—not
a sound—I didn't hear a sound—yes, I did—" "They were gone
while I was doing that big scene with the mother—no they
couldn't have been, because they applauded—oh, God, we

forgot to take our bows—no, no, NO—you dope, we took them, and they applauded and applauded."

I tried to quiet myself enough to call California. "The circuits are busy, madam."

"Good—good—because I can't tell them anything. . . . I'll wait for the notices—I'll wait." The top of my head was thumping so hard I could almost feel it bending with each blow. All night long I rolled and tossed—covers on, covers off; hot, cold, the lines of the play, jumbled, going around and around in my head like a propeller.

"Honey! Honey! Wake up! . . ." It was Mrs. Strong, her arms full of newspapers. Speedily, almost incoherently, we read the notices aloud.

"Nora Marten is a newborn star!"

"A curvy miss named Nora Marten was cheered by the eminent first-nighters!"

". . . A discovery!"

"A talent of gold!"

"Nora Marten, where have you been?"

I leaned back on my bed, exhaling every bit of air from my lungs. "Mrs. Strong," I drawled, "pass me the nail file."

PART
THREE

1

WAS BENT over trying to get a cinder out of my eye. Both eyes were watering, and my nose was running.

"Need some help?" The offer came from a middle-aged man. We were the only two sitting on the outside observation platform of the Chief, California-bound.

"It feels like a boulder in there," I explained.

"I know. Here, let me help." He rose and balanced himself for a moment against the jiggling train.

"Never mind—it's gone—see?" I blinked fiercely, then looked up at him. "Thanks just the same."

He reseated himself. "The roadbed along this part of the country is dusty. We really shouldn't be sitting outside."

"I know, but it's fun to watch the tracks disappear in the distance like a ribbon floating away."

"Mmmmmm," he answered, and became preoccupied with the horizon.

I was bursting to talk. "I'm going to be a movie actress."

"That so?"

"Yes, I got signed up by Kern Brothers studio because I was in a New York play, and everybody in the company came to Grand Central to see me off, and I got weighed in the station, and the scale told fortunes, and mine said, 'Success is yours. Watch out.'"

"That so?" His gaze stayed on the horizon, and we were silent for a while. But I yearned to be heard. My compulsion to talk to strangers . . .

"You see, we didn't run long—in the play, I mean—about four weeks. But that was only because of the crash—all the theaters suffered from it. Mr. Murphy—you know him . . ."

The man nodded imperceptibly.

"Well—his plays have been hits always—but this time—well, anyway, the people in the company were out of a job when they took me to the station, and you know actors don't get jobs one after the other unless they're stars—well, anyway, you know what they did?"

He shook his head.

"They pooled together and bought me this brown suit and this brown hat!"

"That so?"

"Yes, and they got it from Mrs. Olivier. She's famous for selling rich people's clothes—secondhand. They're much cheaper than buying them new—heaven knows how much this cost new. But they're very elegant—from society people and all those kind of rich people." I paused.

He made no comment.

"And they bought me these beautiful brown shoes." I held my feet up. "They don't hurt much—just till I get them broken in—and this brown bag, and this real gardenia. It's kind of brown, too, by now." I giggled. "And stockings and perfume —can you smell it from there?"

"Um hmmm."

"Wasn't that great? I was so happy, them waving at me

when the train pulled out—and you know why they did it?"

He shook his head.

"So I could have what I'd saved to send for my family to come to Hollywood. . . ." I stopped, my eyes squinted against a rain of dust. "I was told I'm going to be in a picture with an actor called Jimmy Cagney. It will be his first picture too." I looked at him and smiled. "People say I don't talk much."

He smiled back.

"What time is it, sir?" I asked.

He took out a pocket watch. "Ten minutes to twelve."

I sighed happily. "Just think," I said, looking skyward, "tomorrow—ten minutes from this very time, we'll be arriving in Los Angeles!"

"Tomorrow?" he bellowed. "Young lady, you've lost a day. Today is Wednesday. Ten minutes from *now* you'll be in Los Angeles."

I jumped to my feet, my hands flailing the air wildly. "Today? Now? Oh, holy smoke! Hollywood, I'm *here!*"

I waited at the station, my suitcase tight in my fist, until the place had almost cleared of people. My agent had said someone from Kern Brothers would meet me. I had watched people joyfully welcoming each other, but now as the crowds dispersed, I became panicky. "Maybe it wasn't me they sent for—or maybe they found somebody else for the part." I saw a man coming toward me. "He couldn't be for me, because he's been standing there looking around ever since the train pulled in." But he was for me.

"You're not Nora Marten?"

"Yes, sir."

He was silent for a long count of ten; then: "What's new?" he asked, daintily flicking something distasteful off his sports jacket.

"I beg your pardon?"

"Nothing." He took my case. "Follow me."

We rode in a bright red, top-down Lincoln convertible. Torn between intense excitement and apprehension, I didn't know what to say. So I waited for him to speak. We were riding along Sunset Boulevard and almost to Western Avenue before he said: "You clammed up."

"I beg your pardon?"

"Nothing. Say, listen—we've got a reservation for you at the Roosevelt Hotel, okay? But we're gonna do the Brown Derby first for lunch—you gotta be *seen* in this town." He inspected me from the top of my hat to my shoes, and nearly ran over a man. "Okay?" he asked again.

"Oh, yes. That sounds nice. I'd like to take a bath first—but yes, that sounds nice."

"My name's Ted Shermfield."

"How do you do," I said. I relaxed my backbone a little and surreptitiously glanced at him. He has a very blond, colorless face, I decided, eyes and all, and he should have a tie on if we're going to the famous Brown Derby. Then I wondered whether he'd take off the beret before we got there. His white-blond, kinky hair was better than that silly-looking tam thing.

The restaurant was noisy and crowded. The maître d' bowed low.

"Ah! Mr. Shermfield, you're here!" he said enthusiastically. "This way, please—and I'll bring the phone—you have been paged several times."

I tagged along. The phone, the waiters, the menu, the napkins, the water, the butter, the rolls, and four people arrived at once, while I sat nervously pulling at my cuticle. We were seated in a large corner booth, and three active waiters, a redhaired girl, and three men in sports jackets swallowed up the light and air surrounding our table. I couldn't keep up with the conversations.

"Yes, Charlie, I read it—great—great . . ." the Beret said into the phone; "Did you see my test, hon?" from the Redhead; "Poker at Joe's tonight?" from the Plaid Jacket; "This is

Nora Marten. What d'ya think?" from the Beret; "Steam room five. Right?" from the other Plaid Jacket; "Who's for tennis Sunday?" from the first Plaid Jacket; "Darryl and Sam and J. L., and Lillian Bond and Toby Wing and Cabot and De Cico and you didn't tell me what you think of her?" from the Beret.

"Who?" There was only one Plaid Jacket left. "Who?" it repeated.

"Her." Shermfield jerked his head toward me.

The last Plaid Jacket stared at "her." I scraped my throat on the French bread crust I was swallowing.

"Drop down to the beach tonight, Ted. We're having some jail-bait and cold cuts." He winked playfully, his whole face contorting, and was gone.

Now we were alone with the salads. "Great guy." Ted smiled, saluting a table of three men on the other side of the room. "This could easily be the night!" he added, then screamed, "Sheely!" and half-stood as the lady stopped at our table.

"This is Nora Marten, Sheely. Kern Brothers signed her for *The Iron Sidewalk*. What d'ya think?"

Sheely looked, then smiled at the wall above my head. "How do you spell your name, honey? I'll put you in the column—Gus!" she cried and put her cheek forward to be kissed by a passing man.

"M-A-R-T-E-N," I spelled.

"Going to Fay's tonight?" Sheely asked Ted.

Sheely only smiles with her mouth, I thought.

"Wherever Darryl goes . . ." he answered gaily.

"You're sooo right—good luck, Dora."

"Nora."

But Sheely's cheek was forward again to be kissed by a lovely blond girl, so she didn't hear.

That night, bathed, a long letter written to the family, and with thoughts of my early-morning appointment to see Mr.

T. L. Kern at the studio, I switched on the radio. I listened to a fanfare of music that segued into the program's theme, "We Love You, We Love You, We Love You." Then a joyous male voice screamed: "Here she is—our very own, Hollywood's favorite columnist—Sheely Dawson!"

After a seeming eternity of rattling papers, a nasal whine slid along the airwaves: "Hello there to *you* from *us* Dora Norton has been signed by Kern Brothers for one picture she's from the New York stage I don't see why we don't stick to our own do you? plenty of beautiful and talented actresses right under our noses why go to such extremities to get them elsewhere Gloria Swanson had noisy words with her marquis shame on you at Ciro's Clara Bow just gave birth to a baby boy all the girls in Hollywood are busy this season and now my good friend Warner Baxter will present to you Dickens' immortal Tale," she took a deep breath and started anew, "Of Two Cities." Musical bridge.

I snapped off the radio. I'm going to make money, I thought, and went to bed.

2

KERN BROTHERS signed my daughter to a long-termer halfway through the rushes of her first day's work," Johnny boasted to his neighbor. "Five years—salary jumps each year—so we're all out here now, including my son. He's got a family, two kids—have a cigar." He continued: "She's made twelve pictures in the eight months we've been here—all leads, and she's starting another one Monday—a big, million-dollar production she's loaned to Goldwyn Studio for."

"Terrific," the neighbor said.

"And just today an aeroplane passed over all of Hollywood with a loudspeaker that said 'See Nora Marten in *Back to Town* at Kern Brothers' Western.'"

"I heard it."

"But what you didn't hear was what happened when she got pneumonia—from overwork, the bastards—while she was finishing *Stay in Circulation*. They took her right off the set and put her in the hospital: hundred-and-four fever. But they didn't even give her a chance to get well. They took her back to our house on a stretcher, shoved her in bed, and brought in the works—camera, crew, director, lights, cables, sound trucks, wardrobe woman, set designer, script girl. Looked like the whole studio swooped down on us. Ceeley almost fainted. There must've been sixty people there, including the man who rewrote the last scene to make it end with Nora in bed gazing lovingly at Pat O'Brien. All that just to wrap up the picture! Thank heavens, she had a rest after that. She didn't have to do another picture for a whole week!

"Now they say they're going to put her feet in Grauman's." Johnny grinned, satisfied that he'd covered all the current events.

I was in bed, but I could hear Johnny's voice as clear as a bell from my ground-floor room just off the porch. He tells everyone about me from Cherokee Street all down Hollywood Boulevard to the Regent Hotel, I thought. Although my movie salary was the same as I'd received for my New York debut, it was for fifty-two weeks a year, and the second year it would jump to three hundred dollars; the third to four hundred dollars; five hundred in the fifth year. Not the huge picture salaries I'd heard about, but I thanked God for what it was. We were together, and it was steady. I looked at the time—9:45. I'd better sleep fast, I told myself; 4:30 A.M. comes awful soon.

A nervousness made me thrash around the bed. I was going to start at a new studio the next day, and having to face strangers had me jittery—almost as jittery as the first day I started in Hollywood. I had played wisecracking chorus girls, sharp-talking reporters, dizzy blonds, temperamental actresses during my eight-month career, but I couldn't overcome my shyness—except in front of a camera. So I faced the next day in new surroundings with anxiety.

And they were indeed new surroundings. At my home

studio the hours were long, and they "shot" fast. No nonsense
—under schedule. So Goldwyn was quite a change: the lavish
sets, the afternoon teas, soft music, individual makeup artists,
hair dressers, dressers, personal maids, special attention from
the prop boy to the producer.

"Well," I told my family when I got home that night, "you
never saw such goings on. We only got two shots done the
whole day, because everybody was busy kissing everybody
and wishing them good luck—and Laura Evans and Ina Eve-
lyn took four hours apiece to get dressed. When everybody
was ready, they called lunch."

We were sitting around the kitchen table.

"Do you like your part, Nora?" Johnny asked.

"They've got me typed, Dad—another gold-digging chorus
girl—only fancier clothes this time."

Johnny didn't say anything to me. But to his ex-vaudeville
cronies he confessed that he didn't really approve of the
types of roles I was doing. One of them told me about it later.

"They've got her as a vampy chorus girl, a flirty reporter,
a wicked gold digger, a wisecracking saleslady. She's not like
that, I swear she isn't," Johnny said. They were gathered in
the lobby of the Regent Hotel on Hollywood Boulevard,
Johnny's favorite meeting place and the hangout for character
actors and others who had been struck down by the Depres-
sion and the demise of vaudeville.

"That's why, fellas," Johnny said to the group around him,
"I'm secretly writing a picture for her myself. She's gonna get
married in the story. She's gonna have the whole wedding
ceremony with everything white—dress, flowers, veil, and
train. I don't want a doubt in the whole world that my Nora
isn't a good girl."

"Will someone stand on her train and yank it off and
show her panties?" the Dwarf asked.

"Nope, no laughs till after the ceremony is over. I want
that gold ring on her finger with nice organ music. Busby
Berkeley can stage it from there."

Cecilia was making the rounds again with the coffeepot. "Nora, I hope at this studio I can visit the set more often."

"Mom, gee, I wish you could, but Laura Evans had a sign put up outside the sound stage: 'No Visitors.'"

"You're a star, too," she said.

"Not really, at this studio, Mom—a leading lady, not the star; Ina is. I get second billing in this one, remember?"

Cecilia slammed the coffeepot on the stove. "Goddamnit, I'm sick of sitting around here doing nothing." She stormed out, banging the kitchen door.

Johnny rose and sighed. "I'll go see, but . . ." He hesitated. "I don't know what she wants—we played bridge last night at Doris and Jim's . . ."

My head was aching.

". . . and the night before," he continued, "we saw a movie, and the night before that, we drove to the beach and played bingo. I dunno . . ." At the door he turned to me. ". . . unless she wants to be in your shoes, Nora. I dunno . . ." He left to find his wife.

"Why don't you sit down, Miss Marten?"

I turned toward the voice and felt my face flush, my heart thump. There was something about that voice, and now, looking at him I thought of the words of a song: ". . . things that happened for the first time, seem to be happening again . . ."

"Sit down," he repeated. "Here's your chair."

I sat, and he stood beside me.

"Sit back," he said, and I sat back. He stayed a moment longer, then walked away. I was looking blindly at my hands folded in my lap. What's wrong with me, I must be crazy, I can hardly swallow.

I was called for a shot, and he was alongside the camera. Yet I had never seen him on the set before. I couldn't trust myself to meet his eyes. His eyes were on me, I knew that. And they stayed on me for the next thirty days of shooting.

I'm—I'm—I'm—he's—he's—he's— I hugged my pillow night after night.

Why? Why can't I talk to him? He asks such simple things: "Do you have sisters and brothers?" "Do you like Hollywood?" "Nice out today, isn't it?" That's all—that's *all!* I thought, kicking the covers off my feet. But my mouth gets dry, and I just mutter to him, or nod. Oh, he must think I'm a dunce. My hands pressed against my hot cheeks. I jumped out of bed and drew a chair to the window, and leaning there, inhaled the night air. I looked at the lawn, the lamppost, the quiet, empty street—then up to the stars. "Listen," I said to them, "I'm in love with David Nolan—I'll spell it for you, D-A-V-I-D N-O-L-A-N—and I don't even know him. Nora Marten loves David Nolan, hear me?" Tears ran down my cheeks as I smiled at the stars. "I'm nuts, huh? But there you are, I'm nuts."

Near the end of the picture, the company was dismissed early one Saturday night. I took a shower, changed to a red-and-white-checked cotton dress, and walked past the Goldwyn stages to the studio auto park. I kept my secondhand 1927 Dodge toward the back of the parking space. Its fenders had been dented by its former owners. The side windshields with the painted multicolored flowers that I couldn't scrape off, and the ripped canvas hood, tied down with rope to keep it from flapping, just didn't belong with the elegant specially built cars that crowded the lot.

As I strode along, I saw a shiny black Cadillac pull out and head toward me. "Wait," the driver called. My heart pounded as I stood there. His car was alongside me. "You're dressed and out of this studio almost before they finish saying 'cut.'"

I looked at him. His soft, dark brown eyes were beautiful in the last ray of sunlight. I smiled and looked down at my shoes.

"Get in," he said, opening the car door. "Please—we'll have some dinner."

I got in. We drove along Wilshire toward the beach. The top was down, and the breeze was soft and warm.

Into the long silence he asked, "Would you like to go some special place, or should we have dinner at my house?"

"I dunno," I answered, and gulped so loud we both laughed.

His home was one story, small, white—and the loveliest I'd ever seen.

"I'll fix us a drink; what would you like?"

My eyes widened in panic. I couldn't think of the name of anything—didn't know one drink from the other.

"I dunno," I answered lamely.

"I'll fix us one," he said, "and sit, for heaven's sake—no, here, where it's comfortable." He put his hands on my shoulders and sat me on the couch. "Now, relax, Nora, I'll put on some music. . . . Do you like chicken?"

I nodded.

"Good—we're having chicken, Southern-fried. I've gotten ahold of a great cook." He turned on his Victrola and waited for several strains of "Summertime" from *Porgy and Bess*. He mixed us a Scotch and soda, then sat in a deep armchair facing me.

"Too strong?" he asked.

I shook my head.

"Okay then?"

I nodded. He's very tan, I thought.

"You're nice and tan," he said aloud.

I must say *something,* I thought desperately, taking another swallow of my drink. "What do you do?" I asked. "I mean, on the set?"

"Pardon me?"

"I mean, well, you're always there, but you're so quiet, and you don't seem to be doing anything."

He laughed in amazement. "Oh, Nora, Nora, I'm your

cinematographer. Fine thing! Don't tell Sam Goldwyn I don't seem to be doing anything!"

"Oh, dear, I'm sorry. You're so quiet I—well, you're so quiet—"

We looked in each other's eyes until I looked down at the floor. "Summertime, and the livin' is . . ." We sat wordless until the record was finished. Then he got up and stood by the window, his back toward me.

"Dinner is served," a man in a white jacket announced.

Oh, God, I hope he has only one fork at each place, I prayed, as David ushered me into the candlelit dining room. I had vaguely heard about more, and wouldn't know which one to take first.

He talked animatedly during dinner, and my nervousness subsided.

When we were back in the living room, he made a fire in the fireplace. He's not an awful lot taller than I am, but he's so straight and slim. . . .

He put "The Way You Look Tonight" on the Victrola. Then he lighted a cigarette and sat next to me on the couch. And his nose is beautiful. A perfect nose, but it's put on the wrong angle, sort of upwards, and it's wonderful and different that way. . . .

"Nora," he interrupted my thoughts, "we're in love."

"Sir, I'm going now," said the man in the white jacket. "I'll be here early Monday. Anything else, sir?"

David shook his head.

"Good night, sir."

David sat looking at me. His arm was along the back of the couch. I was sitting close to the corner of the couch, my eyes on my hands clasped in my lap.

"I'll fix us a liqueur," he said.

I watched him pour a brown-colored liquid into two small glasses.

"Here you are, Nora."

I accepted the drink, then almost at once he set his on the

JOAN BLONDELL   ·   206

coffee table, took my glass, and pulled me slowly to my feet.
He put my drink next to his, and holding my hand, drew me
down a long hallway to his bedroom. He stood me by his bed,
and in the darkness kissed my hands and gently undressed me.

He went around the bed and took off his own clothes. He
eased me onto my back and pulled the covers from under me,
then put them over the two of us—making us one.

I took a deep and powerful breath, and it lasted the whole
sentence: "I'm going to move to a little apartment on Larrabee Street; I'm now entirely grown up, and I'm going to move
tonight, if you don't mind, and please know how much I love
you, but even love sometimes has got to do things on the side
—I mean, separately—I'll still give you my check each week,
and you'll always be safe, and I'll see you every day; and,
well, please, I have to—I have to move to Larrabee Street."

Johnny and Mom and Judy were stunned. And before they
could ask questions, I was gone—one small suitcase stuffed
with whatever was in sight: comb, pink scarf, Bible, chewing
gum, nail file. . . .

I jumped into my Dodge and drove to the studio. My mind
was racing and my heart pounding.

I did it, I did it—just as he asked me to. It's crazy, the way
your whole world can change like lightning, from Saturday
to Monday. Saturday!—that night, all night. I shivered excitedly. He wouldn't let me leave—he just wouldn't. And Mom
believed me when I called at midnight and lied—lied that I
was staying with Sally.

Wonderful, gentle David loves me. He held my body close,
stroked my hair. The kissing was so gentle. All of it was gentle, even the part that I was petrified about, the thing that
Mom said over and over was evil, dirty, wrong. It isn't—it just
isn't, because that's what he wants.

I turned into the Goldwyn lot, parked the car quickly, and
ran to the makeup department. It was empty at this hour. Just
Sally, my hairdresser, waiting to shampoo and set my hair.

"Good gawd!" Sally exclaimed. "Sit still—you got ants?"

I looked at her reflection in the mirror. "Sally?" I asked tentatively.

"Go ahead." Sally smiled. "It's David, isn't it?"

"How d'ya know?"

"Oh, stop now—everyone on the set knows—the atmosphere is thick with it—you couldn't cut the twitch you have for each other with a meat cleaver!"

"Oh, Sally, I didn't know it was like this. I'm so silly and rattled-feeling. . . ."

"He's a helluva nice guy."

"Tell me all you know about him. I don't know anything, anything—except I'm in love."

"Then bang away, kid," she advised pleasantly.

"Oh, Sally!"

"You know he's not free—for a wedding, don't you?"

"I know—he told me. But he hasn't even seen his wife in three years. She lives in New York, and it was over long before then, and he's going to get free now, and we're going to get married."

"Mrs. David Nolan, the fifth. Hooray!"

"What did you say?" I grew pale.

"Four wives so far, and the leading man in two co-respondent cases—didn't you know?"

I didn't answer.

"Hell, kid, I'm not spilling the beans, everybody knows. 'Whattaman Nolan' they call him. Ah, Nora, don't look like that. Listen, I'm going to tell you this, and I betcha I speak for everybody in the industry. David Nolan is the most beloved guy around—both men and women think he's tops. They respect him, too. He's the greatest cameraman in the business—the big stars throw conniptions to get him for their pictures. He can make Marie Dressler look like Dolores Del Rio, and he does it like it's so easy—you know, no snarl, no fuss. Hell, when Goldwyn pays him two grand a week, you know

he's got to be great. And, Nora, he's not a wolf with dames.
It's hard to explain, but he just isn't."

"But, four wives," I mumbled.

"Yeah—well, I tell you something. The dames are after
him like flies. I could go for him myself!" She took a deep
breath. "He's not a wolf, I tell you. I've worked studios for
ten years, and I know." She put the net on my hair and pulled
the dryer over to the chair. "I bet," she continued, "he just
can't say no when they propose to him—he's that damn po-
lite.—" She turned on the dryer, and I sat very still.

Sally gathered up the stray bobby pins, towel, combs from
the dressing table, washed her hands, then pulled up the
dryer so I could hear. "Listen, you're sitting there like you've
been shot. Cut it out. I'm telling you, he's a helluva guy. And
Jesus, he doesn't take his eyes off you—he's in love, man. So,
Nora, be happy and take everything today—screw tomorrow,
okay?"

I swallowed the tears and smiled.

"Sally, you know what I did?"

"What?"

"I told my family I stayed all night with you."

"What else! Say it as often as you wanna."

"I don't have to anymore. I'm moving to my own apartment on Larrabee tonight."

"That's the ole fight. You're a big girl now."

I jumped up and hugged her. "You're my best friend, Sally,
and I love you."

"Okay, now get your ass back under that dryer. You'll be
late on the set."

I was nauseous, and even the touch of sheer nightgown
hurt my breasts. "David?"

He was lying in bed looking up at me. "What is it, baby?
You look frightened."

I scrambled in beside him and put my lips to his ear.

"David," I whispered, "I feel funny, like something's wrong. I have for a month now, and—and, David . . ."

We were close, his arms around me, our bodies pressed tight.

"What, baby?"

"Do you suppose—I don't know, but, maybe—y'see, I passed the time, and . . ."

"Oh, poor Nora, darling." He pulled me closer. "We'll see a doctor tomorrow, after work. Don't be concerned, my little dove; don't you worry your round, silly head. We'll see to-morrow."

I kissed his nose, his forehead, his lips. Oh, I love him so, I thought. He'll find a way to be free fast. I pulled my stomach up closer to him.

He kissed me passionately. We made love, and I fell asleep in his arms.

"I've seen you in several pictures, *Mrs. Smith.*" The doctor's sarcasm did not go unnoticed. He told me that I was about two and a half months pregnant. Words that would have given me such joy threw me into a sickening panic. In his small dressing room, my hands fumbled with my clothes, and my knees shook so violently I had to lean against the wall for balance. But still I hoped. If I write to David's wife and tell her we'll pay the fifteen thousand—both of us saving every penny—just as fast as we can, then we can get married right away and have the baby.

David was waiting in the parking lot beside the Medical Building on Vine Street. As I got in beside him, he took my hands in his and looked at me questioningly.

"Yes, David." I looked at him with desperate hope in my heart.

"Ah—my poor baby," he said, and kissed my nose. Driving toward the apartment on Larrabee, he explained his plans.

"There's a safe doctor someone told me about—he's been in business for years. Office in Los Angeles—he's taken care of a lot of picture people."

I shook violently as he spoke. "David, I can't—I can't do anything to this baby."

"Now, Nora, don't look at it that way, darling. It's such a short time, there's really no baby yet. Besides, Harriet just won't give me a divorce until fifteen thousand is in her tight little fist. Anyway, sweetheart dear," David continued, "no one's ever going to be allowed to come between *us*. You'd give your love to a baby, and I'm a selfish beast, I want all your love for myself, forever. Nora, you hear me?"

I dropped my head to his shoulder. He had talked that way before—not really saying he didn't want children, skirting those words, but suggesting that it would always be just the two of us. But he spoke with such love that I refused to face the possibility that he meant it, that he wouldn't want a child.

"We'll ride to the beach and have some lunch, darling. Let's get our minds off it now—it's not the end of the world, you know. Hundreds of women have it done—there's no danger anymore. You have four days, thank God, before you start the picture. You'll feel great by then, and the whole thing will be back of you."

At one o'clock in the morning, I got out of bed, put on my slacks and sport shirt, and left a note on my pillow in case he woke up: "Dearest David, I've got to go for a ride; my skin is crawling funny, and I can't stay still. Your Nora."

I stopped the car on a ledge overlooking the water between Santa Monica and Ocean Park, took off my sandals, and climbed down the rocks and walked the soft sand to the water's edge. The waves were high and violent. I'll run first, I thought, shivering in my panic. Racing as fast as I could, I cried my prayer aloud: "Oh, God, please forgive me, but have something happen—now, tonight—so there'll be no baby in me. I'm so scared to have that awful thing done. He'll change his mind, my David, soon as we get married." But one part of me wondered why David didn't have fifteen thousand dollars for a divorce when he had made two thousand a week for years.

My heart bursting with fear, I forced my way into the powerful surf. I fought the waves with my body, trying to stand while they banged against my back, my stomach—knocking me down, turning me head over heels, until a tremendous roller carried me onto the sand. I lay there facedown, begging: "Go away, go away, little baby—you can't be born yet, and I can't kill you—I can't—I can't!"

I started the new Kern Brothers picture four days later. My screen popularity had grown to the extent that the studio okayed any request, and my request was that Sally do my hair in all my pictures and that David photograph me.

Sally was with me in my private dressing room.

"You're pooped, kid. Doing it too much?"

I closed my eyes. "Sally," I said, "I've got to tell you. I can't tell things to my mother, and Judy is too young, and . . ."

"Go ahead, kid—spill it. I'm the Sphinx—been in this racket too long to gab."

"I had—I had an abortion."

"When?"

"Three days ago."

"No wonder you look like a ghost. Geez, you look sick as a dog."

"It was gruesome, Sally. I can't get it out of my mind—that creepy office. . . . And, oh, Sally, I was so scared—so desperately scared."

"I know."

"But it wasn't just the awful pain. It was the killing . . ."

"Stop, Nora—your eyes will get red." Sally put her arms around me.

"Sally, maybe you know. What do people do when they don't want—I mean, can't have babies—not yet, I mean?"

"Well, for chrissakes, didn't David tell you, and didn't he . . ."

We talked until I was due on the set, then talked between shots in my dressing room on the set.

"You gals got secrets?" David asked it with an overtone of annoyance.

Two days later, in the middle of the night, I nudged David. "David—David?"

"Ummmm?"

"Please wake up."

He was alert immediately. "What, darling? What?"

"I'm bleeding—hard—and I've never had such terrible cramps in my life."

He switched on the light and jumped out of bed. My skin was gray and my eyes unnaturally bright. My teeth chattered violently. He felt my blazing forehead and, trembling himself, searched the phone book for Dr. Riley's number.

The doctor asked the symptoms and possible cause, then said curtly: "I'll be right there."

David knelt down beside the bed and took my hand in his, pressing it to his heart.

"David!" I cried suddenly. I raised myself to my elbows.

"What is it, darling?" he asked.

"David—listen now, and don't say one word until I finish."

"I won't sweetheart," he promised, though he was sure I was delirious.

"David, think back," I said, very slowly, "it was about four years ago—at the Park Central Hotel. I was at the cashier's window, and I was waiting to buy a stamp, and . . . I . . ."

In amazement he picked up my story: ". . . and you dropped the letter, and we bumped heads. Then you hollered when I tried to mail it for you. Nora, it was you—that dear little girl was *you!* You sailed around the revolving door three times . . ."

"And you smiled at me, David, and I walked on air . . ."

"And I wanted to follow you—couldn't get you out of my mind. Nora, it's crazy—that was us. . . ."

"David, I felt something familiar when you first spoke to me on the set."

"And I knew there was something about your eyes, Nora. Oh, darling." He held me in his arms rocking me back and forth. "Darling—my darling . . ."

A half-hour passed, then Dr. Riley asked David to go into the kitchen. "Peritonitis, Mr. Nolan. I'll have to operate immediately. She's a desperately sick girl. I'll meet you at the hospital. The ambulance should be here soon."

They worked around me in the picture. "Just for a week," David asked them. "She nearly lost her life."

"Nora Marten Bursts Appendix," the newspapers headlined, and my family believed it.

"If you didn't have the constitution of a horse, you'd be dead now," Dr. Riley told me privately. "You were butchered. For your sake, it better not happen again."

David sold his house and sent the money to his wife. Harriet wrote that she was going to the Bahamas for a quick divorce —and he'd be free to remarry in four weeks. "I do hope the new one can stand your silences better than I," she P.S.'ed.

So we were married, in the office of the justice of the peace in Phoenix, Arizona; it was a small, stuffy office, but the only place we could escape the crowds that haunted picture stars.

Johnny, Cecilia, Judy, Scott, and his wife, Janet, were witnesses, squashed against each other.

Just before the ceremony, Johnny took David aside and handed him a well-worn envelope.

"Read this," Johnny said.

"Now?" David asked.

"Now."

David unfolded the letter and read:

To whom it may concern:
Nora Marten, aged eight, daughter of Mr. and Mrs. John

Marten of "The Boy Is Gone" Company, lost her virginity on the edge of a costume trunk while tap-dancing, at the Wabash Theater, Memphis, Tennessee.

Signed,
Dr. Clarence Halsey

David didn't laugh. He grabbed Johnny in a bear hug before he stepped into place alongside me.

There was a small window and a low radiator in back of us as we stood facing the justice. As we took our solemn vows, our backsides were scorched by the steam of the radiator.

We listened intently to the justice.

" . . . Don't forget to be generous with your love; don't forget . . ."

Then I lost the trend of his words and looked at those I loved: Johnny, the veins thick on his brow, his head bent as though in prayer, a prayer that I'd find security and a home; Mom, her posture elegant, her lovely nose in the air as though she were making the best of a bad deal. Cecilia would have been much happier if I had had a tremendous wedding, covered by the newspapers, with her the breathtakingly beautiful mother of the bride.

I looked at Judy and Scott and Janet and thought, what a marvelous troupe I belong to, as the tears dripped down the front of the silk paisley dress I'd borrowed from the studio wardrobe department.

The justice's voice came back to me: ". . . I now pronounce you man and wife. . . ."

As I turned my tear-brimmed eyes toward David, my appendix burst.

Two years later I was standing on the terrace of our house; twenty-three hundred feet below me was Sunset Boulevard. The house was nestled into the top of Lookout Mountain. We could see from Los Angeles proper to the beach at Santa Monica.

I never tired of looking at it—touching the chairs, lamps, drapes, the pictures, the perfectly appointed kitchen, the patio, the lawn, the trees, the flowers. Many times I'd even knelt on the soft rugs and patted them gleefully. "Ours, all ours—as soon as it's paid for!"

Coming in from the terrace, I fluffed the pillows on the couches by the large bay window, then went into the kitchen and took down *The Boston Cook Book*. I was going to make a pot roast and needed a recipe for potato pancakes.

I turned the pages listlessly, then slammed the book shut, dropped it on the floor, and strode back to the bay window. Looking blankly ahead, my legs apart, I started to sway from side to side. The next time something goes wrong—the next time, so help me God, I'm going to have the baby, I promised myself. I straightened a picture over the couch. "I've had four of those torturous things—four—four—four—six counting the two legal ones to correct the bungling," I told the group of men on horseback in the picture.

I went back to the kitchen, got my copper watering can and filled it, then sprayed the two plants in the dining room. David, the doctor warned me that I can't—I can't keep on killing and being deathly sick and terrified like this!

He always answered sympathetically—"Don't worry, baby dear"—and then always found another doctor for the job: Playa del Rey, Long Beach, Palm Springs. He'd take me to the doctor with concern and tenderness—but without fail.

I put my sprinkling can back in the kitchen and poured a glass of milk, then threw it in the sink in a sudden flare of violence. I picked up a tin of fish food and went out to the pond in the patio. I bent over the lilies and sprinkled the food and watched the goldfish scurry to eat it.

The water rippled, and in the reflection I saw Johnny in his rube makeup. "Fish is my favorite food," he said to Cecilia in her white beaded dress.

"Reahaally!" she answered with her pseudo-Southern accent. "Fish is a wonderful brain food. Ah'm sorry to say you don't look very intelligent."

"Jes' think how I'd look if I *didn't* eat fish!"

I smiled at their reflections, those silly, wonderful people I belong to. They'd *answer* me, anyway, not put me off with a "poor baby" that left me limp and lost.

I took a pair of shears and clipped some red geraniums from outside the kitchen door. I put the flowers in a vase in our bedroom.

I walked into the guest suite. It was perfect for a baby: his own living room and bedroom and bath, and a terrace for him to sun. I hummed "Lullaby of Broadway" and cradled my arms as though I held my child.

The kitchen doorbell rang, and I ran to answer it. The grocery boy smiled. "You're seldom home, Miss Marten."

"I know—just lucky today. They're making background shots at the studio."

"I always wanted to be a movie star."

"That so?" I was putting the vegetables in the cooler. "But," he said, "I guess it ain't easy to get to be one, so I got into this business."

"That's wise."

"Oh, say, Miss Marten, could I get your autograph for my boss? He might give me a raise."

"Of course." I smiled.

After he left, I unwrapped the roast and salted and peppered it. I wish David would eat and not just drink, I told myself. Bourbon in his coffee in the morning, a brandy milkshake for lunch, in the afternoon half Coke and half bourbon in a Coke bottle so no one on the set will know he's drinking—then the highballs at night. I get so dawgone starved waiting for him to want his dinner—till ten or eleven o'clock sometimes. I don't understand how he stays sober, but I've never seen him stagger.

I sat by the kitchen window, my chin in my hands. "Twenty-seven pictures so far—my baby would be proud of me," I said to no one.

The phone rang.

"Hello."

"Baby dear?"

"Hi, David."

"I'll be home in half an hour. I'm bringing Jim Wilson for dinner—says he's lonesome."

"Okay."

"Need anything?"

"Nope."

"See you soon, darling—hey! I miss you."

"Me, too."

I hung up. Jim Wilson lonesome—the Dream Boat Movie Star! Why, he has every woman in America clawing over him, for Pete's sake, I thought, irritated that he was coming. I'm just crabby today, I decided. I'll get done up in my new dress and I'll feel better.

3

JIM WILSON'S booming voice halted my jumbled thoughts: "Hallo! Halloooo there! Where's the beauty of the family? Where's the doll-baby?"

"Here, Jim, frosting martini glasses," I called in answer. What a cornball, I thought to myself.

"Ah—there she is! One of the big box office ten—in person! Where's a grizzly bear huggaroo for none other than Jim Wilson!"

His "grizzly bear huggaroo" hurt my breasts, threw something out in the back of my neck, and knocked an earring off. We were both on our hands and knees searching for it as Jim whispered, "Listen, sweetie, May Gould's along—mind? David said you'd have plenty for dinner, so we picked her up. Boy! Did I surprise her—this is not Saturday night, you know."

"Why, sure, Jim, I have a big roast. Get her in here!"

"May, sweetie," he hollered over my answer, "come and

get it—a lil ole Coke for my favorite gal!" Then he lowered his voice again, this time respectfully. "She doesn't drink a drop, Nora—never has."

"I know."

"It's been in all the columns."

"I know."

The perennially young movie actress, May Gould, made her appearance, taking small steps on the tips of her toes. "I never tire of your marvelous view, Nora," she said breathlessly, and smiled, exposing too-white, capped teeth.

"Mee mooo maw-maw, Meee maw mooooo," Jim vocalized. A pain shot through my ears. When my hearing returned to normal, I heard my husband.

"David, where are you?" I called.

Later, I got them to the dining table; David, with his seventh double martini alongside his plate.

"Nora cooks the best damn food I ever wrapped my lips around!" Jim groaned, leaning back and whacking his stomach.

"My baby dear's improving all the time. We like it best on cook's night off, don't we, baby dear?" David smiled at me from the head of the table.

"I wish you'd eat, David; you've had only two bites."

"I checked with my stomach, and that's all it will handle for a while." His answer was always the same. He smiled and rose to fix another martini.

Four Benedictine and brandies later David gathered them in the basement to admire his current hobby—electric trains. It took thousands of dollars and nationwide correspondence to get the "to-scale" trains, tracks, stations, lights, people, mountains, hills, valleys, grass, flowers, dirt, signposts, roads, signals. Nothing missing but the birds and the bees, I thought when I looked at the result of his extravagant indulgence.

The beautifully lighted miniature countryside covered all but five feet of our huge basement. The studio set designer had refused compensation for making the miniature panorama, so David had surprised him with a new Cadillac as a gesture of appreciation.

"David, old pal," Jim said, his eyes following the speeding trains, "you entertain my lil ole gal while I take *your* lil ole gal upstairs for a lil ole private talk. What d'ya say?"

"Right!" David answered, bent double trying to get a stuck train out of a tunnel.

"Right!" May repeated needlessly.

Upstairs, when we were seated in the bay window, Jim said, "I respect you, Nora. You have good common sense. I'm considering marrying May—what's your advice?"

"Do you love her?"

"Well, hell, she's a hell of a gal—not many around like her. And she's got a great reputation—she's a virgin, you know."

"I know."

"It's been in all the columns."

"I know."

"And I'll tell you something else," he continued with growing enthusiasm. "I picked her up the other Saturday morning to grab some chow, and she wanted to know if I'd park by the Bank of America on Highland for a minute, as she had to clip some coupons. Well, Nora"—he leaned toward me intensely—"I sat out there on my big, fat ass for two solid hours while she clipped and clipped."

"My!"

"We didn't wrap our lips around a bite until after three-thirty."

"You must have been starved!"

"Hell, I couldn't guzzle a morsel thinking about what a smart gal she is—hanging on to her dough like that."

"Oh!"

"What do you think about a lil ole wedding?"

I paused. I frankly didn't care much about either of them. My one evening as a guest at May's home was . . . barren: no cocktails, barely enough chicken to go around, no butter for the air-holed bread, weak coffee, lumpy ice cream, and every lamp in the house had strips of cellophane covering the shade, though she had lived there for over ten years.

As for Jim Wilson, well, he was a fabulously popular crooner. Next to Bing Crosby he was tops in the nation. But there seemed something superficial about him.

I answered his question as truthfully as I could. "You'll make a helluva couple."

Jim beamed. "I might just take your advice. After all, a gal with her—er—qualifications—well, the first one drank and didn't have a dime."

"I didn't know you'd been married before!"

"Neither does the press department. Remember me? America's most desirable bachelor?" He playfully grazed my chin with his clenched fist.

"What was she like?"

"A beauty—dark, and from my home town. She was seventeen when I took the leap. She was from a wrong-side-of-the-tracks family, but they were okay. Damn glad about the catch their kid made! After all, Nora, I was a thousand-bucks-a-week m.c. in Detroit, and you know dames, I had 'em swarming over me. So the little babe was in luck, if you'll pardon my French."

I don't think I like you, I thought. "What happened to the marriage?"

"Lasted four years. First two were fair, and then she started to drink. Jesus Christ, what drinking! And crying—Christ! I had an important reputation to live up to, so I sent her to one of those cure places—and a pretty penny that was!"

He paused. "I'll be a son-of-a-bitch if she didn't stop drinking the minute she registered, but as soon as she got home, she'd drain every bottle that wasn't tied down. Murder!"

He lit a cigarette and blew smoke rings. "But I outsmarted her," he continued amiably. "Sent her to visit her mother back in Tyler, Mississippi. You see, I had the Kern Brothers' movie contract in my pokie, and I didn't want her to know it. Then I got a guy I went to high school with who was a lawyer, and I had him get me a divorce, and when it was to be recorded in the newspaper, I had him put the word 'Negro' after my name —so anybody who saw it wouldn't suspect it was me. You know—'James P. Wilson, Negro, divorces Margaret Midland.' See?"

"But why—"

"Why?" he exclaimed in surprise. "So she wouldn't get any of that picture money, that's why! In case she sobered up, she might have. Well, I didn't even have to give her alimony. She just signed the papers in a drunken daze."

I turned my head. "How awful," I murmured.

"I'll say it was awful."

"Any children?"

"Nope." He knocked on the end table. "I'll tell you something, Nora, a guy shouldn't be single in this town. The gals expect too much—and Jesus Christ, the married babes hound a guy to death. I think it's good business if I get married."

"Two can live as cheaply as one," I deadpanned.

"Right!" He grinned.

"Yoo-hooo there, you two-hooo!" May called breathlessly from the foot of the basement stairs. "David wants you to bring the brandy when you come back."

"All right, doll-baby," Jim yelled in answer. He pulled me to my feet and threw both his arms around my neck. "We'll talk about the situation some other time, Nora. I'm not going to rush into anything this serious."

He picked up a bottle of Courvoisier. "Let's go join 'em, you lil ole box-office favorite, you," he said happily. I followed as he vocalized: "Meee mooo maw maw, moo maw maw . . ." all the way down the stairs.

Later that night, lying in bed, I studied my husband's sleeping face in the moonlight. I love my David. I love him so. . . . But why is the pit of my stomach always so heavy with fear, with the uneasiness of not knowing what he's thinking? I turned my back toward him and hung my head over the side of the bed, my hand tugging on the string rug. Even bills, my thoughts continued, he just won't discuss them. "Later, baby dear," he says. But later, full of drinks, he just repeats, "Later, baby dear." And there's just not enough, even with what I make, to catch up—to pay up his extravagances, his weird generosity. It's not fair to anyone, I concluded despondently.

I thought about last month, when one evening after many drinks he suddenly said, "I play the violin, baby dear."

"Really, David?"

"Oh yes, my uncle was a concert violinist. Would have been famous, but he drank himself to death at an early age—around thirty. He paid for my lessons when I was a kid."

"Oh, David—how wonderful—I didn't know." My eyes shone with excitement. David so seldom spoke of anything past—of anything at all.

"We'll run down to Wurlitzer's right now and pick up a fiddle. They're open till nine," he said.

He picked up a fiddle, all right, I thought wryly, one bare leg hanging off the bed kicking back and forth: a Nicolo Amati for six thousand dollars; three hundred dollars for the bow, and one hundred fifty dollars for a practice bow. Nonplussed, I had asked how we were going to pay for it with all the bills due.

"I charged it," he answered conclusively.

Arriving home, he had hurriedly fixed a highball, downed it as a thirsty man does water, and opened the violin case with great care. "Sit there, Nora," he said. I had watched as he stood with his feet firmly apart, professionally placing the violin under his chin. Motionless for a long moment, the bow held midair in his right hand. Closing his eyes and pursing his lips, he drew the bow across the violin strings, and "Way Down Upon the Swanee River" squeaked out of his sawlike movement. I struggled to remain solemn as I applauded the last jerky squawk.

"I'll fix a drink and play it again," he promised me.

Oh, David, I thought now, you're so strange, and awfully funny sometimes—like a little boy. I eased myself out of the bed and tiptoed into the bathroom. There was enough moonlight in the darkness to see my reflection in the mirror, and I spoke to it with my eyes.

Tell me what you think, David. Tell me something—anything. I'm lost. Tell me your secrets—even one. I know you love me . . . but do you? Do you really like the way I am? Do I make you happy? Am I pretty, David? Am I a good movie star? Will we save some money soon? . . . Do you ever say your prayers? Do you know I lie awake every night while you sleep? That I'm afraid of the consequences of the loving—afraid that I'll hate you again, hate you for making me get cut on . . . scraped on . . . so we'll have no baby—no baby.

With great effort I composed myself and quietly tiptoed back to bed.

David moved and murmured, "Spoon fashion, baby dear." I curved my body into his back, he clasped my hands tightly around his waist, and breathed in deep sleep again. My nose was against his skin, and smelling the warmth of it comforted me. Everything will be all right, I told myself, because I love him.

S HEELY DAWSON'S column in the *Los Angeles Examiner* headlined:

The David Nolans (our own Nora Marten, of course) have gone on a camping trip. Kern Brothers have her permission to rest this week because her eyes blinked too much in close-ups. She just completed her forty-ninth picture, one after the other, and she and her cameraman husband are Hollywood's happiest married couple.

T. L. Kern tells me he has twelve other pictures lined up for our Nora. Their best pal, Jim Wilson, the singingest star in the Hollywood heavens, will join them on their vacation. He likes to camp, too. All female hearts will be shredded if Jim marries little May Gould.

An abscessed tooth kept Ruth Chatterton from marrying George Brent Thursday. All Hollywood mourns the death of

Bette Davis' husband, who fell on his head. Marjorie Rambeau ate a lace doily by mistake.

Bye folks—count on me tomorrow.

We were driving through the desert above Indio. I had fixed David another bourbon and gingerale out of the stock in the glove compartment. My hands were sticky, and I was very hungry.

"Will Jim know where you're going to pitch our tent?" I asked.

"Um hum."

"Those beans and hot dogs are going to taste good!"

"Um hum."

"And I'll make us some nice fried potatoes and eggs tomorrow morning."

"Mmmm."

". . . and hot coffee."

My stomach growled long and loud, and I looked at David to see if he'd heard it. He had, and smiled, his eyes on the road ahead. A sickening wave of nausea followed the growl. No—no—NO! I dug my nails into the leather seat of the car. I had to stop thinking about it.

"David," I said, "did you notice I opened in four new pictures all the same day? I saw the marquees when we drove along Hollywood Boulevard: *Miss Army Sue* at Warners; *Good bye All Over* at the Iris; *Sticks and Stones* at Pantages; and *You Were Made to Be Made* at Grauman's. I wonder if they're any good?"

"We'll see them sometime."

I knew differently. David disliked going out. Several times we'd planned to go to a preview or opening of one of my pictures, but by the time David had his cocktails, it was always too late.

"David?"

"Ummm?"

"It's hard to work under yourself—you know what I mean?

I mean, the parts I play are so vacant and dizzy, and wise-cracking . . ."

"You make people laugh."

"Well, I know, but once in a while I'd like a real heavy-weight part, like the kind they give to Garson or Bette. I can do them, too, but I don't fight for them—do I?" David made no comment, so I continued: "Well, it's like—if you know how to build a house, it's hard to just keep building garages all the time."

David smiled. "Your pictures are box office, baby dear."

"It's just that as long as I have to be an actress, I'd like to run instead of walk."

I was silent for a while. "David, I think I see the Big Dipper." David was preoccupied, but I went on. "Gee, I wish I made more money, since I'm so box officey. We could use it."

"Yes, it's a crime, Nora, you should make much more. Want to mix Pappy another little drink, baby dear?"

Pappy! I thought, a rush of tears threatening my eyes.

I mixed another bourbon and gingerale in a fresh paper cup and handed it to him.

"We'll be there in about two hours," he assured me. "Thanks, dearest—you're a great little bartender."

I smiled and put my head on his shoulder.

"It's not cold out, baby dear."

"I know, I have funny chills anyway."

My stomach growled again, and again the wave of nausea crept over me.

Early Sunday morning we heard Jim Wilson's voice bouncing off the trees. "Over the Sea Let's Go, Men . . ."

"Come and get it!" David cupped his hands and called a la Edward Arnold. We had just finished talking about Jim.

"Why does he hang around us so much, David—and stag, to boot?"

"He likes us. He says we're homey . . . he's lonesome, I

guess. But don't worry about the stag part, he gets around—on the Q.T."

"I don't understand why he doesn't take his romances out places."

"They're not that kind!" David grinned. "But he takes May Gould to the Clover Club every Saturday night."

"And to see his pictures over and over."

"Now, Nora."

"It's true. He calls the columnists and tells 'em where they're going so he'll get press shots taken. Honestly, David, I don't think men should be movie actors—'tain't natural." I smiled.

"Shush, here he is. Hi, old pally!" They whacked each other on the back. I picked up the ice bucket to stave off a Wilson hug. "How'd you get here?" I asked.

"Took a plane to Palm Springs—Frank McHugh had an extra ticket he gave me. Taxi wanted twenty-five clams from there, so luckily a fan picked me up and dropped me off about half a mile down the road. You turtle doves having fun?"

"Have a drink." David gave Jim a Coke that had been thoroughly spiked.

"Never touch the stuff," Jim quipped. "Bottoms up." After a swig and a "Wow!" he turned to me. "Brought my new script, sweetie, thought you could cue me on the ride back."

"I will," I promised.

They fixed their fishing rods.

"Yes, Mrs. Nolan, you're pregnant."

I stared at him. "Thank you, doctor, thank you very much," I whispered.

Downstairs David was waiting in the car, studying a road map. My white face made it unnecessary for him to say more than, "Poor baby dear," as I got in beside him. Going north on Crescent Heights Boulevard, he ended the lengthy silence.

"Our house looks great nestled on top of that mountain, doesn't it, sweetheart?"

"David . . ." I paused, then distinctly, slowly, with no intonation, said, "This baby is mine."

He took my hand. "Darling, you're just upset."

I took my hand away and repeated very slowly: "This—baby—is—mine."

Looking straight ahead, I thought, . . . and everything is unknotted now. I feel quiet and—oh—thank You, God, for my baby.

I glanced at my husband's profile. "Yes, David," I agreed, "our home looks great."

I was watching the heavy rain splatter against the bay window. It's only a few more days, I thought nervously, hoping that David would stop demanding sex. The gynecologist had told me to refrain weeks ago, but David had not heeded the warning, nor my pleas. "I'll be careful," he kept saying. I shuddered, and the telephone rang.

"Nora, sweetie? Jim."

"Hi, Jim."

"When's that baby coming, for God's sake? I'm getting to be an old man waiting for it."

"Damn it, Jim, shut up!" I snapped.

"Hey, now, temper, temper. What's everybody's little pal mad about?"

"I'm not 'everybody's little pal,' and I'm sick of being asked 'When's the baby coming?' by everybody who calls—including fan-magazine editors, Sheely, Screelie, Meelie, A.P., U.P., and E.P.—Sheely called minutes ago and whined, 'Nora, dear, I do hope you'll get that baby here in time for my Sunday-night broadcast.' Well, I've got a scoop for all of 'em, including you—my baby will get here when it's supposed to! Just because I'm a movie star is no sign I can whip one up faster than the lucky souls who are *not* movie stars!"

"Hey—hey—hey," he interrupted. "You *are* upset. Where's David?"

"I'm sorry, Jim. Yes, I'm upset. David's having his car fixed in Beverly. I couldn't go with him—I couldn't."

"Nora, did you hear the silly story about the actor that—"

"Jim?"

"Huh?"

"Come over now. Please."

"Well—"

"Please, Jim. I need cheering up."

"Sure. I'll be there before you can say T. L. Kern!" he promised, and hung up.

With the car radio blasting, Jim pulled his Lincoln convertible to a fast stop in the driveway and ducked through the rain. As I opened the front door, his arms were outstretched, and he was singing: "You must have been a beautiful baby, 'cause baby look at you now! . . ."

"Yeah, *look* at me now! And don't give me a hug, for Pete's sake; you'll bump my child!"

He laughed and skimmed his checked cap across the living room to a chair. "Bull's-eye!" he roared.

I took his hand and pulled him toward the nursery. "Come see some of my baby's loot first. See, the beautiful quilt you gave me is on the bassinet. A fan sent this marvelous music box from Germany. Jim, this section will be his living room and den when he grows up—I'm going to add his own kitchen here, and that door will be his private entrance. And look at this fabulous spread that Barbara Stanwyck gave us. It was made by nuns in Czechoslovakia. Gracie Allen gave us this elegant hand-tooled baby book, and this gorgeous gold rattle was from Dorothy Parker. The gossamer cover is from Glenda Farrell. This was Bette's own baby spoon. And Princess Elizabeth sent this royal baby cup—see the teeth marks . . . and this gold plate—see? The President and Mrs. Roosevelt . . ."

Jim said, "WOW!" after inspecting each of the gifts.

"And, Jim, just look at the view he'll have from these windows . . . and Judy hooked this dreamy rug all by herself. It gave her a sore throat from the wool . . . and Mom made these hand-turned sheets with real lace—"

"Nora, my God, Nora," Jim exclaimed in dismay, "what's wrong?"

But my crying was uncontrolled. Confounded, Jim awkwardly attempted to put his arms around my shoulders. I pulled away and ran into the bathroom. He tried to make himself heard through the closed door.

"Nora, baby doll, you're just tired—come on now, David will be home soon—come on, fix me one of those great peanut-butter, sweet-pickle, tomato, bacon, and other goop kinds of sandwiches you make. Don't let ole Jim Wilson feel bad, Nora. 'By a waterfall, I'm calling you hoo hoo hoo . . .'" he sang at the top of his lungs.

I emerged with a damp towel over my face and head. "I feel like a big damn fool jerk," I stuttered, pulling the towel off.

Jim took my hand and gently drew me to the bar in the den.

"You're going to have a drink, gorgeous."

"I don't want one."

"Well, I do, damn it, I can't stand to see you cry like that." He sat me on a stool and went behind the bar.

"Ah—here!" he exclaimed. "Blackberry brandy—it'll tie up your tears; it should, it ties up everything else!" He poured a pony of the brandy, and for himself a double rye. "Here's to that world-famous new baby," he toasted, and downed his drink.

I studied the dismal sky through the antique liqueur bottles that lined the shelves of the window in back of Jim. Then my eyes met his. "Jim," I said quietly, "I can't get into the hospital to have my baby. We haven't the cash—and David won't face it. You have to pay in advance, and because I have a 'name' the cost of everything—doctor, everything—is tripled—more. Jim, I can't listen to 'Don't worry, baby dear' any longer.

David stopped work when I did, and we live up to the hilt, and—"

"Christ—no money! What do you kids do with it, for God's sake?"

"I don't know. This house, our family responsibilities, commissions, alimony, charities, liquor, furniture—"

"How much do you make, Nora?"

"Three hundred and fifty a week."

"Jesus Christ Almighty! And you one of the box office ten? The bastards! Why, Kern Brothers make a pisspot out of your pictures! You ought to walk the hell out until they make a new deal."

"I never could afford to."

"David makes what?"

"Two thousand a week—and has for years, but he's so far in the hole he'll never catch up. He gives everything away, Jim. It's nothing bad he does; he's just so crazy generous it scares me. You know that fifty-seven-foot Chris-Craft he got after we were married?" Jim nodded. "Well, he gave it to his dentist because the dentist canceled all other appointments one Thursday, Friday, and Saturday to devote the time to David's teeth."

"What?"

"Yes, I was there, Jim. Dr. Hammond and David drank bourbon almost continuously during the three days, and while the guy drilled he told us his sad life story. David gave him the boat at the end of the session to cheer him up."

"I'll be a son-of-a . . ."

"Funny part is, we got a whopper of a bill from Dr. Hammond on top of it!"

"I'll be a son . . ."

"And like that six-thousand-dollar fiddle. He only played it that one night, and you know what he told me a few weeks later?"

Jim shook his head.

"He said, 'Baby dear, there's the nicest guy with Ray Heindorf's orchestra at the studio, and while he was parked to run into the post office, somebody stole his violin—his livelihood, y'know—so I gave him mine. God, I felt so sorry for him, he was actually crying, he was so grateful—and he knows it's a museum piece, so he'll take good care of it.'"

"I'll be a . . ." Jim mouthed.

"And we still owe those payments on it, Jim. You see, you can't get mad at David—"

"Who can't?"

"No, really, he's kind, and—and—he gives me presents all the time. Honest to Pete, if a stranger on the street asked him for a thousand dollars, he'd say, 'Wait a minute, pally,' and borrow it from a friend and then give it to the stranger. I've seen him do the most incredible things. I don't know how to manage our money, because I'm bad with money things, but he won't even discuss it with me."

"What a mess."

We were silent for a while. Jim poured himself another drink, and I moved to the couch. Speaking low to the pattern of the chintz, I continued: "I love David. He's my world, and the money worries—well, there'd be a way. We'll always make enough; it's the other—the other, Jim . . ."

"What other?" He came from behind the bar and sat on a stool looking at me. "What other?" he repeated.

"This—my baby that's coming. I want to hear him say something about it—just once. It's a miracle I want to share with him, but when I try, his eyes fade away and his thoughts can't be traced. It's soon, and I'm scared. I have a bum back . . ." I finished lamely.

"Stop it, Nora." Jim stood looking down at my bowed head. "David loves you like a madman. He never takes his eyes off you. Nora, listen to me. I agree he seems vague at times, but that's his way." He paused. "But that you two damn fools don't have enough dough to get into a hospital in style! You're a star, Nora. You owe your public—I'm burned up at Da—"

"No, don't be," I interrupted. "I shouldn't have told you."

"Nora?" David called from the living room.

"Talk to him, Jim; I'll go wash my face again," I said as I ran from the den.

I put on fresh lipstick and a sprinkling of powder; then, composed, I returned to the bar. David and Jim had mixed a highball and were talking about the new Lincoln convertible. David interrupted himself.

"Nora, darling—I have a surprise for you." He smiled.

"A surprise?" I returned his smile.

He took a small jewel box from his pocket and handed it to me. I opened it and stared at the largest square-cut diamond ring I had ever seen.

"David—David!" I said bewilderedly.

"Ten-carat, set in platinum," he told me proudly.

Jim took it out of my trembling hand and inspected it closely as he asked, "Where'd you buy it, pally?"

"A jeweler friend of mine—like it?"

"Well, cut off my legs and call me shorty," Jim said solemnly, looking at me.

"I knew you'd approve, old boy. Let me freshen your drink."

"No thanks, Dave, gotta get on my horse. Publicity stills first thing tomorrow. I'll leave you two lovebirds to yourselves." He tweaked my nose, and made his way out.

Early the next morning, delivered by hand, a letter arrived for Mr. and Mrs. David Nolan:

Dear Kids
    Happy Hospital.
    On me.

                    Love and kisses,
                    Jim

Enclosed was his personal check for a thousand dollars.

5

M Y VISION was blurry. Who is that? I wondered vaguely. "Oh, David." I smiled. But it was too hard to focus, so I closed my eyes.

David's voice seemed muted. "Darling, my darling, I nearly lost you. I love you—I love you, Nora."

"Our baby . . . Where?"

"You have a little boy, Nora, a healthy little boy."

"Oh—oh—oh—oh—" I couldn't stop the sound, nor the gentle pouring tears of the most complete joy I had ever experienced. Then I whirled into a cone of oblivion.

Standing around my bed were three doctors and a nurse. "Your son is thirty-six hours old, Mrs. Nolan, and you may meet him now. No, no, don't move too much—be still," Dr. Winston cautioned. "You had a rough session—seventy-six hours of it, thanks to that back of yours. This is Dr. Namet and Dr. Person—you kept us all very busy, young lady."

"My baby . . . ?"

"Miss Newell"—he turned to the nurse—"get the young man for Mrs. Nolan—but just for five minutes, Nora—then five minutes for your distraught and eager family." He put another pillow under my head. "Later this brigade will be back to check you over." They left the room.

I eased myself to my side, my eyes riveted on the door.

"Here he is!" Miss Newell laid the baby in my waiting arms and left the room.

An eternity of stillness enveloped us. I took shallow breaths so his sleep would be undisturbed. Imperceptibly my arm drew him closer. He must never be hurt. My hand was raised over him, palm down, fingers taut and spread wide, to protect him from everything, everything wrong forevermore.

He smelled like spring to me, and his hair was gold, curving gold. His eyebrows, fine, tiny wisps of the gold. His nose was perfect, and the soft turn of his mouth made for smiling.

I ran my hand down his arm. Strength—great strength—I told myself.

I counted each of his fingers and each of his toes, then let my head drop back on the pillow.

"Attaboy!" I cried exultantly.

6

THE KITCHEN wall was lightly spattered with the icing that had escaped as, with a flourish, I wrote "Happy First Birthday to James Scott Nolan." Licking my fingers, I stood back to survey my masterpiece.

"David?"

"Here, sweetheart." His answer came from the bar. "Want a Scotch?" he asked, as I joined him.

"Not this minute. Now, listen, David—this party's going to be the best ever given, and if I may say so, the groceries cooked by your actress wife are untoppable!" I bragged happily. "I threw in a couple of neighborhood babies to give the party authenticity." I ran my fingers through my hair. "Do you think our birthday boy will be surprised?"

David shrugged his shoulders. "Are one-year-olds surprised?" he asked. He looked at his glass as he raised it to his lips. "To your celebration," he toasted.

My elation faltered. "Hey you?" I asked. "How much love have you got for me?"

"A world full."

"Then kiss me this minute," I demanded gaily.

He came from behind the bar and drew me toward the couch.

"Steady, Tarzan, I said a kiss. . . . Company's due right now."

He dropped my hand and returned to the bar.

"David? No kiss?"

"You'd take time to wallow with your son, but no time for me," he answered blandly.

"I hate it when you say those things," I said. "It's stupid, dumb, nasty." He stared at me but made no reply. I continued, my voice rising: "Oh, David, it makes me sick to have to explain." I felt myself trembling as I watched him light a cigarette, his face calm. "What do you mean, 'no time for you'? You're always at me, with no thoughts of— well, like *I'm* not there—and—and—" My voice broke, and I rapped my knuckles violently on the bar, furious with my incoherence, furious with my frustrated rage.

I watched David take his fifth shot.

A bell rang.

"Ah, your guests are arriving, baby dear," he said detachedly.

I strode to the front door.

7

THE SET was teeming with dress extras, lighting experts, technicians, carpenters, press agents, and camera crew. I entered the huge sound stage followed by Sally, my hairdresser, and Cora, my wardrobe lady. We headed toward Neville Bentley, the director, whose voice was trying to penetrate the racket.

"All right, goddamnit—quiet!" he screamed.

"Quiet!" echoed his first assistant.

"Quiet!" echoed his second assistant.

"Neville is in a snit," I whispered to Sally.

"You're telling me!"

The voices, hammering, and mass industry slackened, then stopped. Neville's glare covered the entire area of the enormous stage.

"Morning, Nev." I had reached him and smiled demurely.

"Wait a minute, sweetie," he said, then addressed the ceiling at the top of his lungs. "Goddamnit, this is a million-dollar production we're starting—a million goddamn dollars —so don't give me any of that goddamn B-picture crap! When I want silence, I want silence!" For the count of ten he listened to the silence. "All right, goddamnit," he continued, "that's better. Now, go about your business. I want to start shooting at nine on the nose, and no crap."

The voices, hammering, and movement picked up where they had left off.

Neville Bentley turned to me and smiled. "Hi, sweetie. Jeez, that dress is a whiz on you—nothing like white fringe, hey!" His smile froze. "Your hair is darker."

"Darker!" I exclaimed.

"Yes, darker," he glowered.

"Well, Nev, maybe a shade or two; we toned it down. It got awful white-looking on that outside location during the last picture. The sun baked it out." If I had said his entire fortune had been carried away on the back of a barracuda in a tidal wave, he couldn't have looked more horrified.

"What have you done to me?" he wailed. "My God, Nora, I saw you day before yesterday, and now you're a different color, and here are three hundred extras standing around, and we're ready to shoot! What have you done to me?" He was addressing the Almighty, through the dome of Stage 27.

I motioned to the prop man for my chair, seated myself comfortably, then asked the assistant cameraman if I could bum a cigarette.

Neville stopped suddenly and stared at me as though I were a coiled reptile. "Maybe I can shoot something else first. How long—Nora, how long, sweetie, will it take to bleach it up—back—like it was day before yesterday—how long?" he pleaded with clasped hands.

Sally and I looked at each other.

"At least three and a half hours, wouldn't you say, Sally?"

"Oh, at least," Sally agreed contritely.

"Oh, God!" Nev lamented, his body bent double as though

a bullet had just been fired through his stomach. "Oh, God!" he moaned wildly. "Why does everyone do this to me?"

The extras and crew were very quiet now, principally to witness the Bentley histrionics.

"All right, sweetie," he said, his voice subdued with hope-lessness, "go do it. I want you like day before yesterday. I'll shoot something in the corridor till you get back." And in the same breath he screeched, "Quiet, everybody!" Immediately the voices, hammering, and industry resumed.

Sally and I left the set.

Later, in my dressing room, we waited for the breakfast we had ordered from the studio commissary. I had peeled off my white fringed dress and was curled up on the brocade chaise in a pink chiffon robe.

"Life-can-be-bee-you-tee-full!" I sighed.

"Yep, three and a half hours of relaxation." Sally grinned. "Imagine that asshole thinking we're gonna change the color of your hair. Gawd, it took what?—about a half a day of mixing different brews to get it this gorgeous shade!"

"We have all these nice hours of—Quiet!" I screeched the word as Neville had.

We ate our food ravenously, lit cigarettes, and listened to the radio.

A news bulletin describing a tragic mine accident inter-rupted the strains of "We're in the Money." I snapped off the sound, and the gay mood that resulted from conspiring against Nev was suddenly gone.

"Go on, kid, spill. You've had something on your chest for a long, long time." Sally spoke slowly, blowing the smoke from her cigarette toward the ceiling. She waited the long silence before I answered.

"I guess I've got to get a divorce."

"I kinda thought it was something like that."

"I'm sick to death inside myself, Sally. Maybe I should be content to live it through this way. Am I a selfish bitch, do you suppose? Am I unreasonable to want David to show signs of loving our child, planning for him? Should I be satisfied with the remote-control lovemaking I get? Is it awful for me to want to see myself in the movies once in a while? Go dancing? Have friends in? I'm no longer flattered that he never takes his eyes off me—they're blank eyes. Is it because David's had it all before—the living, loving, the promises, the romances, weddings, honeymoons? Does he figure because he's saturated with experience, I am, too? What makes him a nice, kind, stone man? What happened to him? I have no way of knowing. He doesn't talk."

I lit a cigarette and took a deep puff before I continued. "Sad part, Sally—he didn't try to fool me—he's the same as he was in the very beginning. I guess my heart pounded so loud then I didn't hear his silence."

"You better get free, Nora, and live the life. It's short as a son-of-a-bitch and there are beaucoup guys that would give their eyeteeth to—"

"I don't want anybody's eyeteeth, or anybody's anything. What I really want is David—a melted David, an unfrozen David, a David I understand."

The phone rang, and Sally answered it. "Yeah? Okay, Pat, we'll be there soon—her hair is almost dry." She hung up and turned to me. "Quit talking about it now, honey. You're starting a big picture."

Back on the set I stood before Neville. He threw his arms in the air exuberantly. "That's the stuff! Now you look like Nora Marten—don't ever do that to me again! All right—let's go, everybody! Quiet!" he screamed.

"Quiet!" echoed the first assistant.

"Quiet!" echoed the second assistant.

8

HELD the flaming, unopened envelope in my fingers and watched the name of the law firm curl up and disappear before I threw the remains into the fireplace.

There you are, Rosenthat, Bentem, and Bryan. Your proclamation is in ashes, where it belongs, I thought belligerently. I do not have to be told that the year is up and today, officially, I am no longer Mrs. David Nolan. I know it, Lawyermen—and thanks a lump!

I went over to the telephone and dialed.

"Mom? Me. Listen, I've got the jumpin jitters. Do me a favor, huh? Gather your beauteous self together and come over and watch Jamie for me. I want to knock off for the day. Go to Santa Barbara."

"Where's Nurse Haines?"

"Here—Chalmeth, and Clarence, too, but you know I don't trust anybody but us when I'm that far away."

"All right, I'll be over in an hour."

"Gee, thanks, Mom."

"Why're you so nervous?"

"I'm free from David—the news just came."

"Maybe you shouldn't go off alone."

"I'm really all right—just want to stretch a bit."

"Okay, see you in an hour."

With the top down on the car and my hair flying in the wind, I ate up the miles past Malibu to Trancas. It was time to see what Jamie was doing, I decided, so I pulled into a small café on the oceanfront.

After being assured by Cecilia that my two-year-old son was playing and laughing and not collapsed with misery over his mother's absence, I took a corner booth and ordered a martini. Then I searched my purse for the address. There it was: Robert Nolan, 1618 Carson Street, Santa Barbara. David's uncle. His father's brother. It had taken me months to trace him after I had found out my ex-husband had a living relative.

Am I nuts to reopen the wound? Why must I still try to decipher the puzzle that is David? To assure myself that I was justified in leaving him?

I watched the seagulls skim the choppy ocean while I sipped the martini. . . . I wonder where David is today? I closed my eyes, hoping to erase my thoughts and to concentrate on making my spine relax. But it didn't work, and I gave in to total recall of the day I told David I wanted a divorce.

It was a rainy Sunday afternoon, and he had been drinking steadily since morning, and quietly listening to records—operatic, classical, and soft. I had brought Jamie to him several times during the day to show how strong and humor-filled his son was. David had motioned me to be quiet—the better to hear the music. I stayed away then, playing with Jamie in the nursery. Later, still trying to make it a communicative day, I made a fire in the fireplace and concocted my own hors d'oeuvres to tempt David. He thanked me and looked pleased, but didn't touch them. I cooked a complete Italian dinner with biscuit tortoni as a surprise. He complimented me but took only a couple of bites.

After dinner it started to thunder and lightning. "Where are you going?" he asked as I jumped up.

"To see if Jamie is all right."

"Miss Haines is in there."

"I know, David, but sometimes babies get scared."

"Please sit down, dear," he said.

The tension that I had been battling all day gripped me, and I stood stiffly. David came forward, led me to the couch, pushed me down, then quickly stretched out on top of me.

"Please don't—I don't want to—now."

"Why not, baby dear?"

I shoved him aside and jumped up, my face pale with resentment.

"David, listen—for God's sake, listen? I don't want you to touch me like that when there's nothing else—" I covered my mouth with my hands while I struggled to be coherent. "David, it's not lovemaking with us. It's a hollowness—it's—David, we're not close or real."

"Since when?"

"David, I've been telling you in every way I know, but you don't seem to listen."

"Don't you love me?"

"Yes, goddamnit, yes," I flared.

"Not so loud, baby dear," he admonished softly. "Miss Haines—"

"When are you going to *look* at your son?" I interrupted. "Touch him? Love him? When are you really going to look at him—and me, and see us—hear us—feel us—?"

"You're upset, dear."

"You're goddamn right I am. I want to operate like a woman—live—function, now, today! I'm sick of guessing, wondering if, wondering why, wondering when—and don't take another drink!" I cried hoarsely as he started to pour.

I ran to the Victrola and snapped off the sound. I pounded my fists together as I prayed for composure. My voice was more subdued when I said, "David, listen. You're sensitive, you have feeling, understanding, and humor, too. I know it. So why don't you open up and let it be shared. I—let me know something—" My sentence was suspended aimlessly.

"I wasn't aware that you didn't know everything about me." His head was tipped back, and he appeared to be looking down his nose. "We're never apart. I've never cheated on you. You have the child you wanted. We don't quarrel, you know I love you. Therefore, I see no reason for you to be so disturbed.—"

"We're never apart, right, but we're never together, either, and you shouldn't bring cheating into it—that's never entered my mind . . . Yes, I have my baby, but I want us to have *our* baby. Don't you see? I want some shared love between us."

David turned on the Victrola, and over the strains of *Aïda* he said compassionately, "This dismal rain has made you irritable. Relax, dearest."

"Stop it, stop it, stop it!" I exploded. "It's not the rain—it's—it's not . . ." My voice petered out hopelessly.

David poured a drink and handed it to me with a smile. Then he kissed my nose. I seated myself on the couch and sipped the drink slowly, as the recording played through and repeated. David leaned back in the armchair, his eyes closed, an expression of calm on his face.

The chimes of the clock made me realize there had been silence between us for half an hour. I walked to the French doors that looked onto our patio. The fish pond was steaming, and my eyes swept the gardens with a pride that was arrested by the pain through my heart. With my back to him I said: "David, I want a divorce."

Moments passed before he asked, "Since when?"

"Since the abortions." My heart was thumping. I was sure he'd take me in his arms now, finally understanding. But he didn't. He gave me the answer that landed me in the hospital bed in Pasadena: "Whatever you say, baby dear."

Six weeks later I was well enough to sign the papers for the sale of our home on the mountaintop, every stick of furniture with it ("No reminders, I want no reminders"), to give the bulk of the sale to David to clear his debts, to rent a furnished house close to the studio in North Hollywood, and to file for divorce. "Make the charges simple, almost nothing, please, Mr. Rosenthat," I told my lawyer. "I don't want anything to hurt David."

The screaming headlines prolonged my breakdown, so that while I worked at the studio each day, each night was spent at the hospital under surveillance and therapeutic treatment —where the night nurse cut out the articles for me to read:

"NORA MARTEN DIVORCES LENS SPOUSE. CHARGES HE READS THE NEWSPAPER IN FRONT OF COMPANY"

"NOLAN READS WHILE MARTEN BURNS."

"CAMERAMAN FOCUSES ON NEWSPAPER INSTEAD OF HER CURVES!"

"GLAMOUR GIRL CAN'T TAKE IT. HUSBAND READS . . ."

And the Sheely Dawson exclusive:

"NORA MARTEN IS IN HIDING AND CAN'T BE REACHED FOR COMMENT. THE INDUSTRY IS SHOCKED THAT HOLLYWOOD'S HAPPIEST MARRIED COUPLE HAVE DIVORCED. A LITTLE BIRD TELLS ME THAT NORA IS FRUSTRATED WITH GRIEF AND IS HIDING IN A HOSPITAL. A STUDIO PUBLICITY MAN GAVE ME A COPY OF A POEM THAT EXPRESSED NORA'S PHILOSOPHY OF LIFE!

Life is phony with baloney
From the start until it's done
Gold or tatters, neither matters
For the strife of life is fun.

"I DIDN'T KNOW OUR NORA WROTE POETRY. SHE HAS JUST COM-
PLETED *Big Town City* AND KERN BROTHERS ARE ANXIOUS FOR HER
TO START *The Dancing Girl and His Nibs.* FRIENDS OF THE FA-
MOUS COUPLE SAY THERE IS NO THIRD PARTY. ISN'T IT AWFUL?"

I sat there with my martini, reminding myself I shouldn't
get all riled up thinking about that trash, nor that idiotic,
vapid rhyme a Kern press agent must have pulled out of a
Cracker Jack box and credited to me. Then I paid the bill
and went back to the car.

As I turned onto the highway and headed toward Santa
Barbara, my train of thought was unbroken. My funny family
was so understanding and gentle. Not shocked, as I expected.
They seemed to have sensed it all along—particularly Mom.
. . . I sighed and switched on the car radio. The recorded
voice of Jim Wilson was singing "A Rose in Her Hair."

. . . Jim's sure been nice this past year, I told myself. Especially to Jamie—playing with him, and raving to everybody
about what a marvelously brilliant boy he is. . . . And he's
tried hard to keep me cheered, taking me to see my pictures
and his. It was fun the night we danced at the Cocoanut
Grove. People swarmed all over us for autographs. I snorted
as I recalled Sheely's miniature scoop: "A little bird tells me
there's a romance lurking between our Jim Wilson and our
Nora Marten."

Some romance, I thought amusedly, the lady pining away
for her ex-husband. . . . My hands tightened on the wheel.
No matter, the ex-husband is married again, illegally, in Mex-
ico—couldn't wait the year for the final papers. . . . He took
unto himself Bride Number Six. But she's a really pretty
girl . . . and nice. I remember her from the chorus of *The
Parade of Lights.* . . . I hope she can penetrate the fog, I
thought, feeling noble.

The strains of Jim's voice over the radio brought my
thoughts back to him. Once in a while I teased him about

Hollywood's worst-kept secrets: Jim Wilson and Teresa Hernandez; she, the world-famous mistress of Him, the world-famous publisher.

"I'm a nervous wreck over her attention. Christ, who needs it," Jim said. "She's even stalling the picture we're doing so she can see me every day."

"The whole studio is on to that," I told him.

"It's not a laughing matter, Nora. The goddamn old bag's schoolgirl crush might get me de-nutted! Besides, if I'm not pleasant, agreeable, attentive, admiring enough to keep her contented, she will damn well tell Him I've been rude or made a pass—or make up any goddamn lie—and I'll be stuck with the fury of Him for that! This mess could easily ruin my career!"

"Well, anyway, she's still lovely to look at," I consoled him.

"Sure, Nora, she's still sultry and beautiful, but the way she inhales the booze, her looks won't be around much longer."

"I feel sorry for her."

"I feel sorry for me," he said.

I turned up the main street of Santa Barbara and brought the car to a stop in front of the El Encanto Hotel.

I found a telephone booth in the lobby and searched the phone book for R. Nolan. Nervously I dialed the number.

"Hello?" a man answered.

"Mr. Robert Nolan?"

"Speaking."

"You're David Nolan's uncle?"

"I am."

"My name's Nora Marten. I used to be David's wife, and I wondered if I could talk to you, if you're not tied up . . ."

"Of course, Nora Marten, I'd be honored to meet you."

"I'll be right there."

I hung up and wandered around the lobby indecisively before I sought the hotel cocktail lounge. I seated myself on a stool at the end of the empty bar.

"You're Nora Marten!" the bartender jubilated, his index finger an inch from my nose.

I nodded. "Please give me something that will settle a thumping stomach." I smiled.

"You're Nora Marten!" he crowed again. I nodded.

"How about a sherry for what ails you?" he advised excitedly.

"Sounds okay."

He poured me the sherry and leaned over the bar uncomfortably close to my face.

"Don't tell me a movie star's got problems."

I grinned vacuously and picked up the glass. He showered me with questions as I sipped. I pantomimed my answers.

"How does it feel to be a movie star?" Shrug.

"You know Jimmy Cagney?" Nod.

"Humphrey Bogart?" Nod.

"Dick Powell?" Nod.

"Errol Flynn?" Nod.

"Edward G. Robinson?" Nod.

"Frank Sinatra?" Nod.

"Ty Power? Clark Gable?" Nods.

"Jesus Christ!" he said admiringly. I nodded for that, too.

"I wanted to get in show business," he informed me as I finished the last of my drink, "but it's tough."

I agreed.

"So I been at this for fifteen years now."

"That so?"

"Well, what can you do?" he wondered.

I didn't know.

"Say," he continued, "my ole lady won't believe I was talkin' to ya unless you sign this—wanna?"

"Sure."

I struggled to get my signature on the sleazy cocktail napkin, then paid my check and walked hesitatingly toward the parking lot.

What will I ask Mr. Nolan? What do I want to know? I wondered, the pit of my stomach hurting, unaided by the sherry.

9

AFTER THREE hours with Robert Nolan, I had the answers I was seeking, knew that no one stood a chance with David because of his merciless mother and what he had experienced with his first wife. "You least of all, Nora, because he wanted you locked with him in his lonely shell so that the nightmare of his young life would not be repeated."

By the time I left him, I had cried, "Oh, my poor David."

Driving homeward along the ocean front, I recapitulated the story of David's youth: Spinal meningitis at the age of seven. Petrified thereafter of sounds: hiding under the bed from the terror of the train whistle, the tracks a half-mile from their cottage.

"What kind of men am I associated with?" was mother Laurene's favorite chant. "A trembling, ineffectual son, and a silent, ineffectual husband—with me, God help me, an invalid."

"That bitch is an invalid, all right—a chronic one—she wouldn't trade her plight for all the health in the U.S.A.," Robert had told me bitterly.

David's mother fractured her foot at her confirmation; had a broken arm at her high-school graduation; dislocated her collarbone at her wedding; and, finally, broke her hip after the birth of David, her first and only child. Her stream of self-willed complaints was unending: migraine headaches, female disorders, chest pains, biliousness, constipation, chills, indigestion. She ruled from her bed or wheelchair, always safe, always protected from reality—her imaginary illness held to her breast to justify the servitude she demanded from her deeply sensitive husband and her sickly child. "Oh, she fooled all who crossed her path," Robert said, "but not me. I saw the comfort she nursed from her plight—the phony, cloying self-pity! What made her want to hide from the world, shirk all the responsibility of a woman, wife, and mother? I don't know. But she did, and the two men in her life paid dearly for her fortress."

David was her slave. Her demands on the little boy were incessant: "Brush my hair . . . rub Mother's arms . . . Mother's head . . . empty the bedpan . . . get Mother's tea . . . Mother's glasses . . . Mother's pills . . . Mother's hanky." The child was left devoid of normalcy, recreation, or friends.

Except for the demanding whine of Laurene, the three Nolans lived in silence and despondency.

David lived with that unholy atmosphere until he was sixteen, Robert had told me, and then his father died. "I was present. He died in the bed next to his wife. A stark, white-faced youngster held his father in his arms, as his father whispered his first and last advice to his son: 'Be a man—I wasn't. Go—run—there's enough time. . . .' When I told Laurene her husband was dead, she screamed in a torment of self-pity, 'No—no—no—I'm helpless!'"

Robert had taken charge then. He hired a woman who, for

her room and board, waited on Laurene. With part of the small legacy George Nolan had managed to put aside from his job as a piano tuner, David bought a secondhand camera and a mangy donkey and left—taking pictures of children astride the animal for his livelihood.

"I'll send half of what I earn to my mother," David had promised Robert.

"She has enough to live on for a long time, my boy. Just set your own life to rights, and no more emptying bedpans, hear? Get some happiness and love in your own cold little bones," Robert advised him.

David still takes care of her, I thought as I drove on. And in style—nurses around the clock. The money we've spent on that woman during our marriage. . . . And yet the bone specialist we had come all the way from New York said that nature had reinforced her hip to such an extent that she could play football if she wanted to. Boy, was Laurene mad at him. . . . No wonder I couldn't ever get close to her. . . .

It was almost nighttime, and I realized I'd had nothing but coffee and drinks all day. I'll pull up to the next clean-looking place and grab a sandwich, I decided. But one by one I passed the eating places, absorbed in David's past.

"Christina was the name of David's first wife," Robert had said. "He met her soon after he was on the road with his camera and donkey. Because it was near Christmastime, he found a lucrative job taking pictures of the children in an orphanage at Del Mar, California, and Christina was one of the orphans. They fell in love, and he hung around the small town, sleeping on the beach at night, and during the day patiently waiting to talk to her through the fence surrounding the play yard."

Robert couldn't fill in the details for me; he just knew that the girl, aged sixteen, ran off and became Mrs. David Nolan. She was musical, self-taught, so was hired to play the organ background music during the silent movies. David took snapshots of the children as they came out of the theater.

Christina had learned the score of *The Big Parade,* so they toured extensively, following the picture from town to town. They made a good living together and were able in about four years to buy a small cottage on the outskirts of Pasadena. David got a job as a still cameraman at F.B.O. studios, and made enough for them to live comfortably and to enjoy the first homelife either had ever experienced. And David was outgoing and happy for the first time in his life.

When Christina told David that they were going to have a child, he was elated. But not more than a month later he left her.

Robert said she had prevailed upon David to get her work as a bit player at F.B.O., and they had worked on the same picture together. "One day David was taken ill on the set with a raging fever, and the studio doctor insisted he go home. He was confined to his bed for four weeks with pneumonia. At David's request, Joe Bekin, the boss of F.B.O., arranged for Christina to occupy a dressing room at the studio rather than risk the possibility of catching his illness while she was carrying their child. They hired a nurse for David, and because they had no telephone, David and Christina wrote loving notes to each other every day.

"One midnight toward the fifth week of his confinement, David became restless, and as weak as he felt, he waited for the rhythmic snoring of his nurse, then dressed and tiptoed out of the house. The studio was dark; the guard told David the company had stopped shooting at ten P.M., and that everyone had left except his wife. He pointed out the direction of her home-away-from-home and let David through the gate.

"But Christina was not in her room, and David, panicked, started his search. He was about to enlist the guard's help when he saw a dim light in one of the suites on the second floor of the Executive Building. Afraid that something was wrong with his wife, he took the stairs two at a time and threw open the door of the lighted office. At a glance he saw it all. Joe Bekin, bossman, leaped to his feet, but Christina lay on the couch, apparently frozen to the spot. Their clothes were intermingled on the floor."

Robert paused in his story. "So a twenty-one-year-old boy's life was shattered. He quietly closed the door and never laid eyes on Christina or his home again. They divorced, and two years later she married someone else and moved to New York."

"What about the baby?"

"Guess it was a false alarm, or something. Anyway, there was no baby."

I came to the main street of Ventura, and without knowing why, I suddenly turned left and pulled to a stop in front of the Piggly Wiggly market that was now standing in place of Marten's Tearoom.

I'm glad they finally cleared those damn trees away, I thought, then crossed my arms over the wheel, and with my head bowed, let my body shake with sobs.

When I was drained of the tears, I renewed my lipstick and combed my hair, and as I turned on the ignition I looked at the dark market, and in my imagination saw an ecstatic group applauding a newly raised sign.

Speeding toward home, I sang without pause: "Alabamy Bound," "Button Up Your Overcoat," "Bye, Bye, Blackbird," "Just a Memory," "This Is My Lucky Day," "You're the Cream in My Coffee," "Birth of the Blues," "It all Depends on You," "The Best Things in Life Are Free," and "Whispering"—making myself relive, not the actual past, but the gay, laughable, hopeful past of that childlike family of five.

Jim was waiting for me. I ran through the living room yelling, "See ya—gotta hug that Jamie first!"

After I had bathed and dressed, I stood before Jim. I had on a white piqué sheath that made my skin look very dark and my hair very light. "You look pretty doggone pretty," he said.

"I feel pretty doggone clean." I smiled at him.

We called good night to Cecilia and were in Jim's convertible, top down.

"It'll be fun doing that next musical together," I said to him. "I read the script, and it's fairly good. I have two lines I've never spoken in a picture before. Do ya think I can manage 'em?"

He laughed. "But I don't get you in the finale, Cagney does."

"Try not to suffer too much, Jim. After all, you've got me off screen, y'know."

"Really?" he asked seriously, slowing the car down.

I fidgeted for my cigarettes to hide my embarrassment, and asked Jim for his lighter. We both lit cigarettes and rode without speaking for several blocks.

"Nora," he said finally, "let's drive to the beach and park along the ocean—I want to talk a bit."

"You've been reading my mind, Jim."

He crossed over Coldwater Canyon and turned on Sunset toward the coast. I like the way he drives, I thought—very sure of himself. Aloud I said, "I'm going to start my talk now —okay?"

"Shoot."

I gave him a brief account of my day with Robert Nolan. "Why did you do it?" he asked. "Still love David?"

"I had to know why he keeps on marrying, why he's so—not in this world. Why he didn't acknowledge Jamie—a million whys."

"You know now?"

"It's clearer. I'm not a psychiatrist, but I understand better. I'd be the same way—almost—I think. . . ." My voice trailed off.

We were making the turns on Sunset and the fresh salt air was getting closer.

"Who knows?" I went on. "Oh, Jim, who knows what's

right or what's meant to be. Sometimes I think God has got little wires attached to all of us, and no matter what we plan, we're going to move where He wants us to move—and it will turn out *right* because He knows—we don't."

"Are you going to miss David always?" he asked.

"Don't let's talk about it anymore. I don't want to feel depressed—the night is too beautiful."

Jim parked the car on a ledge overlooking the waves. We watched the phosphorescent blue and white lights as the water sloshed onto the sand.

"You think with your heart, little stupid," he said gently, "and you'd better start thinking with your head. It's no good otherwise. Regardless of the wire strings the Big Boss is juggling us around on, you've got to face facts. David was no good for you from my way of thinking—no security there. My God, look at the years you've worked hard, and no money to speak of to show for it. I just couldn't believe you didn't have something put aside that David didn't know about."

"He was my husband—why should I keep anything from him?"

"Never let your right hand know what your left hand is doing."

"Huh?"

"Listen, Nora, you've got to have someone protect you against your foolish, overgenerous self. Someone pick up your studio check for you, budget you. Why, your mother has better clothes than you have—and—your sister! My God, giving her everything in sight, and your brother, opening that goddamn florist shop for him. What the hell does he know about a flower shop?"

"Now, listen, Jim, that was to give him and his family a start. Gosh, if you can't help your own—what's the use of anything?"

"It went bust, didn't it? And cost you a couple of years' work."

"Oh, it wasn't nearly as bad as all that," I answered testily.

"Anyway, Scott didn't ask me, he never has. I just wanted to do it—so it was selfishness on my part."

"Your desire, Miss Marten, should be to provide for yourself and your son and stop biting your nails." He smiled at me.

"I know I'm a lousy businesswoman."

"Well," he allowed, "girls are not supposed to be bright."

"How dare you!" I squinted my eyes at him, trying to keep it gay.

"You hungry?" he asked.

"Starved," I answered.

"Well, then," he decided enthusiastically, "let's get some hot dogs!"

"Drive to the Seal place, Jim, get hot dogs and beer, and let's come right back here to eat 'em. I go for familiar places."

Twenty minutes later we had returned with our midnight picnic, and as we ate Jim lectured me about my attitude toward my family concerning money.

"A clean slate, Nora, is what you must start with; deep respect for every penny you make and save. Anticipate your future security, and understand that your haphazard generosity will get you no affection from the recipients. Your policy should be to supervise your expenditures intently."

What a pretty moon, I thought.

"And always think of yourself first—they'll have more respect for you if you let them scrounge for themselves."

Oh, please, let's not overdo this thing, I groaned inwardly. My bunch will have everything they want, old smarty-pants Wilson, no matter how you drone on. But I was nonetheless flattered that he was concerned about me and about Jamie's future. He's right. I'll have to change something. I'm a mess so far, I admitted to myself.

"You behave like a drunken Santa Claus, Nora. Emotion and sentiment are well and good in their places, but business is business. Don't spend a dime without knowing where it goes, and make sure that what you spend will bring back your investment twofold."

Oh, dear, it doesn't sound like fun at all, Nora, does it? I asked myself.

"Skip your family," Jim continued. "They're big kids now. Think of yourself—nobody else *will*. You hear that? *Nobody else ever will*," he emphasized. "You've got to be respected in this world, be important, and the only way to get into that position is to have a pot full!" He chuckled with satisfaction.

"No, sirree-bub," Jim continued enthusiastically. "They're not going to catch this crooner asleep at the switch!"

I dozed a bit, but Jim wasn't aware of it, for his expounding was increasing as the shades of daylight were invading the sky. Finally my head tipped forward, and giving in to my exhaustion from the long, emotional day, I fell asleep. Jim put his arm around me and drew my head to his shoulder. The silence woke me up.

"What happened?" I asked.

Jim laughed. "I put you to sleep."

"Nope. Honestly, Jim, I heard every word, and you're right. I'm going to say, 'Is this really necessary?' to every penny I spend."

"That's my girl."

He smoothed my hair and hummed a few bars of "By a Waterfall." Then he said, "Nora?"

"Ummm?"

"I had a talk with Jamie while I was waiting for you. I said to him, 'I wish to God I had a son like you, Jamie.' He just grinned and whacked me in the nose a couple of times. 'Cut it out, Jamie!' I said. 'I'm not kidding. Let's figure it out. How can I get a son exactly like you?' Jamie didn't come up with an answer, but I did. 'I know, Jamie,' I said, 'I'll marry your mom—it's as simple as that.'" His eyes were moist as he smiled. "Jamie gave me a bear hug."

His head was leaning on mine now, and he tightened his arm around my shoulder. "How about that?" he asked softly. "Good idea, Nora?"

My throat constricted, and tears flooded my heart as I cried alone to my love. "David, oh, David—he wants your son."

Looking at Jim's handsome face, I smiled and answered huskily, "Good idea, Jim."

10

WE WERE to become Mr. and Mrs. Jim Wilson
aboard the SS *Santa Paula,* the reception just before
sailing.

I was standing alongside the crib gazing down upon the
handsome face of my sleeping son.

Jamie's mouth widened in a smile.

"Jamie, am I doing the right thing? Tell me, Jamie . . .
I'm scared. . . ."

The sleeping boy slept on. "Okay," I whispered, tears rolling down my cheeks, "if you open your eyes—or even one eye
—as I stand here, that'll be a sign. I won't go through with it!"

I watched his relaxed face intently.

"Psst, Nora," Mom whispered from the nursery door, "Sally's waiting out front in her car for you."

I told Sally why I was so nervous. "I'll give it to you quick,
Sally. About a week ago, I was about to go to bed when the

JOAN BLONDELL · 266

phone rang. I answered it, and the voice said, 'If you marry
Jim Wilson, your son will be kidnapped, and you will never
see him again.'"

My hands were shaking as I lit a cigarette. "When I could
think sanely at all, it came to me that I knew that voice—I
knew the impediment in that woman's speech."

"Teresa Hernandez," Sally said, shocked.

"Yes, our beloved Teresa. No mistaking that voice, and
she sounded slurred and drunk. I got Jim to the house within
twenty minutes, and we talked until it was daylight. I wanted
to call the damn wedding off—just call it off, period."

"Son-of-a-bitch," Sally whispered.

"Well, as soon as it was nine, we went to see Dawson, the
D.A. He suggested a trained police dog, a night watchman,
and an alarm system. He set up the whole ugly thing for us. I
swear, if you pick up a coffeecup, bells alert the Beverly Hills
Police Department." I attempted a feeble grin.

"It's as puke-making as anything I ever heard," Sally said.
"But be sensible, Nora. Never, ever, would she do anything
like that. She must have been clobbered to call you herself—
and with that unmistakable lisp of hers. . . ."

As we neared our destination, Sally whispered, "Quit thinking about it, kid. Try to find some happiness. Christ, you need
it, and Jamie will be safe as a bug—I'll join the police dog."

I smiled and nodded, but my heart was pounding miserably.

There were a few seconds of silence, then Sally asked:
"Love him?"

"Who?"

"Good Gawd! Your any-minute-now husband!"

"Sally, Jim's going to be just great for Jamie—and we
will always have security, because he's an intelligent businessman."

"And a slow guy with a buck."

I laughed. "That I know. But it's better than just throwing it
away like—like . . ."

"Can't even say his name, can you?"

"No."

"Well, let's get our asses on that boat. Soon you'll have over two hundred intimates with Big Fancy Names waiting to inhale the reception champagne—not to mention Pathé News Reel, Fox Movietone News, Paramount Sound News, and the 'ever-present-at-all-Hollywood-sporting-events Sheely Dawson.' Come on, baby, you're in it too deep."

The city police and studio bodyguards whisked us through the squealing fans that lined the dock, and into the lavish two-bedroom, living-room, bar, terrace, flowered, champagned, fruit-laden suite Kern Brothers gave Jim and me as a wedding present. Two studio wardrobe women were unpacking the bridal array.

After showering and perfuming I was seated at the dressing table in my lacy lingerie looking into the mirror at Sally brushing my hair.

"Sally, I can't—I can't go through with it. I don't love Jim, really love, and he's too nice to hurt."

"Did you ever tell him you loved him?" Sally asked, still brushing my hair.

"No, never. When he asked me if I did, and my answer stuck in my throat, he said, 'Nora, I love *you* enough for both of us—your honesty is one of the reasons I want you for my wife, and because you're a helluva good actress, a helluva good cook, and boy, oh boy, you're beautiful! What more could a guy ask for?' Will I love him in time, Sally? Does that happen?"

"I can give you wisecracks, pal—no answers." Our eyes met in the mirror, and Sally drawled comically out of the side of her mouth, "Fox Movietone News, Paramount, Pathé—"

I jumped up and grabbed my friend, half-laughing, half-crying. "Bring on the wedding drag—I'm getting married!"

11

O N DECK Jim was checking our baggage while I was dressing to face the newsreel cameras and reporters who were meeting the ship an hour before docking time. We had spent seventeen days on the water. If I had made the trip with Jim *before* the wedding, maybe there never would have been one.

He pushed open the door, slammed it, and stood there, apparently stunned. "The Captain has received word that close to one hundred tugboats are going to surround the *Santa Paula* as we enter the harbor, and airplanes will be overhead trailing banners!"

"Why?" I nervously straightened the seam of my stocking.

"Us."

We silently finished last-minute packing.

"Jim?"

"Ummmm?"

"If those guys—the reporters—are putt-putting out here to interview us, we ought to have coffee, toast, pastries—and for sure, some drinks—to warm them."

"That costs money," Jim grumbled.

"It's freezing out, honey, and they must have gotten up at daybreak. We really should do it." I smiled my Sunday best and won.

When the buffet table was set up by the pleased steward and two waiters, Jim put a coin into the steward's hand. "Split it," he said, and waved them out.

What was it? I wondered. Fifty cents?

"You're an extravagant witch." He smiled, looking at the laden table. Then he put his hands on my shoulders. "I'm sure glad we didn't do it the last few nights—your eyes would look glassy now."

"Glassy?"

"From doing it too much." He gave me a playful but solid whack on the behind.

What did I get into? I wondered.

The food, and particularly the drinks, gratified the frozen ladies and gentlemen of the press. Even so, I sensed a slight boredom with their "Movie Star" assignment, and a tinge of sarcasm in their questions.

"You two thrilled with each other?" was one of their goodies.

Jim smiled broadly and clasped his hands over his head like a fighter acknowledging the crowd. The reporters looked at me.

"Yes, indeedy," I said, feeling like a simpering idiot. What would they write if they knew that our first week of the seventeen-day voyage was spent either in our suite or walking fully clothed around and around the deck?

Jim did not want me in any of my divine, custom-made bathing suits until the bruise on my upper thigh had disappeared completely. (I had bumped into a wrought-iron table while playing with Jamie.)

"People will say I did some weird sex thing to you, and I can't have that," Jim told me.

He wouldn't let me go into the sunlight early "because people will think we don't like doing what newlyweds are supposed to do." He wouldn't let me go into the sunlight late "because people will think we're doing it all the time." So I watched passengers having fun swimming, sunning, and playing games around the sparkling saltwater pool.

After many trite questions, and equally trite answers, we were ushered to the upper deck for the newsreel cameras. The whistles from the tugboats and the whir of the overhead planes deafened us; the banners—"Welcome Nora and Jim," "Our Own Jim and Nora," "Congrats Mr. and Mrs. Wilson" —dotted the Hudson River.

Without superb planning by the New York police we never would have gotten through the seething, cheering crowds. En route to the Waldorf-Astoria, we were amazed to see almost all theater marquees with a personal message—"Happy Days Jim and Nora," "Sing it Mr. Wilson," "Swing it Mrs. Wilson" —and it seemed everyone along the way had rice to toss at us.

The Kern Brothers publicity department accumulated about a dozen sob sisters, movie-magazine style, who were waiting in our flower-filled rooms; an array of food, coffee, liquor accompanied the next barrage of shallow questions, the next volley of flash-bulbs.

When we were asked for a picture of us feeding each other, I grinned and whispered to Jim, "We're so adorable!" He gave me a deadpan look.

I excused myself and grabbed the phone in the bedroom. "Beverly Hills operator, please, station call—CR 3–6010." My palms were wet when the connection was made. "Hi, Mom. How's Jamie?"

After about fifteen minutes of assurances that everybody and everything was all right in California, I reluctantly hung up. I cornered a Kern Brothers representative: "Like a good pal, get rid of the press. We want to rest and bathe and dress for the Twenty-one and Stork Club parties." The gentleman rolled his eyes when I said "rest."

Much later that night I thought: Wow! I had no idea we were so popular—it's frightening! Jim was asleep alongside me. I sniffed the skin on his shoulder and wondered how David was.

On the Super Chief, Hollywood bound, I locked the door to our drawing room and hugged Jim. "Oh, honey, isn't it great? Three days, four nights of quiet—just us. Get into p.j.'s, and I'll get into my nightie, and we'll have dinner in here and recap the crazy—"

He interrupted me. "What will the waiter think if we're practically stripped when he takes our dinner order?"

"He'll steam with envy," I smiled as I removed his coat and tie and ruffled his hair.

The night before we were to arrive home I was close to the end of *Gone With the Wind*. George Brent had given me the novel to take on our honeymoon as a joke. "No joke, dear George, I've read every word."

I climbed out of bed and gently smoothed the wavy hair of my sleeping husband. I found a piece of chewing gum, hopped back into bed, and picked up the book again. But my mind flooded with realities to be faced.

So be it—that's the way Jim is, and I'll adjust, and ours will be a good, contented life. He is just what I thought he was when David introduced us—corn-bally. Unsure of himself, pathetically vain. On top of that, he is surprisingly prudish. He will make love only in the dark, furtively, as though we should sit up afterward and smooth ourselves out so teacher won't know. . . .

I finished *Gone With the Wind*.

12

A MERRY, Marten meeting was called to order, and I recounted all the memorable things that happened on our honeymoon. Jim was at Kern Brothers discussing his upcoming picture.

"The day that Jim and I were to make a personal appearance at the Paramount Theater matinee, we were led through dark, cavernous basements and into a service elevator, and up to the fourth-floor dressing room to wait until we were called onstage to bow and throw kisses to the audience." I paused soberly. "We looked out of the window, and from Forty-fifth Street along Broadway to Times Square—the streets, the sidewalks, the side streets and their sidewalks, were dark with people—a sea of people, all still. All traffic stopped, all faces upturned. Never, as long I live, will I forget that, nor will Jim. Oh, kids, listen. Those people—they said there were over a hundred thousand of them—when we leaned out the window and waved, they gave out this thunderous sound as though one powerful voice was calling its love."

Johnny, Judy, Scott, and Cecilia held one another's hands. "You know, Johnny, I've agreed with you about my parts: the happy-go-lucky chorus girl, saucy secretary, flip reporter, dumb-blond waitress, I'll-stick-by-you broad. I've yearned for deeper, more meaningful roles . . ." I walked to a bowl of roses and touched them. "Well, I've just learned plenty! I've just learned that people my age—younger, older—have made me theirs. Maybe I'm their hope, the joy they're going to have, the happy ending. I've shown them that it can happen to them because it's happened to me. And Jim promising: 'Sweetheart, there must be happiness ahead . . . We're in the Money. . . .' What a grave responsibility actors have. We must all always remember that."

13

L IKE A SUDDEN, terrifying earthquake, a series of
events took place.

Johnny went off on a hunting trip—his first—with some ex-
vaudeville cronies. But when he was face to face with a deer,
he could not fire the gun, so he returned home four days earlier than expected. He walked in on them—Cecilia and a man,
asleep. Johnny beat the man to a pulp. Cecilia tried to take
her life with fumes from the car. Johnny pulled her out and
fought to keep her alive until help came.

Kern Brothers and the D.A.'s office, in order to squelch the
whole story, were in on the horrifying mess.

Mom recovered, and Johnny moved to the Regent Hotel.

Jim asked Cecilia to give up her home and move in with
us. It was not a humanitarian request: it was to save money.
Our new house was very large, and there was a suite of four
lovely rooms for Jamie and the governess. Cecilia was to take
the governess' place.

Cecilia sold their house, and I sent my sister to New York, where she studied art, played summer stock, radio, then Broadway. She had blossomed into a beautiful girl and had streams of beaux to share New York's excitement with. We exchanged letters and phone calls, and I was happy that Judy was free to gobble up all the youthful joy that life had to offer —before she bumped into adulthood.

Then came a development for me. My name was no longer to be mentioned in print, in publicity or advertising, in any of the gigantic chain of His newspapers. I walked back and forth in our sitting room. "Jim, my God, do you know what that means? How many newspapers across the U.S.A. my name's off—out of? What did Teresa tell Him about me? We know it was Teresa. . . . What, Jim—what?"

Jim poured himself a double rye and belted it down. "I'm sick, Nora, but what can we do—we're at the mercy of power, tremendous power. Sure it was Teresa—her gal pals warned me I'd better not marry you."

"They did?" I was shocked.

"I laughed it off," he said.

"But *you're* not out of the papers, Jim."

"That would be too obvious, Nora. Ole Teresa's too smart for that."

I sat on the couch. "Fix yourself another drink, and one for me."

We were silent until we had both sipped awhile.

"Jim, okay—we can't dwell on this miserable, contemptible trick. I'll—we'll be okay. . . ."

"Goddamn son-of-a-bitching bastard—just when your career is really zooming!" Jim's voice was tense and low.

I jumped up and whacked my palms together. "Cut it out, honey. Let's zoom into dinner."

It was that night I told Jim the story of what happened to another girl who was after him—told him to cheer both of us up.

I had gone to the studio to watch Jim do his solo in a musical that Busby Berkeley was shooting.

Jim was getting his makeup fixed. Buz was cramped behind the camera on a crane at the top of Stage Seven, about two stories up. He was photographing three tiny newborn birds in a nest. Then the camera pulled away and descended to the stage, where about five hundred girls were swimming in a pond, near water splashing from cliffs. The girls formed beautiful patterns as they mouthed the words of "By a Waterfall." Their voices, already recorded, came at them over loudspeakers. Buz hollered over the sound as he counted out the tempo for them. Then the camera rose and once again focused on the tiny birds in their nest as the music soared to the grand finale.

When the scene was over and Buz was down on the set again, he walked toward me. "See that chorus girl over there —the redhead?" he asked.

"Yep—she's gorgeous."

"Well, yesterday she asked me if I could put in a good word for her to Jim. She's mad for him. 'Sure, sweetie, I'll see what I can do,' I told her. Then I walked over to Jim while she was watching and started talking. I told him I wanted him to have more shading on his face for his solo. We talked about the next scene, and then I went back to La Belle Redhead. I told her it was O.K. with Jim, provided I try her out first."

Buz grinned devilishly. "Needless to say, Nora baby, I'm pooped today."

Jim laughed and said, "That's how he gets most of his girls."

14

I WAS SITTING on the patio looking at my children playing in the distance. Six-year-old Jamie, bent over his tricycle, pursed his lips, making a loud motor sound as he raced around the tennis court. Three-year-old Mary, galloping on a stick with a horse's head, gleefully returned the kiss I threw. God, she was beautiful, as beautiful as Jamie.

"That precious daughter of ours—she's inherited your fabulous skin," I told Mom the day Mary was born. "And she has a special kind of nose. It's just like David's."

"How did David get into the act?" Cecilia laughed.

Mom was in my hospital room when the huge box of flowers was delivered. The card said just "David." The box was filled with forget-me-nots. Mom dried my tears and fluffed my hair so I could look pretty for Jim's visit.

He was delighted with his daughter.

Mom came through the French doors onto the patio. That

touch of white in her hair enhances her beauty, I thought. "Lunchtime, Mom?"

"Yes," Cecilia answered. "I'm going to have Kubu serve the children in their quarters so I can shove them right into bed for an hour. We're going to an early Mickey Mouse movie."

"Hey, little ones," I addressed the children, "next week we're going to be guests of Mr. Disney. He'll show us how and where 'The Three Little Pigs' were born—and maybe Daddy can go with us."

Fat chance, I thought, as they went into the house with their grandmother. He never finds time to be with the children. He's always fuming about his career, his looks, everything! "Is my hair getting thin on top, Nora?" "Is this the best way to part it?" "Is the line okay from both angles?" "It costs too much to run this house." "When are you going to stop spoiling your family?" "I'm not going to sing anymore, I'm going to do straight roles. It's an awful effort for me to sing, I hate it!" "I'm going to sell this house. It's too expensive to run!" "Should I wear this suit to Zanuck's party?—or this?—or this?" "Do you think I'm getting a double chin?" "Goddamnit, food is expensive. In Mountain Lane, Mother fed four on five dollars a week!" "I'm going to trade in our cars. It's cheaper in the long run." "I see where your David Nolan has taken unto himself his seventh wife. All the wives got alimony except you, and all the furniture you turned over to him, the wives have got, not you. And no child support!" "I've got to change agents, the son-of-a-bitch does nothing for his percent!" "We've got to sell this house." "The Bennys spend money like water. That party must have cost them a piss pot. Next time we throw one I'm going to pick the booze myself. After a couple, no one knows the difference anyway." "Did you see the ring Taylor gave Stanwyck? Hell, I hate to think what it costs." "Do I wave my arms too much when I sing?" "What should I wear Saturday night?" "That dress was beautiful on you, but it costs too much." "I've got to call T. L. —I hate the script!" "Hear about the presents Kate Hepburn gave the crew when she finished her picture? She's nuts. Raft, Joan Bennett, Bette, Robinson, Bogie, all of 'em do the same thing. They're all nuts!" "How much was your mother's coat?" "And don't send my folks things, Nora. They're just simple, plain people. They've got a roof over their heads and enough to eat. What more does anyone want?" "Damned Jews run this business! Damned niggers get some fancy salaries now!" "Quite a wedding present you gave your pal Sal. What's she going to do with embroidered sheets, for Christ's sake?" "It's good you're making more money at Kern Brothers, we need it! The years you wasted for so little dough!" "I wish my eyes would photograph a little darker." "Should I get my teeth capped?" "The goddamned government is killing us with taxes!"

I went upstairs to give my children a naptime kiss. Why have I continuously got a depressed gut, I wondered.

Our third house in four years was sold, as always, for a profit. Jim chose another—that, too, in Beverly Hills, and I set about making a home again.

We made another trip to New York, this time to do publicity for our latest pictures.

We went to see a musical. The audience cheered and applauded when we entered, and when the curtain came down the manager led us backstage to meet the cast. We were swamped with enthusiasm.

A young dancer pushed his way through the crowd and addressed me. "I hope you won't mind, Mrs. Wilson, but a friend of mine will die if she doesn't meet your husband."

"We can't have that," I said. "Here he is, where is she?"

The crowd around them was silent now.

"There." He pointed to a girl sitting on the top step of a steep staircase that led to the second-floor dressing rooms.

Everyone looked up at her. I waved and called, "Hey, come on down. Jim can't shake hands with you that far away."

Slowly, like a shy little girl, she descended, and slowly, pigeon-toed, she walked to Jim and stood looking up at him, her hands clasped under her chin as though in prayer. Except for someone whispering, "Oh, brother," in back of me the whole gang of chorus kids were silent witnesses.

"Jim Wilson, with all my heart I worship you, and I sleep with your letters under my pillow, and your pictures are everywhere I look in my little, lonely room." She turned to me. "Forgive me," she whispered.

"Help yourself," I answered, and the company laughed.

Still gazing at Jim, her neck stretched upward, her eyes squinted and shining, she continued: "Always remember my name. Amy O'Brien, Amy O'Brien. Oh, please, please don't forget me."

We were used to goggly fans, but this performance was downright embarrassing. Jim shuffled uncomfortably and broke the spell. "Come on, Nora sweetheart, we're due to join the others." We signed numerous autographs and left.

In the limousine I said, "Holy smoke, that was a creepy kook, that Amy O'Brien!"

"With a voice to match," Jim said.

15

WAS ATTEMPTING to read a recently delivered script, but it was not the proper time. It's so damn silly and delightful the way Mom and Dad have dates now, I kept thinking. He takes her out to dine, then they wind up playing cards or just laughing and talking in the lobby of the Regent.

The Regent lobby was Johnny's living room, for it was the gathering place of ex-vaudevillians, ex-pugilists, ex-everything in show business.

The same old gags, bits, stories, and schticks were updated and kept alive in that lobby. Somebody was always "on," and with an appreciative full house. Cash was given, borrowed, paid back, or absconded with.

Johnny was happiest when he was helping people—and that hotel was full of people who needed help. They called him Johnny-on-the-Spot, because every dime that I insisted he take he shared with the theatrical people who were down on their luck; and those who had children were foremost. He was forever "shelling out," using for himself only enough to get by. His suits were shiny, but some child had new clothes.

Like a gay cavalier Johnny would return Mom to our house after their dates and then go back to his room at the Regent. It was a strange arrangement, but it seemed to work for both of them.

I was dancing with Jim at an elegant soiree given by Claudette Colbert. "My God," he said, "the cost of this jazzed-up tent is a fortune!"

I answered Ty Power's smile over Jim's shoulder. I wondered what it would be like making love with him.

"The flowers alone must be a couple thousand bucks," Jim groused in my ear.

Clark Gable cut in on us and held me so closely I couldn't breathe. I loved it.

The music stopped.

"Jim's over there talking to Sonia," I said with difficulty. As we neared, Jim was saying, "This could set her back a year's salary."

Sonia twirled Clark back onto the dance floor.

Later that night, when Jim had finished his lovemaking, I stretched and thought about Clark, Jim, Henry, Charles, Errol, Ty, Oleg, Bruce, Pasquale, John, George, and Frank. . . .

Steady, girl, I told myself. No cheating. Nothing's secret or sacred in this town, and I have children I must think of. Besides, poor Jim, it would be so insulting—even if he never found out.

I jumped out of bed and headed for the nursery. After I had touched and covered the children, I went into the kitchen for a glass of milk. I sat there, thinking almost detachedly about Jim's pattern for making love:

A. Stand alongside wife's bed and say "Hellooo"—a little lilt on the end of it.

B. Make wife put aside the book she's reading.

C. With no further hullabaloo, jump into bed.

D. As fast as humanly possible, get the damn thing inside wife.

E. Even before she can get her mind off the novel and on the business at hand, cry, "Wow—Wow—Come—Now—Oh-my-God!"

F. Jump up, reshower, regargle, recomb hair, rearrange pajama collar to stand up, hop in own bed, and continue studying the income-tax reports.

Cut.

Print.

I laughed aloud. Who'd believe it?

16

JIM'S AND my long-term contracts with Kern Brothers expired at approximately the same time. I asked Jim to take over the negotiations for a renewal.

"I'll make a stab at the big money, choice of pictures, cast approval, director approval, the whole Big Star shebang," he told me, then added, "I actually hope they don't buy it, we'll be better off free-lancing." Kern Brothers didn't buy it, so we left.

His next plan was to sell our Brentwood home, my favorite. "We'll build a small house at Balboa, cut down expenses, and commute," he decided.

"Build a tepee, for God's sake, Jim, and I'll gussy it up, and we'll live cheaply forevermore. Damnit to hell, this is the sixth divine home I've made perfect for us—I'm sick to death of moving!"

"It's one way to make money, Nora sweetie." He smiled.

So we built the small beach house, and I have to admit I loved it best of all. So did the children and Cecilia.

While it was being built, we made separate pictures, but both at Twentieth-Century Fox.

One work day Jim called me. "My company's slowed up, and we'll break for lunch later than usual. Come over to Stage Ten and we'll go to the commissary together."

I had finished for the day, so I headed for Jim's set.

"Hey, Nora" someone called. "Hi, Faye." I waved to the voice coach. Faye caught up with me. "How's the picture, kid?"

"Who knows until it's in front of an audience?"

"Say, Nora." Faye hesitated. "Let's sit on this bench a minute."

"Anything wrong?" I asked.

Faye lit a cigarette and exhaled swiftly. "Nora, the name Amy O'Brien ring a bell?"

"Nope—let's see—no. Why?"

"I guess I'm a shit to tell you, but hell, I'd want someone to do the same for me."

"What, Faye?"

"Amy O'Brien is a new contractee here from a New York City musical. I've been coaching her for months, so I know her pretty damn well."

"And . . . ?"

She spoke rapidly. "She's after your old man, but I mean *after*. She's beaded down, and she's gonna leave no lil stone unturned. I've watched her operate. I've listened to her phone work, her set work, her commissary work, the whole *megillah*. This dear little starlet is a nose-to-the-grindstone hustler. No more'n she was signed up, she got the lay of executive-land and laid it. Now she's started to work on Jim. She's got a small role in his picture, but she's on-the-spot every minute. I tell you, she's a dangerous, determined tomato."

"Jim's too wise not to see through that. He's always had fans drooling over him."

"Take my word. This one's no fan, she's got an overall plan up her ass."

"Amy O'Brien," I repeated. "Come to think of it, the name does sound familiar."

"Well, watch out for her, or she'll be *very* familiar."

I stood up. "Thanks, Faye."

"Should I feel like a shit?"

"No, I'd do the same for you, or any friend."

"Just keep your orbs open."

We parted, and I continued to Stage Ten.

Amy O'Brien, Amy O'Brien, I said to myself as I walked toward the lights of the scene they were rehearsing.

Jim was standing in front of the camera mee-moo-mauing while the makeup man banged powder on his nose.

"All right, everybody, we shoot," called the director.

It was a long dolly shot. As Jim sang, the camera pulled back, and I saw someone who looked like a little child with a pink babushka tied under her chin perched on the camera stand below the lens. Her hands were clasped prayerfully as she gazed with worship at Jim.

In all my years in pictures, through all the years of Berkeley shots, I never saw anyone sit *there* before, I thought. I turned to a member of the crew standing next to me.

"Who's that sitting on the camera, Bill?"

"Amy O'Brien." He paused. "A pain in the butt."

After the take Jim called to me, "One still, and I'll be right with you, sweetheart." Then added: "Everyone knows my beautiful wife; beautiful wife, this is Amy O'Brien."

Halfway through my "How-do-ya-do," Amy clapped both hands over her mouth as if terrified, and ran off the stage.

"What was that bit with Amy O'Brien?" I asked after we had ordered our lunch.

"She's some kind of a nut," Jim answered, saluting Joe Schenck as he passed our table.

"Hey, Jim—who calls you 'James'?" I asked.

"What?" He looked up from his dinner plate startled.

"We've gotten a dozen or more phone calls here in the last couple of months. The voice is always the same, and so is the conversation—or lack of it. 'James?' *it* says hopefully even when *I* answer. 'James who?' I generally ask. An 'Ooooh' or 'Oh-oh,' or 'Sorry,' is hastily muttered, then *it* hangs up."

"I have no idea," Jim answered, tackling his salad. "A crank or a fan."

"But you're 'Jim,' not 'James'—world-famous Jim—and we have a very unlisted phone number."

"I don't know," he snapped.

We ate our dessert in silence.

Those calls from Amy O'Brien are designed to affect no one but me—just bitchiness, I thought, stabbing the apple pie. Suddenly I giggled, remembering the afternoon I went to see a picture with O'Brien in the cast to find out if the voice came from her.

I bought my ticket and walked down the aisle. In front of me, on the screen, stood Amy, her hair in two braids that stuck out from her head, with bows on the ends of them. She was engulfed in the top of a pair of men's pajamas, her knees knocked together, her toes pigeoned. Handsome Van Johnson unlocked his apartment door and entered. Amy waved the long pajama sleeves happily. Van, startled, asked, "What are you doing here, and what have you got on?"

"Jammeees!" Amy answered, tipping her head to the side.

I never even got to a seat. I just groaned, "Oh, no," did an about-turn, and walked out of the theater.

Now I looked at Jim, intent on his pie. "I feel sorry for James, whoever he is." With an exaggerated hip roll I slunk out of the dining room.

"Hey," Jim called, "what's with you?"

But Amy was soon forgotten in my rush to finish my present picture, do two at R.K.O., then make the final move from our Brentwood house to our Balboa home.

My happiest hours were spent on the weekends there with

the children, decorating, planning to make our new home the prettiest and most livable one on the bay. "No more moving, ever," I warned Jim.

We had our own private beach on the waterfront, and a fleet of small boats was moored at our private U-shaped pier: a sailing dinghy, a canoe, a putt-putt, and a sixty-seven-foot Chris-Craft.

I looked through the bay window at Jim polishing the brass on the big boat, Jamie and Mary helping him. A fried-chicken picnic was packed.

"We're off now, Mom," I called to Cecilia. "We'll be gone for several hours. See if you can get Johnny to drive down and stay for a few days. The weather is gorgeous enough to spread on bread."

We chugged through the glass-clear water. Boy, our collie, sitting on his own director's chair, scanned the horizon. Jim, in his captain's cap, was humming as he steered the boat across the bay. I looked at my happy, tanned children and thought how lucky we were.

Two men were waving frantically at us from another Chris-Craft.

"Bogie and Spence," Jim said, maneuvering toward them. When we drew closer, we could hear the radio. Our friends' faces were tense and white.

"The Japs have just bombed Pearl Harbor," Spence called hoarsely.

"War Effort" became the key phrase, and all our lives changed. Johnny would stand watch for long hours during the night at a mountain outpost overlooking the Pacific. The coastline was dotted with hundreds of these watchtowers, manned by volunteers too old to fight.

Judy flew back from New York and devoted all her days to working for the Armed Forces Radio. Scott gave full time to lighting military training films, Cecilia studied first aid at night school, Jim entertained at the Hollywood Stage Door

Canteen, and I covered the country on a Bond Tour, along with every top star in Hollywood.

When I returned I volunteered to entertain on a two-month tour of the isolated bases in the North Atlantic: Newfoundland, Iceland, and Greenland. I turned down a picture at R.K.O. to rehearse a singing, dancing, and comedy act for the tour. I would make no movies for the time being.

It was while I was touring the North Atlantic that Jim wrote me he'd sold our beach house. "Couldn't get what I wanted for our Brentwood place, so I had to get rid of the other."

I was shocked and sickened.

17

HAD JUST finished my fifth show of the day in Gander, Newfoundland, when General Benson sent for me. "Nora, a call just came through. Your dad is ill—very. My plane will take you to Port-aux-Basques, and from there we'll get you whatever priorities are humanly possible. Somehow, we'll get you there."

The plane was ready for me in forty-five minutes, and we took off.

Over and over on the flight I repeated the general's words: "Your dad is ill—very." How ill? If only I could make a phone call home, but the War Department would not permit calls from a military base, and now there was no time.

They found room for me in baggage cars, trains, and cargo planes that were jammed to capacity with soldiers. I rode four trains and seven planes in two and a half days. And all I did that whole time was repeat over and over the Lord's Prayer.

When I reached Los Angeles, I was told my beloved dad was dead.

Judy, Scott, and Mom were waiting for me at my house. Together we had to choose a final home for the man who had never had one. We wanted it on a hill close to the sky, because he loved the sky, but it had to be a special hill. Johnny had thought California too quiet—he had missed the noise of the cities he had toured. Well, he'd have noise now. We found him a hill near the railroad tracks: we could hear the train whistles as he was buried.

Jim found the church and took care of the other funeral arrangements.

We sat in a private room shielded by sheer curtains. We were touched but not surprised by the number of Hollywood stars who came. And we expected to have the Regent Hotel empty out for Johnny, as it did. But what nobody could expect or even explain was how vaudevillians from all over the country showed up. Down-and-outers, headliners, ex-performers—elderly, middle-aged, young—were there. Midgets, pugilists, old men and women who had been dancing boys and girls on the bill with Johnny were there. With wartime making travel almost impossible, they came: by car, bus, train, plane, and by thumb.

They heard not funeral music, but the songs of their day in vaudeville. The songs we Martens had sung together as we crossed the country. Scott chose them: "At Sundown," "Long, Long Trail," "My Indiana Home," "Swanee," "The Sheik of Araby," "Always," "Moonlight and Roses."

Mom said, "The goodness of Johnny will never die—he has left so much love behind."

And each vaudevillian placed a rose on Johnny's coffin and murmured, "Hail, Trouper."

A week after the funeral I drove Scott, Judy, and Mom to the desert and stopped the car in a desolate area. We all got out and walked, silent, through the thick sand and sparse sagebrush.

I asked, "How did it happen?" We kept on walking until Scott could speak.

"Johnny had made arrangements with the public-relations office at San Diego's Camp Pendleton to do his monologue for the badly wounded soldiers who had been shipped in. The P.R. soldier, a kid named Hank, drove Dad there. Dad stood in the aisle of the huge hospital ward, surrounded by the bedridden boys, and started. He did his act, his pantomime —props, red wig, and all.

"Hank said that at first the soldiers were listless and un-interested, but"—Scott stopped to blow his nose—"but in no time they were listening, then smiling, then trying to sit up, then laughing, then applauding."

He could say no more. We were all drenched in tears.

Our car was a dot in the distance. As though with a spurt of strength, Scott started us back toward it.

"Hank told me," he continued, "that on the drive home Dad was very quiet. After they'd gone several miles, Johnny said, 'Did you see the lights blink just now, son? . . . Well, that means onstage.'

"That was all," Scott said. "He just closed his eyes and was gone."

18

JIM HAD an extremely bad year professionally, while my career was booming. I couldn't have that, I knew. A husband must feel more important.

So, without Jim's knowledge, I turned down several offers, among them a five-picture deal at M-G-M.

"Jim walks around the garden with his hands in his pockets and his head down. That isn't right," I said to Judy.

"Is it because of money?" Judy asked.

"Heck, no, he's quadrupled every penny he's ever made. It's, you know, a man's pride."

Finally Jim got a picture, a small budget, but one that proved a sleeper. It established him as a legitimate actor, instead of the frothy-musical star he loathed.

Somewhere along the line Jim became acquainted with Jeff Flynn, the hottest young producer on Broadway.

"He has four smash hits running in New York right now,"

Jim told me. "He came out here to see if you and I would costar in his new one—music by Cole Porter."

"What did you tell him?"

"No, of course. I want to stick with my new image. Paramount has come up with a hell of a script for me."

We went out to the tennis court to play. When we finished, we sat in the kitchen with Cokes.

I watched him writing figures on a pad.

Jim's a stranger to me most of the time, I thought, as a wave of excruciating aloneness swept over me. He was not affected by Johnny's death. He did not even love the beach house.

I was staring at him when he lifted his eyes.

"How about you working for Flynn?" he asked me. "He told me he's dying to get you. You love the stage—he said if he got you, six months, big pay, would do it."

I gave him an insipid smile. Boy, are you a stranger, I thought again.

I went to New York to do a Flynn show.

The overcrowded office smelled of tobacco, steam heat, body heat, bay rum, and scented soap. My nostrils stretched for fresh air.

A muscular young man was tipped back in a leather swivel chair behind the huge desk, his body covered to his chin with a sheet. A lighted cigar was sticking out of his mouth, surrounded by white, foamy lather, and billows of smoke were choking a barber who was trying valiantly to shave him, while a pretty, white-uniformed girl held his bare foot aloft to give it a massage.

On the wall behind the man hung an oil painting of a life-size near-nude. I recognized the subject as a famous burlesque queen, the author of the play I was about to do.

Then the subject of the painting turned from the window and nodded, almost imperceptibly, toward me. A tall and cadaverous man stepped forward, and in a voice tinged with sarcasm introduced himself. "George Kaufman, Miss Marten, director of the play, if you'll pardon the expression." He bowed solemnly, sighed, and comically used his handkerchief to wipe away mock tears. "You know, of course, our author, Miss Dawn Lyte," he said to me.

"Hey, that's a helluva way to make a dame feel welcome!" the half-beautified man said, ripping the sheet from around his neck.

The manicurist's water bowl was knocked over, and the barber was pressed against the wall as the Wonder Boy of Broadway extracted himself from behind the desk, slid his feet into his shoes, crossed the room, and rapidly pumped my hand. "Pleased-a-meetcha-I'm-Jeff-Flynn. Hey-you-got-a-man-haven't-ya? Wassa-idea-the-low-cut-dress?"

His hand was small, hot, and damp, and when he released mine, I wiped it discreetly along the folds of my silk skirt.

A puff of cigar smoke in my face kept me silent as he addressed the beauticians: "Get that crap outta here."

Mopping the remaining lather from his face, he threw the towel at the barber. He took a wad of bills from his pocket, peeled off several without looking at them, and shoved them in the manicurist's hand.

"Split that, and get outta here, toot sweet. I got big business."

He turned to me, and his eyes were penetrating. "Now, let's make with the meet. How's yer ole man? Great guy."

I assumed he meant Jim, although he suddenly strode over to Miss Lyte and puffed his cigar at her as he finished the question. Miss Lyte turned away from him and looked out the window.

His darting eyes found mine again. "We'll talk it over at chow. St. Regis you're staying, ain't it? You pick the saloon we go to. Seven-thirty's post time."

He rolled his cigar around in his mouth as he continued to no one in particular, ushering me out of his office. "Say goodbye to the lady, you rude bastards, and let's go, ma'am."

He led me swiftly to the elevator. While we waited, he stood uncomfortably close. "What did you say yer name is, miss?" he murmured, his cigar working up and down in his mouth.

I flushed and was annoyed with myself because of it.

"Deposit my star safely on the ground floor," he ordered the elevator boy.

As the door was closing, Jeff Flynn's eyes were on my breasts. "See ya!" he said to them.

Back in my suite at the hotel, I called Jim immediately. "Honey? . . . The Wonder Boy is a prime jerk. He's also the double-talk king. I didn't get to say a word to the director about the revised script or anything. Flynn rattled on and on. He reminds me of a conceited toad and . . ."

Jim laughed. "I told you he's quite a character. Damon Runyon writes about him. . . ."

"That's Damon Runyon's problem."

"Don't get upset, sweetheart. You just arrived. Flynn gets things done, believe me. He's the sharpest producer that's shown up since Ziegfeld. Please don't worry."

I paused before I asked, "How are my two ones?"

"Great. Playing in the yard."

"I'll call them at bedtime."

"Okay."

"Jim? I'm husbandsick, babysick, homesick. I'm coming back. Who needs a play?"

"Now, listen, Nora sweetheart, you just got there today. Give it a whirl. You may love doing the show for a while."

"One week," I said.

"Okay." He laughed. "One week. Cheer up now, sweetheart, you just got there."

"The Great Flynn wants me to go to dinner to talk it over."

"Go."

"I will not. He wears purple suits, and I won't be seen with him."

"Honey, this call's adding up."

"Jim, I miss you."

"I miss you."

"Do you, Jim?"

"Why do you ask that, sweetheart?"

"I dunno. I'm homesick."

"Be a good girl, and I'll call you tonight with the children."

"Bye, Jim."

"Bye, sweetheart."

I hung up and walked over to the mirror. My dress is not too low-cut, I thought.

"We'll knock off for a two-hour dinner break, then rehearse until midnight. I'll give you your plane tickets and instructions before we dismiss later. Okay?" We were opening the next night in Boston.

The stage manager bowed toward us tired actors gathered on the dim theater stage, and we slowly dispersed.

I stopped to brush my hair in the full-length mirror in my dressing room. Reflected in the mirror with me was Jeff Flynn.

"Don't be such a stubborn dame. Lemme take you to dinner. I won't bite—what you afraid of? Hell, I'm the producer. I got some rights."

I smiled. Sometimes he looked so young and nice. "Come on, then, feed me. I'm so hungry I'm liable to bite you."

He took me to Toots Shor's restaurant, and I felt the place come alive as he entered—as did rehearsals or the front of the theater, or the street, or wherever he appeared.

We were ushered to "The Booth" by the captain and several waiters. Flynn called and waved greetings to people at the surrounding tables, drawing all eyes toward us as we were being seated. The obvious bid for attention annoyed me.

"You're an awful show-off," I said.

"Look what I've got to show off," he whispered too closely into my ear.

Toots Shor was looking down at us.

"How come a two-bit bum like you gets to pick up the tab for a lady?" he asked Flynn with a smirk.

"Jes for that you get the tab, and the lady wants champagne," Flynn tossed in answer.

"Great guy," Flynn muttered when Shor had left us. "A soft schmuck—buys drinks for all the drunks. Wish I had the clams that guy owes me to keep this saloon open. I'd buy solid gold moonbeams to hang around your neck."

"I want a martini," I said, fussing with my napkin.

I tossed restlessly through the night, unhappy away from all I loved, and unaccountably uneasy about Flynn. He was in and out of rehearsals, moving fast, catching my eyes and holding them until I, embarrassed, would look away, wondering what the others thought of his marked attention.

In the days that followed, there was not much time to be concerned about anything but the show. Except for my personal notices, the play was pummeled by the Boston critics.

Unperturbed, Flynn went into action. He saw that Miss Lyte had quarts of milk for her ulcers, and the best typewriter money could buy for her rewrite job. He personally took over the direction of the new scenes, which seemed to please the uninterested Mr. Newman. "I find great joy in wandering the sunny streets and playing poker," Newman told me with a wise, old look I couldn't fathom.

Flynn wined and dined the critics who had blasted his show; charmed them into a million dollars' worth of columns and editorials. They all but retracted their sour reviews as the two weeks moved on to "standing room only" for the now well-publicized play.

"I jes put the words in their mouths. They write what I tell 'em!" Flynn bragged so gleefully I had to laugh.

Nevertheless, I felt dissatisfied and discouraged that the play itself was so weak, and I was tired of rehearsing the reams of revised dialogue Miss Lyte was continuously grinding out, tired of going onstage night after night struggling to remember new lines in place of old. The experience was nerve-wracking, and I regretted mightily that I'd left Hollywood—in more ways than one.

But Flynn was alongside me all the time, cheering me on like a football coach. "You're wonderful, Nora—what guts. You're the greatest there is. You're a stand-up dame, if I ever saw one. The going's rough, but we'll lick it because—well, you're a stand-up dame." His eyes would glisten as he searched my face.

I felt flattered and at a loss.

He kept my hotel suite and my theater dressing room banked with flowers. He gave me a delicate, imported music box; a tiny, feathered bird popped out of the cloisonné lid and chirped a love tune. It was an antique from Cartier with his note enclosed: "You're wonderful. Jeff."

He alerted the Ritz-Carlton staff to tend to my every need. He brought me exquisite lace handkerchiefs, seductive perfumes, an elegant makeup case with my name in gold in his handwriting.

During my nightly calls to Jim I'd tell him about the gifts. "I don't feel right about accepting them, but he just won't listen when I ask him not to give them."

"He got a crush on you?"

"I guess so."

After a slight pause Jim said, "I told you he spends money like water."

"That he does."

"Well hell, honey, you might as well get in on it," he said pleasantly.

"Oh, Jim—damn!"

"What's the matter?"

"Nothing."

"What?"

"Nothing, I said—*nothing!*"

"Be a good little girl, and I'll talk to you soon."

I hung up with a bang. Damn it, he could get a whisker burned. How trusting can you get? I threw a pillow against the window and went to bed.

19

ON THE TRAIN to Pittsburgh for another two-week tryout, Flynn asked me if we could dine in my drawing room. He wanted to talk.

"Yes," I answered. "I've finished studying, and I'd like to talk, too."

As always, things happened fast when he came into view. He had the porter rushing for ice and glasses, the steward taking his order for smoked salmon, olive oil, capers, lemon, coarse pepper, and black bread to have with the Scotch he brought in with him.

"Now, beat it. I'll call when we want dinner. Save your best steaks, cool your best Champagne." He pushed the man into the corridor with five-dollar bills.

I looked out the window as he poured the drinks.

"You're quiet," he said. "Quieter than usual, ain't ya? Here, take a swig of this, and gimme your shoes, and relax." He

bent down and took off my shoes as he said it. Then he took
off his own shoes, tie, and jacket.

I laughed. "Making yourself at home?"

He gave me a quizzical look.

"You're a smart gent, Jeff; why do you always say 'ain't'
and things like that?"

"I only went to one-B."

"Oh, stop. You're very bright; brilliant, some people say."

"What do you say?"

"You're a camp." I grinned.

He looked startled. "Wha dat, a fag?"

I took a swallow of my drink. "No, for Pete's sake, it's just
a word to describe a—a sort of a—well, kind of a dishy person
—off the beaten track. It's okay to be a camp, you know—it's
something special."

"Am I something special?"

"You're a camp," I said.

The hors d'oeuvres arrived, and Jeff grabbed the tray
away from the waiter, tossed him another bill, and said he
would ring for him later.

We drank in a silence that made me uneasy. Looking out
the window at the passing lights, I felt his eyes on me. I half
can't stand him, and I'm half-pleased that I never seem to
be out of his thoughts. It's weird and unnerving, I told myself.

He whispered into the silence, "You ever cheat?"

"No," I snapped at him.

"Jes asked," he said sheepishly.

"You?"

"On my girl or my wife?"

I laughed. "Jim told me something about you."

"Yeah? Tell me."

"Well—he said you've been married for years, but didn't
work at it. He said people assumed Dawn Lyte was your girl,
but you said you were just pals."

"Correct. We've never had to-do."

"Who's your girl?"

"Had one for nine years. It's been over for three. Saw her on the street a couple of years ago and—eeeek!" He waved his hands in horror. "I can't imagine me being with her."

He had emphasized the "me."

"Your wife—didn't she mind, about you having someone else?"

"She leads her own life."

"Oh. Pretty country," I said, peering at the passing outline of hills, black against the pale night sky.

"You ever cheated?" he asked again.

"Oh, stop."

The drinks had warmed me, so I added, "A guy got me as far as his bedroom once. He must have been counting on me, because he had the bed covers turned down and a gardenia on the pillow. Unfortunately for him, the cellophane wrapper was still on the gardenia. It struck me so funny I ran from the room laughing, and there's nothing as unsexy as laughing at the wrong time!" I giggled. "Saved by a gardenia wrapper!"

"If it hadn't been for that, you would have?" he asked seriously.

"No. I was acting, overacting, I should say. The guy was nice and flattering, and Jim and I had a problem. . . ."

"What kind—sex?"

"Oh, I don't know—don't ask me. Jim . . ." I paused. "He just seems—anyway, I love Jim. I'm not a cheater. Fix me a drink and shut up."

"You're an exciting dame."

"Shut up."

"You excite me."

Keep it light, I thought. The great Flynn's got a twitch for me, and I'm getting rattled.

We had the best dinner I had ever eaten on a train, served as he demanded it. Then he talked until midnight telling me about his youth. I listened, only half-believing the crazy experiences he related.

He touched my hair tenderly as he left, and I tossed the rest of the night, still feeling the touch.

Unclad Millie opened in Pittsburgh, as in Boston, to full houses and bad reviews. Dawn Lyte typed page after page of new plot and dialogue; the director napped as the cast rehearsed the rewrites, and Flynn again bewitched the fourth estate into reams of gay publicity that kept the SRO sign up.

During one matinee intermission I was called to the backstage phone. "Miss Marten?"

I recognized Flynn's voice immediately. He continued. "Miss Nora Marten—the Box Office Tornado?"

"Oh, stop." I laughed. "What do you want?"

"I gotta surprise for ya. Come out to the front of the theater, manager's office, third floor, toot sweet."

"Mind if I do the second act?"

"No, it ain't that toot sweet, but right after, hurry."

"Okay."

"Bye now." He hung up.

He was pacing back and forth, puffing on a cigar. "Nora Marten, ma'am, the powers that be—such as Strelton, Deans, Newman, and the Wonder Boy here—agree that it's Marten draggin' in the people, not the stinkin' show, or even the publicity. So we're gonna give you a dividend. Money's no good to you, tax-wise, so we're gonna have you pick up the goddamnedest mink coat at Bergdorf's. It's got mink on top of mink—ten thou—a beaut. You deserve it."

He squashed out his cigar and lit a fresh one.

"Now, don't say nothin'," he commanded when I started to speak. "I got it all mapped out. We're makin' a conference call to yer Jim. He'll see it's wiser than a dough bonus. You pleased?"

"Yes." I smiled happily. "Oh, yes, I'd love a new mink coat."

He gave me a quick grin as he picked up the phone and

told his secretary to get Jim Wilson. He puffed on his cigar, blinked his eyes, then told me to get on the extension.

"But," he said, "do yourself a favor and don't talk till I tell ya."

I picked up the extension and leaned back in my chair.

"I can't figure you out," I said.

"Don't." He blinked again.

"Hello?" I heard Jim's voice.

"How's the boy? Flynn, Jeff Flynn."

"Hi there, Jeff. Good to hear from you."

"Say, yer little bride is packin' 'em in, and it's no thanks to the turkey. It's just her."

"That's my girl!"

"Yeah. Well, here's the deal. We want to give her a bonus, me and Newman and them what's got a piece of the show. Money's no good, follow me?—tax-wise."

"I get you."

"So we're gonna have her pick up a mink coat at Bergdorf's—ten thousand clams' worth—how about that?"

"Jeez, great," Jim said enthusiastically. "Absolutely great —she'll love that."

"Yeah, jes wanted to get your nod."

"Marvelous idea. Nora there? . . . Let me talk to her."

"Toot sweet." Jeff covered the mouthpiece of his phone and signaled to me to speak.

"Isn't it dreamy, sweetheart, a new mink coat—I can hardly wa—"

Jim interrupted me, his voice lowered confidently. "Don't let on if he's looking, but, Nora—for God's sake—a mink coat! Make 'em give you a diamond ring or a down payment on some property—a mink coat is perishable."

My temper flared. "I want it."

"Okay, okay," Jim answered, "but it's not very practical."

"I want it."

"Okay—I'm due on the set, talk to you later."

I hung up. Then Flynn did. I took a cigarette out of my

case and lit it myself, although Flynn held a lighted match for me.

Jeff finally spoke. "S'matter? Didn't you know he'd say that? I did—I'd a laid twelve to two—"

"Oh, shut up. Jim thinks differently, that's all. And he's probably right, but . . ."

"Hell, you're a beautiful dame, and beautiful things were made for beautiful dames—who else? Anyways, you got it if you want it. Jes go get it, soon's we hit New York. Ask for Mrs. Gwenivere, second floor, fur saloon."

I laughed. "I want it. And it's very doggone nice of you and your backers—"

"I back myself," he said; "they jes got pieces."

"Well, it's very nice of the pieces. I'm excited, and can't wait to get it on."

"Want some dinner?"

"No thanks, I'm going to the hotel and rest before the night show."

He opened the office door. "Well, go on. Think I got nothin' to do but waste time with dames?"

I smiled at him. "Will you give my sincerest thanks to all of them?"

"Beat it." He grinned.

20

I TALKED to home each night, but despite all the assurances that everybody was fine, I had a foreboding thump in my heart that something was amiss. Jim? He was hard to reach by phone now. "Just left the house." "Just left the studio." "Just left . . ." So when Flynn led me to a quiet booth in an exclusive restaurant on the outskirts of Pittsburgh after the show, I was strangely prepared for what he told me.

"Nora, I got some bad news—don't know how to say it."

"Say it."

"It's about Jim." He paused. "Your mother called me today. She was pretty worked up and had trouble telling what's eatin' her."

"Go on," I demanded nervously.

"Seems Jim's been among the missing too much since you left California—acting strange when he's around the house." He paused again. "This ain't pleasant—can you take it?"

"Go on, I said."

"Your mother thinks he's got some babe. He's out most of the night. He goes out after everyone's in bed, lets the brake off the car and coasts down the driveway. He parks the car down the street and climbs over the brick wall when he gets back before dawn, and tiptoes into the house. Yer ma sees him from the nursery window, and she's sick about it. Afraid for you and the children. . . ."

Jeff's voice faded as I recalled how Faye, the voice coach, had warned me about Amy O'Brien. But Jim wouldn't go for a thing like that—too cutesy, too phony.

Jeff had been talking through my thoughts. Only now did I hear what he was saying.

". . . so I suggest you have 'em followed. I know the guys to do it. You'll have proof of the monkey business in case he wants the children when you get a divorce."

"Divorce?" I felt nauseated.

And I remained nauseated—and sleepless and frightened —during the frantic opening in New York. When the type-written detailed reports of Jim's rendezvous in Amy O'Brien's Wilshire Boulevard apartment started coming in I was too sick to read them. I left that to Jeff. The "detectives" even furnished a recording of what the lovers said to each other.

My face became set. When I went onstage each night, I felt that I carried a heavy trunk on each shoulder.

But I pretended an indifferent "So what? Good riddance! We weren't happy, anyway" attitude; and more and more I met Jeff after the show and made the rounds of the smart clubs. I smiled too broadly, laughed too loud, and remained sleepless through the nights.

Flynn was devotion itself, and I made no effort to discourage it. He telephoned me constantly when we were not together. Then called again when we'd hung up, then called still again. I wondered how he attended to his work, or where his wife was. He watched me from the back of the theater while I was on the stage; from the front seat, the boxes, the aisles. He was in my dressing room every intermission, waiting for me after the show.

Sundays we'd drive to Atlantic City. It was off-season, so we had the boardwalk and restaurants to ourselves. We'd stroll for hours, or ride in the wicker carts as he hummed an unrecognizable tune.

"What is it you're always humming?"

"It's called 'I Love You.' It hasn't been written yet. I'll pick my spot and have some great guy write it someday, and it will be to you," he said lightly.

"Let's close the joint," he'd say when we danced, and we did close it. Currency would fly as he demanded the orchestra remain for us alone. Over and over again he'd request "People Will Say We're in Love" and "All the Things You Are" —and sing them off-key, looking into my eyes. He danced crazily, and I gave in to his craziness. The heat from his body made my body damp. I let myself move along through the days, whirl through them, unable to face the accounting, and using Jeff's adoration as a balm.

21

SITTING in a booth at Chambord near closing time, I drank my third martini, then stared at Jeff while I chewed the olive.

"Wassa matter, Platter Eyes?"

"Holy smoke, they called me that in school."

"I been reading your mail, beautiful."

He looked fuzzy to me. "Jeff"—I took a deep breath to clear my thoughts—"Jeff, we're giving the gossip columns a field day. You know, 'What blond Movie Star (now appearing on Broadway) who is married to what Singing Movie Star, is hiding out in all the hideout hiding places with what married Wonder Boy of Broadway?'"

I giggled meaninglessly, took my mirror out of my bag, and looked at myself.

"You care?" he asked.

"Oh, I dunno. It's not hurting Jim, that's for sure. But what about your wife? Is she getting hurt? I'm cast as the Other Woman, y'know, and I don't like it—don't like it at all."

There was no answer from him.

"I'm getting mulled," I admitted. "But, how come she isn't around? How come I don't hear from her? How come she's not burned up with you missing all the time? How come I've never met her?"

"She's always traveling. She doesn't care."

"I care."

"About me?" he asked.

"About my life being wobbly." My voice rose perceptibly. "I'm sick . . . I ache . . . I dunno how to feel, what to do—and you're messing me up. You're making it easy for me not to think."

He looked at me quietly.

I closed my eyes before I continued. "Jim said something to me once when we had a silly battle over nothing and I told him to leave. He packed one small case, put on his sweatshirt and sailing cap, then stood at the front door and said, 'If you ever get a divorce, I'll get married to somebody else, and she'll be much less than you—and I don't want to end my life like that.' And he choked up, which is unusual for him. And boy, did I choke up, and grab him and throw his cap in the living room, and hug him! I hugged him and he hugged me, and it was over—the silliness—and we were a unit again."

Jeff took my hand in his.

I could feel a crying jag coming on. "Listen, Jeff, I've got to go home."

"I know it, you wonderful dame, and you can go. I'll close the goddamn show—there's plenty more where that came from. I want you happy."

"It's been twelve weeks away from my babies, and I can't take it any longer."

"When you wanna go—tonight?" He was serious.

"Oh, Jeff, no. That's not right to you or the others. Two weeks—okay?"

"You gotta deal."

"You'll be losing a lot, closing the show."

"Screw money—I want you happy."

The following Saturday night, Jeff picked me up at the stage door. And with the top down on his convertible we drove along the Hudson.

We had almost reached Dobbs Ferry before he said softly, "Nora, my darling, I have a surprise for you." He drew my hand to his mouth and kissed it. "Your babies will be here tomorrow."

"What? Oh, Jeff, how do you know?" I grabbed him and shook him.

"Take it easy." He laughed, pulling the car to the side of the road. "How do I know? I'm the guy what done it. I fast-talked Jim, told him you were dying by inches without the kids, and I'd pay for 'em to cross country like royalty. The payin' part's what got his nod. . . . Hey, cut it out, beautiful," he exclaimed as I started to cry.

"Will I have to stay in the show much longer?" I asked into my handkerchief.

"Not if you don't wanna. The notice is up, and you'll have the kids and your ma to go home with."

"It isn't that I don't want to stay. It's—"

"I know. Straighten out your life with the Glamour Boy."

"You're a good man, Jeff. You're kind, like my dad was."

He drove on to a pub in Tarrytown. We sat in a booth, and I talked excitedly.

"The trip will be a great change for Cecilia—and my two ones will love it. And wait till you see them. Jamie was *born* a gentleman and a diplomat, and what a crazy, dry humor for a little guy. I'm sure he'll be president of something important someday—maybe the U.S.A. And my Mary. Oh, the beauty of her, and the independence. There's nothing she can't do. That dream-looking little thing is a nonconformist, if I ever saw one. She's really going to be somebody great and special in this world, wait and see!"

I put my head on Jeff's shoulder. "I'm so grateful and happy."

"Terrific to love your kids like that. My wife wants nothin' to do with kids. Jeez Christ, she's a raging bitch about everything."

"Why don't you separate? It would be better for both of you."

"Who's got that much money?"

"She's holding out for money?"

"Yep, and maybe even that won't do it. She likes the setup, as long as the old man's in the chips. Likes being The Mrs. Jeff Flynn. Big doors open to her, and she's got all the jewels, clothes, furs around, and some left over for company. She travels first-class."

"I'll bet she's lonely."

"My ass. She's got it made as far as she's concerned. And her time's her own, no questions asked—goes her merry way. We ain't got no home life, never did have. It's all battles and turmoil, so I keep outta sight and do the best I can."

I sighed.

"Don't pity me," he warned. "And let's quit and get outta here."

When we returned to New York, we parked the car on Sixty-first Street and walked to Park Avenue. He took my hand and turned abruptly into a building, pulling me along with him.

"Where're we going?"

"My joint. Don't ya wanna see how the other half lives?"

I didn't answer. The elevator took us to the penthouse.

As soon as we entered, I could see that the apartment had been done by a decorator—a bad decorator. Modern, unhomey. Mentally, I redid it immediately: books, the fireplace, deep chairs, flowers, brass. . . .

He sat me on a couch covered in a material that set my teeth on edge, and kneeling down, took off my shoes and slowly rubbed my feet and ankles.

Oh, God! I thought, my heart accelerating uncomfortably.

He got Champagne and glasses and put them on the terrace, then took my hand and led me outside. I looked at the star-studded sky and at the warm lights in the city's windows. Suddenly a great loneliness overcame me, a yearning for a love not yet satisfied.

I seated myself opposite him as he poured the Champagne. We sipped the wine silently, his eyes on me.

"Where is your wife?" I asked. My throat was gritty. I had to clear it.

"We're alone."

I looked down at my hands, clasped tightly in my lap.

He came around the table and stood in back of my chair. He was still for a moment. Then I felt his hands through my hair, and he grabbed it roughly as he pulled me to my feet.

You hurt me, I thought vaguely as he tore at my clothes. His mouth was on mine, opening it, chewing on my lips, drawing the life out of them as he lowered me to the floor.

Afterward, he led me into the bedroom, and with hot towels wrung dry bathed the soot of the terrace from my body. Then he made love to me again, whispering his words of passion, until once again we were drained and quiet. Then he moved his mouth softly along my bare shoulder, along my arm, and sank it into the palm of my hand.

The eerie daylight poured over our nakedness. Again and again we made love until the hot sun covered us.

"I love you, Nora, I love you. I want to be married to you, my Nora. You're mine."

I looked into his large, gray-gold eyes, the lashes thick and black, looked at the slim nose with the hard, distended nostrils. My fingers touched the blue-black hair over his forehead, wet and curly from our night-long lovemaking.

"We're drenched," he said, his mouth on mine.

"Uh huh." I smiled, and he kissed the center of my throat, my ears, held me so tightly I could hardly breathe. Then he leaped to his feet and went into the bathroom.

I heard the shower and his voice above it. "I love you . . . da-da-da-la-la . . ." over and over again. He returned with a towel wrapped around his middle and a damp washcloth in his hand. I did not look at his too-small mouth, his too-small hands. I saw only his tight olive skin, his exciting eyes, as he gently sponged my body.

"Don't move," he said. "I'll fix us some groceries."

"I'll take a shower."

"All right, but get back in bed till I call ya."

"What time is it?" I asked.

"We've got plenty of time. Your kids don't arrive until three-twenty."

Alone in the bedroom, I wondered how I could face the children. Would they know what I had done? Could they sense? Would they forgive me if they ever knew? I put the pillow over my head.

"I've been crazy—I'll make it up to you, my babies," I said aloud. But I felt too whole to plead guilty with honesty.

I jumped out of bed and showered, then spoke into the bathroom mirror. "Nora, you're bad. Your eyes shine, your face is flushed—and brother, what curves you've got!"

He scrambled eggs, onions, and lox together, toasted bagels, and brewed coffee. And we devoured all of it.

"This is a kind of a Jewish breakfast, isn't it?" I asked him.

"Kind of?" He widened his eyes as he chomped on a bagel.

I laughed. "Are you Jewish?"

"Only on my mother's and father's side."

I laughed again. "How come the Irish name?"

"I liked it, and I took it. My real name is Jacob Ginsberg."

"Oh."

"No like?" He stopped chomping and stared at me defiantly.

"I didn't say—"

"I know," he interrupted, resuming the chewing, "some of your best friends are Jews."

"That's true. Only—only I wasn't going to say that at all. . . . You're strange." I looked away uncomfortably.

"I was only teasin' ya. Anyways, people take me for an Eyetalian. Hey, beautiful, come here," he demanded, going around the table to me. He cradled my face in his hands; then his lips were on mine, demanding again.

"No, Jeff."

I really meant it. I wanted to be fresh, keep myself scrubbed to meet my children. It would help rid me of the remorse that was growing in me.

We made love again.

22

EN ROUTE to California two weeks later, I was standing in our drawing room on the Twentieth Century Limited. The children were asleep: Jamie in the upper berth, a special request from his huge, green eyes; beautiful Mary in the lower on the left. And Cecilia was gently snoring in the adjoining compartment.

"My God, I look sick," I whispered into the mirror I held in my trembling hands. "Look at those blue marks under my eyes. It's because I'm frightened—frightened to death. This is the end of something, and I'm afraid. What have I done to Jim? And what have I done to myself?"

Slowly I undressed, put on my nightgown, turned off the light, and crept into the bed opposite my children.

My body hurt as though it had been run over. My mouth was parched, and a chill shook me.

Jeff had seen us off, his arms loaded with presents. He

lifted the children in the air and kissed them and ordered them to take care of their mom. He kissed Cecilia and twirled her around.

"Keep your eye on her for me," he said with a note of demand in his voice.

He tipped all the porters in sight, loudly directing them to give continuous service, to be certain that Miss Marten and family had everything they wanted. That accomplished, he grabbed me and pulled me to the rear platform and pressed his body against mine. He kissed my eyes, nose, mouth, hands, then suddenly straightened his shoulders and was still, just looking at me.

"The train's going to start, Jeff. Get off."

"I love you, Nora, I want to marry you."

"The train's moving!"

It *was* moving, and the porter was warning him.

He jumped off and walked along, faster and faster, until he was running, his eyes never off mine.

When he was out of sight, I had felt relief, as though it were the finish of a movie I had made, and now I could go home. But then I saw his cigar lying on the floor, and picked it up. I put it to my nose, inhaling the aroma as I slowly walked toward the drawing room. "Smells like Johnny." I smiled, but felt like crying.

Telegrams greeted me at each stop. "I love you," they cried in one form or another. At Albuquerque, personally delivered by a colorful Indian chief, were toys for the children, Navaho rugs, hammered silver jewelry for Mom and me. The delivery of a pound of Beluga caviar held the train up ten minutes. Iced Champagne was brought in by the delighted steward.

My secretary was at the train to meet us as we pulled into Pasadena. He relayed Jim's message: "Working and will see you at the house this evening."

While we were waiting for our luggage to be loaded into the car, the station loudspeaker paged me. My heart was pounding as I picked up the phone. "What shall I say to Jim?

How shall I act? Hurt? Mad? Cold? Sarcastic? Indifferent? How?"

My panic was momentary, because it was Jeff's voice. "Where've ya been all my life, huh? You been hiding? When am I gonna see ya?"

When I got into the car and started toward home, I thought of the call with amusement and decided, you're dull, Jim, wow—you're dull. I pity the Peter Pan-collared prize you've won. She ain't gonna have no surprises!

But the amusement was short-lived. The scenery was getting familiar, and I felt ill again.

Home finally, I hugged, kissed, and petted Boy, our collie, greeted the help, put playclothes on the children, then walked slowly through each room, touching the furniture, the plants, the paintings. I was in the bedroom when I called Cecilia: "Mom!"

She came to me. "What is it? What's wrong?"

"Mom, my arms are dead, they won't move."

"They're like ice!" Cecilia cried, rubbing them. "I'm going to call Dr. Ralston."

"No, maybe if I just lie down awhile . . ."

But Cecilia did call the doctor, and he was sitting beside my bed when the door opened so suddenly I jumped.

"Jim!"

"Hi," he said; then, "Hi, Doc, what's wrong?"

"You've got a sick girl on your hands, Jim."

Jim went over to the bed and looked down at me. "What's wrong with you?" he asked.

"Don't know." I tried to smile. "How are you, Jim?"

He went into his dressing room without answering me.

"Nora, I'll leave you now. That shot should make you sleep. I'll drop by in the morning," I heard Dr. Ralston say over the pounding in my ears.

After he left, I kept my fast-fogging eyes on Jim's dressing-room door. When he came out he had changed to his jeans and T-shirt. He didn't come close to the bed this time, but stood in the center of the room looking down at his wristwatch, winding it as he asked nonchalantly, "How's the mink coat?"

I turned my face toward the pillow, not answering. I felt weighted down, and sank helplessly into unconsciousness.

When I awakened the next day, Dr. Ralston was sitting by my bed and Cecilia was standing next to him.

"Where's Jim?" I mumbled.

"At work, honey; he hopes to get home early."

"My eyes are funny—what time is it?"

"Afternoon of the day after—you slept long," the doctor said.

"A day and night and day away." I tried to smile, and wondered why I was so tired—as though I hadn't slept at all.

"Where are my two ones?" I directed the question toward Cecilia.

"Playing—horses at the moment," she said.

I closed my eyes and slept again.

Later that night I was sitting in an armchair close to the fireplace in our bedroom, talking to Cecilia.

"Oh, Mom, I feel so strange—like I've had a long sickness."

"Nora, you shouldn't be up. Please get back in bed," Cecilia begged.

"What's wrong with me, Mom?"

"A—well, a nervous breakdown they call it." She turned her head away.

"Stop crying now; please don't cry. I'm as strong as a bull, and you know it. Just a few days . . ." I tried to comfort my mother.

Cecilia finally answered. "Jim will be home soon, honey. He just phoned. Chalmer will serve dinner to both of you here, but you mustn't use up energy. Dr. Ralston said you are not to get upset—not to talk."

"I'm okay, Mom. Just let me kiss my two ones before they pack in for the night."

But before Jim reached home, I was in bed again. I tried desperately to think clearly, but my thoughts were like dreams: drifting, disunited, inconsistent.

Don't let us lose our home, our life. . . . It's a nightmare, see? See it Jim? You cheat! You made me a cheat. I don't give a good goddamn—you're a dead fish. The only joy you feel is when you touch money! I've got a guy, and you would die of envy if you knew how we feel. . . .

Get in bed with me, Jim, just get in without taking a shower and combing your hair and brushing your teeth and gargling and spitting and putting perfume on your privates. . . . You cold-assed Don Juan, you—made—us—have—no—home—and —I—did—too. I'm—sorry. . . . Say—you're—sorry. I—hate—you—for—not—trying—

Jim was shaking me as I opened my eyes and wildly grabbed his arms to pull him toward me. He extricated himself and stood stiffly as he said, "You're making a racket—what's up?"

"I want a divorce, now, quick," I said, and closed my eyes again.

23

CECILIA was, as always, a giant in a crisis. For fourteen weeks she ran interference for me. She kept the studios, agents, friends, even family from knowing how desperately ill I was.

She pretended gaiety as she turned down pictures for me. "She's vacationing, and deserves it—flying all over Europe, and won't be back for several months."

And she kept from my sight the newspaper headlines that squealed "HOLLYWOOD'S HAPPIEST MARRIED COUPLE SPLIT" and the gossip columnists' endless second-guessing for public consumption.

I lay in a darkened room.

"My eyes jump, and I see all blurry," I told Mom.

"Dr. Ralston, I'm afraid to brush my hair. It falls out in buckets—look! Will it ever grow back?"

"Yes, Nora, yes."

"Will I ever stop stuttering?"

"Yes, Nora, yes."

Sometimes I cried with pain at sounds, so Cecilia kept it soundless around me. The weight of the bedclothing hurt my body, so Cecilia devised ways of suspending the covers over me. And she cooked delicacies to tempt me into eating.

Whatever energy I had I used when the children came into the room—listening to them, kissing their hands, nodding, smiling, then I'd sink back into the loneliness of confusion.

Mom was hounded by Jeff, who gave her a number to call collect in New York three times a day. When she didn't call, a messenger would come to the house with a note from him, which he had ordered written by someone in California, demanding that she call immediately.

"What's she doin'? How's she feel? She's got to get outta there. Did she get the bracelet? The flowers? The earrings? Did you tell her to get the hell up? When will that jerk get outta the house and leave her alone so I can get to her, that phony bastard! Tell her if she gets up, I'll meet her somewheres—anywheres. Tell her if she won't get up, I'll come there anyways and get her up. . . ."

Cecilia tried to inject a word of explanation, but it was no use.

"Call me back in five minutes with answers. Bye now," he'd say, and hang up.

"Sally says Jim makes the rounds every night—Mocambo, Chasen's, Ciro's, Romanoff's—a loner with a long face and a busted head for the newspapers. He declaims to the nearest ears that I've destroyed his life, his home—and how would they feel if a New York producer gave their wife a mink coat that costs a fortune?"

"I know," Cecilia answered. "It's been in all the columns about his despair."

"I'm filled with shame for him—he knows what I know. Mom, it's our battle. Why should he talk it out to everyone but me?" It was difficult to breathe. "I'm tired, Mom, tired of pretending."

Cecilia straightened the bedcovers. "Stop talking, Nora, please rest."

"He's always whistling, hammering, slamming doors or vocalizing at the top of his lungs—living on here until the money settlement, living here, yet never speaking to me."

"Stop talking, Nora."

"I don't stutter quite as much, do I, Mom?"

"No, thank God."

"And my eyes are better."

"Yes, thank God."

I turned onto my stomach, put the pillow over my head, and started sobbing.

"Don't, Nora, don't," Cecilia said.

But I couldn't stop crying, and I couldn't stop talking. "I want Jim to be kind and warm. That's what I want, Mom. It doesn't matter about the little crumb who's after him. I heard their voices on the detectives' recording, and she's so corny—pleading with him to marry her, guide her career. It's like a cheesy, B-picture. And he just 'now-nowed' her. . . . Doesn't he know about his Amy? Everybody else does. Her reputation is in the public domain. She's a tramp dressed like a little kid. She was a call girl in New York—exhibitions her specialty. Flynn, and even a New York doctor, told me they knew some of the guys she 'entertained.' She's using Jim—can't he see? It would be a giant step for her to get the Star Husband of a Star. . . . You know something crazy? I can't get myself to mention her to Jim. He thinks I don't know about her. And he doesn't mention Jeff—does he know? . . . We're both silent —we should *talk*. Mom, help me."

Cecilia got a cold cloth, turned me around, and pressed it to my eyes. She gave me a pill the doctor had prescribed, then sat by the bed humming a lullaby until I cried myself to sleep.

Later that night I got up, bathed, fixed my hair as best I could, put on lipstick carefully, then waited for Jim. When I heard him coming up the stairs, I prayed for the right words.

"Jim, I must talk to you," I said as he entered.

"What about?"

The stuttering started again. "P-p-please, Jim. Don't let's go through with this—no divorce, Jim."

"Make up your mind what you want," he snapped.

"I want—I want—"

"For Christ's sake," he interrupted, "you ask for a divorce, disrupt my life, uproot everything I built up, and now you whine!"

"Jim, stop it!" I rose and screamed at him, "Don't be such a —a liar—a phony!"

"A liar, a phony, she says! What the hell are you?"

That was as close as we had ever come to the heart of the matter. We stared at each other momentarily, then Jim stalked into his dressing room.

I sat in the armchair and listened as he whistled a medley of the tunes he had made famous. I heard him in the shower, changing his clothes, still whistling—that continuous, determined, feelingless whistling.

When he was finally dressed, he walked past me and muttered, "Guild meeting."

I pulled myself out of the chair and said firmly. "Jim, stop. I don't want a divorce. I want to stay here, home—with you. I just want kindness and warmth from you; then we—"

"Kindness? Warmth? Jesus, what are you talking about? I'm the best husband you'll ever get!"

I interrupted him. "Jim, listen—"

"Warmth?" he topped me. "You've had everything you wanted, haven't you? Take a look in that garage; it's wartime remember?" His voice rose, "Anybody else got fifty pounds of coffee? Another thing"—his voice was at a wild pitch—"another thing," he repeated, pointing his finger in my face, "plenty of people are talking about you and Flynn, but it's not true—*it—is—not—true*—because I, Jim Wilson, did not marry a bum! You hear that?" he yelled. "I, Jim Wilson, did not marry a bum!"

He slammed the door shut and was gone.

I was sitting up in bed, my lawyer standing by the window. He had been talking to me for over an hour about the division of property and finances. By law, everything we had should be divided between us, but Jim wanted every cent that had been spent on me, my family, and friends deducted from my share. And he had kept records over all these years.

The lawyer was urging me to use the proof I had against Amy O'Brien to get what was coming to me.

But all I could think of was one item the lawyer had told me: Jim wanted back the one thousand dollars he had given David and me when Jamie was born. "Happy Hospital"—hah!

"I'll sign it, whatever it is—let's get it over with. I can't stand the sight of him around the house any longer," I said.

"Are you sure, Nora? We can fight."

"No fights. I'll sign the thing."

24

JIM MOVED to a rented house in Beverly Hills, and my family made a concentrated effort to get me on my feet again, but it was Jeff who forced the change.

Ten, twelve, sometimes twenty times a day he talked to me from New York.

"How come I never hear from ya?" he would say, calling me back a minute after he had hung up.

One day, with even more than his customary elation, he told me of his plan.

"Got an idea, baby. Since I'm stuck with rehearsals for *Up in the Bowery,* why don't you get that round, beautiful ass outta that bed and do *Anything for You* in Chicago? I'll pay you more'n I do Townsend, and that's more'n the mint's got. You'll be great in it."

"Wait, Jeff—"

"And you only hafta play it a little while—little as you want,

six weeks, four, two. I can just see you in it. Those beautiful
—Oh, God, when I think of 'em, you know what happens to
me! C'mon, now. Leave Monday. I'll meet ya in Chicago.
We'll get lost for a few days—then you can start rehearsals."

"Jeff, I can't."

"Do you know how long it's been since we got lost? Jeez
Christ, think I'm made outta stone?"

"Jeff—"

"The tickets will be at the house Monday, and don't bring
any clothes. I wanna buy you new ones. Anyways, who needs
clothes wit what I got in mind."

"I can't."

"Never say 'can't'—it's all set. You open in three weeks."

"I'm still weak, Jeff; I can't work."

"I'll make you strong, sweetheart, it's all set."

"The children—"

"They'll be safe with your mother for the little you'll be
gone. You only hafta play it two weeks if you wanna—give
you my word."

"I can't sing very well—not like—"

"Who needs singing?"

"Stop it, Jeff, it's a singing role, and nobody can touch
Townsend."

"Screw Townsend and singin'. Just swing that pretty ass
and be there." He hung up.

My family encouraged me to leave.

"A change of scene may be the best for you," my doctor
said. So I left.

On the train the grave sense of panic still clung to me, so
I welcomed the messages from Jeff: "I'll take care of my darling. You know something? I love you."

He had a limousine meet me in Chicago and take me to a
flower-filled suite at the Ambassador East.

"I'll be with you," his note read, "as soon as you get your
coat off, darling."

I dropped the note on the table and stood toward the window, not seeing the view, trying to stop the gripping desire to escape—to run, run, run—but to where and from what, I didn't know. I was shaking violently as Jeff rushed in and gripped me tightly. His body trembled against mine.

"Jeez," he said sheepishly. "It happened the second I touched you—emergency case."

He gave me a necklace with a large, gold heart pendant, studded with rubies. And on the back it was engraved, "You know something? I love you." He ordered our breakfast, but before it arrived, we made love—and again before we dressed. He hired a limousine. . . .

"We're gonna go to Milwaukee for lamb shanks—great German restaurant."

He couldn't keep his hands off me in the car, and I was embarrassed in case the chauffeur was conscious of us.

"I'll stake him," he whispered in my ear.

And so it went for days. He took me everywhere—we hid out everywhere—we made love everywhere.

He flew to New York when I started rehearsing his show, but flew back that night, then left early the next morning and flew back again at night. He ordered the rehearsals stopped Friday afternoon, and we flew to Bermuda one weekend, then he chartered a yacht the next.

In a letter to Sally, I confided:

> Things happen so fast around him that I haven't time to be sick—yet I can't shake the screwy fear that hits me when I have a moment to myself. Perhaps that's how a breakdown leaves you for a while. I'm free, so it couldn't be my conscience; but it's funny, I don't feel free.
>
> Anyway, no lover has ever loved so! When we're not making love, or on the move, he's telephoning, telephoning, telephoning. And he won't let me out of his sight. I have to listen to him transact business, stay with him, look at him— and I like it, Sal. He has a scary temper with people now and

again—I don't like that at all. But most of the time he's a darling.

It's incredible how fast and furiously he gets things done. He doesn't take no for an answer from anybody. He seems always to be racing, like there's no time left, and he's got to get it all in!

Sometimes, though, Sally, I can hardly keep from laughing at him. He *is* funny—unbelievably funny; almost like a joke you've heard.

Example: Those four-hundred-dollar suits he wears come a-flyin' off the minute he hits a room. The Sulka ties are thrown in the air, the hand-turned shoes, the sheer, expensive hose—all are thrown any which way, and he plumps himself on the bed in his handkerchief-linen undershorts and pulls me down with him. After the fantastic lovemaking, he lights a two-dollar cigar, grabs the phone, and calls everywhere in this world of ours. He's fame-happy, crazy, a caricature of a big shot—but I'm swinging along with it, and why not? It's just what the doctor ordered. I don't have to think or cry.

25

So I MARRIED him: twice. The first time he didn't even bother to ask me. He pulled me off a train in Chicago and took me to a church—an empty one. He had picked a bookie friend to do the honors. When the ersatz priest started to read the Lord's Prayer, Jeff told him to jump to the finish. "I pronounce yez man and wife," the bookie said dutifully. Jeff put the ring on my finger and bent me backward: we almost disappeared on the floor behind the pews.

All of this because I was to stay away from other guys until we could get married "legit." He was, of course, still married to his first wife.

The second time was a year after his wife's death—and after I knew him well enough to know better. I had felt his violence, suffered his jealousies—he suspected every leading man I worked with—had been followed by his detectives. He ran his own shuttle from New York to Los Angeles. He went from coast to coast the way most people cross town. One trip to scream at me for being out so long on a shopping spree, unreachable by phone; another trip laden with gifts, delicious plans, and undying love; still another to sneak up on me while I was at the studio working with Clark Gable—to pelt me with his accusations and fury.

Each time I ran away from him, he found me, and I couldn't fight his kind of magnetism, in bed or out. He broke three of my fingers once and I almost lost consciousness from the pain: but he got on his knees to beg me to forgive him, then raced me to a hospital. He ended one argument with a platinum-and-diamond heart and chain for me—another with Christmas-in-July gifts for my children. What was money to a man who lost ninety thousand on one race at Santa Anita without a tremor?

He made all the decisions for me. Including the one that got us to Las Vegas for our wedding.

He called me late one night. "Nora . . . my wife. You hear that. That's what you're gonna be tomorrow night. We've waited long enough."

"Jeff, I can't."

"I know how you feel. I've been rotten to you, but I'll make it all up. You believe in me, you give me strength. Class. There's nothing wrong with us that a wedding won't cure. You're my stand-up dame, and I want you to be my wife."

"Jeff . . ."

"I'll be there around four tomorrow afternoon. Get packed. Vegas is up all night, so we'll tie the knot there—stay a few days having fun. We'll map out the rest when we get home."

"Listen, Jeff . . ."

"I mean it, Nora, you're gonna be married to me tomorrow, because I worship you—and that's no bullshit."

The top was down on Jeff's Cadillac as we drove into the early-evening colors of the desert. "For a long time you've been trying to get rid of me, haven't ya?" he asked. "But now you're gonna be my wife, so it's too late, sweetheart, the show's on the road."

I smiled, then started to cry. He pulled well off the side of the highway and behind a cluster of trees and took me in his arms. He made love to me gently, almost shyly, as though it were our first time together. "Nora, don't be afraid of me, I know I've been rough on you, but no more, my darling, we're gonna have a full and exciting life together."

On the way once again, he planned our future: "We're gonna move you and the kids bag and baggage to the East Coast. No more pictures—you're jes gonna be Mrs. Flynn and take care of us. I'll get you out of the Fox deal through Kenworth. We're gonna find a mansion outside New York, and I'm gonna commute like an ordinary husband—we'll put your house up for sale."

"My family?"

"Did I ever stint on anything? They'll visit us—I'll spring for the trips, and Ceeley can live with us—I'll see that our home has a terrific guest house. Then she can keep track of the kids while we go to Europe, Australia, everywhere. Jesus Christ, what happens to me when I think of us makin' love in all those foreign places."

He turned into a motel and pulled me out of the car. "I don't want that vacancy sign to go to waste," he said.

Showered and freshened, we were on our way once again, but now I felt relaxed and content—until he continued with his plans: "I might have to borrow that fifty G's deferment check that's due you from Columbia—jes for about two weeks. Some unexpected things have come up—we might even hafta dip into that insurance fund you've got."

"Oh, my God, no, Jeff. Ronald Colman set that up for me before I married David—he was David's best friend. It's with Lloyd's of London, and when I'm forty-seven I'll get money enough to live on the rest of my life. No, Jeff, I've got to keep paying on that." I shivered in the warm air.

"Don't worry about it, baby, I'm gonna quit gambling from now on—I'm jes gonna gamble on us. You'll have more than any dame has ever had." He paused and changed his tone. "I think I might buy the Ringling Brothers' Circus."

We rode for another hour listening to the radio, my head on his shoulder. Finally he said, "Nora, I've got somethin' goin' for us that'll make us millionaires. There's a guy in Oyster Bay that's invented a circular movie screen. It's enormous, wait till you see it. You'll get chills, it's so exciting. So far he's jes made home movies with his family walking around and playing the piano—and he's got one scene he took in a local church of choir boys walking in from either side, and the music is three-dimensional too—stereophonic—it's the Goddamnedest thrill. Well, I'm goin' to nab it and call it Thearina—like that name?"

I nodded.

"Nora, it's not perfected yet. It's got three seams I gotta get rid of. But I'm gonna grab the son-of-a-bitch—and I'll force 'em to widen every fuckin' movie screen in every theater across this nation to keep up with me."

"My God, it sounds exciting, Jeff."

"Wait'll you see. The inventor, Williams, uses his garage to show it and work on it—biggest thing to come along since the advent of talkies, and I'm grabbin' it, baby, for us."

I loved listening to those elaborate dreams that usually came true.

We pulled into a gas station, and while the attendant was filling the tank, we walked around. Suddenly Jeff stopped and looked at me as though I were a stranger and said, "Nora, feel this." He put his forefinger and thumb on my Adam's apple and gently moved it back and forth. "See, I know how to do it. It's so easy—no one would ever know."

"Do what?" I tried to take his hand away.

"Kill you. It's so easy—feel? That's in case you ever cheat on me."

"Shut up, Jeff, you're giving me the creeps—stop that rotten kind of talk." I walked away from him, then turned back. "Jeff, I want to go home. Maybe some other time we can work it out, but now I want to go home."

"Cut it out. I was only kiddin'." He grabbed my hand and took me back to the car. We rode in silence.

He pulled into an inn called Casa Español, registered us as Mr. and Mrs. Jeff Flynn, and got an attractive room. "We need to grab an hour's sleep," he said to me.

When we were in bed, he said, "We can't waste this soft mattress sleeping."

"I'm terrified, Jeff."

He grabbed me and covered me with kisses. "I was a rat to frighten you. I'm sorry, honest to God I am." He made love to me with nonstop words of endearment and promises. We took a short nap, showered, and were again on our way.

He was singing along with the car radio, when suddenly he switched off the music. "Nora, did you know Harry Truman went into bankruptcy while he was in the clothing business— then went on to become President of the United States?"

I shook my head.

"Well, he did—got a whole fresh start, wiped the slate clean. I may do that one of these days."

"Bankruptcy!" I was shocked.

"Don't worry, darling. I won't do anything wrong for us. I always land on my feet—nobody loses around me."

We were facing the lights of Las Vegas.

We were married in a private room. The decor was arranged by Jake Dillon, a big-time gambler. The room was packed with badly arranged, multicolored baskets of flowers. It looked and smelled more like a funeral parlor than a wedding. "I'm doubling as best man," Jake told me.

Just before the ceremony, I took Jeff to one side and presented him with my wedding present, a tattered, yellowing letter: To whom it may concern:

> Nora Marten, aged eight, daughter of Mr. and Mrs. John Marten of "The Boy Is Gone" Company, lost her virginity . . .

There wasn't a chance of hearing the vows, for the man

at the organ sang his way through the whole ceremony in a loud, nasal voice: "The girl that I marry will have to be as soft and as pink as a nursery . . ."

Instead of the final "I do," I whispered "Oh, God."

How right I was.

Four years later I had to get away from what had become a nightmare of unreason and brutality. The best parts of Jeff Flynn reminded me of Johnny: his optimism, his strength, his delight in children, the confidence he gave me that everything we wanted would come true. But there were too many ugly parts to this man. The turbulence, the rages were more than I could bear even though I loved him.

So I left heartsick and drained. It was the toughest thing I ever did. It meant trying to reactivate a career. It meant pulling up stakes and looking for a home again. But we Martens were good at that.